TO BEASLEY
WITH DEEPEST +
TO MBFIA -
FOR 49 YEARS —
NEED I SAY MORE ?

Love, Donovan Milley
(Donnie)

LEMON GULCH
THIRD EDITION

First published 2000 by Gay Men's Press
Millivres Ltd and Millivres Prowler Group, London UK.

Cover art by Donovan O'Malley
Cover design by Leif Södergren

ISBN 978-91-979188-0-0

LEMONGULCHBOOKS
www.lemongulchbooks.com

For Keif.
He knows why.

DONOVAN O'MALLEY

LEMON GULCH
THIRD EDITION

LEMONGULCHBOOKS

CONTENTS

CONTENTS

1. MY HUMANE CONDITION

My name is Danny O'Rourke. I am A Only Child which resides with My Beauteous Mom and my old poor Dad which is a Inebriant as he got Thwarted due to a Deleterious lack of one leg. Plus My Beauteous Mom desires to be called Jarleen instead of Mom as it don't sound so darn motherly. Which she ain't. Mean Aunt Edna May says Jarleen ain't got proficient time to be a accurate mother as she was in a Acute State Of Orgasms from a early age on due to A Hormonal Unbalance Of The Highest Order which has ran in our family for Eons. I *myself* am impelled to Onanate a Maximum of 4 times per day and sometimes a whole alots more. Whenever Applicable.

You ought to note me. What a site! I am as fat as one hog and busting out from all my garb plus got red greasy hair and Multifarious pimples plus keel over exceptionally easy when nerve racked and stutter Dire while Chatting. I am 6 feet tall almost although 12 years of age only. But I purport to appear like 18 plus am additionally purported to wet my bed sporadically when Somnolent.

Plus I did not blubber at my dead Granddad's funeral to which I did not go to as the insides of my fat big 2 Thighs was exceptionally chafed and sore as a chicken with their head chopped off. But I would not of blubbered even if I had of went. As said Granddad was not kind. Plus promised to bequeath me his battery radio when he croaked. But did not do said as promised as my cousin Gregory which is a Gasoline Sniffer was gave said battery radio. As he is the all time favorite football playing grandson of this Deeply Departed Mendacious Granddad which additionally traditionally blowed cigarette smoke on to my piglet face plus emitted Dire farts immediately Prior To Departure.

But worst of all said Granddad was not kind. PERSONS SHOULD BE KIND. ALL OF THEM! As all Individuals desires to be treated kind. Explicitly we fat big Sissies which ain't able to defend theirselves!

Said Granddad did not like me a whole alots neither. Even although I had brung him his multiple cigarettes plus fresh Liverwurst and Raisins on my Schwinn blue bicycle underneath of a merciless sun. Plus he called me Sister Sue and said I waddle like a girl. Yes! I waddle! But can not do nothing to impede it. As I am exceedingly obese said fat 2 thighs flops together which impels my fat heinie to shake which impels my fat tummy to jiggle which impels me to stick out both of my 2 hands like a girl so as to procure my Perfect Balance.

However. I feel excessively blue and lowly as per this Granddad when sometimes I ponder him sporadically. But I would not blubber if he croaked again today even. And I blubber exceedingly easy as I am a fat big Sissy. (As said.) (Ask any person which knows me.) It is excessively fortuitous that I got a behemoth Vocabulary!

Bull is my Dad's nick name as he was a almost championship Prize Fight Boxer prior to losing one right leg while he was a Occupational Troop in Tokio Japan subsequential To World War 2 due to falling on to a train's tracks during Inebriation and become Thwarted. (As said.) Which is why he become a Inebriant. (As said.) Which is what my sick Lying Granddad said immediately prior to croaking.

Poor Bull don't never say nothing to me excepting: Hello Joe. What do you know? What are a-cookin' in Tokio? Plus squints his eyes slitty like a Japanese Individual as said Phrase is uttered as he is Inebriated and sleeps all day in our front room on our Davenport as Jarleen don't never permit him to limp in to her bedroom and relax hisself upon her bed which is preserved for her and Jack Shanks habitually while I am at school and Bull is in the Inebriation Unit which Jack Shanks hisself runs and Jarleen is off from work early from her job at the Tangy Mayo factory as they have ran out of lemons which is the Tangy segmant in Tangy Mayonnaise which grows in Lemon Gulch which is my Home Town. Jack Shanks is Indubitably My Beauteous Mom's Paramount. (But I Digress.)

However. When Bull is present plus sleeping on our Davenport Jack Shanks and My Beauteous Mom habitually fuck under a starry sky on top of a mattress in the Rear of Jack Shank's Chevy Pick-up Deluxe. They think I do not know nothing about their Fucking Information. (Ha. Ha.) (I do!)

We come to Lemon Gulch which is a excessively little town crammed down in between 2 exceptionally brown big hills in Southern California underneath of a merciless sun one year ago in 1946 so as for Bull (Our Inebriant.) (As said.) to purchase our new small home in which we currantly reside in with his World War 2 G.I. loan plus Missing Limbs Benefit. (one limb only.) (As said.)

Plus so as Jarleen can work at Tangy Mayo.

Almost every resident which resides in Lemon Gulch has came from Oklahoma or Texas or Arkansas plus works at the Tangy Mayonnaise factory. (Our town's Major Statistical Employer.) However. Jarleen My Beauteous Mom is born in Tennessee and Bull hisself is born in Oregon which makes them A Exemption To The Rules.

I am me myself one farther Exemption as I was born from a Caesarian approximately 20 miles away in Port City California which is a Navy town chock-full of loitering sailors with protrusive weenies at The Tales Of Hoffman Memorial Hospital which makes me a California Native Son which is a relentlessly Scarce Item.

Jarleen says that after World War 2 every fool plus their brother which did not croak in said war was dyin' to reside in Southern California. She is correct in the extremes. Jarleen always is. Excepting when she ain't. Which is a whole alots. But I love her like a mother as she is My Beauteous Mom plus hope that she loves me but ponder if this is so as she don't never say a whole alots to me nor hugs me nor kisses me due to one burning need not to smear her Raging Ruby Lipstick. (Unfortunately.)

Did I utter that Jarleen was beauteous? **OH MY GOSH!** She is more then jist Beauteous! She is the loveliest lady of all the ladies which works at said Mayonnaise Factory. Plus possesses also a whole alots of admirers including the weeniless Jack Shanks. (Which ain't weeniless in real actuality as how could My Beauteous Mom fuck him if he was?!) (Joke!)

My Beauteous Mom likes weenies a whole alots as she is A Mature Lady With Sharp Appetites. (Due to said Hormonal Unbalance.) (As said.) Everybody loves My Beauteous Mom! (Inclusive of me.) (To say the least!)

However. Almost no person explicitly likes *me*. Not my teachers nor Bull nor said Granddad. (Before Departure.) (Obviously!) And Jarleen is Preternaturally preoccupied with Motion Picture magazines plus bowling and fucking under the stars. Whenever Applicable.

However. I ponder that Miranda Cosmonopolis personally likes me. She is a girl which is even fatter then I of which I am a Devotee of. However. Mr Jimmy which is Little Norman's father which resides up the street and which possesses a conspicuously perky weenie might like me somewhat. (More about Mr Jimmy and his weenie later.)

When I am not pondering the horrid bully Paul K Benderson (More about the Inexorable PK later.) or Fred Foster's convivial weenie (More about Fred which jist moved in prior later.) (He lives adjacent next door.) (As said.) (And is 14!) I listen to The Lonely Gal which is a lady which tells me that she loves me on *my* battery radio which I found in a trash can behind of the Piggly Wiggly Market which is lucky for me as my Lying Granddad did not keep his promise and bequeath me *his* battery radio prior to croaking. (As sadly prior said.)

As all electrical wires has been blew down by a Ravenous storm a battery radio is Vitally Essential. We even purchased a used Ice Box for $5.25 which utilizes Authentic Ice to reserve our Household Combustibles such as Ketchup and Mustard and Butter and Eggs plus Dr Peppers which must be ice cold as their habitually drank underneath of a merciless sun.

I got Granddad's bedroom now which is a whole alots better then sleeping on a Cot in the kitchen where I was impelled to sleep during his lifetime as he resided with us while living plus never Scrutinized one singular Solitary book. (Which is Profoundly Shocking!)

However. *I* read Voluminously plus Cohabit my school's library Perusing Multitudes of beauteous words in variegated Volumes and ain't interested in nothing which ain't Literal as Reprehensable items like Arithmetic plus Science plus Sports bores me Shitless. So my school grades ain't the greatest as they do not grade on new words. Unfortunately my teachers only notes my reddish obeseness plus horrid pimples and girly waddle which ain't appealing to The Multitudes. One teacher said I got the Anti Grammar Syndrome. (Which don't sound none too good plus which I ain't able to find under the A's on my Webster's Severely Abridged Dictionary.) However. I should be graded on what lays deep insides of me which is many wondrous words plus Infinitely kind feelings as then I would be right on the top of my class.

However. This is my horrid Humane Condition: I am the Scapegoat of the Inexorable Paul K Benderson which is called PK and there ain't nothing I can do to impede his mean Demeanor.

I firstly noted this Inexorable Bully one year prior while he was beating up on a small poor boy which was a whole alots littler then he. I give said Bully 10 cents to terminate said beating up on. (Which kind Lottie Venables had gave me for trimming the

4

edges of her skinny lawn.) I was going to purchase 2 Milky-Ways with said cents but I real soon ascertained that this small poor boy required not to get beat up on a whole alots more then I required 2 Milky-Ways. Now PK habitually beats up on *me*! Which is exceptionally sad as it is excessively urgent that persons will like me as us fat Sissies got explicit Humane Conditions and desires all the friends which one can procure. Explicitly the boy next door which is 14 (As said!) and which jist moved in last month which is My Divine Fred Foster with whom I am in love with to a exceptionally High Degree.

2. A OFTEN UNCARING WORLD

"Fred ain't waked up as of yet, Danny," says Fred's Mom which is loitering with her wet 2 hands in their front door of their next door home.

"I w-w-wish to s-show him m-my B-B...B-B...B-B...B-B-Black Widows," I say plus poke my jar of spiders out at her.

"My! Ain't they pretty! Well, come on in then."

Said Mom wipes her wet 2 hands on her apron and leads me to Fred's bedroom door.

"Time Fred waked up, anyhooo. Jist go on in, honey."

Fred's Mom hangs her apron up on to their door hook and gets her purse plus says:

"I got to do me some shoppin' right away."

Their front door slams shut and I and Fred is Fully Insulated insides of his home!

I waddle in to Fred's bedroom pondering his weenie among my brains. He is asleep! My fat tummy jiggles like a hound sucking eggs! My brows sweats like a stuck pig! My heinie wobbles like a cow's titties! My weenie twitches like a chicken with their head chopped off! I stick out my fat 2 hands so as to procure my Perfect Balance plus ain't hardly able to hold my jar of 3 exceptionally poisonous spiders steady!

"Hi, F-F-Fred my old p-pal!" I holler which feasibly comes as a big surprise on Fred as I do not think he considers hisself My Old Pal as of per yet as him and his family only moved next door one month prior. (As said.) (Twice.) (The last month of school previous to summer's vacation to be implicit.)

I stick out my jar of spiders at Fred but he don't note them as both of his blue beauteous eyes is closed shut tightly.

"Danny," utters Fred which maintains said 2 eyes closed shut.

I suddenly note a wiggly Lump underneath of his sheets! My heart stops it's beating! Fred's Lump wiggles! I take a deep breath jist so as to keep from keeling right over! My fat arms flaps up and down! My weenie flops sideways among my Y-fronts! Has Fred saw me noting him through my bedroom curtains as he waters their lawn in his cut-off Dungarees with his jangly keys on a ring on his belt loop?!

I am so filled up with love that my yellow little teeth commences to chatter!

Fred's blue beauteous 2 eyes opens.

"Set down, Danny," he utters soft and lowly, "before y'all fall down." (Variegated individuals is incessantly uttering said to me due to my jiggly waddle.)

I set down on to his bed contiguous. Fred which is 14 yawns and sets up and his sheet flops off so as I can note his variegated curly chest hairs!

"Whatcha got there, Danny?"

He grabs my jar of spiders.

With my 2 eyes clamped on to Fred's wiggling Lump I holler insides of my brains: "What have *you* got there, Fred?!"

Even although I desire to grab right ahold of his Lump I can only utter "b-b...b-b...b-b...b-black w-w-widows," and I almost can't hardly even utter that!

"Big ones," says Fred which rubs said twitching Lump *again!* My weenie wiggles and protrudes! It *don't* go unnoted!

"Wanna get..." Fred licks his 2 lips as he is real nerve racked too, "...in to bed?"

Me? That Fat Big Sissy in bed with My Divine Fred Foster?! I literately flop right down on to his bed adjacent besides of him!

"Please take off your Dungarees first."

Fred is Eager But Courteous.

"S-sure, F-Fred, w-whatever you s-say, m-my old p-pal."

I unbutton my Dungarees and peel said down off from my fat sausage 2 legs. My Boner snaps out from the access slot of my Y-fronts as I crawl underneath of Fred's sheets.

Fred is a literate oven! I slam my fat tummy right up contiguous and he grabs my hand and yanks it down on to his relentlessly hot Genitalias! My piglet nose sniffs a delighted swampy fragrance which whooshes out from underneath of said sheets.

6

"Please feel me up, Danny."

DO I COMPLY!

I might as well come right out and utter it as you will Perceive it sooner or later anyhow. I am Acutely attracted to weenies. (The Humane Penis.) Please do not ask me why. As I can not tell you. As I do not know.

Fred is excessively naked underneath of said sheets. I grab him! His Boner pokes right out from his tummy plus is warm and sticky!

"Put your mouth on it, *please*, Danny!"

Fred grabs away his sheets!

"S-Sure, F-Fred, my old p-pal!"

DO I COMPLY! I ain't had my mouth that full since last Thanksgiving! I almost suffocate then Fred's Boner flips right out from my mouth with one big slurp and he hunches over and rolls my Y-fronts down plus slaps his tongue on to the tip of my Boner!

I squirt exceptionally promptly!

Fred smiles and politely requests for me to rub at his Gonads as he desires to Onanate immediately.

He squirts promptly too all over his 2 sheets then wipes hisself up with 3 Kleenexs subsequential plus additionally says:

"I guess I better get these sheets in the washer before Mom comes back!"

Now ain't that kind of Fred not to desire to impede his Mom with the Daily Grinds in washing his 2 sheets?

"Y-Yeah", I say to Fred, "d-darn g-g-good ideal, F-Fred, m-my old p-pal".

ALAS! I wisht said was occuring in real actuality... **BUT IT AIN'T!**

As at this Dire currant minute of my life what is occuring is: **PK BENDERSON'S BIG BOOT IS PLANTED ON MY HEAD WHICH IS PINNED DOWN CONTIGUOUS ON TO THE SIDEWALK JIST OUTSIDE OF THE GULCH THEATER OUT FROM WHICH I HAVE JIST CAME OUT FROM!** And if I move even a inch said Bully will twist my left arm behind of my back which will hurt a whole alots more. So I jist lay here flat on my heinie pronely plus fight him back in the only way which I can which is to pump my brains so full of My Divine Fred Foster's convivial weenie that there ain't no more room left for this poor misguided PK Benderson!

"FAT SISSY! FAAAAAAT SISSY!" hollers PK which I can

not hardly hear no more due to Fred's dear Genitalias which is printed on my darn 2 eyeballs. (Fortunately!)

PK spits on the sidewalk plus lifts his boot off from my head and permits me to arise up and bicycle away. What a Reprehensable Mode in which to spend the 2nd day of Summer's Vacation in.

It is exceedingly dark and hot. I bicycle to our home which is empty as My Beauteous Mom is out bowling as per as usual with Jack Shanks. (Ha. Ha.)

My Dad Bull is Inebriated so don't count as a accurate person plus the icebox is empty of Combustibles but I ain't hungry anyhow as I gobbled down 5 Milky-Ways at said Major Motion Picture. I always gobble food due to my Relentless Pubescence which impels me to be Rapacious.

With my flashlight as we ain't got no electricity due to prior said lack of Electrical wires I waddle through our living room past my Inebriated one legged snoring Dad to my bedroom and light my kerosene lamp plus open my window and sneak in Tinker which is my black and white small dog. She lays down at the bottom of my bed and goes right to sleep as she is Ostensibly sleepy.

I unbutton and bust out from my horridly tight Dungarees and keel over on to my bed and rub the sore Hump on the side of my head plus scrape out variegated sidewalk gritty bits from my greasy hair and as per as usual old big tears squirts out from my piglet 2 eyes as I ponder said boot on head. (PK's.) (Boot.) (Unfortunately.) (Alas!)

To excape this Inexorable Bully I ceaselessly exit prior to the termination of all Major Motion Pictures and jump on my bicycle and pedal away before he notes that I have went prior to his noting. Fortunately Miranda Cosmonopolis is a Major Motion Picture avid goer and incessantly tells me said Picture's Denouements. (A French word which means Ends Of.) (Miranda taught me it.) (As her Army Uncle married a French lady in Paris France.) (Which taught her.) (Miranda.) (In Lemon Gulch not Paris!)

Anyhow. I jist could not exit out early from tonight's Motion Picture as it stars 2 young brothers with protrusive weenies which hugs a whole alots as their Orphans. The Swimming Coach at their Orphanage possesses one additional protrusive weenie jist like Mr Jimmy's conspicuous one although Mr Jimmy's weenie is more conspicuous then protrusive but it does protrude Contemporaneously. (A whole alots due to it's tucked sideways up posture.) Conspicuous weenies like Mr Jimmy's do not grow on trees! (More about Mr Jimmy and his weenie later.) (I failed to additionally add that it is perky also.) (As said.) (But I Digress.)

This Swimming Coach in said Picture is incessantly garbed in a white tight swimming suit jist like Fred Foster's although the Coach's weenie protrudes more as said is more Mature then Fred's as he is 32 years of age which I ascertained as he had to answer a age question on a Adaption Questionnaire prior to his adaption of said Orphaned 2 brothers and wrote 32.

Anyhow. Said Coach which lost his wife and 2 children in the same airplane crash which Annihilated said Orphan's parents is in Crucial danger of becoming Dangerously Cynical which the kind principal of their Orphanage tells him. So he ascertains to adapt the 2 brothers so as to Know Love and procure A New Lease On To Life instead. Which is what *I* need. (A Lease!) However. There is big trouble as it ain't Seemly for a singular bachelor to adapt 2 Pubescent boys. Please do not ask me why. As I can not tell you. As I do not know. As said Coach would of made a much more Scrupulous father then my Dad Bull. (The Inebriant.)

However. Said coach is Scrutinized by The Adaptation Society which has a Meeting and *finally* Peruses Newspaper clippings which Divulges that this Coach is a War Hero which rescued Colleagues In Distress In The Line Of Duty so the adaption is Allocated jist as all implicated is climbing out from the Orphanage's swimming pool. This Heart Rendering news is brung right to their poolside by the kind janitor which answered the Swimming Coach's telephone as he was sweeping said Coach's office out which is why he was there in the 1st place.

The Coach and the Orphaned 2 brothers hug each other like chickens with their heads chopped off plus one of the Orphans says to this Swimming Coach:

"**OH MY GOSH!** What should we call you now, Dad or Coach?!"

"Jist call me Dad!" answers their new Dad with a kind smile instantaneously. Do my tears squirt out!

"Let me show you my breast-stroke...Dad!" hollers the additional Orphan.

I wisht my Dad Bull would utter something besides Hello Joe. What do you know? What are a-cookin' in Tokio?! But he don't as he is Thwarted. (As sadly said.)

Then all implicated swim Hectically among the Orphanage's swimming pool. The kind janitor even takes off his janitor's

Coveralls and jumps in without no swimming suit and one can note with Exceptional Ease that he possesses a protrusive weenie even although he is garbed in boxer shorts in which it is hard to note weenies in. (Excepting when wet.)

Then this kind janitor's tormented Spouse turns up unexpectantly as she has finally Pinpointed her kind janitor Co-Spouse's exact location. (He works at the Orphanage part time only as he is a Scientist which desires to get back to Basics which he tells this wife when she asks why the heck he up and disappeared so sudden. "To get back to Basics, honey," he says.) (As said.)

The poster says this Major Motion Picture is:

"A FRANK EXAMINATION OF THE HUMANE CONDITION IN A OFTEN UNCARING WORLD!"

DO I CONCUR!

Contentment tears squirt out from my piglet 2 eyes as I exit out from the Gulch Theater. But I am not on the look-out for PK which sneaks up from behind of the Popcorn machine and grabs me. Naturally I keel right on over like traditional and down slams PK's boot on to my head!

This is the 7th time PK has pinned my head down contiguous in one month. Twice at the Motion Pictures plus 4 times in the school cafeteria and once contiguous by The Big Lemon. (More about The Big Lemon later.) (As said.)

THIS MEAN BRUTALITY HAS GOT TO BE TERMINATED! BUT HOW?!

I squash myself down deep in my bed and yank my blanket right over my head plus strive to forget PK which ain't easy as I am Peace Loving and long for Domestic Tranquility.

Anyhow. I plant my 2 feet up adjacent besides of my black and white small dog Tinker's tender soft sides and turn on my battery radio and listen to The Lonely Gal which now comes on plus utters real soft and lowly:

"How I have missed you, Lonely Guy."

I wipe a additional fat big tear out from my piglet eye.

"Are you as lonely as I?" says The Lonely Gal which sighs a sweet big sigh.

"Y-Yes, d-darling," I utter.

"I've got a big surprise for you," says The Lonely Gal, "for you alone."

Now ain't that a kind thing which to say?!

"Just a few moments ago I was looking through a book all about American heroes and I saw a hero who looked just like you."

I ponder that said hero better not look *jist* like me or he is in for a whole alots of trouble!

"And I said to myself," says said Gal, "I'll bet that my Lonely Guy is as brave as this hero!"

OH MY GOSH!

"So I got me a pencil and a piece of paper and the paper is pink and perfumy and when I smell it I think of you thinking of me."

A additional fat big tear squirts out from one more of my piglet eyes.

"And on my pink, perfumy paper I wrote a song. Dedicated to you, Lonely Guy. To you and you alone. And here it is."

Beauteous music commences to play plus said Gal sings:

"Hi, brave guy
I smiled at you a moment ago
Didn't you know?
Brave guy
I'm kinda shy
But it wouldn't take a spy to tell
I think you're swell."

I jist lay here on my bed with my 2 feet squashed up adjacent on to my black and white small dog plus my battery radio smashed contiguous on to my ear as said Gal sings:

"Brave guy
You're a man now!
And how!
And I was wonderingggggg
If you'd do a little thingggg for meeeeeee!"

"Anyth-thing, L-Lonely G-Gal, d-darling."

"You seeeeee
I haven't got a date
And it's getting mighty late

To get one for my dreams tonight.
So, all right?
Will you be mine?"

"I s-sure w-will!"

"You will?!
What a thrill!
Oh brave guy, geeee!
That'll beeeee
Just fine!"

Now ain't that a kind song which to sing?

Then The Lonely Gal plays variegated other songs plus converses with me soft and lowly for a full duration which abates me up from feeling blue and lowly due to my PK Deprecations. Then said Gal utters:

"Goodnight Honey, sleep tight, don't let the bed bugs bite. And remember that I love you."

Now if that ain't a kind thing which to utter I don't know which is!

Then comes her Commercial plus joyous persons sings all about exceptional water heaters in Bliss. After this commercial I ponder Fred Foster's weenie plus attain a instantaneous Erection and Onanate with Peanut Oil and squirt Lubriciously and dab myself dry with a Kleenex then stick my can of Peanut Oil way back underneath of my bed.

I am now relaxed proficient.

I ponder a whole alots on how I can get my fat 10 fingers on Fred Foster's weenie in real actuality which impedes my Dire thoughts about PK plus impels me to commence to get sleepy. Although I smell like Peanut Oil I doze in Bliss as I always liked Peanuts and their entertaining smells.

My Humane Condition traditionally feels a whole alots better after The Lonely Gal's Radio Program and Onanation.

3. MY BEAUTEOUS MOM AND
MY THWARTED DAD

I currantly ponder Fred Foster's weenie as I stir a Aluminum pot of Oatmeal as it is morning and I always make my own breakfast plus My Beauteous Mom's coffee as she is impelled to shave her legs for the Daily Grinds but ain't able to use her electrical leg shaver due to our Dearth of electricity and is impelled to use a Archaic razor which is Time Consuming. (But I traditionally make her coffee anyhow even while electricity is Omniscient.) (As she is My Beauteous Mom.)

"Your Aunt Edna May caught your cousin Gregory sniffin' gasoline out of the tank of their automobile with his fingers stuck up some little bad girl's panties," says My Beauteous Mom like it is ALL TIME BIG NEWS which it surely ain't as I have already knew about said cousin's Sniffing as he throwed me on to the ground and sat on my tummy and told me so. (Unauthorized persons habitually throws me on to the ground and sits on my tummy and/or slams their boot on to my head.) (Please do not ask me why. As I can not tell you. As I do not know.)

"He'll end up as exhibit "A" one day. On a aut-topsy slab in a court room!" says My Beauteous Mom which Infers to said Illicit Sniffer finding hisself in a State of Incarceration. (Like in The Keyhole.) (More about The Keyhole which is a Periodical later.)

Jarleen has now shaved both of her legs and is smoking a cigarette and chewing Dentyne gum plus combing Glorious Lavender Wave-Set on to her platinum blonde Pompadour like Betty Grable which is my all time favorite movie star due to her Million-Dollar Legs. However. Jarleen jerks her wad of pink Dentyne out from her mouth and flings it at a ash tray in which she has sat her smelling old cigarette in. I wish to heck Jarleen would terminate smoking as it makes my greasy hair stink Abominable.

"Promise me you won't never stick none o' yer fingers up no little bad girl's panties," says Jarleen.

IS THIS FUNNY! I almost keel over like a chicken with their head chopped off!

"The only pants I want my fingers up is Fred's!" I holler deep among my brains.

"Little bad girls ain't nice," adds Jarleen additionally and as I am a Exemplary Sissy I utter:

13

"I p-promise, J-Jarleen."

Girls?! Heck! Miranda Cosmonopolis incessantly pokes her fat 2 titties right on to my face while bending over contiguous on to my school desk.

"SORRY, MIRANDA!" I traditionally holler among my brains, "I myself am partial to weenies!"

But of course I never utter said out loud as I do not wish to wound Miranda as I cherish her plus feel excessively sorry that she is jist as fat as I not counting her titties. Plus her heinie is as big as mine and I am 6 feet tall almost! (As said.) (Alas!)

It is Propitious for Miranda that she takes singing lessons from Miss Fishlock plus has Rapturous success as a Opera Singer lined up to propel her in to the future as she ain't the most popularest girl in school! And I which is the most unpopularest boy ought to know!

However. As Miranda is my only childhood friend besides of Little Norman with which I onanated with (Mr Jimmy's Offspring.) I cherish her but do not wish to tell her so as it might impel her to grunt and close her eyes and get all heightened up like which occurs when I touch her waste with my hand during dances.

In Any Case I do not also wish to tell Miranda that I myself attain Erections only for the male's sex as it would not be Prudent. (Plus could get me in a whole alots of trouble.) (As said is Frowned Upon by The Multitudes plus The Keyhole.) (More about The Keyhole later.) Sometimes I sporadically ponder that my weenie Affiliations is handed straight down to me from Jarleen which is OK co-incidentally by me. (However.)

"Good," says Jarleen which now answers my answer that I will not stick none of my fingers up no little bad girl's pants.

Jarleen opens the door to our hall closet which smells Strikingly Similar to Bull's Lurid socks as our laundry hamper contains said socks. (P!U!) The only thing my Dad Bull has ever gave me is Athlete's Foot as I borrowed his socks once plus got a savage infection which Flares Up habitually.

I now commence to ponder Fred Foster again in joy as I stir my Oatmeal but Jarleen yanks a pair of exceedingly high heeled shoes out from said closet plus hollers:

"I will fall offa these highest of my heels one day and bust my sweet ass!"

Which butts right in to my Fred's weenie pondering again! It is increasingly arduous to concentrate on Fred's weenie among all

14

this abrupt impedence.

Jarleen keeps Sensible Shoes in her locker at Tangy Mayo but don't hardly never ever wear them. Anyhow she has got to look her best while coming and going as she is so munificent who knows where a Talent Scout might literately lurk? And Motion Picture Magazines do not lie as Jarleen says which Scrutinizes Motion Picture Magazines like a hound sucking eggs as we ain't got no television set as of per yet and said regular electrical wires ain't to be situated prior to next week. (As said.) However we got a gas stove upon which to cook upon but upon which Jarleen don't desire to upon as she don't relish the State of Cooking but jist cooks a sporadic stew sometimes and leaves it on said stove for me to help one's self.

Therefour no eating Ritual is Extant. No setting down at no collective table communally. But as My Beauteous Mom is a working Woman which is impelled to Face The Daily Bumps And Grinds I excuse her happily from Housemaker Drudgery inclusive of cooking variegated foods.

Jarleen smears her Raging Ruby lipstick on in front of our hall mirror plus looks sublime in her Palest Of Yellows yellow Tangy Mayonnaise Factory uniform. Her behemoth platinum Pompadour is now fully dry and hard like a rock. She taps said with her Carmen Red long fingernail. "Suu-purb," she utters, "jist suuuu-perb."

I wisht I was beauteous like My Beauteous Mom instead of fat and big and pimply and reddish. (Misfortune Is My Lott.) (Alas.)

Jarleen currantly smears her cheeks up with Tangy's new fine product of vegetable oil for humane faces and glitters wondrous as I stir Oatmeal plus continue to ponder dear Fred's weenie. Then **FLOP-CRASH!**

"Your drunk of a father has fell to our goddamn floor again!" hollers Jarleen.

I do not relish when My Beauteous Mom Infers to me that Bull is a drunk as he only falls on to our floor a whole alots as he possesses one leg which impedes his Perfect Balance. He is a Thwarted Inebriant and should be treated As Such.

Poor misguided Bull sleeps on the top of our Davenport in our front room on a crunchy Bevy of Hydrox chocolate cookie crumbs and curly dried up bread crusts almost most of every day plus night with his bottle of Vat 69 whiskey and his Petite Picnic Size empty Tangy Mayo jar from which he drinks it from. Right over

Bull's head on the wall is a old poster from a Prize Fight in which Bull has fought in while 2-legged. On said poster is a behemoth photo of Bull when he was young plus handsome and underneath of this photo it says:

"WATCH THIS BOY GO PLACES!"

I ain't never seen him go nowheres excepting from our Davenport where he sleeps to our kitchen where he eats to our collective toilet where he poops plus back to our Davenport. Of course this don't Encompass his traditional Perennial Pilgrimages to Jack Shanks' Inebriation Unit.

I set down at our kitchen table and gobble my Oatmeal as food is my only comfort excepting weenies and words plus ponder how I am going to get my piglet fingers insides of Fred Foster's Y-fronts. Then comes a additional big Flop-Crash!

"For chrissake! Where has he went and fell to now, Danny? Go see!"

I drop my Oatmeal spoon and instantaneously terminate pondering Fred's weenie and waddle to our front room plus note that Bull has yanked his phony leg off in his sleep and broke a itsy-bitsy Statuette of Bambi which is Jarleen's all time favorite Statuette as it is her Solitary surviving Statuette as all the other variegated Statuettes of our Household had MADE IN JAPAN stamped on their bottoms and was destoyed by I and Grandma in a Patriotic Tantrum while WW2 was In Situ. (2 years prior.) (I was 10 years of age.) (Then.) (And Unformed.) (Mostly.) (But fat as one hog.)

Bull's 2 eyes open up and he notes me plus sticks his fingers on to said 2 eyes and pulls them up like slits plus says:

"Hello Joe. What do you know? What are a-cookin' in Tokio?"

"Who c-cares, B-Bull?" I holler, "S-So what?!"

Every fool plus their brother knows that said Jap War was terminated in 1945 but he don't hear me as his 2 eyes is shut again. I only sass him when he is exceedingly Inebriated and ain't able to grab me even although my sassing ain't totally kind. But as he sporadically slams me with his phony leg he don't deserve total incessant kindness although most of the time he procures said from me. As Kindness is my Motto.

Once when Bull wasn't so Inebriated as I pondered he was he propelled hisself sideways instantaneously on his Stump and grabbed his phony leg up from our floor and whacked me on my

16

head so hard that my piglet 2 ears rung for one week! I still got implications on my left ear. But he did not mean to. He jist did it as he ain't trustworthy when Inebriated which is ceaseless due to Thwarting. (Unfortunately for all implicated.) (Explicitly me!)

Once I even told Bull that it is my Tantamount Wish to suck weenies. I guess I was impelled to utter it as I was blue plus lowly. He must of not heard nothing or he would of whacked me. As he feasibly might not relish one Cocksucker for a son as Cocksucking is Frowned Upon by The Keyhole. (A Sex Crime Periodical Dedicated To All Right Thinking People.)

I feel real sorry for Bull sporadically as Jarleen don't even like him and she is his Spouse. No Individuals likes him not even me. What a Humane Condition! Explicitly for a Dad with one Offspring. (Me.) My heart bleeds habitually for Bull *and* me as we got Not Being Liked in common. Me not by him plus him not by me. Although we got nothing else in common in common. (Sad But True.)

Jarleen only lets Bull hang around so as she can Amass his Veteran's Missing Limb Benefit funds and go out bowling. (Ha. Ha.) Plus purchase Slow Gin Fizzes for Jack Shanks on which to sip on underneath of a merciless sun.

I sweep up My Beauteous Mom's broke Bambi Statuette and disperse of it so as she will not know it is broke plus be blue and lowly as it breaks my heart to see persons blue and lowly explicitly My Beauteous Mom Jarleen.

Back in our kitchen I Divulge that Bull has yanked off his phony leg again.

"Ain't that jist like him," says Jarleen which now smears on her purplish eye shadow plus says:

"I'm a-goin' bowlin' tonight with Jack Shanks which has kindly gave us a five pound Texas Rainbow Fruit Cake in a decorative genuine tin box which he ordered direct from Waco, Texas. It ain't arrived as of yet but I seen it's photo in his full color brochure."

"W-Why d-did J-Jack S-Shanks g-give us a T-Texas R-Rainbow F-Fruit C-Cake?" I utter as I am striving to be Conversational although still pondering Fred's delighted Y-fronts.

"Because..."

Jarleen looks exceptionally suspicious plus squinty, "...because Jack Shanks jist happens to be a bosom friend of our family's!"

How dumb do they think I am?! (Ha. Ha.)

Jarleen lights a additional cigarette and takes one big puff plus says:

"Jack Shanks is a gentleman. Which is more'n I can say for your father!"

Jarleen notes herself on our hall mirror plus grins From Ear To Ear. "You know what a real gentleman is? A real gentleman is a guy which removes my douche bag from our kitchen sink before he pisses in it! Ain't that funny?! Jack Shanks told me it."

Jarleen laughs like a Laughing-Hyena for one interval. It contents me to note My Beauteous Mom in a State of Full Bliss.

She now yanks a leaf of tobacco off from a glamorous tooth. Jarleen's glamorous teeth is eternally white and perfect and commented on by strangers whom she enjoys.

I scoop Oatmeal with a whole alots of sugar in to my piglet mouth and Jarleen glues on her last phony eyelash plus washes her fingers in our kitchen sink and plumps up her fluffy sleeves on her Tangy uniform blouse which is the only item she ever irons (She is currantly impelled to Utilize our gas stove iron which must be heated upon said due to said Dearth.) (Of electrical wires.) (As said.)

Jarleen enters our bathroom for her morning Defecations and I hear a additional Flop-Crash from our front room. I find Bull bleeding from his head on our floor while Somnolent plus Relay this information to Jarleen which is alleviating through our bathroom door and she flushes our toilet and jumps right out plus runs to our front room and takes one Deleterious look at Bull then telephones Jack Shanks at his Inebriation Unit which comes right on over like a accurate Paramount should ought to of.

"He has fell to our floor once too often this morning," says My Beauteous Mom to Jack Shanks which currantly enters in to our home. Jack is also a Laborer which Labors for hisself when he ain't Laboring for other persons or running said Inebriation Unit which was set up by Municipal Funds as Jack's Dad is the Mayor of Lemon Gulch which set up said. My Beauteous Mom says that Jack is a wondrous Laborer which is more'n she can say for Bull.

Jack Shanks wears big floppy Zoot Suit pants with 33 million pleats on each side of them and ain't got no weenie Lump which you can note but I ascertain that he possesses at least one. (Ha. Ha.)

"Thanks, sugar," says Jarleen to Jack Shanks after he flexes his old big muscles and dumps my Thwarted poor Dad down on to the mattress in the Rear of his Chevy Pick-up Deluxe.

"Hello Joe. What do you know?" says Bull pronely to Jack,

"What are a-cookin' in Tokio?"

"Yeah," says Jack Shanks, "sure thing."

"Your a real life-saver, Mr Jack!" hollers Jarleen which exhibits one Bevy of perfectly glamorous teeth.

"Yeah, sure thing," says Jack Shanks which climbs in to his Deluxe and slams it's door.

Jarleen wiggles and waves all over the darn place as Jack drives off plus hollers:

"See you tonight, sugar!" for the darn whole neighborhood which to hear! Jarleen can be real embarrassing! As every fool plus their brother already looks at me anyhow a whole alots of hollering don't help none but she don't mean to embarrass nobody. She jist don't ponder nothing suitable while conversing to Jack Shanks as she is all heightened up and it is real hard to get her heightened down. I wisht she would act so kind when she talks to poor misguided Bull even if I do not like him much but Jarleen don't *never* say nothing kind to Bull.

However. I know how My Beauteous Mom feels as it is arduous to be kind to a relentless Inebriant which strives to whack you when one gets too contiguously adjacent.

4. DIVINE FRED FOSTER

Jarleen goes off to Tangy Mayo in her clear plastic high heels with the little Polka Dot roses on their opened toes. (My All-Time favorites!) I am now Fully Insulated at our home as Bull is in the Inebriation Unit so I can ponder in Domestic Tranquility without no Obtrusions from Jarleen nor floor-floppings due to Bull on how to get some of my piglet fingers on to Fred Foster's convivial weenie as my Relentless Pubescence is Rapacious.

I rinse out a empty Regular Size Tangy Mayo jar and punch holes in it's lid for air and stick it in my pocket plus sneak around outsides of our home to make sure that PK ain't on my Vicinity nor adjacent nor even contiguous. He ain't. So I bicycle to my school which is desserted for summer vacation and crawl on my knees underneath of the Baseball Bleachers where I and Little Norman Tomlin traditionally Onanated and trapped Black Widow spiders while hiding out from Coach Jackson which was a Drilling Sergeant in the War and impels us to do Military Callisthenics which is Mutually Repellent to both of us as we're Conscientous Objectives which loathe Violent Disarray.

I trap 3 spiders insides of my Tangy jar and return with said to our home and find a half pint bottle of Bull's Vat 69 Whiskey hid in one of his Lurid socks in our laundry hamper.

I pour some Whiskey in to a additional newly rinsed Tangy jar and screw it's lid on tight and cram it in to the back pocket of my Dungarees.

My bright ideal is to get Fred over to our desserted garage and Inebriate him so as he don't know what the heck he's doing and Feel-Up his convivial weenie.

So I waddle next door to Fred's home with my jar of spiders in one hand and the jar of Whiskey in my back pocket and knock on Fred's front door. His Mom which opens their door says:

"Fred ain't up as of yet, Danny"

"I w-want to s-show him s-something."

I stick my spider jar out to Mrs Foster which takes it but screams when she notes what is insides plus keeps on screaming and throws said jar down which breaks on their cement porch. one of my 3 Black Widows crawls over her shoeless bare foot and she jumps up real high then slams down real hard plus screams exceptionally loud then jist stands still like a Ceramic Statuette. Then she commences to shake and a whole alots of little puffs of air comes out from her mouth but she still don't move. Then her neck gets red and her brows gets white and her nose gets purple!

"G-Gosh, am I *s-sorry*, M-Mrs Foster! I d-didn't m-mean t-to...!"

Fred runs out from their home. I note that he ain't got nothing on but his Y-fronts in which his convivial weenie flops around in plus a broom in his hand.

"What the heck is going on out here anyhow?!"

"Spiders!" hollers Fred's Mom, "That big fat Sissy bastard tried to kill me!"

Now ain't that a unkind thing which to say?!

She runs in to their home and slams their door which leaves jist I and Divine Fred and my 3 spiders Fully Insulated on his front porch.

"Now why'd you have to go and do that, Danny?"

Fred makes a unkind face.

"I didn't m-mean to, F-Fred, m-my old p-pal."

I strive to yank my 2 eyes off from his Y-fronted Genitalias as my weenie is twitching like a chicken with their head chopped off.

"I j-jist w-wanted to s-show you m-my s-s-spiders! I ain't g-got n-no intentions on k-killing y-your M-Mom!"

"Well you've went and scared the heck outta Mom and she's as mad as a wet hen and I think you oughta better jist go home now," says My Divine Fred which is 14.

"Y-You c-can keep the sp-spiders. And th-this t-too!"

I twist the Tangy jar of Whiskey out from my back pocket and hand it to him. He looks unkind at me and my heart breaks in 2 plus a old big tear flops off from my piglet nose. It is bad enough jist being fat and pimply and heightened up Compassionate but to blubber in front of Fred is Dire! I oscillate sideways so he ain't able to note my horrid tears and snotted nose.

As I waddle away I hear My Divine Fred Foster whacking my 3 spiders to death with his broom.

5. MIRANDA COSMONOPOLIS AND THE "SHE'S SO FAT POLKA"

I am blue and lowly for 2 subsequential days about Fred and his poor misguided Mom's unkind words. How could I ascertain that she was a **ARACHNIDAPHOBIC?!** (A Flighty Individual which is a-scared of spiders!)

I am so blue and lowly that I can only listen to The Lonely Gal which is as blue and lowly as I on my battery radio. But said's battery is excessively weak which saddens me still farther.

So I ascertain to sit Fred's weenie on my back burner as I got Other Fish To Fry as The Wednesday Club is to give one of their Wednesday summer dances for us 7th graders today and I promised to meet dear Miranda Cosmonopolis there as no person won't dance with neither of us if we don't come. So we traditionally do so as to dance with each other hopefully in our Insulations.

Dear Miranda is exceedingly short and excessively wide from the front and sideways additionally as her 2 titties and heinie is big in all 5 Dimensions. She is not no fatter then I but seems a whole alots fatter due to said 2 titties which wobbles worst then my own tragic heinie and makes her arms and hands stick out plus flutter all over like mine does. However. It is Infinitely Admissible for a *girl's* arms plus hands to stick out and flutter as it don't denote no Sissification whatsoever when emanating from females but is

21

Anathema for we Sissies. Girls is lucky as no person can never call them Sissies with Impunity.

Dear Miranda is my only almost friend. (As said.) I am exceedingly glad on her Proximity as there would not be no Individual at school to converse with lacking her as at Lemon Gulch Elementary no person will touch me with a 10 foot pole. No person will touch dear Miranda with a pole neither as we Cohabit the same Communal Conundrum. (So to speak.)

So here is dear Miranda setting in a corner with her black long hair in 2 pigtails which is tied tight up over the top of her round little head which makes said head look exceedingly littler and a site to beseech. I myself do not look as horridly as traditional as I am wearing my 100 Percent red nylon seersucker long-sleeved no-iron shirt.

Anyhow. I note dear Miranda setting in a corner contiguous behind of a big palm tree planted in a Tin can. Dear Miranda habitually sets adjacent besides of big items so as that she don't seem so behemoth in comparison to said items. This propels her to purport to appear more Diminutive.

I now set down adjacent besides of her plus utter:

"W-Why the heck d-do th-they c-call this p-place the W-Wednesday C-Club anyhow?"

"I don't know," says dear Miranda real Courteous like always, "Maybe it is because it is Wednesday today?"

"Y-Yeah, I g-guess th-that's it."

I knew this prior however but jist wished to converse Amicably to cheer dear Miranda up as she is relentlessly nerve racked at these here dances and I am her Devotee plus am additionally nerve racked. So a Chat is required.

I ask her if she would desire to dance as I know the box step as kind Lottie Venables taught me it.

"I would be delighted," says dear Miranda which grabs on to a segmant on my arm as we waddle out on to the little dance floor. My right hand is impelled to rest on the top of her side underneath of her arm where I can procure a good grip as I ain't able to get close enough to her due to her 2 titties plus my fat tummy to put my arm totally around her waste in it's Entirety. Also I am 6 feet tall almost and she is approximately 5 feet which is additionally Disadvantageous.

When my hand touches Miranda she grunts and shuts her little eyes. You would have thunk it is the 1st time she got touched by a male on her waste! And she grunts every time she is touched which is repetitious. However. As I am a Devotee I do not mind at all.

Then PK Benderson which is a 8th grader and should not even of been here at our 7th grader's dance comes in with a record and puts it on the phonograph plus looks a unkind look at me also giving me The Finger Contemporaneously. I am Accustomized to said unkind looks and Fingers however and as long as PK loiters contiguous by the phonograph I ain't in no Immortal Danger.

I and dear Miranda grin at each other and commence to dance. I am sweating like a stuck pig but dear Miranda is as dry as a dog's bone and smells sweet like a Rose. (My all time favorite blooms.)

But PK's record is a Polka plus Brisk so we suddenly got to dance Brisk and Miranda's fat 2 titties and my fat tummy and heinie wobbles like a chicken with their head chopped off and the box step which kind Lottie Venables taught me don't work. But none of the other kids ascertains what their doing neither and it is fun. Then a Vocalist on the record sings:

> "She's so fat
> That nobody wants her!
> Nobody wants her!
> Nobody wants her!"

OH MY GOSH! PK'S RECORD IS "SHE'S SO FAT THAT NOBODY WANTS HER POLKA"!

> "She's so fat
> That nobody wants her!
> Nobody wants her!
> Do you?!"

A couple of girls dancing on our Vicinity notes I and dear Miranda wobbling and flapping plus giggles and a boy and a girl contiguous strives to not giggle but anyhow does. Plus PK gives me The Finger. If I was not so Accustomized to The Fingers I could jist set right down and blubber!

> "She's so fat
> That nobody wants her!
> Nobody wants her!

Nobody wants her!
She's so fat
That nobody wants her!
Nobody wants her!
Do you?!"
(Vocalizes said Vocalist.)

Pretty soon a whole alots of kids is laughing. I do not care as
they are always laughing at me anyhow and as sadly said I am
Fully Accustomized but poor Miranda ain't and the look on the
front of her round little head is horrifying in the extremes!

The Wednesday Club lady yanks PK's record instantaneously
off from the phonograph but Miranda commences to blubber real
hard anyhow and one of her 2 pigtails comes loose from the top of
her round little head upon which it was tied down upon plus flops
all over the place and she covers up her face with her big lacey
collar and literately runs in to the ladies's restroom like a chicken
with their head chopped off! PK is laughing like a hound sucking
eggs! I myself am still sweating like a stuck pig!

I waddle over to a bench against the wall and set down and
wipe said Prespiration off from my brows which is profuse. The
Wednesday Club Lady which is real mad impels every Individual
to stop laughing plus throws PK out from The Wednesday Club
and puts "To Each His Own" on to the phonograph. (one of my
favorite melodies.) It's about a rose which is impelled to remain
in the sun and rain in order for it's lovely promises to come true.
I myself am similar to said remaining rose. But as per me no
promises ain't never came true. As a rule it is better not to take no
promises from nobody. As they ain't hardly never kept. Which has
been my experiences with battery radios. (And promises.)

Every Individual calms down and dances along to this soft
nice music. Said song is sang by Mr Nat King Cole. I keep setting
on this bench up against the wall however as nobody but dear
Miranda will dance with me anyhow. (Not even with said pole.)

Suddenly I note the ladies's restroom door opening one small
bit and dear Miranda pokes her round little head out and her eyes
is all red and puffy although her pigtail is currently tied up where
it belongs with it's hairy Colleague.

Dear Miranda points at me to meet her jist outside on the big
Veranda and I ascertain that she don't desire to come back in to the
dancing room as she is in a State of Full Humiliation.

Dear Miranda which is exceedingly red-eyed sets down adjacent besides of me and I pat her genteel on the top of her head plus say:

"P-Please do not w-worry, dear M-Miranda."

Miranda instantaneously covers her round little face with her hands for one interval and snivels and whines which impels her titties to jiggle something awful!

After one additional interval she uncovers her face and wipes a Bevy of tears from her eyes with a hanky. Then she notes me for a duration and takes a additional hanky out from another pocket over her left tittie and wipes the Prespiration off from my Prespiring brows plus says:

"Thank you, Danny, you're a real nice boy."

I and Miranda do not go back to the dance as dear Miranda remains on a State of exceptional Humiliation so we jist set here on the Rear Veranda so as that I can impede my Prespiring and my danger of keeling over is Terminant.

However. Dear Miranda wipes my brows off 2 more times plus desires to wipe said once more even. But 3 times is proficient so I oscillate my brows away which impedes one additional sweat wipe plus say as kindly as feasible:

"Th-Thank you M-Miranda. Your r-real considerate b-but Th-Thrice is enough."

I waddle dear Miranda towards her home which is way up on the side of one of the dry 2 hills in which Lemon Gulch is crammed down in between on plus sing to her in hopes of alleviating said State. (Of Humiliation.) The song I sing is from the Major Motion Picture WHO CARES WHAT THE WORLD SAYS which features a Heart Rendering story about a Filthy Rich Individual which is in love with a Poverty Stricken girl which is Far Below him currantly playing at The Gulch Theater which I have jist saw. Said song goes:

> "Who cares what the world says
> *I* sure don't
> I'm in love with you
> Who cares what the world says
> I sure don't
> I know you love me too..."

After "I know you love me too" I look around to note if PK Benderson is following I and Miranda. He ain't. So I breathe a collective sigh of relief plus continue to sing:

> "Who cares what may happen
> *I* sure don't
> Your mine my whole life through..."

After "Whole Life Through" I terminate singing abruptly and tell Miranda for Safety's Sake that this is jist a song which don't Infer to I nor she personal but she don't seem to hear me and jist looks real sleepy at me plus grunts. Then I continue to sing and yank my hand back from her as she has jist grabbed it plus squeezed it exceptionally hard. Plus I sing:

> "So who cares what the world says
> *I* sure don't
> And I know you feel
> That way too."

I do not stutter none as I ain't never stuttered during song's singing.

By this currant minute we are contiguous of dear Miranda's home. It is dark almost and Miranda utters:

"That's a really pretty song, Danny."

"Th-Thank you, M-Miranda."

"Goodnight, Danny,"

"G-Goodnight, d-dear M-Miranda."

She opens her front door and goes in to her home which is a whole alots bigger and nicer then mine but I am glad for dear Miranda that her home is nicer and bigger as she requires a nicer bigger home as her Humane Condition is feasibly worst then mine as she is a girl plus is exceptionally Sensible. Girls suffers more then boys due to their most tender Sensitivities.

I waddle along plus ponder what it would be like to possess a real pal like Fred Foster with which to sleep in the same bed with. And with which to cuddle at night with and suck weenies with plus utter kind words To And Fro. Like Lottie Venables and Miss McCoy. Although neither of those kind ladies ain't got weenies. (Obviously!) Plus would not suck said even if they did possess one as ladies ain't got no desires to suck no weenies anyhow. Feasibly. (Probably Jarleen would suck Jack Shanks's weenie due to her Sharp Appetites.) (If Applicable.) (I ain't sure.)

As I waddle on home I note PK Benderson which loiters acrosst the street from The Big Lemon in front of the Saga Of The West Drugstore And Fountain Grill. But he don't note me as it is dark and I ain't on my bike as per as usual but am Fully Pedestrianized.

6. BURT AND OUR DROUGHT

It is Thursday morning which is the day on which I mow Lottie Venables lawn on every week. Lottie Venables is the kind music teacher on Palm Street which is jist around the corner from our home. I am currantly laying on the top of my bed as I ponder her and her grass.

Lottie possesses a friend which is named Miss Lela McCoy which is excessively lucky for me as Miss McCoy is the owneresse of LG Radios where I purchase square batteries for my battery radio which costs a total of one dollar each. For mowing Lottie's lawn I receive 25 cents as it ain't a big lawn but is skinny. However. As it slants up hill it impels me to sweat like a stuck pig but I Prespire exceedingly easy anyhow and can not blame no lawn for that. Nor don't.

It requires 4 weeks plus 4 mowings of said lawn to earn profi-cient funds for one new battery but as one battery lasts for only 2 weeks I know why I found said radio insides of a trash can! So I got to either mow more lawns which I do not relish to do as mowing lawns gets me excessively overheated up explicitly underneath of a merciless sun or else I got to find me a additional way to earn the other dollar to keep my radio perpetually co-operative on which I listen to The Lonely Gal's radio program on which is a Vital Necessity.

Plus without no radio I can not also listen to Bulldog Drummond and Superman. Or Portia Faces Life and Captain Midnight and Young Widder Brown. Or I Love a Mystery and Lux Radio Theater (Sunday afternoons only.) and Fibber McGee and Molly (Wednesday nights only.) and Baby Snooks! Plus Let's Pretend (Saturday mornings only.) and The Shadow which knows what evil lurks insides of the hearts of men! (And so do I.) (Explicitly PK Benderson's!) (Unfortunately.) And Inner Sanctum Mysteries (Sunday nights only.) and Lorenzo Jones and His Wife Bell and Mary Noble Backstage Wife. Plus Junior Miss. (Sunday mornings only.) So Lottie Venable's friend Miss McCoy is a God's Send and here is why:

Poor Miss McCoy possesses one lung only as it's Colleague collapsed unexpectantly in childhood so she wheezes Tempestuously and it is excessively arduous for her to squat and create radio displays in LG Radio's little display window. She can squat *down* OK but it is the squatting *up* which gets her wheezing out of controls. I know jist how she feels as I ain't able to do nothing about my keeling over neither nor my waddle plus I puff proficiently when it is too hot which is a whole alots and as often as not. (Explicitly underneath of a merciless sun.) (As said.)

Lottie Venables anyhow told Miss McCoy that I got a artistic talent as I showed Lottie a drawing I had drew of a large tittied lady in a Space Suit. (Which Little Norman requested that I draw so as he could note it and Onanate Contemporaneously.) So then Miss McCoy asked if I would create her a window display. I sure would and I complied suddenly with a exceedingly brilliant ideal. I made 24 little stick men out of pipe-cleaners plus stuck them down on their little feet acrosst the LG Radio's display window. Said feet was created by me with green Never-Harden Plasticine clay. Each little pipe cleaner man had a cut-out white paper face glued on with a delighted smile. In all of their 48 little Plasticine Never-Harden fists my stick men was holding a long and skinny winding cardboard sign which zig-zagged acrosst said display window upon which was painted upon:

> Purchase your radios from LG!
> Purchase your radios from LG!
> Purchase your radios from LG!

Was I a hit! Miss McCoy was delightful with my ideal plus I currantly get 25 cents every week to make new winding signs such as:

> Gosh! We sell batteries too!
> Gosh! We sell batteries too!
> Gosh! We sell batteries too!

> and (Upon Their Inception.)

> Clock-Radios Galore!

Clock-Radios Galore!
Clock-Radios Galore!
Clock-Radios Galore!
Clock-Radios Galore!

It is still Thursday morning. I made cinnamon toast with a whole alots of butter and sugar as there is butter and sugar now as Jarleen has jist boughten said. (Plus I charged one bread from the Busy Baker Truck but they was all out of Jelly doughnuts.) (Unfortunately.)

I am currantly sweating like a stuck pig as I bicycle down to LG Radios with my new sign as Miss McCoy closes early on Thursdays plus I got Lottie's lawn to additionally mow. I am on the look-out like always for the horrid PK which left a Dog's Turd and a dirty note:

BIG FAT SISSIES EAT SHIT

on our front porch which I immediately dispersed of Prior To Departure.

Miss McCoy which is wheezing Tempestuously and holding her sides like she Perennially does when the temperature accedes 85 degrees F gives me a ice cold Dr Pepper from her LG Radios Office icebox upon my arrival plus shows me the new clock radio with which I am to feature my new Serpentine sign with which says:

Another Clock Radio! Wow!
Another Clock Radio! Wow!
Another Clock Radio! Wow!

I gulp my Dr P down. I always gulp said down as it is more refreshing implicitly after a bicycle ride underneath of a merciless sun. Then I crawl slow as it is a exceedingly tight squeeze in to Miss McCoy's display window and yank my prior Serpentine sign out from the 48 little green Never Harden Plasticine fists of my 24 pipe cleaner stick men.

Then the bell on the LG Radios entrance door clinkles and in walks a guy in a pair of Levi-Dungarees! As I am laying down in said display window my piglet 2 eyes clamps explicitly on to his fly. A Levi buttoned fly! And every fool plus their brother knows that Levi's has got one less button then they require as their Denim Textile habitually bunches out and one can freely note right on to the convivial Y-fronts of the occupant insides which is exclusively what I am currently doing!

OH MY GOSH! Said guy is additionally wearing weenie-creeper jockey shorts which tugs one's weenie right out through their access-slots! So what I note is: **ONE SEGMANT OF SILKEN FOURSKIN POKING RIGHT IN TO MY EYE ALMOST! OH MY GOSH!**

I oscillate my head right up plus note out from the display window's little door the face of this Levi-wearer which has got curly brown hair and a gap between his front 2 teeth plus a exceedingly dark sun tan. He is a whole alots older then me but ain't no taller as I am inordinantly. (Tall.) (As said.) (one vital segmant of My Humane Condition.) (Besides my weenie Affiliations.)

"Danny," wheezes Miss McCoy, "this is Burt. Burt, this is Danny."

I got to oscillate way over on to my fat tummy to propel my fat heinie out from the little door of this display window to shake Burt's hot big hand.

"Hi, Danny," says Burt which smiles and squeezes my sweaty fingers and looks jist like the Pepsodent Toothpaste ad of the guy on the beach! The one with all them girls crowding contiguous plus grinning and poking their fingers on to his sun tanned tummy. This darn advertisement makes me eternally Irascible as every fool plus their brother would go bananas if I even put my thumb on to this Pepsodent Toothpaste's guy's sun tanned tummy. **WHY?! BECAUSE I AM A MALE, THAT'S WHY!** And one ain't permitted to touch other males on the top of their tummy nor on their Genitalias even if our Humane Conditions propels their-selves to! (Jist ask The Keyhole!)

Anyhow. "Hi, B-B-B-B..." I say.

"Burt," he says real Courteous then oscillates around to converse with Miss McCoy.

"B-B-B-B-B-B-B-B-B-Burt!" I continue to say untill I can say it plus go real red. Then I purport to tie my shoe so as to procure a long good peep through the gap on his Levi's fly which Features his Silken Fourskin to great Advantage. Said long good peep is Duly procured and then Miss McCoy wheezes Tempestuously:

"Danny, Burt is to help me take inventory of our stock. He'll move the big boxes for me."

I yank my piglet 2 eyes off from Burt's weenie but not prior to him noting me noting said bodily segmant!

"Burt," says Miss McCoy, "there's a new box of radios by the back door. Can you please unpack them, dear? I must go around the corner to the bank. You and Danny can take care of each other for a few minutes, can't you?"

"Sure, Miss McCoy, we sure can," says Burt which looks me right straight on to my piglet 2 eyes like he knows The Truth The Whole Truth And Nothing But The Truth about my Affiliations! I got to bend down and purport to tie my other shoelace so as every fool plus their brother will not note my weenie twitch!

"Be glad t-to, M-Miss M-McCoy," I utter real Courteous which Infers to Miss McCoy's kind taking-care-of each-other demand.

Miss McCoy gets a envelope from behind of the LG Radios Official counter and waves at us plus wheezes as she exits out from her door. Poor Miss McCoy. I know jist how she feels as the currant temperature is way on over her 85 degrees F wheezing borderlines.

"Danny," suddenly utters Burt, "can you please show me where the toilet is? I got to pee somethin' awful!"

"Sure, B-Burt, my old p-pal."

Burt slaps his hot big hand on my shoulder and I waddle him through the stock room back to said toilet. **OH MY GOSH IS THIS CONTENTING!**

"You don't, by no chance got to pee too, do you, Danny?"

"H-HUH?!" I say.

"If you got to pee too, old buddy," he says, "we could save us one whole toilet flush if we done it together. They're sayin' on the radio that we got to save water 'count of our drought this summer."

"Y-Yes, B-Burt," I utter, "th-that's a darn good ideal all r-right!"

I ain't hardly able to believe my luck! firstly his weenie-creepers! 2ndly his hot big hand right on to my shoulders! 3rdly one invitation for mutual alleviation!

My fat 2 legs wobble and my yellow little teeth chatter and I attain a Erection which snaps right out through the access-slot of my own weenie-creeper Y-fronts plus bumps on to a cold rivet insides of my Dungarees in Bliss.

Burt goes in to the toilet. I waddle in contiguous and he shoves the door shut and *locks* it and unbuttons *all* of his Dungaree buttons right from the top and yanks down his Y-fronts and the sweetest Boner I have ever saw flops right up adjacent against his sun-tanned tummy with a behemoth WHACK!

"Gosh, Danny, this heat always gives me a Boner when I got to pee!"

I could jist loiter here noting Burt's Boner untill the cows come home.

"Hey? Ain't you going to unbutton?"

I continue to loiter with my piglet 2 eyes clamped on to the shiny tip of Burt's clean sweet Genitalias in a Mute State of Full Imfatuation.

"Here, let me unbutton you, dear old buddy."

Burt unbuttons my Dungarees and yanks down my Y-fronts and my Boner pops up like a chicken with their head chopped off and then he kisses me right on the top of my nose!

Now ain't that a kind thing which to do?

Then he pushes his Boner down with one hand and shoves it between my fat 2 thighs right underneath of my Genitalias plus squirms it real slow insides of it's squirmy Silken Fourskin back and fourth and back and fourth in exceptional Bliss!

"Gee, don't that jist feel good, Danny?!"

"Oh, y-yes!" I holler, **"OH Y-Y-Y-Y-Y-Y-Y-Y-YES!"**

7. INFINITELY KIND LOTTIE VENABLES AND HER TRUE FRIEND OF HER HEART

"OH, YES, *WHAT*?!" hollers PK Benderson.

"OH Y-YES, I'M A F-FAT BIG S-SISSY!" I holler as my head is underneath of PK's big boot which is planted on top of it again plus am impelled to. (Holler.)

I try real hard to ponder my new pal Burt's Silken Fourskin again but I ain't able to Visualize it among my brains no more as PK hollers so **LOUD!**

Mr Snatchfold comes running out from his tool shop where he is sharpening and Lubricating Lottie Venables' lawn mower plus Divulges that said mower is Fully Lubricious and ready to Mow Up A Storm. His Divulging is real hard to hear as one of my ears is smashed contiguous on to the sidewalk and the other one is contiguous underneath of PK's boot. (As said.)

PK releases my head due to Mr Snatchfold's mean look at him and walks away plus gives me The Finger as per as usual.

Mr Snatchfold helps me to stand up as I feel woozy and fully ready to keel right on over. But don't and wheel Lottie's fresh sharpened and Lubricious lawn mower to her nice home.

I had took said lawn mower to Mr Snatchfold's for sharpening and Lubrication after I finished up with Miss McCoy's display window plus noted Burt's weenie segmant which however did not require no communal alleviation even although Lemon Gulch *is* Drought Ravished.

I suddenly note PK which leans contiguous on a mail box acrosst the street from Lottie's smoking a cigarette and giving me The Finger but commence to mow Lottie's grass anyhow as I got a Acute requirement for battery funds as my currant battery is on it's last 2 legs like a chicken with their head chopped off.

As it is exceedingly hot Lottie has got all of her windows wide opened and I can hear her playing her piano which is exceptionally soothing explicitly while mowing lawns underneath of a merciless sun.

After a duration when I am finished almost mowing Miss McCoy walks right up to Lottie's gate as it is Thursday and LG Radios always closes at 1PM which Sanctions Miss McCoy's currant presence.

"Your display is simply wonderful, Danny," says Miss McCoy, "Several customers have commented on it already and it's only been up an hour!"

What a Kind Bearer Of Glad Tidings she is!

"Lottie, dar-linggggg," wheezes Miss McCoy through Lottie's opened window subsequential, "I've brought cupcakes for two!"

Lottie's beauteous piano music terminates abruptly and Lottie's head comes poking right out from her window with a big smile right on the front of it!

"Oh, I do hope it's cupcakes for *three*, Lela, as Danny has been such a hard-working boy today! Isn't he handsome? See his red hair shine like flames?!"

Now ain't that a kind thing which to say?! Flames! 2 excessively kind things in one day and one right after the other! I push said red greasy hair out from my piglet 2 eyes plus Resolute that from now on I will view said red greasy hair much more favorable. (Like Flames.)

I am sweating like a stuck pig when I terminate mowing so Lottie takes me to her shiny bathroom and gives me a wash rag which smells like Roses plus a towel and says that I should freshen myself up for Tea For 3. **OH MY GOSH!** I ain't even never had Tea For one! As Jarleen don't never cook tea. (She don't hardly ever never cook *nothing*!) (As said.)

I take my T-shirt off plus wash the Prespiration off from my face and out from underneath of my fat 2 arms and off from my jiggly tummy plus note my red head-hair in Lottie's wash basin mirror which makes me contented for once to view it. I will ponder my good hair again tonight if I am blue and lowly which is Highly Feasible.

As I am combing said hair I hear beauteous music coming out from Lottie's piano in her front room plus hear a beauteous voice which commences to sing:

"Believe me
If all those endearing young charms
Which I gaze on so fondly today..."

I terminate hair-combing and waddle down the hall and peep on to Lottie's front room. As Lottie plays her piano Miss McCoy loiters contiguous with her 2 hands on top of Lottie's shoulders plus sings incessantly:

"...Were to change by tomorrow
And fleet in my arms
Like fairy gifts fading away..."

I had never even knew that Miss McCoy could sing plus ponder if she takes lessons from Miss Fishlock like dear Miranda Cosmonopolis as her singing is Flawless!

However. She commences to wheeze Tempestuously as the temperature currantly accedes her borderlines but anyhow bends over and looks right in Lottie's face and sings relentlessly.

"Thou would'st still be adored
As this moment thou art..."

Lottie's blue 2 eyes gets all wet from tear-squirting and she terminates her playing and reaches up from the piano and grabs one of Miss McCoy's hands and kisses it tender. Then Miss McCoy bends over farther and hugs her real genteel. Then Lottie commences to play again and Miss McCoy bends back up and commences to sing again plus wheezes as bending up is jist as arduous as squatting up due to one's breathing implications.

"Let thy loveliness fade
As it will..."
(Sings Miss McCoy.)

I am exceptionally contented to note these Infinitely kind 2 affectionants which gives me great Bliss!

"And around the dear ruin..."
(Sings Miss McCoy.)

My piglet 2 eyes is wet with tears of lonely kindness which squirts right out as I know jist how Lottie and Miss McCoy feel. I wisht I had someone with which to feel this way with. Even *one* parent would be proficient. (But one male friend on my own Bracket would be Preferable.)

Miss McCoy currantly notes down at the top of Lottie's head as Lottie plays her piano and shoots a exceptionally tender look at Lottie's hair feasibly noting the Fading Loveliness in The Dear Ruin of said. Plus sings and wheezes:

"...Each wish of my heart
Would entwine itself
Verdantly still."

I await untill they terminate their song and hug again then I waddle in to Lottie's front room as I do not wish to scare nobody by coming up contiguous unexpectantly like a German spy.

Lottie requests me to set down which I do as I am real wore out from lawn mowing.

Lottie and Miss McCoy set down adjacent besides of Lottie's coffee table and Lottie notes Miss McCoy with Devotion as she pours I and Miss McCoy one tea Per each of us plus hands me a Cupcake from a big dish of 8 with pink and light blue frosted tops.

Then Lottie suddenly yanks her 2 eyes off from Miss McCoy and interrogates me as to how is my display window creation job going?

"He is brilliant!" wheezes Miss McCoy which chews on a exceptionally nice light blue Cupcake, "He is just brilliant! Danny has a definite future in display window decor."

"I am *so* glad for you," says Lottie which touches my hand, "Life is occasionally difficult, isn't it, Danny?"

"Y-Yes, M-Miss V-V-V-V-V-V..."

"For people like us," says Lottie real quick so as I ain't got to finish pronouncing her last name due to my pronounciation implication of which she is real Vigilant of.

"Yes," says Miss McCoy which possesses a real far away look in one of her eyes.

"But we persevere, do we not, Lela?" says Lottie, "Do we not, Lela dear, the true friend of my heart?"

"We do indeed, Lottie dear, my kindred spirit."

"And so will you too, Danny," says Lottie. "Won't he, Lela? Persevere?"

Miss Lela McCoy literately shakes said far-away look right out from her eye plus says:

"Indeed he will, Lottie, persevere."

I do not know what the heck they are Chatting on as I do not know what Persevere Infers to. However. I make Mental Notations to look it up on my Severely Abridged Webster's.

Lottie gives me a additional Cupcake and I chew away in between swallowing gulps of suu-perrb sweet tea as I added Multitudes of sugar.

"Have you...errr, got a special girlfriend, Danny?" wheezes Miss McCoy.

I terminate chewing my pink Cupcake plus ponder whether dear Miranda Cosmonopolis comes underneath of the Heading of Special Girlfriend even although she is my *only* girlfriend and my only almost friend besides my black and white small dog Tinker and Little Norman Tomlin. I decide that Miranda don't come underneath of Special Girlfriend Heading but belongs under the *Only* Girlfriend Bracket so I say:

"N-No."

"Good," says Lottie, "No use begging for heartache."

"Have you got any special...errr, boyfriends?" wheezes Miss McCoy.

"F-Fred F-Foster," I utter joyously.

"Good," says Lottie.

"I'm in l-love w-with him," I additionally utter before I even can impede myself! Which is a excessively STUPID item to utter right out in front of other Individuals but said jist flops out as I feel so delightful with these contenting 2 friends of their hearts.

"Y-Yes. F-Fred F-Foster!" I utter repetitiously as I instantaneously do not care which knows it!

"Good," says Lottie.

Good?! You could of knocked me over on a feather!

"Good," says Miss McCoy additionally which also says:

"Burt is an exceptionally nice young man and seems also to be other-directed."

"But Burt is seventeen. Danny is a bit young for..." utters Lottie.

"Of course," says Miss McCoy which gets real red for one full interval plus says:

"Whatever was I thinking? Danny is just so...well...tall for his age."

She really Infers to that I am obese but as she is so kind she don't utter said as it might insult me even although I am Fully Accustomized. But ain't that a kind thing which not to say? (Talk about perpetual Courtesy!)

During the rest of our Tea for 3 Lottie and Miss McCoy plays me a record from A Long Diseased Composer of which I ain't never heard of. They also give me 3 more Cupcakes from the kitchen even although I have ate 3 plus they look in to their 4 eyes and pat the hands of each other a whole alots in a State of Full Bliss.

Alas! As I ain't Vigilant PK Benderson grabs me jist as I am exiting out from Lottie's front gate. Miss McCoy has stayed so as her and Lottie can compare notes about our new Lemon Gulch librarian which is A Tall And Handsome Unmarried Lady Of A Certain Age.

PK which has grabbed me now commences to poke me with a sharp stick and impels me to waddle in front of him underneath of a merciless sun all the way to The Big Lemon. (More about The Big Lemon later.) I get exceptionally purple and PK lets me go without slamming his boot on to my head as he is a-scared I might keel right over and croak as Croaking runs in our family right along with Hormonal Unbalances and Relentless Pubescences. (For Eons.) (As said.)

I waddle past Lottie's on my way home from The Big Lemon plus hear beauteous music Emanating from her phonograph. I got a behemoth desire to join them 2 kind affectionants in that house of contentment but do not as their happiness is Sublime and I do not wish to spoil nothing by being reddishly present even if they got beauteous music and Multi-Colored Cupcakes.

Anyhow. I ascertain that from now on when I hear beauteous music I will ponder in Bliss on Lottie Venables and her true friend of her heart Miss Lela McCoy and their Long Diseased composer.

8. PLEASE DO NOT B-BLUBBER
POOR W-W-WOLFGANG

As I am laying on my bed tonight I ponder what Miss McCoy Infers to when she says that Burt is Other Directed. She did not say which direction. There is 4. West. South. East. North. Ladies is a Enigma.

I am exceedingly jaded from lawn mowing plus walking clear to The Big Lemon being poked with said sharp stick by the Inexorable PK. (More about The Big Lemon later.) (As said.) So my brains jist wanders all over the place and I ain't able to sleep plus I do not feel like no Onanation is Eminent.

I can not ascertain why I suddenly ponder poor Wolfgang which is A Misplaced Boy from Germany and one year older then I. But I do anyhow.

Poor Wolfgang was On Approval in Mrs. Godwin's class of which he is a whole alots older then. Not in my class of which Mrs Vealfoy is the teacher of and which don't like me as her United States Marine husband was caught with a additional United States Marine 2 years prior which makes her eternally bitter. Which is what Little Norman told me although he did not utter what Mrs Vealfoy's Marine husband and the additional United States Marine had did during which they was caught doing it plus Little Norman did not know who caught said nor whom told him that said was caught in the 1st place. Little Norman really don't know much at all but is immature which is Explicable. (Although he is sporadically Erudite.) (Sometimes.) (Fortunately!) (But only on Esoteric items.) (Sex. Ect. Ect. Ect.)

Mrs Vealfoy said that Wolfgang was supposed to learn about America 1st plus get hisself Fully Accustomized to our Proclivities prior to being submitted to a class with his own age. But every person pondered that Wolfgang was goofy insides of his brains as he jist loitered around on the playground during recess looking nothing but. He smiled kindly a whole alots although which is contenting but he never said nothing implicit when you conversed to him due to said goofiness.

Anyhow. I ponder him currantly as he is real tall with black hair which hangs down right on to his brows like that Madman

38

Hitler's unfortunately done plus he possesses a protrusive weenie which I noted habitually. (Wolfgang's not Hitler's!) But poor Wolfgang don't reside here no more anyhow as he has went plus took that convivial weenie with him. (Alas.)

PK Benderson did not like poor Wolfgang. Plus marched on Nazi Goose Steps adjacent behind of him and hollered Heil Hitler which ain't a excessively kind item which to holler at no poor Misplaced German boy which has feasibly jist excaped from said Madman's Clutches!

PK is Infinitely Unkind and I jist can not ascertain why and I hate to utter this as it ain't kind neither but I Loathe poor misguided PK with great compassion as he is **A GOD DAMNED SON OF A BITCH!** I am sorry I said that but was impelled to by Righteousness. (Please ignore said Impudent Epigram.)

Anyhow one day I waddle by and note poor Wolfgang setting behind of the Bleachers after school which is let out for the day and I ponder that Wolfgang might be striving to Onanate behind of said when all us kids has went home. This is of interest to me. It can not be denied that he currantly sets on a popular Onanistic district and I could be impelled to Onanate with him at the drop of one hat. However. He *could* be feasibly commencing to catch Black Widows. So I waddle over to him plus say:

"Hi W-Wolfgang! G-Going to catch you s-some b-black w-widow s-spiders?"

He jist looks up at me like he don't know what the heck I am talking about and I am Chatting plain English! I ponder that I must of been stuttering a whole alots. However. I set down adjacent and jist set here for a full duration. Suddenly he commences to blubber.

"W-Why are y-you blubbering, W-Wolfgang?" I utter soft.

Well he jist looks at me with this goofy look. So. As I can not stand to see nobody blubbering I put my arm on his neck plus am I shocked when he flops his head right down on to my shoulder plus blubbers louder even!

I oscillate around real quick to note if said school-exiting out kids has saw us but they ain't as all have went home prior. So I utter real soft and genteel:

"P-Please d-do n-not b-blubber poor W-Wolfgang."

Well. Wolfgang jist notes me for one interval and his eyes gets all goofy and he grabs me and puts his 2 arms around me and squeezes me like a hound sucking eggs plus blubbers additionally harder.

AM I MORTIFIED! Lucky for me we set behind of said Bleachers and every fool plus their brother has went home. (As said.)

Poor Wolfgang squeezes me untill it is real hard to breathe and I smother almost plus ponder that this is some sort of German Wrassling of which I ain't framiliar of. But as poor Wolfgang is blubbering this don't seem to be The Case.

Then I really got to admit that I commence to note poor Wolfgang's protrusive weenie as he is setting extemely contiguous. Said protrusive weenie however is of the same Dimension as per as usual and ain't in the least Tumescent in any way Whatsoever. However. I myself have attained a Boner due to all of these hugging Fricasees plus ponder for one interval about unbuttoning Wolfgang's brown corduroys and yanking out his German weenie and slamming my piglet mouth right down on to said like a chicken with their head chopped off! **OH MY GOSH!** It would be the 1st German weenie I had ever saw plus as poor Wolfgang is older and even taller then me his Genitalias will be feasibly ripened Unto Their Majority. Like mine is due to my Hormonal Unbalance which impels my Relentless Pubescence. (**ET AL!**) (As said!)

This is what I ponder as poor Wolfgang sets there hugging me plus blubbering. Although I am sad that he is blubbering and desire to ascertain why plus comfort him I jist can't keep his weenie out from among my brains while I wiggle Tumultuously in my Y-fronts.

Anyhow. I permit Wolfgang to hug me plus hug him back as I wish seriously to alleviate his blubbering but ponder suddenly on what would occur if PK Benderson seen us!

Then poor Wolfgang puts his mouth real close to my ear plus says:

"V-Vee h-high sun s-see?"

And I say:

"S-See wh-what?!"

Wolfgang jist looks goofy at me and blubbers. So I hug him additionally which makes him blubber harder! Have I jist did something wrong? Hugging should impel sad Individuals to be content. Hugging would perpetually content *me* in the extremes. But *I* ain't no German Misplaced Boy like Wolfgang. (Obviously!) As although I am a sissy I am a American Sissy through and through!

Wolfgang finally stops blubbering and takes his 2 arms off from contiguous around my neck plus says:

"V-Veeder S-Sane" and exits out from behind of said Bleachers. Unfortunately I ain't able to waddle out Contemporaneous as I got a behemoth Erection which impedes Vicarious motion so I got to hunch low and loiter. But as said Boner will not dwindle down I am impelled to crawl way back underneath of said Bleachers and ponder Fred Foster's weenie plus Onanate. When abruptly content I shrink down plus crawl out from underneath of the Bleachers and note if PK Benderson is lurking on my district. He ain't so I waddle on home with Impunity.

The day before school lets out for summer vacation my teacher Mrs Vealfoy requests me to stay after the other kids has went home and I get excessively worried as I ponder that Mrs Vealfoy has detected my weenie Affiliations and I do not desire for their Divulgence like in The Keyhole. (That unkind Periodical with variegated Sex Crimes.) (Mentioned sadly prior.)

"Danny," says Mrs Vealfoy exceedingly Courteous but not kind as she ain't never due to her bitterness on her United States Marine husband which was caught with that additional one, "I have a message for you from Wolfgang's mother."

OH MY GOSH! Am I shocked as I do not know Wolfgang's mother from Adam which is German. Plus do not know no other German Misplaced Persons neither excepting for Wolfgang plus hope Wolfgang ain't Divulged that I noted his weenie Acutely.

"Wolfgang is being moved to another school," says Mrs Vealfoy.

"F-For goofy k-kids?"

"Goofy?" says Mrs Vealfoy, "Goofy?! Wolfgang isn't goofy. Do you mean that he stutters? You stutter too. That does not necessarily make you goofy. Although I *do* sometimes wonder."

"W-Wolfgang s-stutters?!"

"No more than *you* do."

"W-Why is he being m-moved to another s-school?"

"He is going to a special school to learn to speak English."

"Is he d-dumb or s-something?"

"Wolfgang is an *extremely* bright boy," says Mrs Vealfoy which looks right at me plus turns her mouth down due to exceptional bitterness. (As said.) "It is a real pity we don't have *more* like him!" she adds additionally with her bitter 2 eyes Glaring right on to me!

"Th-Then why d-don't he talk English? All th-the G-Germans

in th-the M-Motion P-Pictures t-talk English only f-funny l-like G-Germans t-talk English."

Mrs Vealfoy jist notes me with her 2 eyebrows all squinched up in a Heightening State. "Wolfgang liked you very much. His mother told me to tell you. And she said that he said to say goodbye to you."

This was the most Mrs Vealfoy conversed at me in the darn whole year excepting for telling me not to squeeze pimples on my brows in her classroom.

It is still Thurday night plus here I am still laying on my bed still pondering poor Wolfgang. **OH MY GOSH!** Why didn't some teacher tell us that he can not talk our English Language from his Inception at our school? *Any* Individual would blubber if every fool plus their brother at school can talk English and one's own self ain't able to! Poor Wolfgang. I know jist how he feels as no person will Chat with me due to my Humane Condition In A Often Uncaring World plus I talk the English Language and Utilize multiple Intriguing words!

Anyhow. I am content as Wolfgang liked me. Now I got a total of 3 friends. Dear Miranda Cosmonopolis and Little Norman plus Wolfgang but not including Lottie Venables and Miss McCoy which ain't on my own age Bracket although their kind friends. Oh yes. My black and white small dog adores me but ain't humane. And My Divine Fred Foster is on a back burner with his poor misguided Mom which swears horrid.

OH MY GOSH! I jist remembered that I forgot to procure my Urination Protecto-Sheet from our Clothesline. I sincerely hope I do not pee my bed tonight as I am too fatigued to procure said Protecto Sheet momentarily.

Anyhow. Wolfgang has went. Plus took his sweet weenie with him. I wisht he had not of went to this other school as I could of been a excessively good friend of his. Maybe We'll Meet Again Don't Know Where Don't Know When.

9. THE LONELY GAL

I have became exceptionally blue and lowly due to all of these Ruminations on poor Wolfgang and what the horrid PK Benderson done to him plus what us other unspecified persons done as we ascertained he was goofy as he could not Chat on our Mother's Tongue.

I am additionally blue and lowly about Fred Foster's poor misguided swearing Mom plus been pondering about her a whole alots as Fred Foster's Mom is a adult neighbor which should of ought to of knew better.

Lucky for me it is almost time for The Lonely Gal which always heightens me right up when I am blue and lowly and Fully Insulated.

My black and white small dog Tinker which adores me is sleeping on the top of my blankets adjacent besides of my feet currantly so I turn out our kerosene lamp which smokes like a hound sucking eggs and turn on my battery radio as it is 10 PM and The Lonely Gal's soft kind voice instantaneously utters:

"Hello, Lonely Guy. This is your own Lonely Gal speaking to you from Port City. Lonely Guy, are you out there, honey? Are you?"

"Y-Yes, d-darling."

"Did you miss me, Lonely Guy?" utters The Lonely Gal.

I nod my greasy head Yes.

"Then say it, Baby, say it! Say you missed your own Lonely Gal!"

"I m-missed you a wh-whole alots, L-Lonely G-Gal!" I say although I do not really miss her a whole alots currantly as I got a exceptional sum of items among my brains. Anyhow. I know in real actuality that she ain't able to hear me. But I always strive to be kind even to persons which can not hear me as persons should be kind. **ALL OF THEM.** (My Motto.) (As said.)

So here I am all reddish and fat and pimply and Fully Insulated with my right ear smashed up contiguous against my battery radio listening to this lonely kind lady which says she loves me sporadically as I ponder items such as:

Is she fat too?
A possesser of pimples too?
A jiggly big tummy too?
A Floppy heinie too?
Is she Cruelly Incapacitated too?
Why is *she* lonely?

43

"I saw you, Baby," says said Gal real soft and lowly, "just after lunch yesterday. I prayed you'd turn around and look at me. My little old heart did flip-flops, Sugar. But you just continued to stride along in all your manly grace."

Me? Manly?! She would surely change her mind if she had *really* saw me as I am a far fling from Manly as I waddle habitually to procure My Perfect Balance!

"To love and to be loved," says The Lonely Gal, "It is The Human Condition, baby."

OH MY GOSH! THE HUMANE CONDITION!

I commence to Prespire! She knows about Humane Conditions In A Often Uncaring World!

Then said Gal sticks on a record which plays soft and sweet.

> "I've got a thing for you
> Baby
> Hope every day and every night
> Maybe
> I'll rush down the street
> We'll chance to meet
> Our fingers'll entwine
> And I'll feel so fine
> 'Cause Baby
> You'll be mine
> All mine..."

As this considerate kind song continues I get all heightened up! I will find the address of The Lonely Gal's broadcast studio in the yellow pages! I will catch the cheap (Non-Expressive.) bus to Port City and meet The Lonely Gal face to face tomorrow and **FRIENDSHIPS WILL BLOOM!**

I can get the bus's fare out from underneath of our Davenport's Cushions when Bull fastens on his phony leg and alleviates one's self tomorrow morning as a Bevy of loose funds invariantly falls out from his pockets in to between said Cushions as he lays there snoring all day. (Due to his Expulsion from Jarleen's Exclusive bedroom.) (As sadly said.) (Prior.) (I collect said loose funds once a month only as I wish for them to Conglomerate.)

But! Then I instantaneously remember that Bull is in the Inebriation Unit and I ain't got to await for said morning alleviation. So I waddle out to our front room and root through our

44

Davenport's Cushions like a hound sucking eggs plus find a whole alots of cookie crumbs and dried up old curly bread crusts and a big piece of brown lettuce which don't look even like lettuce no more. **OH MY GOSH!** There ain't nothing here but garbage! Then I note a 2 dollar bill stuck real far back contiguous on to a rusty spring plus grab it out and waddle back to my bedroom and stick it in to my Bright Blue Corduroys which lays on a chair and climb back on to my bed jist as The Lonely Gal Signs-Off with her traditional song which she herself has wrote:

"Who knows
what may happen tomorrow?
Will it be happiness?
Will it be sorrow?"

If PK Benderson grabs me it will surely be sorrow tomorrow! *WHY* **DO I PERMIT SUCH ACTS OF BRUTALITY?!**

"Who knows
what may happen next week?"
A kick in the pants?
A peck on the cheek?"

Feasibly a kick in the pants if PK Benderson is contiguous. As no person never Pecks me on my cheeks. None of 'em.

My tears squirt out and I find a Kleenex underneath of my bed which is Severely stiff from dried-up Spermatozoans. I blow my nose on said Kleenex irregardless of said Mélange while The Lonely Gal sings:

"Will a new love
take the place of the old?
Will happiness
paint the clouds gold?
Or will this longing for you
fill me with sorrow and pain?
Will it be only... honey, be honest...
Will it be only, more lonnnnnnnely?"

The Lonely Gal terminates with a little sweet kiss and I switch off my radio as it's so late and it's battery is low. However. I stop blubbering and suddenly feel exceedingly heightened up about my bright ideal to visit The Gal!

As I do not wish to ponder Fred Foster' weenie as said is currantly on my back burner I ponder instead on the Pepsodent Toothpaste ad guy's Lower Pelvic Torsal Regions and attain a Erection plus Onanate and am abruptly contented.

Then as my black and white small dog Tinker is Somnolent she emits one traditional fart which instantaneously impels me to open my window wide plus poke my head out for Oxygen as it is a exceedingly hot night in Lemon Gulch.

If you do not desire to get overheated up do not sleep in no Gulch! Jarleen says that Lemon Gulch is a behemoth ditch with real steep sides which you can not climb out of even if you could! But my deeply departed Grandma says that Lemon Gulch is jist like any other place on Our Cosmos which is jist like Mayonnaise which is a Colloidull Admixture of Lemons and Vinegar which is bitter (Like Mrs Vealfoy due to her United States Marine husband which got caught.) and Egg Yolks and Soothing Variegated Oils which is soft and comforting. (Like Lottie Venables and Miss McCoy and their Long Diseased Composer.) However. It has been my Experiences that there is a whole alots more Lemons and Vinegar in Lemon Gulch's Mayonnaise then there is Egg Yolks and Soothing Variegated Oils.

Anyhow. I mount back on to my bed and commence to go right to sleep plus hope I will not pee insides of my bed while Somnolent but will dream about The Lonely Gal instead of. Mayhaps she can tell me why My Humane Condition ain't inclusive with Humane Love.

10. THE FATTER EVEN THEN I BOY

In the morning excessively early I waddle in to Jarleen's bedroom (After having took my pee-soaked sheet to the garage to soak in a Wash Tub.) and tell her I got to study with a friend for the Gulch Annual Spelling Bee as I require a excuse to go to Port City to meet The Lonely Gal and I might be out exceedingly late tonight. But My Beauteous Mom ain't Acutely interested anyhow as my studying ain't got nothing to do with my Genitalias in which she possesses a Acute Interest in. But I bring her a coffee in bed anyhow. I would of loved to of brung her a jelly doughnut but we didn't have none as I have ate them all and I would of feasibly ate *it* too even if we had of had one additional one. (Know Thyself!) (I do!) (Unfortunately.)

As Bull is interred at The Inebriation Unit I ponder if Jack Shanks is underneath of Jarleen's bed hiding. He probably ain't as no Irreconcilable noises was heard last night. But they are exceptionally Secretive these 2 about their Esoteric Ventures.

After coffee and garbing plus makeup Jarleen commences to exit out from our home on her journey to Tangy Mayo to which she always walks to as there ain't never Adequate funds for gasoline as our funds is perpetually Squandered on vital purchases of Vat 69 Whiskey for Bull. But Tangy Mayo ain't real far away anyhow as Lemon Gulch ain't behemoth but is only Modest And Unassuming like Clark Kent is. (Superman!)

I now loiter by our front door jist as Jarleen passes by as if I am contiguously adjacent it is feasible that she might Peck me goodbye. However. She don't. (I better not hold my breath untill she does!) (Ha. Ha.) (I would suffocate!) (Joke.)

I watch Jarleen sashay down our street like I always do as she looks simply suu-perrb when a merciless sun beats down on to her glittery Pompadour. What a Beauteous Mom I got! I wisht she would Chat with me about anything excepting whether I stick my fat fingers up some little bad girl's pants.

I take a bath and garb one's self in my Bright Blue Corduroys and 100 Percent red nylon seersucker no-iron long sleeved shirt which sets off my new shampooed and Brylcreemed flaming hair which I don't no longer consider as no Distinct Liability. (Due to Lottie Venable's kind utterances about said.) (Hair.) (Mine.) (Flames.)

I make sure I got said 2 dollar bill safe insides of my pocket then jist as I am waddling out from our front door our darn telephone rings so I waddle back plus answer it like I always do as Bull is Inebriated in Perpetuity and Jarleen answers said telephone only when she is occupying our home which she currently ain't but she don't like to answer said even while she is in occupation as the only almost person which ever calls her is mean Aunt Edna May which as Jarleen says bores her Shitless. Anyhow I pick up said telephone.

"H-Hello?"

"Would you so kindly put Mr Bull on to the telephone, if you please," says this here lady's voice, "I wish to converse with he."

"M-Mr B-Bull is in Th-The I-Inebriation Unit but he is t-traditionally b-back home by 2 P-PM."

"To whom do I have the pleasure of speaking to?" she utters, "is this Danny? Bull's little son?"

I do not like the Little because I ain't. As I am proficiently fat plus tall. However I utter back:

"Y-Yes, I am s-said s-son."

"Huh?!" says this here lady's voice, "To whom am I speaking to?"

"D-Danny."

"Pleased to meet yer acquaintance, Danny. Bull has often spoke to me of you quite endlessly."

I ponder that she wishes to converse as why would she tell a lie if she don't as Bull ain't never spoke endlessly of me to nobody even hisself as he never says nothing but Hello Joe. What do you know? What are a-cookin' in Tokio? (As said.) (Alas.)

"Nice day we're havin', ain't it, Danny?" says this unspecified lady.

"Y-Yes."

"It ain't so hot as yesterday, though."

"N-No."

"You could of flushed me right down the toilet yesterday and I wouldn't of minded."

As I am currently pondering about that bus which I got to catch to Port City I do not say nothing kind like I ought to of but am silently Mute. I guess she notes my intense desires to get off of our telephone as she says right after one behemoth sigh:

"Well, Danny, when Jack Shanks brings Bull back from the Inebriation Unit could you so kindly tell him that Flo called?"

"I'm exiting out n-now f-for P-Port C-City."

Which sounds real important.

"Oh, you *are*!?"

"Y-Yes m-ma'am," I say real kind as I strive to hide the Assertion that I am in a big great hurry to catch that bus as it ain't kind to cut her off, "B-But I will w-write B-Bull a n-note however."

"You *are* kind."

Now don't this prior sentence jist fill me up with joyous Bliss! (As kindness is my motto.) (As said.) (Innumerous times!)

"It has been a great pleasure to talk with you, Danny. Maybe one day we will meet face to face. Goodbye, honey," says Flo.

"G-Goodbye, Miss F-Flo."

"Please call me 'Flo', Danny, everbody does. My name is Firenze but they call me Flo."

Although I might miss my bus I do not wish to disappoint her expectations so I say excessively conversational:

"I g-get woozy in the h-heat w-when it is s-so h-hot. I h-hope to g-gosh it is c-cooler t-tomorrow...F-Flo."

"Me too," says Flo which laughs real long and joyous then hangs up the telephone.

I got real deep feelings for lonely unspecified Individuals.

I exit out and lock our home up and release my black and white small dog Tinker from our garage so as she can joyously get fucked by 3 dogs which loiter around like hounds sucking eggs and can have puppies whom I adore.

I am jist rolling my bicycle out from said garage when I note poor misguided PK Benderson which comes by about 4 times per week to Razz me from the middle of our street in front of our home. He ain't seen me so I squat down behind of our garage and hide for a half hour as he sets there on a yellow fire Hydrant plus smokes 3 cigarettes as he is jist dying for me to prance out on to his site and attempt to procure my Perfect Balance.

PK leaves finally without detecting me and I bicycle down to the Bus's Station. Because of this horrid Bully I miss the cheap Non-Expressive bus and got to await 2 hours as the next 2 buses is expressly non-stopping to Port City and cost too much.

I set down at the Serving Counter in the Saga Of The West Drugstore And Fountain Grill/Bus's Station and consume a complementary Marshmallow Sundae and Peruse Funnybooks. (I am allowed this Largesse as I sweep the sidewalk which lays contiguous sporadically.) (The Bus's Station segmant is maintained by Michelangelo Ricardito Da Vinci Martinez which sweeps it up hisself and Labors for Mr Sebastien and Miss Violet Melmoth which is the proprietors of The Drugstore And Fountain Grill segmant of The Saga Of The West Drugstore And Fountain Grill/ Bus's Station.) (To be Implicit.)

It is almost 2 PM as I embark on to the cheap bus to Port City plus am soaking wet with sweaty Prespiration and am surprised to note a boy which is even fatter then I which is additionally sweating like a stuck pig plus looks hot and miserable. I know jist how he feels as my own dear Genitalias is currently exceptionally raw due to their traditional merciless chafing among my fat 2 thighs.

I ponder if this fatter even then I boy desires to discuss his

Humane Condition with I and The Lonely Gal so as our bus pulls out from said station I kindly smile at said boy plus say:

"H-Hello, old p-pal!"

Plus set down right adjacent besides of. As I am fat he will not seem like he is so fat by comparison to fat me even although I am a whole alots skinnier then he. But I ain't doing myself no harm neither setting down contiguous of such a fat boy as I will appear thinner next to he which is fatter. (In A Manner Of Speaking.)

The bus stops unexpectantly and I flop right up against this obese boy's heinie! (As said heinie covers the total bus's seat almost!)

"Hey, Fatso!" he hollers "Leave my butt be! What are you, a dirty queer or somethin'?!"

A DIRTY QUEER?! What the heck is **A QUEER?!**

The bus starts up again and the fatter even then I boy suddenly removes hisself from off of our communal bus's seat and squeezes his fat big heinie right by me and sets in the rear segmant of our bus from where he currantly notes me real unkind from!

As if I ain't got enough on my brains our bus breaks down so we are impelled to jist set here in the heat. The fatter even then I boy finally flops right over on to his bus's seat and commences to snore Barbariously.

The only other person on the bus not counting me and said unkind boy plus the Handsome Bus's Driver is a old blind lady which is Perusing a Volume with her fingers. I know jist how she must feel in her Dire darkness and I right away got to ponder something else or I might blubber so I ponder Fred Foster's weenie. But blubber anyhow.

11. THE HANDSOME CARELESS BUS'S DRIVER

Then I get a bright ideal! So I blow my nose on a wadded-up Kleenex and wipe my eyes on the long sleeve of my 100 Percent red nylon seersucker no-iron shirt plus waddle down the aisle of our bus to the Handsome Bus's Driver which possesses curly black hair on his head.

"C-Can you p-please tell me, s-sir, how s-soon will they s-send another b-bus?" I utter exceptionally Courteous.

The Handsome Bus's Driver which is setting in his Driver's

Seat with his back on to me don't say nothing so I utter additionally Courteous:

"S-Sir? I wonder s-sir if we got to s-set here all d-darn d-day?"

I converse soft and lowly so as not to wake up the fatter even
then I boy nor disturb the blind poor lady which is Vicariously
Perusing with her Heroic fingers. (As said.)

Prespiration is literately pouring right off from me and I am
sure I will be impelled to pee real hard real soon. I ponder that if
the Temperature gets any hotter I might additionally jist keel over.
Said Temperature is way over Miss Lela McCoy's wheezing borderlines so I am exceptionally glad she ain't here as no Co-Sufferer
which is a comfort!

Said Handsome Bus's Driver still don't answer my interroga-
tions and don't even oscillate his head around to do so. So I waddle
farther down said bus's aisle and squat contiguous plus note that
he is sleeping with his 2 legs stuck right out in front of him.

THAT AIN'T ALL THAT I NOTE! This Handsome careless
Bus's Driver ain't even buttoned up his pants the last time he alleviated hisself! Plus **OH MY GOSH** the access slot is wide open
on his boxer shorts! My weenie wiggles like a chicken with their
head chopped off so I purport to tie my shoe and squat closer for a
better peep. (A old trick of mine.)

Said Bus's Driver is breathing genteel plus his breath smells
good like a Top Quality Root-Beer. I check if that fat poor rude boy
is still sleeping on the Rear segmant of our bus. He is. So I take one
deep breath of Oxygen for comfort and stick my piglet hand in to
the cozy unbuttoned gap on said sleeping Driver's pants and cup
my fingers around 2 of his plump gonads which huddle adjacent
besides of his sweet weenie in a warm nest of curly black hairs.
Suddenly his weenie twitches plus flops sideways and so does
mine!

I oscillate my head and look over my shoulder to see if it is safe
for me to proceed with Impunity. It is. As all persons (2 in number.)
is either sleeping or blind. So I joyously Feel-Up our Handsome
Bus's Driver's 2 gonads and his weenie abruptly Tumesces plus a
little shiny bead pops right out from the pink tip on it. I touch
said bead which spins a skinny thread from my finger then poke
my piglet nose right in to said hair's nest like a hound sucking
eggs and am jist about to Accomodate his convivial Boner in to my
piglet mouth when I feel a joyous hot squirt insides of my Y-fronts
and wake up!

OH MY GOSH! Here I am flopped over on my bus's seat with my wet weenie between my fat 2 legs and passengers is dismounting off from said bus and I am at the Port City Bus's Station and it is almost 4 PM!

The fatter even then I boy makes a mean face as he passes by me. The last time I seen a heinie that big it was on the back of a elephant at The Port City Zoo! (Excuse me, please!)

I permit a Bevy of variegated Individuals to walk by then I waddle out behind of them plus keep a safe distance between me and that Barbarious fat boy. I ponder calling him a bad name but don't as it would be unkind. Plus he might beat me up.

12. THE KIND ELEVATER LADY AND THE UNKIND RECEPTIONIST

I waddle through the Bus's Station where a whole alots of handsome sailors with protrusive weenies loiter even although a whole alots of signs says No Loitering!

I would adore to loiter untill the cows come home as I am Acutely drew to variegated weenies of all renditions. (As said.) But I do not loiter as I abide by legitimate laws Whenever Applicable. So I purchase 3 Milky-ways at the Confectionary Counter and exit out from the Port City Bus's Station and waddle past the hospital at which I was born at which was The Tales Of Hoffman Memorial Hospital. (As said.) Jarleen had me there on a Caesarean so I was not impelled to squeeze out through no Pewdendas but was Surgically Removed plus was not impelled to make no unnecessary journey down no Utilitarian canal.

Said Beauteous Mom did not desire to have me at the County Hospital at which most of we Babies Of The Great Depression was born at as she says that it was unsanitary. Jarleen is real picky about her Pewdendas.

Anyhow. Now I am supposed to be lucky as when every fool plus their brother asks me at which hospital I was born at I ain't got to say County but can utter instead of: The Tales Of Hoffman Memorial. But all persons always says "Huh?!" As nobody ain't never heard of The Tales Of Hoffman Memorial which is currently a Old Folks Home which is re-named The St James Home For The Recalcitrant Elderly.

The Lonely Gal's broadcasting room is clear acrosst town in a grey big building on B street. I almost keel over approximately 3 or 4 times as it is so hot due to a merciless sun but finally arrive there Victorious.

"Excuse m-me -please, c-can you please tell me where I c-can f-find The L-Lonely G-Gal?," I say exceptionally Courteous to a lady with behemoth horn rim glasses which sets up on a real high stool adjacent behind of a counter with a sign on it which says: RECEPTIONIST.

As I am woozy from the heat she looks fuzzy to me so I thump my head with my piglet fist and she Focusses plus says:

"The Lonely Gal ain't here."

Then said Receptionist looks down on me with her big magnified 2 eyes and her skinny black eyebrows squinch up horrid and she says:

"Whaddaya want with *her*?"

"I g-got a message f-for her."

I utter Afoursaid as polite as feasible as I hope the horn rim lady will like me as I can always use a friend. (*Which* can't?!)

"I can take *any* message," says this lady.

"Th-This is a exceptionally p-personal m-message," I say as I ain't able to Chat about Humane Conditions with totally unspecified Individuals which nerve racks me.

"Well The Lonely Gal doesn't take no personal messages."

"She d-don't?."

"No, she *doesn't*. Write a letter, chubby."

This poor misguided lady ain't never going to be my friend plus is as bitter as Mrs Vealfoy! Which impels me to ponder with whom *this* lady's husband got caught with! I strive to think up a new good word with which to utter to surprise and delight her with and which might impel said to be contented. But I can not due to the sunburn on the back of my neck. But I grin anyhow as I do not desire to be mean to nobody even unkind persons. As they are humane too.

"*What* is the message?!"

Said lady clacks her red long fingernails on her Receptionist's counter.

"I g-got to say it to her p-personal."

My neck stings something awful and I got to pee even although I alleviated myself at the Bus's Station prior. (But did not formally Infer to it.)

53

However. I note that a elevater lady is watching me from her elevater which smiles kindly plus possesses white gloves. She is as kind looking as the horn rim lady ain't. I am exceedingly Pacified by her kind smile as kindness has always went a long way with one's Sissies.

"Oh, come off it, Mary Eleanor", says this smiling elevater lady, "don't be a party pooper. Tell the boy where she is at."

This kind elevater lady shakes her finger at Mary Eleanor plus adds:

"Or I will!"

The unkind receptionist (Mary Eleanor.) aims her red lips right at me and blurts out:

"Well, for your information, fatty, she is at The Jolly Jug!"

She pokes out her thumb without even looking at me plus utters:

"Just around the corner."

But the elevater lady smiles real kind and tells said directions to me in Loving Detail. I thank her Courteous and as I exit out from said building I hear the unkind Receptionist say loud to the kind elevater lady:

"Now why would you want to send that big fat Sissy down there for?!"

This unkind Receptionist has even knew that I can hear her unkind currant words!

Why do persons talk so mean to We Children?! Even although I am almost 6 feet of height plus look a whole alots older due to Deportment and Premature Pubescence then 12 I am only one humane boy!

13. THE STEAMROLLERS AND THE SOMNOLENT INEBRIANT

I look up at the sign over the door.

THE JOLLY JUG
Formerly The Maiden's Head

Plus underneath of this sign is another sign which says:

There ain't no other place
just like this place
anywhere near this place.
So this must be the place.

I gobble down the last one of my 3 Milky-Ways plus enter in and look around for The Lonely Gal. The jukebox which is red and orange sits in a exceptionally dark segmant of this Quasi-dark big room plus plays:

"You broke my heart
And throwed its little pieces on the dirty, stinkin' floor..."

My yellow little teeth commences to chatter like they traditionally do while nerve racked plus this Quasi-dark big room is roasting! (Due to the external merciless sun Indubitably.)

On the right side of said room is a pool table and 2 beauteous ladies is rubbing blue chalk on to the tips of their pool sticks and drinking beer from cans. Neither of said is The Lonely Gal as neither of said is lonely as they got each other as Colleagues. Hence ain't.

On the left side of said room is a green shuffleboard with 6 skinny Chromized legs. A short-haired lady in a red baseball cap which also holds a can of beer has jist made a shot plus is leaning over said shuffleboard laughing with one of her 2 feet kicking up in the air. She ain't The Lonely Gal neither as said Gal don't never laugh as Loneliness ain't no Laughing Matter. (Sadly.)

A contiguous lady claps her hands and wipes her Prespiring face on to her sleeve plus takes a swallow from her can of beer which she grabs off from a table. This lady ain't The Lonely Gal neither as how can she be lonely if she possesses one laughing friend?

OH MY GOSH! If none of these indeterminant Individuals is The Lonely Gal then where is she?!

All of said 4 ladies is garbed in satin black shirts with "THE STEAMROLLERS" printed in red big print acrosst their respectable 4 backs. All of said 4 ladies wear black slacks plus all of said 4 oscillates their multiple heads and notes me. This ain't no big surprise as every fool plus their brother always notes me in Incomprehensible Ways whenever I am On The Scene so to speak.

"Yeah?" says the short-haired lady in the red baseball cap

which leans on this green skinny legged shuffleboard, "What can we do you for?"

"I'm l-looking for The L-Lonely G-Gal," I utter as Courteous as feasible.

"Get the kid a coke, Lorraine," says said lady to her Colleague at said shuffleboard, "He's gonna need it!"

"Sure, Babe," says Lorraine, "The poor kid is burnin' up! See how red he is?"

"Th-Thank you for your c-concern," I utter plus hope I ain't about to Fervantly keel over, "b-but I am always r-reddish like thus p-plus I ain't got enough m-money to p-purchase no c-coke."

This ain't explicitly a Truism as I got a Modicum of funds but said is preserved for purchasing additional Milky-Ways for dinner as I am getting hungry already.

Said lady smiles. "It's on me, kid. I'm Babe".

"Th-Then I w-would p-prefer a D-Dr P-Pepper, ma'am." (As Dr Peppers is my all time favorite beverage even although Coke is The Favorite Of Millions The World Over.) (I adore Ice cold milk also.) (Whenever Applicable.)

"Get the kid a Dr P, Lorraine," says Babe which takes a red bandana out from her hip pocket plus wipes it back and fourth on to her Prespiring brows.

"Th-Thank you v-very much, Miss B-Babe." I utter grateful.

"Don't think nothin' of it, kiddo, but can the "Miss" stuff. I'm jist plain Babe."

Babe smiles and Dislodges away my bitter reminiscences of the unkind Receptionist which was fresh among my brains as unkind items habitually loiter where No Loitering is preferred.

As I await for my Dr Pepper I oscillate my head and peer Eagerly in variegated directions in this dark big room and can now jist make out the head of a Somnolent lady which is laying with same (The head.) on a table contiguous by the bar. My brains zoom! Is this The Lonely Gal?! The jukebox plays :

> "On the night I was born
> My pore daddy was torn
> With a sorrow as great as could be..."

This must be The Lonely Gal as even although Somnolent she looks as lonely as all heck.

"...I was the apple of Dad's eye
But I caused him to cry
'Cause the Good Lord took Mama, you see..."
(Plays said jukebox.)

I ponder if The Lonely Gal lost her mother or father or some Individual Dear and Near with her. When persons asks about my Dad Bull I always say that Bull is croaked instead of a Thwarted Inebriant as I do not desire to answer Probing Questions as Prolongated Chat on my one legged Dad Bull traditionally impels me to blubber. Please do not ask me why. As I can not tell you. As I do not know.

Lorraine brings me my Dr Pepper spilled over 3 ice cubes. I thank her Courteous and take one behemoth swallow and consume nearly all of said then point one finger and suddenly say:

"Ain't th-that The L-Lonely G-Gal over th-there?"

"The one and only, hon," says Lorraine, "In all her glory. She is resting up for her broadcast tonight and there she is."

"Sleepin' it off," says Babe which notes Lorraine with Infinite kindness.

"Always sleepin' it off," says Lorraine. "Poor thing."

I ain't able to yank my piglet 2 eyes off from that Somnolent lady. "I g-got a m-m...m-m...m-message..."

"Set down before you fall down, honey," says Babe.

I feel excessively woozy so I set down on a high stool with a hot leatherette plastic red seat and although my heinie commences to itch Rapaciously I utter repetitiously:

"I g-got a m-message for h-her."

I am currantly woozier even plus hope I do not keel over before I can utter what I have came to utter.

"She'll wake up in a minute, kiddo," says Babe. "What's your name?"

"D-Danny."

"You in love with her too, Danny Boy?" says Lorraine.

"Everybody's in love with The Lonely Gal, Danny," says Babe, "But she don't love *nobody*. Not since..."

Lorraine shakes her head at Babe which terminates her prior sentence instantaneously.

"N-Not since w-what?" I say.

We hear glass smashing and oscillate our multiple heads. It is The Lonely Gal which has half-raised her head up from her table and shoved a empty beer mug off from it. She looks at I and the 4 additional ladies and hollers:

"What the fuck are you five fuckers gawking at?!"

"Ain't nobody here but us chickens," says Babe.

"Oh?!" says The Lonely Gal, "Oh!? Is that fucking so?!"

The Lonely Gal's head flops sideways plus says:

"How I loathe the contact of your fucking hostile eyes!"

Said head whacks right down on to the table then arises right up again like she is going to utter some additional item. But don't. Then said head whacks down plus comes up then whacks down again. I hope she ain't hurt herself! If I was not so woozy I would of waddled right up to her sleeping sides and patted her on her head genteel.

The 2 ladies at the pool table terminate their playing and Glare at her. I Ruminate that The Lonely Gal is all wrung out from sincere longing which is why she must of spoke fowl language as Jarleen sporadically Chats in these fowl Modes but don't mean nothing vital by it unless she is conversing with Bull and then she is fowl on purpose.

Anyhow. The Lonely Gal requires her strength as she has got her broadcast show tonight plus will benefit from a additional Cat-Nap as it is so darn hot and Enervating. (Said hotness nor Enervation can not never be Over Emphasized.) (As Southern California is severely Situated in a Sub-Tropical Climactic Belt.)

I myself am sweating like a stuck pig plus better not move from my leatherette red stool as I might weaken and flop to the floor. (Weight is heavy!)

However. I can not yank my piglet eyes off from said Gal plus am delightful that she ain't deformed nor Transfigured in no way whatsoever nor obese in the extremes like I myself which often impels brutal loneliness which I would not wish on no living Individual even me. (Nor don't!)

However. The Lonely Gal seems to be a Inebriant.

A concerned short lady comes out from a back room and commences to sweep up said Gal's broke beer mug which is scattered wide and far.

However. I know exactly what said Gal Inferred to when she uttered Hostile Eyes prior as a whole Bevy of said eyes Glares at me every day and I Loathe them. They follow me everywheres I go. I noted said Eyes on the horn-rim lady Receptionist and on that fatter even then I boy on the bus and Last But Not Least on the

Inexorable PK Benderson. Eternally if not Incessantly!

So my heart fills right up for The Lonely Gal as I note her head laying there on that table in the Quasi-darkness adjacent besides of the bar. And I ponder The Multitudes of kind items which she utters habitually to me from my battery radio while the Jukebox plays:

"Operator,
Please connect me to Paradise
I want to speak to Grandma
Again..."

I pretend that I myself am a Orphan like them adapted 2 brothers in the Motion Picture and am watched over by The Lonely Gal which at this very minute commences to snore. I suddenly feel so heightened up that I holler:

"I L-LOVE TH-THAT L-LONELY G-GAL! I L-LOVE TH-THAT L-LONELY G-GAL!"

I must be a Madman to holler like this as all 4 said ladies abruptly oscillates and notes me With Alacrity!

Then everything gets woozy and I feel like I will either pee or keel over. I do both of those Simultaneous.

14. SOME EXCEEDINGLY KIND LADIES

When I awaken up the jukebox is playing:

"She was only a cowgirl in love..."

The room wobbles all over for one full interval then Little By Little I note all items more easy (Variegated objects like light bulbs and Ect. Ect. Ect.)

"...But her love was as big
as that big sky above..."

I am laying flat on my back pronely on the pool table with one pair of smelling bowling shoes underneath of my head for a pillow. Babe is fanning me with her red baseball cap and Lorraine is noting me with Overpowering Conjectures. I feel a Dire wetness on my Lower Pelvic Torsal Regions. **AM I ABASHED!**

"He has went and peed hisself, that poor fat kid," says one of the 2 ladies which has been playing pool. She squats down with her pool stick right besides of her pool table Compatriot which squats down similar approximately one foot behind of Babe.

"But it could of been worse, Reggie," says this squatting lady, "He could of pooped hisself."

Reggie kindly laughs. "We better get him offa this table, Marie, 'fore he wets it. Or somethin' even worse!"

Said 2 ladies desires to remove me off from the pool table top but Babe keeps fanning me and won't let them come contiguous plus utters:

"Let the poor kid cool off for a minute, gals, he's all fagged out."

"Well if you say so, Babe," says Reggie which Infers to my Heat Prostation. I myself am not excessively worried as I keel over a whole alots plus am Fully Accustomized. (As said.)

Lorraine brings me a additional Dr P spilled over 3 ice cubes plus says:

"On the house!"

Now ain't that a kind thing which to do? I set up and she smiles at me and hands me the Dr P. I am now brimming over with gratuities plus am totally conscionable.

I thank Lorraine then complement all 4 of these exceedingly kind ladies on their Gorgeous black shirts with "The Steamrollers" in red acrosst their respectable backs.

"Oh, these old things," says Marie, "They're jist somethin' the cat drug in."

"She don't mean that," says Reggie, "She's jist joshin' you. We're all real proud of our new git-ups!"

"We got us a bowlin' team, Danny," says Babe.

"This here's our outfits," says Marie which yanks at her pointed simply Gorgeous floppy collar.

"Glad you like 'em," says Babe to me, "My baby Lorraine designed 'em."

"Drink your Dr P, Danny," says Lorraine which turns red and shoots a kindly embarrassed look at Babe plus bends her head over contiguous and sings soft to me:

"Little boy, you've had a busy day..."

Now ain't that a kind thing which to sing? Even although I am every item but little? Her Angel voice matches her Angel face Impeccable and she is singing a song which The Lonely Gal played on her radio program which instantaneously impels a unspecified number of tears to squirt out from my piglet 2 eyes. Big surprise. (Ha. Ha.)

Then I suddenly reminisce said Gal and oscillate my head around to find her. But her table is desserted!

"W-Where'd she g-go to?" I ask Babe which dips her red bandana in to a glass of ice water and swats my brows.

"She has went to get some sleep before her broadcast, Danny. She jist snuck off while you was sleepin'. But she'll be back tomorrow night at 7 PM 'cause it's Gala Talent Night and she's gonna sing a song she has wrote herself. You can come back then and hear her sing and meet her in person if she's sober."

"If he's able to," utters Lorraine. "You don't look real good, Danny boy. Maybe we should jist call your folks?"

I want to sink right on through the green Textile top on this pool table! **OH MY GOSH!** Am I Mortified! I peed myself and blubbered plus keeled over plus lost The Lonely Gal! Plus bus's tickets don't grow on no trees and I ain't got proficient funds to come back to Port City to see The Lonely Gal ever again as I hardly got funds left to purchase one battery for my battery radio! (Which is exceptionally low currantly.)

I slurp from my Dr P plus am nauseating Poste Haste.

"You oughta better lay back down agin, Danny boy," says Babe, "You've went all green!"

Lorraine grabs my Dr P glass and I lay back on to the pool table with my head on these smelling 2 bowling shoes which do not stink nearly so bad as prior as I am Fully Accustomized. However. I am currantly blue and lowly from said abrupt dessertion of The Lonely Gal.

From the corner of my eye I note Marie and Reggie which is playing their pool on the opposite segmant of this pool table Courteously so as to evade Disconcerting me. How Infinitely kind!

I feel a whole alots better untill a Bevy of pool balls comes whizzing acrosst said table and whizzes between the 2 bowling shoes and whacks me right on my head one after the other! Jist prior to when I pass out for the 2nd time I hear Reggie hollering:
"FOR CHRIST'S SAKES, MARIE, WHAT HAVE YOU WENT

AND DID?!"

Babe and Lorraine slaps me awake. What a wondrous feeling for one to have kind persons which care about you slapping us awake. A sore big bump has arosen through my red newly Revered Flaming hair.

Marie says that she is real sorry for braining me with her balls. I accept her apology gratuitously and insure her that worst items has occurred to me. (Such as PK Benderson **ET. AL!**) (To be Implicit!)

Reggie gives me a Milky-Way and Babe and Lorraine offers to drive me home in their blue beauteous 1941 Plymouth Convertible which was jist painted prior plus smells new. Babe and Lorraine has cut off the smashed roof of this auto which was wrecked with their Acetylene Torch theirselves which made it as good as new excepting for it's roof which is lacking.

"Who needs a car roof?" says Babe which is a Short Order cook plus enjoys spray painting in her spare time, "Hell, it never rains in Southern California!"

"And Lord knows," utters Lorraine which is a Reinforcement Engineer at Duff Mesh Wire Fences and a expert in Acetylene Torches and Bowling Shirts, "we got us a bitchin' car for a song!"

However. They keep a Tarpaulin in the trunk of this 1941 Plymouth jist in case of Reciprocation. Said Tarpaulin currantly lays right underneath of my damp heinie. (Jist in case.)

A excessively hot wind slams through Lemon Gulch tonight. The yellow shiny paint on The Big Lemon is flaking all over the darn place and shoots straight in to my piglet 2 eyes as we zoom past. Said Big Lemon is 8 feet tall and cement and is a monument to Lemon Gulch and sets in the middle of our town plus a tin sign which sits in front of it says:

LEMON GULCH
BEST CLIMATE IN THE COSMOS
COURTESY OF TANGY MAYONNAISE

Which is our town's biggest Statistical Employer. (As proudly prior said.)

Babe and Lorraine sing as we zoom along:

"I don't want no phony ro-mance
I don't want no triflin' love!
If your gonna be unfaithful
Get yourself another turtle-dove!"

Babe possesses a strong voice and is a fast but careful driver and I adore her more every time she is cussed out by variegated other drivers and pedestrians with fowl language.

"It ain't necessarily so!" she sings at said drivers and pedestrians as we zoom right along.

I lay on their Rear seat pronely underneath of a starry sky with my fat sausage 2 legs propped up on Babe and Lorraine's genuine leather bowling ball carrying bags and I am only a small bit uncomfortable due to said wetness of my Lower Pelvic Torsal Regions but I feel excessively content with my 2 kind and glamorous lady friends on who's satin black backs I read with exceptional joy:

"THE STEAMROLLERS"

The Best Climate In The Cosmos tin sign has became blowed off from The Big Lemon and lays on the road flopping up and down like a chicken with their head chopped off plus tangled up in a Tumbleweed. (A Dessert Growth.)

Babe jist misses the Best Climate sign with a real sharp swerve of our auto but only gets cussed-out for her efforts from a pedestrian which shouldn't of been loitering right in front of us in that darn pedestrian cross walk so late at night!

"It ain't necessarily so!" sings Babe right back at him as we zoom right by! Boy do we all laugh!

Babe and Lorraine kindly drive me up to the almost new Galvanized Wire Mesh gate of my home plus tells me that every fool plus their brother sporadically pees hisself sometimes and keels over which is a great comfort.

"And don't forget, Danny," utters Lorraine, "Gala Talent Night is tomorrow night at 7 PM."

I tell them that I will be there but I sadly do not ascertain how one can. I am real contented all the same as Babe and Lorraine likes me even although they ain't got no ideal that I am only 12 years of age and must ponder that I am 18 like most persons due to my inordinant height and growed-up Deportment. Anyhow. What a jolly Trio us 3 make!

I am Aghast when I ponder that I ain't even thunk of The

Lonely Gal for about approximately a hour and a half precisely and she is the reason that I had went to Port City in the 1st darn place! I do not pride myself on this here Absent-Mindness.

I Dare Not to waddle through our front door as it is very late and Bull jist might be awake plus try to whack me with his phony leg so I climb through my bedroom window which is eternally unlocked plus ungarb and pee and climb on to my bed.

I have missed out on The Lonely Gal's radio program due to all of prior said plus am suddenly blue and lowly as I ain't got no ideal how to procure a bus's ticket for the trip to Gala Talent Night where I and The Lonely Gal can discuss our Humane Conditions In A Often Uncaring World after she has sang her song and is Leisurely Inclined.

However. I am exceedingly concerned on her Inebriation plus am so nerve racked that I ain't able to sleep so I reach way underneath of my bed for my traditional Peanut Oil and commence to ponder Fred Foster's weenie even although I am keeping it on my back burner.

After a Lubricious plus contenting Onanation I stick my Peanut Oil way back underneath of my bed and shift abruptly to Somnolence. Plus slumber sleepily.

15. BULL'S HEENOUS CRIME!

I awake up the next morning and rub my sore Billiard-Ball-whacked head and waddle adjacent towards our kitchen so as to make Oatmeal and My Beauteous Mom's traditional coffee as it is a Ritual to which I Adhere To Scrupulous.

But here is said Mom in our front room which is dripping Prespiration and flopped right down on her Komfo-Lounger Chair with one behemoth white plaster casted leg stuck up on said Komfo's E-Z-Pull-Out Foot-Stool! Plus Bull ain't nowhere to be saw!

"Well good morning to *you!*" hollers Jarleen right at me, "Where the hell was *you* all day yesterday?!"

"I t-told y-you I was s-studying for my S-Spelling B-Bee with a f-friend, Jarleen," I fib with Impunity. (As I jist had to meet The Lonely Gal for Humanity's sake.)

"Oh. I guess you did," says Jarleen, "Well. While you was

a-studyin' I was at the factory a-slippin' on a broke jar of Tangy and skiddin' on my ass right acrosst the floor into the goddamn Petite Convenient Picnic Size display and breakin' my pore leg in three places!"

My Beauteous Mom is exceptionally Irascible!

"And your sonofabitch father," she hollers, "has went and committed hisself a heenous crime!"

I do not relish her calling my Dad a Son Of A Bitch as he is only a Thwarted Inebriant.

"I shoulda oughta hadda of called the *po*-lice and got his ass interred! But I called Mr Shanks instead!" hollers Jarleen, "Lucky for Bull, that heenous sonofabitch!"

I commence to ask her about Bull's heenous crime but she ain't on a Conversant disposition. So don't.

After I make her morning coffee she impels me to Retire in to our back yard so as to check if my black and white small dog Tinker is currantly interred in our garage due to her Oestrus Mode.

OH MY GOSH! Poor Tinker requires desperately her dog little friends! I am a Devotee of my black and white small dog and Insulating her away from other dogs is Infinitely unkind and don't produce no puppies neither. However. Poor Tinker procures joy by Onanating with our small Old-Rose colored front room Throw-Rug which she bunches up Capriciously insides of her back 2 legs and whacks away at. When said Onanation is terminant she perpetually abandons said rug in this bunched up State and we are habitually tripping over it. Jarleen has nicknamed said rug Tinker's Friggin' Rug and says that said routine is a whole alots better then Tinker getting fermented every other month of the calender.

As I waddle among our back yard I ponder how I am going to excape from our home for Gala Talent Night tonight as I require a bus's ticket and Milky-Way funds Over And Above of the price of a new battery plus how in the heck am I going to allude my Irascible Beauteous Mom?

I jist *got* to see The Lonely Gal and interrogate her although I am seriously concerned on her Inebriation plus fowl language which reminds me of certain members of my family which can remain nameless. (But who's initials is B-U-L-L and J-A-R-L-E-E-N!)

I chase a Mean Spirited dash-hound which snaps at me out through a hole underneath of our almost new Mesh Wire Fence and end up by a open window of our home's front room through which I hear the chimes of our door bell chiming through.

Who can it be?! I am excessively Prudential and conceal my head from the Gawk of my scowling Beauteous Mom which has inserted a straightened out wire coat hanger underneath of the top edge of her plaster cast plus scratches insides of it as she sips on her can of beer. Our doorbell rings Thrice more.

"Come on in, goddammit!" hollers Jarleen, "the sucker's unlocked!"

Said front door opens and a real skinny lady garbed in exceedingly thick red lipstick and a black Pheasant Skirt and a low necked Pheasant Blouse plus net black stockings and Ballerina Slippers enters in. She possesses a exceptionally pock marked face plus stringy black hair right down to her waste.

"Well, well, *well!*" says Jarleen, "If it ain't Flo, that poor old street whoor from Port City! I thought I throwed you out yesterday with the rest of the garbage!"

"I come to apologize," utters Flo which is Indubitably the lady with which I Chatted with yesterday on the telephone to!

"Then apologize and git yer skinny ass outta our happy home!" hollers My Beauteous Mom at poor broke down old Flo.

"I am *real* sorry," says Flo.

"What for?" hollers Jarleen.

"You *know* what for."

"I want to hear you say it with your own pocky mouth!" hollers My Beauteous Mom in one Frenzy.

As I watch I keep one's self real low contiguous on our window sill so as not to be noted.

"Sorry for *what*, you lousy chippie!"

"I am sorry for fuckin' yer husband!"

I am so surprised I flop with a whack on to a Exterior wall of our home.

"It give me a *terrible* start!" says Jarleen which scratches away insides of her plaster cast with the wire coat hanger, "Your obscene act, Miss Port City whoor, almost drove me straight back to my physician!"

"It *did?*" says Flo.

"I seen you layin' on your back on our bed with your old black dyed muff a-stickin' up heavenwards like you thunk it was a sacred shrine!"

"Bull stuck a pillow underneath of my butt," says Flo, "Fer

comfort's sake."

"It give me a real shock!"

"I said I was sorry. That's why I come here today. I walked in the awful hot sun all the way from the Bus Station to say I was sorry."

"I seen it all through my own bedroom window," says Jarleen, "Bull was on our toilet and there you was, muff up, a-sleepin' on my marriage bed!"

Jarleen pokes the coat hanger back insides of her cast and scratches vicariously. "Lucky for me I was leanin' on my crutches or I would of fell directly to our cement driveway and harmed myself!"

"I said I was sorry."

Flo wipes her Prespiring brows with a black hanky.

"Git yourself a goddamned beer out from the ice-box and set down!" hollers My Beauteous Mom, there is something which I wish to tell you."

"Well it *is* real hot. A cold beer might jist hit the spot."

Flo goes to our kitchen and gets a can of beer out from our ice-box and comes back and sets down on Jarleen's favorite chenille yellow chair.

My Beauteous Mom ain't nearly so Beauteous currantly as her platinum Pompadour has broke in 2 segmants plus flops back and fourth every time she oscillates her head around fast of which she is doing a whole alots of. She pokes her coat hanger deep down in to her plaster leg cast for comfort plus utters:

"As I stood there leanin' on my crutches lookin' through my own bedroom window at your crime I felt somethin' funny happenin' to me. I thought at first it was them pain pills which my physician had gave me for I did feel woozy."

Jarleen gives the insides of her plaster cast a additional delighted scratch. "But it wasn't no pain pills! What was makin' me so woozy was that due to the shock of seein' you layin' there, I aged ten years on the spot!"

"You poor kid."

Flo wipes Prespiration and runny black hair dye off from the Rear of her neck with her black hanky, "I know what you mean. I could lose a whole lipstick in this big crease by the side of my mouth. And things ain't gettin' no better."

Flo touches her red long fingernail on to her lip and a old big tear squirts out from her eye and shoots down in to this big pock hole.

"Then the toilet flushed," says Jarleen which don't wish to be discommoded, "and out come Bull from our bathroom which climbed back upon you and proceeded to pump away at your sleepin' form."

A horrid scream rants in the air!

"I wasn't takin' nothin' away from you that you ain't lost already!" screams Flo which instantaneously explodes!

"You and Bull was adulteratin! You shouldn'ta hadda oughta never of done that!" screams My Beauteous Mom!

"I done a service for your drunk husband for which he give me a stinkin' little cardboard box of minor items of which there was one wilty lettuce, one leaky, half pint of semi-sour milk, one rotten peach, one economy size packet of 2 kotex for next week *if* I am lucky enough to require 'em, and one bottle of cheap shampoo which dried my hair up somethin' awful!"

"Them was *my* kotexes!," hollers Jarleen, "And if you ask me that was more'n you deserved!"

"Well I didn't ask you, did I?" hollers Flo, "Why don't you jist telephone your spouse and ask him what he has got to say about this matter?!"

"For your information, you cheap slut, they ain't got no telephones insides of no Inebriation Units!"

"I was real sorry fer you jist a minute ago," hollers Flo, "But I don't feel sorry no more!"

"I feel real sorry for you! Too!"

"Well you can jist stop! Too!"

"No," hollers Jarleen, "I do. I feel real sorry fer a broke down, black dyed old street whoor for which there ain't no future for!"

"Don't you talk to me about no futures! Tangy Mayo ain't the fucking Waldorf As-toria Ho-tel!"

"You poor, dried up old hooker! Your jist gonna dye your old black hair till it falls right out by its skinny, grey roots!"

"Don't you talk that way 'bout my hair! My hair is my crownin' glory and you know it! And your the one's dried up! Your as dry as desert sand! Bull's pecker bleeds! Bull told me so!"

"*Did* he? *Did* the sonofabitch?! Well I'll tell you why," hollers Jarleen which looks like she is going to kill Miss Flo! "Bull's pecker bleeds 'cause he has got the Sy-phillius! And I will not let him touch me with a ten foot pole! That is why he give you a old cardboard box of minor items and throwed you down and stuck a pillow underneath of yer skinny ass and stuck his Sy-phillistical tool right up you! 'Cause *I* will not let him touch *me* with a ten foot pole! Bull has got the Lemon Gulch Shit Sy-phillius!"

I got to look that up too! Sy-phillius. Sy-phillius.

Flo goes real goofy plus gets a a-scared look on her face and her beer can hits the floor with a behemoth splat which sprays me right through our window's screen! She hollers:

"Your a Liar!" and jumps right at Jarleen which whacks her on her nose with the wire coat hanger! This scares a Minor Quantity of pee out from me which I can feel leaking down my left Dungaree's pant's leg.

Flo's nose commences to bleed from said whack and she backs away from Jarleen. I jist squat there peeing down my Dungaree's pant's leg and peeping over our window sill. I wisht said 2 ladies would attain their dignities and not fight. Explicitly My Beauteous Mom.

Jarleen grabs her crutches and hoists herself up from her Komfo-Lounge Chair.

"Your gonna croak from Sy-phillius!" she hollers plus clumps towards Flo which jumps back and grabs her purse and yanks a item out from it plus pushes a shiny button on said item and a sharp long knife blade jumps out with a behemoth snap!

"J-Jarleen!" I holler! But nobody hears me!

Said 2 ladies notes each other with real unkind Glares and Jarleen raises her crutch and aims it at Flo which wiggles her knife around in the air then hunches down low and crawls adjacent towards Jarleen like a alley cat!

"You come jist one inch closer to me and I'll kick you with my big white leg!" hollers Jarleen which leans on her crutches and swings her plastered big leg back and fourth. "Don't say I didn't warn you, you black-dyed bitch!"

Flo stabs up in the air with her knife! "To think that I had came here today to apologize to you! Why your no better then Bull is! Your both jist poor white trash!"

"Your nose will rot right off from your chippie face!" hollers Jarleen, "You got Sy-phillius! And you got it from Bull! Consult your physician!"

"Your a Liar!"

"Why, honey!" says Jarleen which smiles real unkind, "jist you have a look at yourself in that mirror by our kitchen sink."

Jarleen points Flo to the kitchen and follows real slow behind of her.

"Your a Liar," additionally utters Flo which stares in to the mirror. "I don't see *nothin'*!"

"You gotta squat *way* over to see," says Jarleen, "as our mirror is all rusted on it's top. You have went all purplish at your nostrils! See? That's one of the primal signs."

Flo squats over and looks real close plus says:

"I don't see *nothin'*!" She squats lower even plus looks closer even, "Your a Liar!"

While Flo is squatting plus looking Jarleen creeps up behind of her and leans herself on to her crutches and raises her plaster cast leg real high up in to the air! Before Flo can jump away Jarleen slams said leg right down on Flo's head with one behemoth **WHACK** and Flo flops down on to our kitchen floor!

Jarleen clumps back to her Komfo Lounger and flops herself on to it and jerks on it's lever and it's Foot stool shoots out and yanks her plaster leg right up and she hollers over her shoulder to our kitchen:

"Now git yer Sy-phillistical ass outta our happy home!"

But Flo don't move!

"I said," hollers Jarleen," to get your skinny ass outta our home!"

But Flo still don't move even a inch!

"Goddamn it!" hollers My Beauteous Mom, "I said for you to get your ass outta here!"

But Flo *still* don't move!

Jarleen grunts and makes a goofy face and yanks the Lounger Lever and lowers her white big leg down on to our floor and pulls herself up on to her crutches again plus clumps back in to our kitchen and jabs Flo on her skinny heinie with said crutch. But Flo jist lays there.

"Whoor?!" utters Jarleen real soft which sounds like she is a-scared, "Git up."

But Flo *still* don't move!

Jarleen jabs at Flo's skinny heinie again. "Git up, I said!"

But Flo *still* don't move!

OH MY GOSH! Am I a-scared!
"Jesus!" utters My Beauteous Mom, **"JESUS H. CHRIST! I'VE KILLT THE FUCKER!"**

16. FLO IN ONE HEAP

I waddle instantaneously on to our front porch and loiter insides of my wet Dungarees peeing plus peering through our screen door in to our home. Jarleen hunches over Flo which lays in one heap on our floor adjacent besides of our kitchen sink. I loiter and feel real goofy as one murder has feasibly jist took place. So I jist loiter and loiter feeling goofy plus wet. Then!

"Ohhhhh....Ohhhhh....you crippled sonofabitch! You... savage brute!"

It is Flo! Which squats up excessively slow on to her 2 knees! Jarleen jumps back so fast that she almost flops off from her crutches.

"You mean, crippled, sonofabitch!" hollers Flo at My Beauteous Mom which commences to hunch down from her crutches to help old poor Flo up.

"Don't you dare touch me!" hollers Flo which Indubitably suffers horrid from Concussion. She jumps on to her 2 feet and grabs her knife from our floor and snaps it shut plus grabs her purse and crams said knife right in to it and Glares horrid at Jarleen!

"Self defense," hollers Jarleen. "You was brandishin' a lethal weapon at me! I call that attimpted assault with intint to commit mayhim! I was only defendin' myself! "

Jarleen suddenly notes me loitering outsides of our screen door. "Danny!" she hollers, "You seen her do it too! You seen her unsolicited assault upon my persona! Zip-knives is illegal contraband!"

My Beauteous Mom uses said Legalistical sentence which she has read in The Keyhole's Judicial Sex Crimes Section so as to scare

Flo off.

Flo looks real a-scared plus holds tight on to her purse with her 2 hands and sways back and fourth Concussively towards our screen door besides of which I continually loiter on the other side of. I politely open it for her and she flops right in to my fat 2 arms! It is lucky she is skinny or we could of both keeled over as I ain't real steady on my feet due to exceptional Shock plus said heat. (Exceptional Shocks of any rendition traditionally unsteadies me.) (Implicitly while peeing right down my leg!)

"Sorry, Danny, I didn't mean to almost knock you down," says Flo, "I feel woozy."

I know jist how old poor Flo feels but I suddenly reminisce my peed-in Dungarees and set her down quick on to our front porch and lean her head contiguous on to our mailbox plus waddle like lightning in to my bedroom and slam my door.

"She has jist tripped and fell over your little dog's friggin' rug and lit on her head," hollers Jarleen through my bedroom door, "I am a innocent party!"

"I could sue yer ass off!" hollers Flo through our screen door at Jarleen which I can hear as my bedroom window is contiguously adjacent to our front porch.

"Sue his little dog," hollers Jarleen at Flo, "It's her friggin' rug which you have fell over!"

Jarleen jist pretends to laugh but I know she is jist as a-scared like I am.

I waddle in to our front room in my 100 Percent red nylon seersucker no-iron long-sleeved shirt and clean Bright Blue Corduroys which I washed and ironed myself before I Retired but did not mention formally. Jarleen currantly looks at me to see if I believe her about Flo tripping over Tinker's Rug. Well. I *got* to believe her ain't I? As she is My Beauteous Mom. And I love her.

I waddle out from our screen door to Flo which is still setting on our cement porch leaning her whacked head on to our mailbox where I laid her genteely prior. I kindly pat her tenderly right on the top of her black stringy hair.

"I h-hope your f-feeling better, Miss F-Flo," I utter kind as feasible as she has jist went through a Ordeal.

"Thank you, Danny," says Flo, "Your awful kind to inquire."

Jarleen looks goofy then exits away for one interval and comes right back and hands me 2 dollars plus says:

"Danny, take this here indecent street whoor back to Port City

72

and make sure she don't fall flat on her chippie face! Otherwise she might jist sue your dog Tinker! Ha! Ha! Ha!"

Jarleen laughs but I sure can note that she is *still* a-scared.

Then a behemoth ideal hits me right in between my piglet 2 eyes! **OH MY GOSH!** I jist ain't able to believe my luck! one interval ago I pondered that My Beauteous Mom was a Homocidal Maniac plus I did not know how I was going to get to Gala Talent Night at The Jolly Jug! But now I got the bus's ticket money right here in my own fat darn hand and Jarleen ain't no Maniac plus even impels me to embark to Port City Poste Haste! As my Deeply Departed Grandma traditionally uttered: It Is Always Darkest Jist Prior To One's Dawn.

At the Lemon Gulch Bus's Station I purchase 2 tickets on the next cheap (Non-Expressive.) bus to Port City with a whole alots of change to spare! I now possess funds for Dr Peppers and Milky-Ways plus my round trip ticket clear back to Lemon Gulch!

But **OH MY GOSH** here is PK Benderson right smack in the middle of the Bus's Station and when Flo goes to a locker to procure her cardboard box of minor items PK shoves hisself right in front of me and gives me The Finger and will not permit no Unobstructed Passage adjacent plus 2 behemoth stacks of Ipana Toothpastes impedes me from going around him!

"Fat Sissy Fairy!" he hollers, "got hisself a old whoor baby-sitter!"

This puzzles me. I ain't nothing like a fairy which is a dainty item of which I am Diagonally Opposed of. (As I am fat as one hog.) But suddenly Flo jumps in front of me and makes a exceptionally nasty knife stab at PK which jumps sideways quick!

"Get lost, you drip!" she hollers at PK, "or I'll cut off your fucking balls!"

PK gives her a unkind but a-scared look and backs hisself away real fast plus Glares at us and gives me The Finger. I ascertain that I am Indubitably in for it sooner or later. (**ET. AL!**) (As said.) (Alas!)

I and Flo embark up on to the bus with me carrying her cardboard box of minor items which she procured from the locker in the Bus's Station insides of which she slept last night in. I sit Flo's box up on to the bus's luggage wrack and we set ourselves down on to our 2 Bus's seats. Then Flo closes her eyes and clinches her fists real tight plus says in a excessively high scratchy voice:

"The only reason I come to your home today, Danny, was because I ain't got no busfare back to Port City where I live. I thought your Mom was in the hospital where she belonged. As she had fell off her crutches when she seen I and Bull in bed. I thought Bull would give the busfare to me but he wasn't there. And then when I seen your Mom I thought if I apologized then she might give me the busfare. I was real desperate!"

I nod my head as I ain't got nothing stimulating to additionally add but am real sorry that Flo was Fully Insulated without no bus's fare as I reminisce once when we lived in Port City and I was 10 years of age plus 5 feet 7 inches tall and fat as one hog and after a Major Motion Picture I got Marooned downtown in a behemoth crowd of hollering Individuals which jiggled my bus's fare right out from my piglet fingers and said fare fell in to a sewer as World War 2 had jist terminated one minute prior. And this was all the funds which I possessed. And my piglet fat arm got stuck in the sewer grate trying to Re-Procure said funds! Anyhow. Here I was Fully Insulated from my home! What a horrid feeling to be blue and lowly and Fully Insulated when every fool plus their brother is delightful due to a whole World War termination! However. A protrusive sailor yanked my stuck arm out from said grate and give me bus's fare as I was blubbering. I could of noted his delighted weenie all day as my Relentless Pubescence was On The Rise even although I was Marooned insides of a Effulgent crowd! (But I Digress.)

17. THE LIVID
INTER-PRE-TAH-TIVE DANCER

Our bus commences to go but old poor Flo jist sets there in her bus's seat besides of me with her 2 eyes squinched tight shut and her 2 fists squinched Ditto. After one interval she rubs the Rear of her head where Jarleen whacked her and I can hardly keep from squirting tears as I know explicitly jist how she must feel. However. Jist as I am commencing to ask her Intimant Items about her Daily Life as a Street Whoor she oscillates her head towards me with a behemoth jerk and opens her shut eyes and grabs my shoulders with her skinny hands and commences to blubber big gurgly blubbers! **AM I MORTIFIED!**

As she blubbers she wobbles back and fourth plus yanks me right along with her. As I am currently nauseating due to said heat this yanking ain't Beneficial. (To say the least!)

"I done a service for your Dad," hollers Flo real loud plus yanks me back and fourth and farther adds:

"And he give me a stinkin' little cardboard box of minor items, includin' one peach and one bottle of cheap shampoo which I used this morning in the Saga of the West washroom which dried my hair up somethin' awful! And the damned peach was mushy! I ain't accustomed to bein' paid off with inferior toiletries and rotten fruit!"

Even although I am in a Full State of sympathy with her I ponder that I am going to keel over due to being yanked rapaciously back and fourth.

Lucky for me our bus possesses a Air Cooling Accoutrements which alleviates my discomfort In Small Degree.

Flo finally stops blubbering although she is still relentlessly yanking me back and fourth.

"W-Where do you w-work at?" I utter and strive to soothe her by Transmogrifying her sad thoughts. She stops sniveling and whining plus makes a additional gurgly noise down insides of her throat plus yanks her skinny big hands off from my shoulders and wipes her streaky black Mascara off from her pocky cheeks and utters:

"I am a inter-pre-tah-tive dancer."

"I kn-know w-what that m-m-m-m-m-m-m... Infers to," I utter, "T-To interpret is t-to expound th-the m-meaning of. W-What do y-you interpret?"

"Moods, hon."

I instantaneously note she is impressed with my Literalness.

"My bodily movements," says Flo which wipes a behemoth Mascara hunk from besides of her nose, "emulate various human moods such as love and sadness and joy and sexiness. And various vital urges. And others."

She squinches up her face and body segments a variety of variegated ways such as hunching her skinny 2 shoulders up high or opening her eyes exceedingly big or making her hands look like Buzzard's feet.

"Oh," I say, "I s-see."

"I recite," she says, "Too."

"Y-You d-do?"

75

"Yes indeedy. I write my own material...well mostly. Know what I mean?"

Flo waits for my answer but I ain't got one for this here explicit question.

"God damn!" she says, "I had me some future in the past."

"Oh p-please tell m-me about it!"

"I was a real good student," snivels Flo and I hope she ain't going to yank my shoulders again.

"I am a g-good *L-Literal* s-student," I say as I know that this is the only good thing about me excepting what which lays deep insides of me which is literately even better.

"Look, kid," she says, "we're talkin' about *me!*" She grabs her black hanky from her purse and blows her red pocky nose.

"I'm s-so s-sorry," I utter real Courteous, "b-by all m-means, p-please c-continue Unabated."

"You bein' a smart-ass?" she says. "I seen lots of smart-asses. So I sure as hell know a smart-ass when I see one!"

"P-Please," I say, "I am v-very interested in your p-past."

"That's what it is, all right."

Her Mascara is running again as tears of lonely sadness has squirted out from her eyes so she takes a mirror out from her purse and wipes said eyes with a Kleenex plus tosses said Kleenex on to our bus's floor Irresponsibly. I instantaneously yank said up from the floor and stick it in my pocket Responsibly.

"Gee, ain't *you* a good boy," utters Flo which makes me Blissful then continues:

"When I was seventeen I was first runner-up in our high school short story contest. I was *real* gifted."

OH MY GOSH! Am I Engrossed! A real writer! So I utter:

"W-What a honor!"

Flo likes my utter and squinches her eyes shut and leans her head back contiguous on to her bus's seat.

"I had wrote a story called 'Hitch Hiking To Hollywood' about a girl who hitch hikes to Hollywood and transforms herself in to a hooker by a appalling mistake. Although I ain't never went to Hollywood me myself although it is jist up the coast, my story proved itself to be a livin' profligacy."

"A l-livin' w-what?" I say plus make Mental Notations on Profligacy.

"It all come true, hon. With yours truly. Eighteen long long years ago to be exact."

She opens her eyes and notes me, "About the time that you was born."

I told you every fool plus their brother thinks I am 18!

"But now," says Flo, "my precious gift has flew the coop."

She grabs her black snotted hanky out from her purse and blows her nose hardly.

"I was forced in to my present life by bossy men who do not understand the inner desires of nobody. I was farther depressed down by beers and diet pills until now all I got left is my crowning glory."

She yanks her black stringy long hair away from her Prespiry neck and re-wipes both of her 2 eyes with said snotted hanky plus says:

"And, of course, what's still hot and slippy right here between my skinny legs."

She pokes her thumb right up her Pewdendas and I note her lap for a Tell-Tail coffee stain or something but do not see nothing Irreconcilable.

"Metaphorically speaking," says Flo, "*He* used to say that, 'Metaphorically speaking,' That bossy old guy I shacked up with."

Flo looks Dementing for one interval and I ain't got no ideal what the heck she is Chatting on but make Mental Notations on Metaphorically Speaking plus utter real kind:

"Y-Your L-Literal sk-skills is still th-there d-deep insides of y-you, Miss F-Flo."

She heightens up.

"Oh do you think so? Do you really think so?"

Then she heightens down and looks sad and I ponder she will blubber or yank my shoulders again. But don't do neither. (Fortunately!)

"You sure my skills are still here?" says Flo which slaps her right hand on her heart. I grab her hand off from her heart genteel plus stick it on to her head.

"N-No. H-Here."

I thump her on her head soft with my thumb as no matter what occurs you always got your brains to fall back on to.

"Your a real smart kid, Danny."

Now ain't that a kind thing which to say?!

Flo pokes her face real close and notes me for a interval then looks out from our bus window as the dessert sites whizzes by and a old big tear flops down her pocky poor cheek.

"I wrote me a epic pome," she says, "Well. Me and this real bossy old guy I shacked up with wrote it. He was a reporter in the newspapers which had became a drunk. I helped him as he was down and out. But..."

"H-How k-kind," I utter as it is real kind for Flo to help you when one is Down And Out.

"But he got bossy. *Real* bossy."

Flo squinches up her brows and looks Dementing for a additional interval. "And, well, the sonofabitch wrote my epic pome hisself. All of it. But I learned it by heart. Which ain't easy! It deals with my anger that this bossy old guy said I was born with. At first I thought it was bullshit. But now I don't. As..."

Flo looks like she is going to utter something additional but don't but jist oscillates her head and stares out the bus's window again then re-oscillates at me plus utters:

"It rhymes good. My epic pome. I make up new words too, sometimes," she says, "as I go along. And they ain't so bad. I got what is known as Residual Talents."

Am I heightened up! I can't hardly await to get Flo to Gala Talent Night to Recite her Pome but I do not tell her nothing yet as she might get all heightened up and grab my shoulders again or yank out her scary knife.

"I got another pome too," says Flo which is smiling for the 1st time since I met her while her stringy black hair wiggles in a squirt of cool air which shoots down from a air vent on the Air-Cooling Accoutrements.

"This other pome is about God. I wrote this one a hundred Percent by my lonesome after this old guy had...well... went. Know what I mean?"

"Y-Yes. W-Where'd he g-go to?"

"He...died."

Flo gives me a excessively goofy look and hunches her shoulders up plus looks like she is going to shiver or blubber but don't do neither.

"Like to hear it?"

I nod up and down exceedingly enthusiastic as I always like items about god as I and Jarleen and Bull ain't never went to church as we ain't Reverential.

"I will interpret the moods of my pome with my entire body as I recite it."

Flo sets up real straight on to her bus's seat and commences.

"Oh, Godddddd!"

she hollers which makes me jump.

"Oh, Godddddd!
Did you not hear me say hello?!"

She cups her hands to to her mouth to interpret a explicit Mood of hollering at almighty god. Lucky for us the only other passengers on our bus is a old couple which don't seem to hear exceedingly good.

"I been hollerin' at the top of my lungs all day
tryin' to find a way
To say
Come down, God
And join we two together,"

hollers Flo which wraps her skinny 2 arms right around herself plus wiggles from side to side which interprets a additional Mood Mode of being joined together with the almighty. (I *think*!) (Ain't sure.)

"You, God, don't care a feather
Whether
I been bad or had or what have you!
And I read a *bro*-chure..."

Flo interprets reading a brochure which she pretends to hold real close to her eyes plus squints. This is Dramatic in the extremes!

"A *bro*-chure called:
Jesus Is Your Sidekick and..."

She grabs my shoulders plus yanks me back and fourth and hollers:
"But he *ain't* your sidekick, Danny! 'Cause where was this Jesus guy when Bull give me that rotten peach?! Huh?! And that inferior shampoo that dried up my beautiful hair?! Huh?! Where was Jesus when your Mom whacked me on my head?! And where

was Jesus when that goddamn sailor beat me up in the park and give me two great big black eyes and a broke wrist?! Where was Jesus then?! Huh?! **HUH?!**"

I jerk back from her and wipe my face off on to the sleeve of my 100 Percent red nylon seersucker no-iron shirt as old poor Flo is Livid plus spitting spit at me during said hollering. Then she squints her eyes again and continues to interpret the Reading *Bro*-chure Mood Mode:

> "And Jesus don't care where
> says this *bro*-chure
> You been
> Or what you done..."

She throws her arms all over like a chicken with their head chopped off!

"But he *must* care, Danny!"

OH MY GOSH! Firstly she says Jesus *don't* care then she says Jesus *must* care!

"He don't like what he sees neither!"

Her 2 eyes currently go all Dementing in a See Mood Mode.

> "Geez, it was a crazy book.
> But I took a look
> and did what it said
> And my face sure is red
> from hollering!
> And though I holler with all my might
> Your never nowheres
> anywheres in sight!"

She cups her 2 hands to her mouth and interprets hollering again.

> "And goddamn it, God,
> I have hollered long enough,
> So I'm goin' out
> to get a beer
> And if your here
> when I get back
> We can talk business!"

80

"That's it," says Flo, "That's my Jesus Pome."

"F-Flo! Th-That is a excellent P-Pome!"

"No shit?"

Flo shows all of her teeth which feasibly wasn't brushed this morning neither as she slept at the Bus's Station which ain't got proper Faculties although she washed her crowning glory but not real affectively due to said Inferior Shampoo which was gave to her by my Dad Bull. (As said.) (But I Digress)

"A e-e-exceedingly e-excellent P-P-Pome!" I utter for a additional kind emphasis. **OH MY GOSH!** You jist never know what one will find on the Non-Expressive Bus to Port City!

Flo grins at me and I grin right back plus tell her all about Gala Talent Night at the Jolly Jug which commences promptly at 7 PM.

"The Jolly Jug," says Flo, "Didn't it used to be called The Maiden's Head?"

"Y-Yes!" I utter, "F-Formerly."

"Is this Jolly Jug one o' *them* places?"

Both of Flo's eyes Transmogrifys theirselves in to 2 skinny slits, "One o' them places that is always gettin' closed down by the Police Department?"

"It is th-the n-nicest p-place I ever b-been in m-my whole d-darn l-life!"

Flo don't utter nothing for one interval then looks goofy then squinches up her brows.

"Your daddy really got Sy-phillius?"

"W-What's S-Sy-ph-phillius?"

"Never mind."

I make Mental Notations to look up Sy-phillius on my Webster's then our darn bus breaks down as it possesses The Vapor Lock which is implicitly what our Bus's Driver utters.

Babe should be here as her and Lorraine would know jist what to do so as to get this darn bus back on to the road. I ain't had good luck with Major Motor Vehicles belatedly. (To say the least!)

They do not send us no other bus neither as this is the cheap bus. So we jist set here for hours in the hot heat as the Air Cooling Accoutrements don't work when said bus ain't In Motion.

I got to go out behind of a big Tumbleweed (A dessert growth.) (As said.) 3 times to alleviate as I have drank 3 Dr P's subsequential to Embarkation and Dr P's goes right on through me as one segmant of said is a Pejorative. (Prune Juice!)

81

Flo goes right to sleep and as she twitches and moans a whole alots I ponder that she is still suffering of Concussions procured from Jarleen's white-legged whack. I myself concentrate on not keeling over. Us obese boys Abhor heat as said is Anathema while fat.

Our bus finally gets to the Port City Bus's Station in Twilight and Flo dismounts and says she will be only one minute plus will I jist set down in the Waiting Room while she procures some funds? I ponder that she resides real near this Bus's Station but don't desire for me to note her abode which is feasibly a shack as she was Shacked-Up in said with that Old Bossy Man which had wrote her Epic Pome for her so I say:

"I s-sure w-will!" even although I desire to waddle to the NO LOITERING Vicinity and loiter untill the cows come home while Contemporaneously noting protrusive loitering sailor's weenies. But I don't. As there ain't no loitering permitted and I obey legal laws Whenever Applicable. (As said.)

18. THE CONVIVIAL MEN'S ROOM AT THE PORT CITY BUS'S STATION

I set my fat heinie down in the Waiting Room plus ponder how lucky I am that Flo says I am a real smart kid which is the kindest thing which any person ever said to me except for My Deeply Departed Grandma which uttered I am a Ugly Duckling which ain't became Fully Swanified. Now ain't that a kind thing which to say? Although said Grandma Neglected to utter when this State of Full Swanification would duly occur.

Anyhow. I currently got a new friend (Flo.) which to add to my list which includes Babe and Lorraine and Marie and Reggie and the concerned short lady and feasibly even the kind elevater lady at The Lonely Gal's broadcasting studio's building. Oh yes! And dear Miranda Cosmonopolis plus Lottie Venables and Miss Lela McCoy plus My Divine Fred Foster which don't count currantly as his Mom hollered at me and he is on my back burner. (Where *she* sets contiguous!) (As prior said sadly.) But I relentlessly ponder Fred's weenie anyhow plus his blue 2 eyes and am propelled to profess that I love him Extravagant even Back-Burner-wise. (But I Digress.)

As I set here adjacent besides of Flo's cardboard box of minor items and await for her I joyously ponder with excessive relief that PK Benderson is way the heck back in Lemon Gulch and ain't here in Port City to protrude on me nor stick his boot on to my head. I additionally ponder joyous about The Lonely Gal which could be my very best friend in A Often Uncaring World when she is proficiently rested.

As I ponder The Afourgoing said I get so hungry I purchase 6 Milky-Ways at the Bus's Station's Confectionary Counter and gobble down 2 and put the other 4 insides of my front 2 pockets. (2 Per Pocket.) Plus pat my fat contented tummy even although I disapprove of said Acutely due to it's obese floppy fatness.

What can be keeping Flo which is taking a real long time to return?! Anyhow. I arise up and waddle towards the Men's Restroom to alleviate a Call of Nature (To pee.) plus reminisce a delighted saying my Deeply Departed Grandma taught me as I waddle along:

> "When Nature calls
> at either door
> one should not attempt to bluff her!
> But haste away
> night or day
> or one's health is sure
> to suffer!"

DO I CONCUR!

I stand alleviating one's self at the white 3 Anchors Double Urinal which has got a Dearth of sailors as they are all loitering in the NO LOITERING Vicinity. However. I hear one person enter in but do not look up as I got a Dilemma alleviating in the presence of variegated unspecified Individuals and desire to reserve my Equilibrium.

This unseen but heard person comes over contiguous and unbuttons hisself and yanks out one weenie.

Like a spy I oscillate my piglet 2 eyes on to this peeing stranger's Genitalias. What a weenie! Jist the sort of convivial weenie I habitually ponder My Divine Fred Foster possesses! I inch my piglet eyes up from said dear weenie towards it's righteous owner's face. **OH MY GOSH!** It *is* Fred Foster!

"Hi, F-Fred, my old p-pal!" I holler plus surprise Fred a whole alots and he pees right on to his Ked's Tennis Shoe!

"Danny!" he says, "What are *you* doing here?!"

Fred possesses sunglasses and a baseball cap and a red bandana which is tied around his neck plus his bundle of keys is hooked traditionally on to the belt loop of his Dungarees.

"I c-come here to m-meet The Lonely G-Gal at The J-Jolly Jug. I'm t-traveling w-with a interpre-t-t-tah-tive d-dancer which is to r-recite a Epic Autobiographical P-Pome!" I utter With Alacrity.

If that don't impress Fred then nothing will!

"Gee, that sounds great, Danny!"

Fred adjusts his Silken Fourskin to Explicate his Urine. His jolly weenie seems to wink joyously at me as I relentlessly note it in Bliss plus forget all about Fred's occupying my back burner while my own dear weenie twitches and snaps in to a Boner Poste Haste!

"W-What are y-you doing here, F-Fred, my old p-pal?"

"I uhhhhh..."

"A M-Major M-Motion P-P-Picture?"

"Yeah, Danny, that's it, a Motion Picture."

"What M-Motion Picture, F-Fred, my old p-pal?"

He don't utter nothing but "Errrrr...".

"C-Carnival in C-Costa R-Rica with V-Vera-Ellen? It's p-p-playing at The Orpheum. I I-love V-Vera-Ellen! Explicitly wh-when s-she d-dances on the top of them g-giant C-Costa R-Rica M-Marimbas!"

Which she don't in this explicit Motion Picture but said sounds Dramatic and I desire to Overwhelm Fred.

"Danny," says Fred which ain't Overwhelmed, "it is awful hard to pee while your staring at my peter like that."

However! Fred's weenie is Tumescing Up and he instantaneously oscillates sideways so as it ain't so accessible as prior to my Glare.

"Gosh, I'm s-sorry, F-Fred, m-my old p-pal, I didn't m-mean..."

I yank my piglet eyes off from Fred's convivial Genitalias.

"That's all right, Danny. Hey, I'm awful sorry my Mom hollered at you the other day."

Fred is Strenuously noting my Boner and yanking his Silken Fourskin back and fourth over his pink hard weenie head. As this is a Primal sign of Onanation I commence to Onanate additionally then we change hands abruptly and he Onanates me and I Onanate him plus I can hardly get my fingers around his convivial Boner!

We squirt Loquaciously as Fred's belt-looped keys clanks

Clamorous on the white 3 Anchors Double Urinal in Bliss!

I wipe myself up with 3 subsequential paper towels and consider myself lucky that every fool plus their brother ain't came in to relieve hisself during my Fully Insulated Onanation. Plus wish Stringently that Fred could of been here in real actuality.

I button my fly and exit out from this desserted Men's Room and am jist in time to note a policeman leading Flo and her box of minor items out from the Bus's Station! What has she went and did?! I commence to follow her and said policeman but she tells me to go away with variegated winks of her eyes as she feasibly don't wish to Inhibit me in no Police Preceding which is a kind thing which not to do.

So I aim my fat big tummy towards said Jug. Plus waddle right on. Fully Insulated. As per like always.

19. GALA TALENT NIGHT AT THE JOLLY JUG!

It is excessively dark as a merciless sun has sat. I waddle down variegated streets puffing plus pondering sadly what happened to old poor Flo.

After one duration I hear music! It is the twanging guitar of a Sad Cowboy who's Cowgirl Compatriot has left him in The Lurch and is a song which I adore. Said Sad Cowboy Croons:

> "Even though it is summer
> It is winter in my heart
> The stars has lost all their glitter
> As you've upset my applecart..."

I waddle around a corner and see the neon yellow sign THE JOLLY JUG and pat the 2 Milky-Ways insides of each of my front 2 pockets in joy plus smile to one's self as I will be among variegated exceedingly kind ladies real soon. The Sad Cowboy's voice gets louder plus louder and sadder and sadder:

> "...We pledged our love
> Through thick and thin, Lu-ceeel
> But time run out
> Miss Fortune spun her wheeel..."

I am instantaneously real sad that Flo ain't here to recite her Epic Pome plus hope Fervantly that she can get this police matter sorted out to his satisfaction so's as she can join us later at her own convenience. Said Sad Cowboy Croons unabated:

> "...The cards was stacked against us
> From the start
> I shoulda known to love you
> it weren't smart
> You said you loved me
> But you told a lie
> I'm so dah-gone lonely
> I could lay right down and die..."

I know jist how this sad Crooning Cowboy feels as Fred Foster's poor misguided Mom called me a fat big Sissy Bastard! Plus if I wasn't so fat and inordinantly tall PK might not even note me plus I would not acquire so many Hostile Eyes contacting me on every available opportunity!

Also it is excessively Mortifying that I am jist as big as PK and it don't make no difference as regards Self-Defense as I am a additional coward. (Multitudes of we Sissies Abhor violent Tactics which goes Hand-In-Hand with one's being Conscientous Objectives.) (As said?) But I ain't no *Bastard* as my parents was married one week prior to my birthday which is what my Deeply Departed Grandma told me. Which makes Fred's poor misguided Mom inaccurate in the extremes.

"DANNY!" hollers this here screaming voice!

I am so a-scared I darn near alleviate! It is Flo and here she is running out from a alley with her cardboard box of minor items underneath of her arm and waving a Bevy of dollars right at me!

She comes running up and grabs me and pokes her skinny arm right through my fat arm and hugs me which is contenting as I adore embraces of all renditions.

"I screwed that fuckin' cop!"

Flo's head oscillates right around and she points up a alley. "In there! The sonofabitch didn't want to pay me but I scared him with my zip knife!"

She laughs real goofy. "Jist imagine, Danny, threatenin' a real cop with a real knife! He must of thought I was a Loony! Hah!

Hah! Hah! Hah! Hah!"

Flo sticks a indeterminant sum of dollars insides of my 100 Percent red nylon no-iron seersucker shirt's pocket and I ponder contented how many more Milky-Ways and Dr Peppers and/or batteries I can purchase with said as she flops her arm around my neck and we enter in to the The Jolly Jug.

The Quasi-dark smoky and big room is chock full of ladies's voices which is laughing and grinning plus festooned with twisty Duplicitous colored crepe paper streamers!

A lady turns the jukebox down so as a 3 lady band can practice on their instruments on a little stage which is surrounded by approximately thirty folding chairs and feasibly more all of which which is filled with Vivacious ladies garbed in Dungarees and slacks and one or 2 colorful sporadic Dresses or Pheasant Skirts. (Plus the Odd Ballerina Slipper.) They all got cigarettes and cans of beer as beer is the only alcoholic beverage which is served among The Jolly Jug's premises.

A whole alots of said smoking ladies oscillate their multiple heads so as to note us as we enter in as Flo's stringy black long hair plus low cut Pheasant blouse plus exceedingly small waste is one Big Plus. For once it ain't me which is being Glared at but **OH MY GOSH** these ladies *is* Observant as Flo sits down her cardboard box of minor items and commences to graciously swing her skinny hips to and fourth.

"Danny!"

It is Babe which is about as nice a site as I have saw this total nerve racked day.

"Danny boy! Wow! Is that a lollypop in your pocket or are you jist glad to see me?!"

Babe laughs real happy and loud which contents me and I utter:

"Oh, n-no, B-Babe. These ain't l-lollypops!"

I stick my 2 hands insides of my 2 pockets for proof. "Th-These is M-Milky-Ways! (Which is getting exceptionally soft and gooey on my hot fat 2 thighs.) B-But I s-sure am glad to s-see you, B-Babe!"

Babe hugs me tight. I jist can't *never* be hugged too tight. *Never!* Then Babe stands back and gives Flo one real long look plus says to me:

"Who is your lady friend, Danny?"

"My name is Firenze but they call me Flo," utters Flo which stands real straight and pushes out her little 2 titties, "I am from

87

Italian origin."

"Now ain't that nice!" says Babe which sticks out her hand. Flo sticks out hers and Babe takes it and shakes it.

"Pleased to meet yer acquaintance, Flo," says Babe which smiles Gregoriously, "Any friend of Danny Boy's is a friend of mine."

"Likewise, I *think*," says Flo.

"F-Flo desires to r-recite her P-Pome tonight, B-Babe, if th-that's OK."

"That sounds real good, Danny. Jist what sort of Pome is it, Flo?"

"It is a Epic Pome."

Flo sticks her nose up snooty and looks down on to Babe which grins jolly and don't note nothing Irreconcilable.

"We ain't got no poet-tesses performin' tonight so that would round off our program jist fine," says Babe.

"I would like a rhythm accompaniment as I am also a inter-prah-tat-tive dancer. And I intind to extemporize."

"Consider it done!" says Babe which gives me a goofy look. I make Mental Notations on Extemporize plus Glare In Vain for The Lonely Gal which should of been here by now but can not see her no where in this crowd of smoking oscillating ladies.

"Why, hello, Danny Boy!" shrieks Lorraine which walks right up contiguous, "Feeling better I see?"

"I f-feel f-fine!" I utter, "Is The L-Lonely G-Gal here as of y-yet?"

"She ain't arrived as of yet," says Babe which looks exceedingly worried as she Consults her Wristwatch.

"She's s'pose-ta sing the first and last songs too," says Lorraine with her knitting brows, "She is our star attraction."

"This is Danny's friend Flo," says Babe, "She is goin' to recite us a epic pome."

"How exciting, I can't remember when I last heard a me epic pome!"

Lorraine's eyes should be painted and put insides of a Art Museum as their so Gorgeous. (Almost as Dazzling as My Beauteous Mom's!)

"Welcome to Gala Talent Night, Flo!" says Lorraine. "There's prizes, you know, for the winners! Maybe you'll be a winner?"

"Well, I'm a loser now. I sure as hell don't know how I can be a winner and a loser at the same time," says Flo, "Maybe I will jist stick to bein' a loser, Honey. It pays more."

Flo laughs a goofy laugh.

"Well, you jist never know," says Lorraine.

"And that's for sure," says Babe which pats Lorraine's cheeks. "Ain't it, honey?"?

"That's fer darned sure!" says Lorraine which lays her arm on to Babe's shoulders real tender plus genteel.

Flo gives both of these kind 2 ladies a Dementing Glare plus pokes her thumb at a Artistic table of variegated fruits plus says:

"I could sure use me a big fat banana. Is this here fruit free?"

"Free as the air, hon!" says Babe, "Compliments of the house except for the pineapple and watermelon which is jist for looks. You and Danny go help yourselves. Lorraine and me has got to make a announcement."

Babe and Lorraine which holds each other's hands mounts up on to the little stage and announces that Gala Talent Night will suffer a slight delay as their waiting for The Lonely Gal which is to sing the 1st song but said delay will be Accentuated with a special Melody performed by this 3 lady band.

"I am real sorry to keep you ladies in waiting," says Lorraine which laughs. One or 2 variegated ladies laugh additional but not a whole alots as they desire for Gala Talent Night to get it's show on to the road. I myself laugh as I Ruminate that Lorraine is making a joke. (Ladies in Waiting!) (From History.) (**ET. AL!**)

I and Flo help ourselves to a indeterminant sum of bananas from the Fruit-Art Table on which we 2 set on the edges of and Flo snaps her knife open and hacks off a hunk of pineapple from this elegant Fruit-Art display which is exceedingly rude as said Unique pineapple is meant to be saw and not ate.

As I and Flo eat our fruit the lights go down for the Special Melody then **OH MY GOSH!** I note from the corners of my piglet eyes 2 feet in Gorgeous Patent Leather high heeled shoes poking out from underneath of this Fruit-Art table upon which we set upon!

20. COMFORTING IN THE BACK ROOM

I jump right off from said table and squat down and look underneath of it. There laying on her back supinely prone is a real tall lady which is garbed in black nice slacks. I crawl underneath and squat over said lady which smiles up at me.

"Hi, Lonely Guy," she utters.

OH MY GOSH! It is The Lonely Gal which I did not recognize as she ain't got no sunglasses on!

"This is a real fucker, isn't it?" she says in her framiliar voice and her breath ain't as fragrant as feasible due to Multiple indeterminant alcoholic beverages. (A smell Historically framiliar to me due to my inebriated Dad.) (Bull.)

Said Gal says:

"I am supposed to fuckin' sing the first fuckin' song but these fuckers can just all of 'em go fuck their fuckin' selves before they'll get a fuckin' song out of fuckin' me!"

I am devoted to her due to her affectionant radio talk prior but am shocked as fowl language is Anathema to me irregardless of which utters it. (Inclusive of My Beauteous Mom!) (Or others!)

Suddenly from my Cramped Location underneath of the Fruit-Art table I note walking towards us the feet of Babe and Lorraine which is searching all over the darn place and looking worried so I crawl out from underneath of said table jist as a wet big hunk of Flo's illicit pineapple whizzes right by my nose on it's way in to her cardboard box of minor items. Flo don't even note me but jist sets there with her skinny legs dangling over said Table hacking at what is left of the beauteous watermelon and winking at every lady which Glares her way.

I hastily waddle over to Babe and tell her that I found The Lonely Gal so Babe and Lorraine and me come back and yank said Gal out from underneath of said table and in to the back room. Flo don't note nothing but jist oscillates her head plus smiles at all the smoking ladies and chews watermelon and pineapple. (Exceptional messy I might additionally add!)

In the back room the concerned short lady gives The Lonely Gal a big cup of coffee from which she takes a sip from but spits out!

"Fuck you all!" hollers said Gal, "Fuck every last fuckin' one of you except that big fat Sissy!"

"Geez, hon, y'all don't have to talk so mean," says Babe, "Specially in front of this boy. Why he can't be more than eighteen."

"Get the fuckin' hell outta here, all of you! But leave the fat cocksucker with me!" hollers The Lonely Gal implicitly.

OH MY GOSH!

Her eyes roll right back in to her head and all I can note is their 2 whites.

"He's so goddamned ugly he's cute! I *like* 'em Sissified!"

She likes me Sissified!

Babe puts her mouth real near The Lonely Gal's ear plus utters soft and lowly:

"Geez, hon, your s'pose-ta sing the first song."

"Get the hell out!"

OH MY GOSH! Said Gal ain't nothing at all like on her kind radio show!

Babe, Lorraine and the concerned short lady exit out and shut the door real soft.

The Lonely Gal opens one of her squinched shut eyes and squints at me plus says:

"So what's your story, fat-stuff?"

"I love y-you!" I scream.

Said Dire Outburst is due to the shock of her fowl language plus maybe if I tell her loud enough that I love her she might jist sober up and love me back plus then we could be friends feasibly and Chat on our Humane Conditions amicable.

However. The Lonely Gal's alcoholical demeanor is real disappointing and she ain't even Thwarted as she possesses 2 Fully Legitimate legs. But as her fowl language and Inebriation is due to her Humane Condition I still love her plus additionally holler:

"Y-Your m-my comforting w-when I am b-blue and l-lowly!"

Hot big tears splashes on to my 100 Percent red seersucker nylon shirt in agony!

"Are you for real, fat boy?"

Said Gal yanks a hanky out from her hip pocket and throws it right at my face, "Whaddaya mean, you love me?!"

I commence to blubber like a darn 8 year old person not the 18 year old person I purport to Emulate and tears keeps squirting out and said Gal's hanky don't help none.

"Whaddaya mean, you love me?" says said Gal real soft and lowly this time, "whaddaya mean by that, huh?"

Her eyes twitch and go crossed and she sets up in her chair plus makes a grab at her cup of coffee but misses it and jist sets there Glaring at it so I waddle in and hand said coffee to her although I am still blubbering.

"Thanks," she says and takes a slurp.

"Y-Your w-welcome."

"*Are* you a cocksucker?"

"I s-sure d-desire to b-be," I utter with relief that she has prior knew all about my Affiliations, "W-Weenies is all I ever p-ponder on besides y-you and F-Fred F-Foster."

"What's your name?"

"D-Danny."

"How old are you?"

"T-Twelve."

"You're lying!

"I a-ain't!"

Said Gal takes a additional slurp of coffee. "You look *eighteen*! FUCK!"

"I g-got the H-Hormonal Uh-Unbalance. M-My Aunt Edna M-May says it has r-ran in our f-family f-for Eons."

"Yeah? Well, *something* has *ran* in your family for eons, you're sure an ugly kid, aren't you?"

"Y-Yes. Every p-person th-thinks so."

"The gals tell me you have an important message for me."

"Y-Yes."

"Well what is it?"

"I love y-you. B-But I already s-said it p-prior."

"Yeah. Well, Sugar, love bores me shitless."

"B-But w-we g-got the s-same H-Humane C-Condition!"

"Humane Condition?! What the *fuck* is that?!"

"Ain't you s-seen T-TWO ORPHANS AND A W-WAR H-HERO which p-played at all m-major theaters last w-week? It is about life in a o-often un-c-caring w-world!

"Life?! What the fuck do *you* know about life?!

"It's the H-Humane C-Condition. L-Life is!"

"Listen to me, my fat young sissy! If anybody ever asks you about what *life* is you just tell 'em that The Lonely Gal says you gotta fuck *life* up the butthole and stop all the shit before it shoots out and drowns you!"

"B-But I love y-you!" I yell repetitiously as things ain't going the way I desire them to plus I can not think of nothing else which to holler.

"Everybody loves me, fatstuff. Or *did*. No future in that, is there?"

"Y-Your e-excessively l-lonely and I'm e-excessively l-lonely..."

"*I'm* a sonofabitch!"

"N-No, y-your n-not!"

"I've driven everyone who ever mattered straight out of my fucking life. I'm a selfish, cruel, megalomaniacal sonofabitch!

There *are* people like us, you know!"

"Mega-lom...w-what?" I say as I wish to add this Magnificent word to my vocabulary.

"I'm no good for anybody, my fat, young Sissy boy. I intend to end it all tonight after I sing my fucking song. I have nothing to live for!"

"*I* am s-somebody t-to live f-for! Y-You t-tell me you l-love me e-every n-night on the r-radio!" I holler.

"I say that to everybody!"

The Lonely Gal takes a big gulp of coffee and slams it's cup on the table.

"Let's get the hell outta here! I gotta sing my fuckin' song, for chrissake!"

She jumps up off from her chair and I waddle quick and open the door like a gentleman and she commences to exit out but misses said door and slams right in to the wall and jist stands there goofy and her nose is bleeding like a chicken with their head chopped off. I pat said blood off from said nose with the hanky she has flang at me plus hand it back to her. She notes me for one interval then grabs me and hugs me real tight contiguous and as she is almost one half foot taller even then me which is almost fully six feet tall my nose gets buried in between of her 2 titties which smells perfumy and delighted.

Then she pushes me away rough but grabs me right back and kisses me a big spitty kiss square on my upper lip.

"I *do* love you, my fat Sissy," she hollers and wobbles right out through the door. Now ain't that a kind thing which to holler? No person ain't never hollered I Love You to me! (Nor whispered it neither!)

Said Gal wobbles towards the smoking ladies which commences to scream:

"LONE-LY GAL!
LONE-LY GAL!
LONE-LY GAL!"

I pull myself up on to the Fruit-Art Table adjacent besides of Flo who's eyes is glued right on to the heinie of The Lonely Gal which wobbles among the cheering Bevy of ladies and climbs up on to said stage and grabs a chair on which to steady herself on plus grabs the microphone and smiles and hollers:

93

"Hi, Regina! Hi, Marie! Hello there, Babe and Lorraine!"

Babe and Lorraine looks excessively nerve racked and holds hands.

"You there!" hollers said Gal which points at Flo, "You with the black hair to your waist! Welcome to Gala Talent Night at The Jolly Jug!"

Flo smiles real big at The Gal and her teeth literately shine and Flo whispers to me:

"Do you think she'll like my pome?"

"I h-hope s-so."

"She better if she knows what's good for her!" says Flo which pats her knife which sticks in her black shiny belt.

"Great to see you, Ellen! Dry those tears, Dolores and forget her! How's the wife, Lily?! Divorce final, Cindy?!" hollers The Lonely Gal like she really cares a whole alots about these variegated smoking and beer drinking ladies.

Then this here lady grins and pokes her thumb at herself then one finger at The Lonely Gal which grins right back plus says:

"Sorry Deirdre, not tonight. I've... got a headache!"

Deirdre makes a sorrowful look on her face then takes a sad big puff from her cigarette and the crowd laughs and claps and so does Deirdre which was jist teasing in the 1st place.

"As many of you gals know," says The Lonely Gal, I've had a minor upset recently. But life's like that, isn't it, gals?"

"YEAH! LIFE'S LIKE THAT!" hollers variegated smoking ladies which nods their multiple heads. The Lonely Gal smiles and don't seem lonely currantly although she is still wobbling due to Residual Inebriation.

"I'll just come out and say it," she says, "I've been left in the lurch, haven't I?"

The crowd is silent instantaneously and said Gal don't smile and I note Babe and Lorraine which oscillate their nerve racked heads all over.

"Yes, I've been left in the lurch," says said Gal, "Not that I didn't deserve it."

She wobbles reeeeeeal far over plus grabs hard on to her contiguous chair so as to impede a Impending Calamity.

"But enough of this!" hollers The Lonely Gal, "We're here to have fun! We're here to show the world what we can do!"

All the ladies clap and whistle and holler real loud that their here to show the world what we can do!

"However, I have written a song to express my keen sense of loss," says said Gal, "So I'll say it... with music, gals!"

She makes a motion to the 3 lady band. "Hit it, gals!"

The band commences to start to play one soft Melody slow. Suddenly The Lonely Gal drops the microphone and flops right down on to her 2 knees! The band terminates playing as she pulls herself up and grins and hollers "Coffee break!" and points at the concerned short lady which brings her a cup of coffee Poste Haste.

A Bevy of variegated smoking ladies laughs. But it ain't funny! As The Lonely Gal could of hurt one's self severe!

21. FIFI AND COLLETTE AND THE MUCH MALIGNED ANOMALY

Babe and Lorraine and the concerned short lady jumps up on to the little stage and crowd around contiguous. The Lonely Gal squinches her eyes shut and waves her arms all over and hollers: "What the *fuck*?!" as she has jist spilled said hot coffee right on to the top of one of her Ample 2 titties.

Lorraine and the concerned short lady props The Gal up and disperses her down off from said stage and in to the back room.

Babe which still loiters on the stage utters:

"Sorry, gals, but we got to have a short intermission while The Lonely Gal drinks her coffee. And meanwhile we..."

But Babe ain't allowed to finish uttering what she is uttering as a tall lady with sunglasses jumps up on to the little stage and Gesticulates her hands all around and whispers something in to Babe's left ear.

"No, Fifi," says Babe, "I don't think so because..."

But Fifi keeps on Gesticulating her hands and then shoots around and whispers in to Babe's right ear.

Another unspecified lady jumps up on to the stage which Gesticulates additionally and whispers in to Babe's left ear which Fifi has jist abandoned plus is approximately half as tall as Fifi which is behemoth.

After a full duration Babe which looks worried nods her head Yes to said 2 ladies.

"Well, gals," says Babe over her microphone, "It seems like we got a song to be sang by Fifi and Collette who also have wrote it theirselves. As some of you gals know, Fifi and Collette teach French at two Junior Colleges but jist for safety's sake I ain't sayin' which ones."

There is a whole alots of laughs and Fifi and Collette bows to the assorted smoking laughing ladies which sits their beer cans contiguous so as to clap their Manifold hands.

"As I have heard their song before I want to warn all of you to jist stay calm and don't throw nothing. We all of us feel real strong about this here situation," says Babe, "but throwing objects such as beer cans don't solve nothing."

The said Assorted claps a additional time then sips their multiple beers and smokes their Omniscient cigarettes. Babe which don't look real contented Relinquishes the microphone to Fifi plus dismounts down off from said stage.

Fifi and Collette move in real close to each other and sits their arms on top of each other's shoulders which ain't easy as Fifi is behemoth (As said.) and Collette is shorter even then the concerned short lady. But they commence to sing anyhow. **LOUD!**

> "We're suffering
> From the much maligned anomaly!"

What the heck is The Much Maligned Anomaly?! I make Mental Notations as these 2 French teachers sing unabated:

> "We're feeling So *de trop*!
> We're questioning
> Furiously and phenomenally
> Society that treats us so!"

I remember how The Society treated the Orphanage Coach when he desired to adapt them two Orphan boys. (*Before* they detected that he was a war hero and they was mean and unkind!) I know explicitly how these 2 French teachers feels!

> "But our questions don't do any good!
> Our behavior is not what it should be
> They tell us we're bad or we're mad
> Or we're sick!
> And a doctor could make us tick
> Properly!

Oui! Oui! Oui!"

"Yeah!" hollers one smoking lady! "Oui! Oui! Oui! and make that doctor a gy-necologis*tess*!"

Everybody laughs real goofy but I ain't got no ideal what the heck Fifi and Collette is singing about. I ascertain it is Female Troubles of which Mean Aunt Edna May says ladies has got a whole alots of. Them 2 French Teachers sings on relentlessly:

> "We're suffering
> From the much maligned anomaly!
> We're feeling
> so *de trop*!
> We're yelling
> furiously and phenomenally
> At the Vice Squad
> that treats us so!"

Variegated smoking ladies grumbles and growls plus bangs their beer cans together and blows their cigarette smoke out from between of their communal teeth as Fifi and Collette continually sings:

> "We're not sick!
> Well, no sicker than you!
> But we simply don't screw as
> You do!
> Our erogenous zones are complex!
> Won't ignite with the touch
> Of the opposite sex!
> Non! Non! Non!"

"NON! NON! NON!" hollers all of the smoking ladies which is getting *real* riled up and so am I but please do not ask me why! As I can not tell you! As I do not know!

Collette does a little dance around Fifi which stands still and shakes her one finger like a jitterbug then they sing collectively:

> "We're harassed!
> We're entrapped!
> We're enraged!

97

The Vice Squad could be
So much better engaged!
We don't mean any harm to no one!
But the day is approaching
We'll carry a gun!"

"Bang-bang-bang!" hollers a smoking lady which has glittery eyes and pretends like she is shooting a gun.

"Or a knife!" hollers Flo which waves said over her head, "Slash-slash-slash!"

Fifi and Collette nevertheless sings:

"Oui! Oui! Oui!"

"OUI! OUI! OUI!" hollers more smoking ladies and Fifi and Collette additionally sings:

"Oui! Oui! Oui!
We're suffering
From the much maligned anomaly!"

There's that word again!

"A practice that has not found favor in our day!"

one real heightened up lady throws a beer can almost but Babe points at her and she don't.

"Nature's ways
are a mystery!
We appear down
through history!"
(Sings Fifi and Collette.)

All of the ladies is currently standing up and hollering and banging their beer cans and stamping out their cigarettes on the floor with their variegated feet!

"We're as natural as Hets!
(Sings Fifi and Collette.)
And we're kind to our pets!

98

But we're suffering!
Suffer-innnnnng!
Suffer-innnnnnnnnnnnnnng!"

Then Fifi and Collette which teaches the French Language at
two Junior Colleges sticks their arms around each other's wastes
and Fifi takes off her sunglasses and they look real hard right on
to each other's 4 eyes plus sings:

"Sweet Sappho
was one of us!
Yet mankind likes
none of us!
"We're *sooooo*
de *troooooop*!"

I am real sorry about all that suffering as I know jist how they
feel due to PK Benderson's Inhumane Acts Upon My Persona.
Anyhow. I make Mental Notations on Saffo plus Mankind. (**ET.
AL!**)

All of the smoking ladies plus Babe herself and Reggie and
Marie is all jumping up and down. But Flo jist sets there on the
Fruit-Art table swinging her skinny legs in their black net stockings and gobbling watermelon and pineapple and waving her
knife sporadically up in the air sometimes.

Then Babe jumps up on to the little stage plus yells:

"Thank you, Fifi and Collette! That was real rousing!"

Fifi and Collette bows plus looks contented and dismounts
down off from the little stage and sets on 2 chairs and multiple
ladies runs up and hugs and kisses them like chickens with their
heads chopped off.

Then all persons cheers again as The Lonely Gal comes out
from the back room and she ain't wobbling so much as prior plus
has got a big coffee cup in her 2 hands from which she takes a
swallow from and sits the cup down and climbs up on to the
little stage plus makes a sign with her hand and the 3 lady band
commences to play again. Real slow and real soft and lowly.
Splendiforously.

22. THEM CRAZY ACHES

"We've all experienced loss, gals, at one time or another," says The Lonely Gal, "so you'll know exactly what I mean when I say..." She commences in her low voice to sing her very own unique original song which she herself has wrote:

> "I ache at midnight, honey
> When the moon is high
> To say I didn't ache
> Would be to tell a lie..."

A goofy look comes on to the front of her sweat drinched face as it Prespires.

> "I ache at noontime, baby
> When the sun is hot
> It's jus' a crazy Hell
> To be where you are not."

"Know how you feel, Lonely Gal," says Flo which whacks off a additional hunk of illicit pineapple from the Once Magnificent Fruit-Art display.

As I am excessively embarrassed I move a small bit away from Flo plus yank a Milky-Way out from my hot pocket which is exceptionally soft and gooey. I take one big bite and commence to chew but the Lonely Gal looks right at me so I terminate chewing while she sings:

> "I got them crazy crazy aches
> I got them crazy crazy aches
> I got the shakes
> I got the shakes
> From them craaaazy aches
> From them crazy crazy aches."

I re-wrap said Way and stuff it back insides of my pocket as it is currently exceedingly squishy plus Destined to become More So due to it's incongruity on my fat hot leg.

"Them gosh-awful aches,"
sings The Lonely Gal.

I ascertain to ignore her fowl language and Inebriation as she sings so good. I will be her stout friend plus Remunerate her for them multiple Fully Insulated nights in which she was my only comfort in. Her soft singing is incessant:

"I ache in summer, sweetie,
In fall and winter too
And springtime is a horror
'Cause I ache to be with you
Oh I shiver like a jelly
From my bosom to my belly..."

Our friendship's blooming will give I and said Gal A New Lease On To Life.

"...I got them crazy crazy aches
I got them crazy crazy aches
I got the shakes
I got the shakes
From them craaaazy aches
From them crazy crazy aches..." (Sings said Gal real Mellifluously.)

I oscillate my piglet face on to Flo and utter:
"Wh-What y-you need, F-Flo, is A N-New L-Lease On To L-Life."
"'Zat so?" says Flo which is Deliriously noting The Lonely Gal plus drinking a Surfeit of beers and is currently one Persona Non Gratin even although she has gave me 2 dollars prior. (I counted it!)
Flo wipes pineapple juice off from her mouth with a piece of purple crepe paper tore off from the Fruit-Art display and giggles With Alacrity. Multiple ladies oscillates their heads sideways and shushes her.
"Up yours, mister!" she hollers real rude.
The Lonely Gal currently sways with deep feelings back and fourth as the band plays a soft music-only segmant and I can smell her perfume from where I set as I long to be hugged by her in a State of Bliss. (Feasibly with my piglet nose in between of her

101

perfumy delighted titties.)

"Get me another beer," says Flo which hands me fifty cents, "And get yourself a coke."

I waddle over and purchase a beer and a Dr P (Although Coke Is The Favorite The World Over.) plus set down by Flo and give her her beer and change and thank her Courteous for my Dr P but she don't say Thank You back. I guess she thinks as she paid for our 2 beverages she ain't got to be Courteous which ain't polite.

My Deeply Departed Grandma taught me manners and I am habitually gratuitous as Bull ain't got none and Jarleen ain't Courteous to no Individuals which don't possess at least one protrusive weenie on their persons. (Except for Jack Shanks which feasibly hides his in one Plethora of Zoot suit pleats.) (As said.)

The soft music-only segmant terminates and The Lonely Gal additionally sings:

> "...When I was just a little girl
> My mama said to me
> You pay for everything you get
> 'Cause nothin's ever free
> Then I fell in love with you, Babe..."

"Yes *you*, Babe!" hollers The Gal which points her finger straight at Babe which has her arm on Lorraine's shoulder and looks Mortified as who wouldn't be if they got a finger poking straight at them Before The Multitudes.

The band stops playing and a whole alots of the ladies whispers but not so loud that I can hear their words so I do not know what said say. Poor Babe is nerve racked and Lorraine suffers Infinitely too. The Lonely Gal points at the band for their music to commence again and Babe and Lorraine looks alleviated. However I got to admit I myself do not know what the heck is going on!

> "Then I fell in love with you, Babe,
> And mama's words came true
> 'cause I pay for every minute
> That I cannot be with you..."

sings said Gal which currantly puts a great Momentum on to said aches and shakes!

"I got them crazy crazy aches!
I got them crazy crazy aches!
I got the shakes!
I got the shakes!
From them crazy aches!
From them crazy crazy aches!"

I shiver Dire plus desire to climb right up on to that little stage
with her and Ache And Shake away jist like her as I know jist what
it is like to ache as I ache to be handsome plus adored but can not
never be even although I ache! Aching jist never helps as it only
impels persons to ache even more like chickens with their heads
chopped off.

My piglet 2 eyes fills right up and I commence to blubber. **OH
MY GOSH!** Will I be a blubbering fat heinied Sissy eternally?!

"...Love is the Devil's bargain
You pay for with your guts
To fall in love forever
You gotta be half-nuts
'Cause even if your love's returned
In equal measure, 'Sighhhhhhh'
(Sings The Lonely Gal.)
The Devil's compensated
When one or the other of you die.
I got them crazy crazy aches
I got them crazy crazy aches.
I got the shakes
I got the shakes
From them craaaazy aches
From them crazy crazy aches!"

I myself commence to acquire them crazy aches and shakes
and am blubbering exceptionally Dire. I grab a handfull of paper
napkins from the Fruit-Art table and blow my piglet red nose. I
have blubbered so many times currantly that I have lost all count
but as blubbering is a vital segmant of My Humane Condition I
allow it to go Unchallenged.

Then a whole alots of blubbering busts out! Babe and Lorraine
is both blubbering and so is Marie and Reggie plus the concerned
short lady.

All the smoking ladies jumps up and claps and whistles and cheers and The Lonely Gal bows Thrice but suddenly shivers awful and shakes and falls backwords over her chair with one big flop!

The smoking ladies Gasps and blows smoke through their noses and Babe jumps up on to the little stage with Lorraine exceptionally contiguous. I waddle up to them and volunteer my service.

Babe squats over The Lonely Gal which lays there wiggling something awful with her 2 eyes all white and her mouth foaming with froth and her arms and legs flopping around like a chicken with their head chopped off!

The concerned short lady comes running up with a magazine and hands it to Babe which rolls it up and pokes it in between The Lonely Gal's teeth then Babe and Lorraine and me carries The Lonely Gal and lies her down on to the pool table.

Flo which is still chopping up the Fruit-Art pineapple jist hunches up her 2 shoulders and gives us all a goofy look. And all the smoking ladies whispers Amidst theirselves.

"The Gal'll be OK, Danny," says Babe.

"Real soon," says Lorraine.

"She always sleeps a little after one of her fits," utters Marie which has came running up.

The short lady which is exceedingly concerned jist loiters here and fumbles her fingers around in her apron's pockets. Reggie runs up with a behemoth glass of ice water.

"Jist set that water down, Regina," says Babe. "She cain't drink none while she's a-sleepin'."

"Pore thang," says the concerned short lady.

Lorraine dabs at her own red eyes plus says:

"She doesn't take her pills on purpose! Her doctor says not taking them can be fatal as she has complications!"

"She done this on purpose, gals. She jist don't want to live sometimes," says Babe, "She told me so."

They all snivel for a duration then The Lonely Gal opens one of her eyes plus burps plus utters:

"What the *fuck*?!"

But passes right out again.

"She has got so much to live for too," says Babe.

"But she's real down in the dumps," says Reggie.

"God in heaven!" hollers Lorraine at every fool plus their brother at Gala Talent Night, "Babe can't help it if The Lonely Gal

104

falls in love with her, can she?"

"It sure ain't Babe's fault," says Marie.

"It sure ain't," says Reggie.

"That's fer darned sure!" says Marie.

"I seen this comin' fer months and months," says Lorraine.

"Let's jist leave her in peace for awhile, gals," says Babe, "Let's jist give our gal some air."

I do not wish to exit away from The Lonely Gal explicitly as her face looks so greenish. But Babe yanks me plus the sad others away.

"Well," says Babe which looks around at the concerned smoking ladies which sets on their chairs drinking beer, "We sure got to git this show on the road and fast! Me and the gals was to sing the next song, Danny, but we gotta have some time to git ourselves together, don't we gals?"

"We sure do," says Reggie which wipes her eye on the shining black sleeve of her THE STEAMROLLERS shirt.

"That's fer darned sure!" says Marie.

"Danny, can your friend Flo recite her epic pome right this very minute?" says Babe.

I oscillate around and note Flo which lays on her back pronely almost on the Fruit-Art table hacking at the last hunk of Fruit-Art watermelon with her knife. She stuffs some in to her mouth and 14 million black little watermelon seeds shoots out all over her tummy. However. I utter real Courteous:

"I'm s-sure F-Flo'd be r-real delightful."

I waddle fast over to Flo.

"Flo!" I holler nerve racked in the extremes, "C-Could you p-please Interpret y-your Epic P-Pome right th-this v-very minute?!"

23. "MY NAME IS FIRENZE BUT THEY CALL ME FLO"

"*Dee*-lighted!" hollers Flo which jumps right off from the Fruit-Art table and wipes said watermelon seeds off from her tummy with her black hanky plus snaps her big knife shut and tucks it behind of her black shiny belt.

Babe climbs up on to the little stage and grabs the microphone plus says:

"Here is a real interesting newcomer to The Jolly Jug, gals. She is a inter-pre-tah-tive dancer and will recite and simultaneous interpret her own epic pome."

There is a couple of moans from smoking ladies which feasibly do not relish Epic Pomes or maybe which can not ascertain what a accurate Epic Pome is. (Neither can I although I got no trouble with the Pome segment.) However. Their moans ceases instantaneously as Flo swings her skinny hips back and fourth and climbs on to the little stage and says something to the lady Drummeresse which is garbed in green satin which commences to beat out a slow rhythm beat on to her Drums. The Base Fiddle is Strummed by a tall lady garbed in a yellow chiffon dress with a knitted hair Snood to match which joins right in.

Flo makes a sign for the Trumpeteresse garbed in her brown Kulots to play whenever she feels a Impetus to then swings her skinny hips to said slow rhythm and winks at the smoking ladies and commences to Chant: (Talk slow due to said Rhythm Drum Beats.)

> "My name is Firenze
> But they call me Flo
> I got hips of wrath
> I got tits of woe!"

Flo wiggles her pointed little titties and skinny hips to interpret what she has jist sang plus licks her lips and sticks her skinny 2 legs in her netted black stockings right straight out in the front of her like a Nazi soldier which is Goose Stepping. (I am glad poor Wolfgang ain't here to see this Stunning Site!)

Flo takes one big step then one more then one more then one more plus Chants as the drum beats incessant:

> "I strut down the street
> At night 'til I'm spent
> Crying crudely,
> Lewdly:
> Body for rent!"

She jumps around real crazy for one full interval and pokes her arms and legs out all over the place then terminates suddenly and swings her stringy black long hair real slow to and fourth and licks her lips in a exceptionally Dementing mode.

> "My bodice is a-ged
> My stockings are shred-ded
> I had been enga-ged
> But my lover has fled-ed
> On the eve of the day
> That we were to be wed-ded!"

Flo pokes out her little pointed titties plus Chants: (Talks slow Ect. Ect. Ect.) (As said.)

> "A man is the reason
> I walk the night!
> A man is the reason
> I look a fright!"

What wondrous words this old bossy guy with which Flo was shacked up with but which died has wrote for Flo! Plus I know how hard they was to learn by heart!

> "A man is the reason
> I lost my pride
> A man is the reason
> I'm dead inside!"

Flo stops and pats her knife which is tucked insides of her belt (As said.) and unties the string on her low neck Pheasant's Blouse plus yanks this Blouse right over her head and pokes out her titties which ain't covered by nothing but a black Skimpy brassiere with a hole right over one tittie's nipple which pokes right out! The smoking ladies Gasps and whistles and claps and so do I and Flo Chants:

> "I twist, I sway,
> the crowd smacks their lips!"

Her pink little tongue goes in and out repetitiously like a Rattlesnake as she smacks her 2 lips to interpret said Crowd of her Pome which smacks theirs.

"Their ravenous eyes
On my relevant hips!"

Do *her* hips get shook! (Plus her little 2 titties too!) Then off comes her black skirt from under her black belt and the ladies claps and waves their beer cans and Flo's lacey black panties flap as their excessively loose and fluttery on her skinny heinie! She grins and pats the knife in her black belt plus Chants (**ET. AL!**):

"I ask in return
But small payment from each
A sack of potatoes
Shampoo
Or a peach
To munch and forget
While I rest my hips
And they rest their eyes
And they rest their lips!"

Off comes her black little brassiere with the nipple hole! She tosses it up in to the air and the Trumpeteresse catches it right on her Trumpet and the smoking ladies gasps plus clinches their cigarettes in between their teeth and claps!

Flo yanks her black long hair over her naked titties instantaneously and Lorraine runs and dims the regular lights and turns on a spotlight and Flo's little sharp teeth shines bright and her hips wiggles and she opens her 2 eyes wide plus screams horrid!

"My name is Firenze!
But they call me Flo!"

The band gets louder and louder and the drum pounds faster and faster and Flo hollers:
"I got hips of wrath
And tits of woe!
A man is the reason
I walk the night!
A man is the reason
I look a fright!"

"Kill the dirty bastard!" screams a indeterminant oscillating lady! (Which feasibly Infers to the man which is the reason Flo looks a Fright!)

Flo sticks her knife in between her teeth and makes mean faces at the ladies which sets in the 1st row of chairs plus kicks off her Ballerina Slippers and yanks her knife out from her belt and snaps it open and slashes her net black stockings right off from her skinny 2 legs and throws them at a clapping lady which hollers:

"Screw him!"

"Screw the desertin' sonofabitch!" hollers a additional lady which takes a slurp of beer!

"I second it!" hollers another lady!

"Fuck his goddamn eyes out!" screams a lady in a sequinned black Snood with a cigarette in a behemoth holder!

> "A man is the reason
> I lost my pride
> A man is the reason
> I'm dead inside!" (Chants Flo.)

"They're all alike!" hollers a obese uncontented smoking lady, "Boil 'em in oil!"

Flo squats way over and grabs a cigarette from the obese uncontented smoking lady's mouth plus salutes her like a soldier then sticks the cigarette in her own lip and takes a long puff then jumps up and down and around and around and impels every person to laugh. Plus so do I!

Then Flo commences to Chant again and takes little steps which go faster and faster with every singular word and makes puffing little noises like a Japanese Locomotive in a Newsreel.

> "Years later I ponder
> While dying my hair
> Dull, ebony-black, that if he'd been there
> I'd of bound that mean bastard by his dick to our bed!
> And twisted his testicles
> until they bled!"

"You get him, Flo baby!" screams a smoking lady with goofy eyes and beer slopping out from her can.

"They're all alike!" yells the obese uncontented lady.

"I'd batter his butt
with a stick till he shouts!
(Chants Flo!)
What a lesson he'd get
For the morals he flouts!"

"Why the dirty sonofabitch!" hollers a lady in a purple
moo-moo with a Anchor tattoo on her arm.

"But vengeance is mine! saith the Lord
And Flo pales!
She sets down her beer
To polish her nails
(*Interprets* Flo.)
She'll ponder revenge, God,
Some other time, later
Tonight she is slated
To trick with a waiter!"

Flo takes another puff on her cigarette and flops back on to her
chair.

"Saith the Lord God once more:
But Vengeance is mine!
Saith Flo as she polishes her nails:
That's jist fine!
For you do it better, God,
Then anybody I know!
Saith the beer drinking,
nail polishing, wrathful Flo!"

All of the sudden Flo jumps up and yanks off her lace black
panties and throws them right at me!
A whole alots of ladies laughs crazy! I pick the sweaty panties
up off from the floor as I ain't a good catcher. (I play Execrable
Baseball!) (But only when impelled to.) I stuff said panties insides
of my pocket but almost keel over as I Ruminate that 2 gooey
Milky-Ways lays in this Self-Same front pocket so I yank said lace
black panties out from said front pocket but it is too late as the
panties and said Ways is all one chocolatey gooey mess!
Suddenly I hear the scariest holler I ever heard! Flo is as naked

110

as a plucked goose and howling up at the ceiling like a hound sucking eggs!

Variegated bevies of smoking ladies is hissing and hollering at each other and cussing and is all real real angry jist like Flo!

Flo screams at a explicit Individual in said crowd and points her finger at this person! And a whole alots of smoking ladies oscillates their multiple heads and Glares horrid! And here is the unkind policeman which did not wish to pay Flo for her service plus he is jingling a pair of handcuffs and striving to break through one Bevy of smoking ladies which is currantly holding hands and guarding said stage from his Reproach!

"I'll catch you some night!"

Screams Flo at this striving policeman,

"And di-sect your dick!
I'll twist off your balls,
You miserable prick!
I'll yank out your nails!
I'll hiss in your ear!
I'll gouge out your entrails!
I'll piss in your beer!
My name is Firenze
But they call me Flo
I got hips of wrath
I got tits of woe!"

Flo sticks her arm up high and with all of her might throws her knife right at the policeman! Lucky for him it misses and slashes over the Textile green top of the pool table plus stops jist contiguous by The Lonely Gal's sleeping head about which I forgot about untill the currant minute but which ain't surprising as every fool plus their brother is hollering like chickens with their heads chopped off which makes concentration Difficult If Not Incredible!

I waddle instantaneously to The Lonely Gal's sleeping sides and note that she is still Somnolent and not nearly so greenish as prior plus snoring which is a comfort.

A Multitude of the Manifold has currantly grabbed the policeman by his 2 arms and a Bevy of smoking said are pouring beer in to his mouth plus all over his blue uniform! Lorraine turns off all of the lights but I can still note Babe and the concerned short lady which throws a blanket over Flo and runs her out the back door due to Silvery Moonlight.

A additional Bevy of ladies is hissing and booing at the policeman and one of his pants legs is ripped in which I note a protrusive weenie in and my own said twitches although it don't attain no Erection Per Se as said policeman is being Manhandled by these smoking ladies and unkindness traditionally impedes my Erections on one.

The policeman finally rips off his badge and holds it up for all to note that he is Certified and is hollering fowl language like a chicken with their head chopped off as he is a-scared and mad but no person gives a darn and I don't neither as he was so unkind to Flo prior. Which reminds me that Flo's cardboard box of minor items is still laying underneath of the Fruit-Art table and she will need it so I grab it and waddle fast as feasible towards the back door!

A exceedingly mad smoking lady yanks off the police-man's boxer shorts as many mad others pins his 2 arms adjacent behinds of him! As I waddle by I jist got time to note that this policeman's weenie is Fully Circumscribed plus don't possess no Silken Fourskin neither but I ain't able to loiter by said but **OH MY GOSH**! even although I do not wish to I acquire a behemoth Erection! Please do not ask me why! As I can not tell you! As I do not know! However! This Erection is Fully Unauthorized!

I waddle out from the back door with my illicit Erection and Flo's cardboard box of minor items and Flo kisses me when I hand her said box which impels my Erection to shrink down instan-taneously as she smells like beer although I love to be kissed by Any And All persons Whenever Applicable but not by Individuals which drinks alcohol to access although explicit allowances was made pertaining to The Lonely Gal which kissed me on my upper lip prior. (And wasn't that a kind thing which to do?!) (But I Digress.)

Babe and Lorraine which is in said alley grab Flo and literately throws her on to their beauteous convertible blue auto plus tells me I better not come with them as they got serious doubts as regards my legalistic age irregardless of my 6 feet almost of floppy height.

Babe starts up said blue beauteous Plymouth and her and Lorraine and Flo wrapped in a blanket zooms away!

I waddle fast back in to the Jolly Jug to check on the

Configuration of The Lonely Gal.

Said smoking ladies has got the policeman cornered and he is currently as naked as Flo but ain't got no blanket with which to Cloak his protrusions with. I take a long good note of said protrusion (Weenie.) which is contenting plus reinstates my Erection as it is too dark for it to be saw but I feel guilty in the extremes anyhow.

Then I waddle up alongsides of the pool table but The Lonely Gal has went! All which is left is a Miniscule puddle of Barf where her head was laying prone and prior.

Then Marie and Reggie comes running up and grabs me and Clutches me adjacent in between them and runs me out through the back door in to the alley again and Marie hollers:

"The Lonely Gal has went, Danny!"

"She can't afford to get caught here by the whole Port City Vice Squad!" says Reggie, "It would ruin her reputation and that's for sure!"

"That's for darn sure!" hollers Marie.

I can jist hear the Police's sirens currently protruding out from the distance.

"It was a set-up," says Marie, "The cops was gonna raid us tonight anyhow!"

"Somebody kicked that sonofabitch cop in the nuts," says Reggie and laughs real hard.

"And he got jist what he deserved," says Marie.

"That's fer sure!" says Reggie.

"That's fer darn sure!" says Marie.

"Who was your friend, Danny?" says Reggie.

"That Flo gal," says Marie, "she was kinda nervous, wasn't she? With her knife and all?"

"Sh-She's a f-friend of My B-Beauteous M-Mom's," I say as I ain't propelled to say no more currantly as I am blue and lowly and got to pee.

"She shore is pretty," says Reggie which Infers to Flo. Marie squints her 2 eyes at Reggie.

"But not as pretty as you, hon," says Reggie real fast which squeezes Marie's cheek real hard in between her 2 fingers, "That's fer darn sure!"

Marie and Reggie drive me to the Port City Bus's Station in their auto which ain't as nice as Babe and Lorraine's but is OK by me.

As it is only 9 PM I ascertain that My Beauteous Mom is still out somewheres with Jack Shanks laying on his mattress in the Rear of said Pick-up Deluxe and Glaring up at a starry sky. So I do not bother to telephone to my home as it would not be To No Avail. Besides I wish to save the funds which Jarleen and Flo has gave me which added up together is a sum total of almost 3 dollars and is the most funds I ever got ahold of of my own Spontaneously. Plus which will purchase multiple batteries and Multitudinous Milky-Ways.

I got to pee like a hound sucking eggs so I waddle to the Bus Station's Men's Room. Plus **WHOM** do I note there?!

24. FRED FOSTER'S WONDROUS SECRET!

IT IS MY DIVINE FRED FOSTER which is garbed in his sunglasses and cut off Dungarees with his keys jangling and a red bandana right around his neck!

"Hi, F-Fred, my old p-pal!" I holler real convivial and scare said right out from his wits!

"Danny!" he hollers, "What the heck are *you* doing here?!"

"I come to m-meet The L-Lonely G-Gal," I say, "at The J-Jolly J-Jug and I brung w-with m-me a d-dancing p-poetess which r-recited a auto-b-biographical Epic P-Pome with a original in-ter-p-pre-t-ta-t-t-tive d-dance!"

If *that* don't impress Fred, nothing will!

"Gee, that sounds jist great, Danny."

Fred adjusts the Silken Fourskin on his convivial weenie and I forget all about my *back* burner and Re-Instate him instantaneously on to my *front* burner.

"W-What are y-you d-doing h-here, F-Fred, m-my old p-pal?" I utter as my piglet eyes oscillate on to Fred's dear weenie and stay clamped plus my own dear said Lurches like a chicken with their head chopped off!

"I uhhhhh..."

"A M-Major M-Motion P-Picture?" I utter real helpful plus hide my tumescing Boner underneath of my fat piglet fingers.

"No. I come here to visit with my errrr... girlfriend."

A *girlfriend*! **OH MY GOSH!**

"Danny," says Fred, "It is *awful* hard to pee while your lookin' at my peter like that."

"Gosh, am I s-sorry, F-Fred, my old p-pal, I didn't m-mean..."

"Danny," says Fred with his eyebrows all squinched up Dire, **"YOU GOT A *BONER!*"**

My heart jumps up and down and I am so scared that I can't hardly breathe!

"As there's only me and you here, Danny, and ain't no ladies present," utters My Divine Fred, "Why have you got a Boner?"

I ponder real fast plus say:

"I h-had a ex-c-cessively ex-c-citing night, F-Fred, my old p-pal. I b-been s-surrounded by 45 rampaging f-females!" (This is a indeterminant number only but 45 is feasible factually.) "My B-Boner is jist n-nerve r-racked"

"Oh," says Fred which *believes* me! "I didn't know guy's Boners got that."

The bell rings for our bus and Fred shakes his sweet weenie dry plus Reinstates it's Silken Fourskin and installs said back insides of his dear Y-fronts plus buttons up his fly.

My own Wayward weenie has reserved it's Erection so I got to smash it back down insides of my Bright Blue Corduroys fly which hurts plus hold said down while I button up so as to not catch one of my Relentless Pubescent hairs in the button holes. I hope Fred ain't saw this Minor Alteration.

I and Fred exit out from the Men's Room and embark on to our bus back to Lemon Gulch.

"I'm awful sorry my Mom hollered at you the other day," says Fred while we are setting down in a *real* dark segmant on the Rear of our empty bus.

"Oh th-that's OK, F-Fred, m-my old p-pal."

"I'm *awful* sleepy," utters Fred which yawns a behemoth yawn, "*Girlfriends* can sure tire a guy out."

Fred lays way back on our bus's seat and pokes his hand insides of his Dungarees and scoops up his weenie on to the other side of his crotch where I guess he ascertains it will Repose more contented. (I know jist how it feels when *my* weenie ain't Tranquilized.) Fred don't note me noting his weenie but I could be wrong as I am wrong excessively often which I admit Without Remorse. (One has got to be honest with theirselves!)

Fred stretches and closes his eyes. "I think I'll get me some shut-eye, Danny. I am so darned tired that *nothing* could wake me up!"

Fred is breathing soft and lowly instantaneously and is Fully Somnolent so I jist set here and feast my piglet 2 eyes on his pants leg which is full of weenie with Impunity as we are both hid from the Bus's Driver by a excessively behemoth baggage wrack.

Fred's Dungarees is real tight which propels his weenie to poke right up for every fool plus their brother to note plus his 2 legs is all muscley as he is a top runner which traditionally comes in 1st.

Our bus finally starts up and jiggles Fred right up adjacent contiguous of my fat big hot thigh and I note his dear weenie as it Tumesces and creeps slow down his left leg. (All of we boys gets Boners during Somnolence throughout one's Life It's self.) (Due to our Exigencies.)

As I ain't able to impede one's self I reach over and unbutton My Divine Fred's fly as he is so darned tired that *nothing could wake him up* and his Boner pops right up through his Y-fronts and his Silken Fourskin snaps right back plus his pink Boner head glows Merry underneath of The Silvery Moon.

Our bus bounces in to a big road pothole and Fred's dear Boner wobbles back and fourth like a telephone pole in a Earthquake of which California has a whole alots of bi-yearly.

I slam my mouth down suddenly on said Boner and the convivial results is quick in cumming!

I wake up from a road bump and suddenly here is Fred which is red like a beet and sticking his hand insides of his Y-fronts and his crotch is all wetted! Well! Fred jist looks right at me which is looking right at his wetted crotch.

"Don't go thinkin' I peed myself, Danny. I had me one heck of a wet dream! And it was a lulu!"

Darn it! I was asleep and I missed it but I feel one Sublime hot stickiness insides of my own Y-fronts and ascertain I had me a lulu of a Wet Dream additionally. Lucky for me my Wet Dream don't show through my Bright Blue Corduroys.

At the Saga Of The West Drugstore And Fountain Grill I purchase I and Fred which waits outside so as his dream-wetted crotch ain't noted one Milky-Way each and then I and Fred walk home together underneath of The Silvery Moon. I wish I could hold his hand and sing to Fred like I sung to Miranda Cosmonopolis but do not as it would be Frowned Upon by The Multitudes Indubitably.

Anyhow. I and Fred loiters on the street in front of our respectable homes and Fred thanks me Courteous for the Milky-Way plus utters:

"Danny, if you don't tell nobody about my wet dream on the bus I promise I won't tell nobody about how you stared right at my peter at the urinal and got a Boner."

"I w-won't tell n-nobody, F-Fred, m-my old p-pal. I p-promise!"

I would defend Fred's weenie with my Very Life!

Fred is content and tells me that he will talk to his Mom and tell said that I did not mean to scare her with my spiders which was for Fred's Delectation only.

Fred waves at me from his front porch and said Silvery Moon shines right down on to the top of his shining hair which is real Dramatic like in a Major Motion Picture.

I am so full of love and weenie longing that I ponder my poor Sissy heart will bust! But fortunately I got this here contenting secret with which to share with Fred with. Anyhow. I waddle in to my bedroom jist in time for The Lonely Gal's radio program which says:

"Hello, Lonely guy," as I peel my Bright Blue Corduroys down off from my sausage fat legs. "Did you miss me, Lonely Guy?"

I do not answer her like traditional and say Yes Darling as I feel blue and lowly as heck the minute I hear her voice. However. She currently talks the words of a sweet song real soft:

"Although they sing of love
Love's not for me."

As I am Courteous I listen even although she impels me to feel so bad. I ain't soothed by her no more as her conversing is phony and she only means it on the radio even although she said I Love You to me in person and kissed me on my upper lip as she was in a Advanced State of Inebriation. And I keep on noting her feet poking out from underneath of the Fruit-Art table and her wobbling and foaming all over the darn place as she don't take her Anti-Fit medicine on purpose as she desires to End It All.

"Let them write poems of Love
Love's not for me."

She can certainly say that again!

"Love led me far astray
Through days that were as grey

117

as any gloomy play
Could ever be."

Well. Love ain't led *me* nowheres!

Suddenly I reminisce Flo's Pome and how scary it was implicitly that segmant with her knife! **OH MY GOSH!** With all this heightened up pondering I ain't able to heighten down and sleep and I even commence to ponder PK's stinking boot stuck on my head.

"Did you miss me alot?" says The Lonely Gal from my battery radio.

"Why s-should I miss you, L-Lonely G-Gal?!" I blubber as fat big tears instantaneously shoot right down my piglet cheeks, "I jist l-left y-you 2 hours ago. In a p-puddle of B-Barf! (At least *Bull* don't never barf!)

I turn off my radio and blubber hard for one full interval then sop my tears up on a old stiffened Kleenex and ponder hard on Fred's weenie and attain a Erection plus Onanate with Peanut Oil. After said Onanation I waddle to my bedroom window plus holler for my black and white small dog Tinker. But she don't come. So I got to go to sleep without no warm soft black and white small dog's sides on to which to poke my 2 feet on to.

25. A ACCURATE FAMILY

I awaken up as it is 8 AM in the morning plus rub my eyes which is Smoke Agitated as every singular smoking lady plus their brother smoked like a hound sucking eggs at The Jolly Jug!

I lift up my blanket and note my sheets In Perpetuity to ascertain if I peed on my bed during somnolence. But ain't. **THANK GOSH!** So I arise up off from my bed and tuck my big tummy in to my orange horridly tight pajamas plus waddle to our collective toilet to alleviate one's self.

All items is Back To Normal almost as Jarleen is still in her plaster big cast plus is to visit her physician in one interval with the muscular Jack Shanks which is to come and pick her up in his Deluxe. They are going subsequential out bowling after said physician's visit. (Ha. Ha.) **(HA!)**

Bull is laying on top of our Davenport with a old dried up

cheese and mayonnaise sandwich sitting on his chest plus snoring. Mayonnaise is one item of which we got plenty of as it is free due to one Complementary Tangy Crate delivered Factory-Fresh every Christmas.

Anyhow. Here lays Bull right underneath of his old Prize Fighting Poster which says as per as usual: "WATCH THIS BOY GO PLACES!" which impels me to feel blue and lowly every singular time I view it as this photo on said poster Bears No Resemblance on to his present State of Affairs. (Unfortunately.)

Anyhow I got Fred's Wet Dream on which to ponder on which makes me feel so joyous in Bliss that I waddle back to my bedroom and set there pondering jovial and Feeling-Up my dear weenie which twitches and attains a full Erection which ain't surprising where Divine Fred is implicated.

Our telephone rings With Alacrity so I tuck said Boner underneath of my pajama draw strings plus yank those afourmentioned strings tight so as to compress said Boner painfully down and away from Prying Eyes such as Jarleen's. I waddle to our front room and answer said telephone as I know Jarleen is currantly Perpetrating her morning alleviation as she has jist flushed our toilet one time so far.

Jarleen traditionally flushes our toilet one time prior to each alleviation so as not to splash Septic water on to her Pewdendas. Plus 2 additional times subsequential to piddling for politeness's sake to the next alleviater but mostly for Hygienic considerations as Jarleen is startlingly Solicitous to her Pewdendas plus the Private Segmants of other Individuals.

As Jarleen ain't flushed said toilet 3 times as per yet I know that she is piddling and/or pooping relentlessly plus Perusing a Motion Picture magazine and even if she ain't she don't traditionally desire to answer no telephones when I am in Occupation of our home as the caller is always almost Mean Aunt Edna May anyhow to whom Jarleen don't like to Chat to as Aunt Edna May bores My Beauteous Mom Shitless. (As said.) (Explicitly on telephones.) So I pick up said telephone. Plus utter:

"H-Hello?"

"Danny?" says this voice which is Flo. Lucky it is me which answers our telephone!

"H-Hello, F-Flo!" I utter exceptionally jovial as I am still heightened up from savouring Fred's Wondrous Dream, "W-What d-do you know? W-What are a-c-cookin' in T-Tokio?"

119

Please do not ask me why I utter this. As I can not tell you. As I do not know. But I feel excessively content as I still got one Quasi-Erection even although it is interred tight underneath of my pajama's knotted draw strings.

"Danny? Is your Dad there?"

"H-He's s-sleepin' on our D-Davenport."

"Is your Mom there?"

"N-No. S-She is on the t-toilet."

"Good," says Flo, "I was going to hang up if she answered. Don't tell no body I called, okay?"

"OK" I say plus additionally add:

"M-My B-Beauteous M-Mom's goin' bowling with M-Mr Shanks."

But I do not add Ha Ha like traditionally as I ain't got no desires to rat on Jarleen as I love My Beauteous Mom although every fool plus their brother anyhow knows she is eternally either adjacent besides Jack in his Pick-Up Deluxe or underneath of him on said Deluxe's mattress in it's Rear.

"Bowlin'?! With *Jack Shanks*?!" says Flo, "With that big ole cast on her leg?! Ha! Ha!"

Anyhow. I ascertain to meet Flo later even although she scares me as her knife gives me The Willies. But she promises to purchase me a Marshmallow Ice Cream Soda at The Saga Of The West Drugstore And Fountain Grill which is right acrosst the street from The Big Lemon. (As said.) At that time I am required to give her her chocolatey lace black panties which she throwed at me BC (Before Chocolate!) (Joke!) during her Epic Pome at The Jolly Jug back.

"That bossy old guy that wrote me my Pome give 'em to me a real long time ago," says Flo which Infers to said lace black panties, "I jist wouldn't never want to lose 'em."

"They g-got ch-chocolate all over them from m-my M-Milky-W-Ways. I am e-exceedingly s-sorry."

"Chocolate? Milky-Ways?"

"Y-Yes, ma'am. M-Milky-Ways. Y-Your p-panties w-was in m-my p-pocket and g-got m-melted on b-by m-my M-M-Milky-Ways."

"Oh, that's all right, honey. I guess it ain't the first time they been in some guy's pocket *or* got chocolate on 'em. See you in a little while!"

So I am supposed to meet Flo but jist now I got to feed Little

Norman's brown big dog which is named Rags.

I play monopoly sporadically with Little Norman Tomlin which possesses the only weenie I ever sucked in real actuality which resides jist up the street. (As said.) He is one year younger then I but a whole alots littler plus possesses no pubescent hairs. Not one! At least I never noted none when we Onanated communally underneath of the school Bleachers where said prior sucking and variegated Onanations occurred Perennially. However. It is feasible that Little Norman has sprouted one Bevy since. (Of hairs.)

Little Norman's handsome Dad is as said Mr Jimmy which possesses wavy black hair and brown big eyes and one conspicuous delighted weenie which always lays head up and sideways plus pointed joyous off to the left insides of his exceedingly tight Dungarees in a State of Bliss.

I surprised Mr Jimmy once in his garage when I was looking for Little Norman. Mr Jimmy had his suu-perrb weenie out plus was peeing right in to their floor drain. Wow! He whipped said back insides of his Dungarees as quick as a chicken with their head chopped off but not prior to me noting it Assiduously! I ain't never saw such a perky weenie and stuck right on to the lower Abdomenal Torsal Regions of such a kind man which always kindly smiles plus pats me right on the top of my head every time he notes me like I am a accurate person and habitually says:

"Hi, Danny, how ya keepin'?"

But Mr Jimmy looks at me jist a small bit goofy currantly. He is real friendly and all but jist a small bit goofy acting. I guess it ain't the best ideal in the world to surprise persons Unsolicited during peeing like a spy.

Little Norman's mother which is named Miss Brenda makes the best Pecan Panochy fudge on our Cosmos and possesses a brown big mole right adjacent besides of her lower lip which don't Retract from her beauteous looks none as she is so kind so I do not traditionally note said brown mole which ain't nothing like Miss Snelgrove's hairy wart anyhow. (More about Miss Snelgrove's wart later.) She is from Texas. (Miss Brenda not Miss Snelgrove.) (But I Digress.)

I traditionally show up to Little Norman's Happy Home jist as the whole darn Tomlin family is terminating their dinner which includes Miss Brenda and Little Norman and Little Norman's sister Bunny Lois plus Mr Jimmy with his conspicuous weenie hitched up sideways. Perky like always. Which contents me.

Anyhow. There they all are all plopped down at one dining table together jist like a accurate family.

I set there on their front porch awaiting for Little Norman while they eat plus I get fatter by the hour as I gobble down Miss Brenda's wondrous Pecan Panochy fudge which she gives me on my own yellow pretty dish with flowers painted on it as I am a growing boy. (In all directions! East! North! South! And West!) (To say the least!) (Unfortunately!)

Jarleen hates to cook variegated foods of any description plus will do so Underneath Of Duress only. Like when she is hungry. But as My Beauteous Mom is a working lady with a Dearth of leisures due to The Daily Bumps And Grinds she don't have proficient time for a whole alots of variegated foods cooking. So don't. (As said.)

Anyhow. When I ain't currently pondering Fred Foster's glorious Boner nor Mr Jimmy's conspicuous weenie nor The Lonely Gal's Inebriation nor Miranda Cosmonopolis's tender Sensitivities nor Flo's scary knife nor horrid PK Benderson's boot on top of my head I ponder Bull and Jarleen and me all setting down at a **DINING TABLE** Contemporaneous at one time. **DINING** from a yellow big bowl of beef stew with flowers painted on it and Textile napkins from napkin rings with our little initials setting on our knees. Like a accurate family. Like the dear Tomlins.

But even in my dreams Bull always passes out plus kicks off his phony leg and falls off from his chair on to our floor. (Which ain't his fault as he got Thwarted.) (As said.) And Jarleen always runs in to her Exclusive bedroom with her bowl of stew plus one big soup spoon and her darn Motion Picture magazines and I end up habitually unaccompanied. At said dining table. Dining *alone*. (As per as usual.) **EVEN IN MY OLD DARN DREAMS!**

26. MR JIMMY PLUS DIVINE FRED.
HA. HA.

It is a exceedingly hot summer day. The *same* day. As currently it is only 2 minutes since I said that I end up habitually unaccompanied at said dining table dining alone. (Even in my old darn dreams!)

Little Norman and his total Tomlin family is currently visiting his Aunt Clio in Port City and I got requested to water Little

Norman's brown big dog Rags which is tied up adjacent besides of her dog house. As said dog was fed Prior To Departure of her owners water only is required In This Instance.

As I waddle by the Tomlin's bathroom's window on my Pilgrimage to Rags's dog house I hear noises coming out from their home in which no person is imputed to be in so I climb up on to their Sears and Roebuck's Pre-fabrocaded green cement Barbeque Grill which is contiguous on to said bathroom's window plus look in.

Mr Jimmy is jist coming out from their shower as naked as a plucked goose and Vicariously toweling hisself off. He looks up and notes me noting him and comes to said window and I additionally note that his conspicuous weenie wags in a exceptionally convivial plus perky Mode.

"Hi, Danny! How're ya keepin'?" says Mr Jimmy which kindly smiles and shows his white shiny teeth which is even whiter almost then My Beauteous Mom's.

"Come on in and have a Dr Pepper!" says Mr Jimmy like he knows that I got a Preferential desire for Dr Peppers. He must be one good mind reader! He opens their back door and Bades me to enter in to their Happy Home plus gets me a ice cold Dr Pepper from their icebox as they got a icebox like us as one's electrical wires ain't installed on this here Vicinity as yet neither.

Mr Jimmy leads me in to their bedroom plus utters:

"Set yourself down, Danny, while I towel off."

So I flop down on to a soft nice chair.

OH MY GOSH! Mr Jimmy looks so Slim And Trim! So Neat And Hard To Beat and his perky weenie flops all around so nice right underneath of his flat nice tummy which is being Vicariously toweled off! (As said joyous prior.)

In their wall mirror I note my own Prespiring Lower Pelvic Torsal Regions which has soaked right through my T-shirt plus my piglet face which is more reddish today even then yesterday and even more pimply. However. I am heightened up and warmish on my weenie which is currantly twitching and flopping due to the convivial site of Mr Jimmy's perky prior said.

"I stayed home today, Danny."

Mr Jimmy kindly smiles and additionally towels hisself off, "Jist couldn't waste a whole Sunday in Port City with Little Norman's Aunt Clio, Danny. So I guess I'm a lonely old bachelor."

Mr Jimmy's eyes sparkle like Gene Kelly's when Mr Kelly

dances with Miss Vera Ellen which is my all time favorite dancing lady. (With the Notable Exemption of the exceedingly Glorious Miss Ann Miller which I additionally love as her Tap Dancing is Second to None as well as her Glittering Smile!) (Also I adore when Mr Kelly sings with Miss Judy Garland which is my all time almost favorite songstress excepting for Miss Ella Fitzgerald which sings Embraceable You and makes me blubber on my battery radio as I desire Embracing but traditionally lack said.) (In Aces!)

Mr Jimmy smiles and drops his towel on to a chair and pulls on some white nice Y-fronts. **OH MY GOSH!** He only pulls said Fronts halfways up on to him which leaves his conspicuous weenie only halfways covered up which glows exceptionally pink from it's recent toweling off plus lays soft but perky contiguous against Mr Jimmy's tummy and reaches right up to said's belly button. **IT IS A SIMPLY SUU-PERRB WEENIE!** And Worthy Of Admiration Of The Highest Order!

I feel exceedingly hot among my Genitalias. (Chafing. **ET. AL!**) So I take a deep big gulp from my Dr P and nearly choke one's self to death due to my heightened up State of Affairs.

Mr Jimmy sets down on their bed and pulls his socks on to his 2 feet and the bed's springs bobs up and down underneath of his heinie and the Ejection Slit on his halfway covered up weenie winks right at me! I commence to Prespire and turn redder even then traditional plus my prior acquired Boner Throbs horrid and I am close to keeling over with exceptional desires. I take a additional swig of Dr P to heighten down but choke again.

"Having trouble, Danny?" utters Mr Jimmy which loiters here half insides and half outsides of his Y-fronts and splashes Mennen's Skin Bracer on to his handsome face plus chest. I do not answer as I am Mute plus can only note his exposed weenie segmant and not say nothing. Why don't he pull up his darn Y-fronts and tuck in his Extremities?! Don't he know I am a Bonified Sissy with Affiliations?!

I arise suddenly up from my chair and waddle right over to him. Lucky for me my shirttails is outsides of my Dungarees which conceals my Boner from being saw which would of Divulged said Affiliations. Anyhow. I utter:

"M-Mr Jimmy, that M-Mennen's S-Skin Bracer sure does s-smell g-good!"

"Real glad you like it, Danny boy. Try some for yourself."

Mr Jimmy laughs convivial plus scoots in exceedingly close

contiguous behind of me and pours a amount of green fragrant Skin Bracer on to his hand and reaches right over the top of my shoulder and rubs said Bracer on to my piglet face which burns my Reprehensable pimples something awful but I do not utter nothing as it smells so good plus I do not wish to look a Gift Horse Up It's Throat! (So to speak.)

Mr Jimmy keeps patting Mennen Skin Bracer on to my face real genteel. As I am nearly jist as tall almost as he is I feel his soft joyous weenie bump right against my fat big heinie! **BUMP! BUMP! BUMP! OH MY GOSH!** I suddenly lose my controls and poke one of my 2 hands right out behind of me and grab his weenie plus yank his squirmy Silken Fourskin backwords and fourwords and backwords and fourwords!

"Hey, Danny! What the heck do you think your doin'?!" hollers Mr Jimmy.

However. His weenie Tumesces right up insides of my fat piglet fingers like a balloon with a squirt of helium which is a lighter then air gas Readily Available to fill up the average Circus Balloon.

I keep rubbing Mr Jimmy's Silken Fourskin and Mr Jimmy don't utter nothing implicit but jist sort of mumbles out variegated items like:

"This ain't right. This ain't right," plus: "What the heck do you think your doin'?! What the heck do you think your doin'?!"

However. As he is mumbling he rolls his Y-fronts down plus yanks me around towards him and pushes me genteely on to my piglet 2 knees and sticks his convivial Boner right in to my piglet mouth!

OH MY GOSH! Mr Jimmy's clean soap smell is so contenting and his joyous Boner is so sweet and warm from it's prior dousing in their shower! He now commences to Courteously shove said Boner in and out and in and out and in and out.

"**OH MY G-GOSH!** I'm g-gonna squirt! M-Mr Jimmy I'm g-gonna squirt!" I holler plus squirt!

"DANNY!" screams Jarleen right through my bedroom door, "Don't you forget I'm goin' bowlin' with Jack Shanks after my physician's!"

Our front door slams. I wipe myself dry instantaneously with 2 subsequential semi-stiff used Kleenexs and stick my can of Peanut Oil back underneath of my bed plus am real careful to shove it way *way* back as I ain't contented with the ideal of Jarleen

125

uprooting my Onanistic Accoutrements.

However. Jist now I got to water Little Norman's brown big dog Rags.

Underneath of a merciless sun I waddle by the Tomlin's front room window on my way to said dog's dog house. My fat heinie wobbles even more then traditionally as my body lays in a State of exceptional Fatigue due to recent relentless Onanations.

I hear voices Emanating from the Tomlin's front room. But **HEY!** All Residents is reputed to have went to Port City to visit Little Norman's Aunt Clio!

I waddle to a window and am careful not to be saw plus look in and this is what I note! **OH MY GOSH!** Here is Mr Jimmy plus My Divine Fred Foster! They are setting on Mr Jimmy's Davenport together Perusing What Every Young Man Should Know. I got a Volume jist like it which was detected insides of dear Miranda Cosmonopolis's Granddad's garage which she give to me as he was Diseased.

Mr Jimmy's perky weenie as per as usual is tucked sideways in his tight Dungarees plus he has got his hand right on to Fred Foster's bare glittering thigh as Fred is garbed in his white swim trunks *only.*

"Wet Dreams, Fred," reads Mr Jimmy from What Every Young Man Should Know, "are a natural function. Plus nothing of which to be ashamed of. Indeed, they are every healthy young man's Happy Heritage."

At least I think this is what he says. As said front room window is closed I ain't able to hear implicit word tones.

As Fred listens avid I squat low and crawl around to a open window right contiguous where I can hear better.

What a site! I note the pink tip of My Divine Fred Foster's weenie creeping right up over the top of his white swim trunks in a State of Dire Distention!

Mr Jimmy lies said Volume down and snuggles up adjacent besides of Fred on said Davenport and yanks open the top of Fred's swimming trunks and grabs Fred's Boner with one hand and pulls back it's Silken Fourskin with the other!

Mr Jimmy's own convivial Boner now twitches and plunges out from his unbuttoned fly as he rubs the friendly little Ejection Slit on the tip of Fred's said with one thumb plus 2 fingers. After a Suitable duration he pokes his fingers which has became sticky from Esoteric Secretions underneath of Fred's nose.

"You see, Fred, this here is known as Young Man's Pre-Coital Slippage. Taste it," smiles Mr Jimmy real kind, "It's jist great!"

"YOU FAT-ASSED, SISSY BASTARD!"

27. THE LACE BLACK CHOCOLATEY PANTIES.

"YOU FAT-ASSED SISSY BASTARD!" hollers PK repetitiously!

So here I am! Fat big Sissy me! Mr Jimmy and Fred Foster has shot right out from my brains! I strive to yank them two shining Angels back in to said brains but PK slams his boot on to my head even harder. I would of keeled right over if I wasn't already so supine plus flat on my back on the dry dirty grass which grows contiguous on to The Big Lemon which is right acrosst the street from The Saga Of The West Drugstore And Fountain Grill where I am supposed to meet with Flo any moment.

"What the *hell* is that in your fat-ass pocket?!" hollers PK which grabs out from my heinie pocket the black lace chocolatey panties which I promised to give back to Flo. In a Full State of Desperation I strive a additional time to yank Mr Jimmy and Divine Fred back into my brains but it ain't currently feasible.

Suddenly I hear a horrid holler which *ain't* PK's!

"THEM'S *MY* PANTIES!"

It is Flo! I hear a framiliar snap of her horrid knife and PK jumps away with Flo's lace black chocolatey panties and hollers at her:

"Your a whoor! Everbody knows your a dirty old whoor!"

Flo stabs her knife up in the air and her 2 eyes goes Dementing and she zips away after PK in her black net stockings! (Plus completely garbed of course!) **OH MY GOSH!** is she fast in her Ballerina Slippers! PK runs up a alley hollering back at me.

"I'll get even with you, you fat Sissy bastard!"

Get even with *me*?! **OH MY GOSH!** *I* am the innocent boy on this situation and he is the darn Bully! Don't he know *nothing*?!

Then I get blue and lowly instantaneous plus ponder that maybe I ain't such of a darn innocent boy after all as I know it is Diagonally Opposed against the law to suck weenies plus maybe even pondering about said in a Esoteric Mode is a Heenous Crime? (The Keyhole says so!) Even for girls?

So here I set on my fat big heinie on this horrid dry old grass plus sniveling and noting instantaneously that I got stinking dog shit on my all time favorite 100 Percent red nylon seersucker no-iron long-sleeved shirt's sleeve. This is a literate tragedy! Lemon Gulch must be the shittiest town on the Cosmos!

My piglet 2 eyes puffs up! **OH MY GOSH!** I am adjacent besides of a blubber! Then Flo comes back which is waving her lace black chocolatey panties at me.

"That little sonofabitch! I'll cut off his prick next time! **SLAUGHTER HIM!** I'll cut him up in to little pieces like..."

Then she stops instantaneously and looks Dementing up at the blue clear sky for a full interval. I ponder Alacrously if Flo would of feasibly Decapitated PK's ugly weenie in real actuality if she could of captivated him as it would of hurt like a chicken with their head chopped off! As I Abhor Violent Disarray I commence to blubber!

"What the *hell*?" says Flo which oscillates her head away from said sky and stares at me goofy but helps me up from this shitty grass anyhow.

"PK g-got dog s-shit on my all t-time f-favorite s-shirt," I snivel among my shooting tears plus snot.

"Hell, Danny, we can take care o' that in no time! Come on. Let's go get us a ice cream soda. My inter-pre-tah-tive dancin' went real good last night so I'm payin'. There's some things I wish to ask you."

Flo picks up my bicycle from where it had fell to when PK jumped on to me and we head jist acrosst the street to the Saga Of The West. (Drugstore And Fountain Grill/Bus's Station.) (As said.)

Flo orders 2 Marshmallow Ice Cream Sodas and takes me in to the Ladies's Rest Room and washes the dog shit off from my shirt which is easier then I pondered as said shirt is 100 Percent nylon which is a non-absorbent Textile plus she tells me that she had came to Lemon Gulch last night as she was invited for some inter-pre-tah-tive dancing at a Rotary Club Barbeque by a old customer which picked her up from the corner of her traditional Port City alley to which Babe and Lorraine had kindly took her to after a short trip to her shack for re-garbing and make-up.

"What I wanna know," says Flo while we eat variegated gooey ice cream chunks out from our exceptionally delicious Marshmallow Ice Cream sodas with skinny long spoons, "is jist what do you know about The Lonely Gal?"

"I like h-her v-v-v-v-very m-m-m-m-m-m-m-m-m-much," I say without hesitation.

"You do?"

"B-But sh-she is Inebriated. L-Like B-Bull. C-Ceaselessly."

"She is?"

"C-Ceaselessly. At least every t-time I s-seen her sh-she w-was."

"Do you know her real name, Danny? I phoned her radio station and their mean receptionist wouldn't tell me nothin' about her."

"I d-do not know her r-real n-name. B-But B-Babe maybe m-might.

Flo says she will contact with Babe if she can find her at The Jug. We terminate eating our Marshmallow Ice Cream Sodas and I accompany Flo to the next door Lemon Gulch Bus's Station plus thank her for my delicious Marshmallow Ice Cream Soda gratuitously noting Spontaneously my Vicinity exceptionally Vigilant so as not to Blunder Into PK if he is contiguous. He ain't. (Fortunately!)

As Flo's bus is leaving we utter goodbye as she embarks up on to said plus hollers:

"You take care of yourself, Danny, and don't pay no attention when they call you a big fat Sissy. 'Cause there's worse things in life then bein' big fat sissies!"

"L-Like w-w-w-what?!" I holler.

"Like bein' a woman," she hollers back, "in a fucking man's world!"

I know exactly how old poor Flo feels as I am a Devoted Cocksucker plus fat and big and Reviled of Bullies and variegated rude Individuals and their Hostile Eyes of which I Loathe the contact of. This State of Affairs possesses explicit Similarities with Female Troubles as The Keyhole is chock filled of rapings and every fool plus their brother knows Females must face The Daily Bumps And Grinds inclusive of bossy men which can not keep one's Greasy Paws off from ladies's heinies and titties **AGAINST THEIR WILLS**!

Flo's bus commences to drive away and she rolls down it's window and pokes her head out plus hollers:

"I had me a Wasserman test at the Gulch Clinic and I ain't got no Sy-phillius! You can jist tell Jarleen to put that in to her pipe and smoke it!"

Flo rolls up said bus's window and I that note she is laughing real hard behind of said. It is joyous to see Flo laugh as other

129

person's joys habitually fills me with Ditto.

I make additional Mental Notations to look up Sy-phillius on my Webster's which I ain't done as of per yet plus ponder if said has got anything to do with Syphilis which is a Venerable Disease.

28. MR JIMMY!

I waddle back to the Saga Of The West to procure my bicycle. **BUT OH MY GOSH!** Here is PK Benderson setting right on top of it giving me The Finger!

"You fat Sissy bastard!" he hollers, "Now you ain't got no broke down old whoor with no zip-knife to stick up for you!"

PK grabs my fat arm and twists it behind of me and pushes my bicycle along with his other hand and drags me up a alley plus in to a back doorway of the Tangy Mayo old desserted Warehouse and throws I and my bicycle down on to the cement floor with a clash!

"What's that there in your pocket?!" hollers PK which pokes his finger at 2 dollars which sets in the front pocket of my 100 Percent red nylon seersucker no-iron shirt which he ain't noted prior.

"T-Two d-dollars."

"Gimmee it!"

PK yanks said funds right out from my pocket which I should of took out from said last night and reserved in a safe place but did not plus unbuttons his Dungarees and pokes the ugliest weenie I have ever saw right on to my face!

"Eat this, you fat assed Sissy queer!"

I oscillate my poor head away abruptly from his ugly Protrubince!

"Ain't hungry?!" hollers PK.

I wiggle away on my heinie on the cold cement floor untill it whacks up contiguous on to a cold dirty wall and I ain't able to wiggle no farther.

"Oh heavens! Poor fat-ass Sissy ain't hungry! Then maybe he's thirsty, huh?!"

PK aims his ugly weenie right at me and commences to pee yellow bright pee! He pees all over my 100 Percent red nylon seersucker no-iron long-sleeved shirt! He pees all over my Bright Blue

Corduroys! He pees on my shoes! He pees on my bicycle! He pees right on to the front of my face! Then he pees right on the top of my head! I ain't never seen no poor misguided Individual with so much yellow Reprehensable pee!

PLUS DO I BLUBBER! DO I WHINE! DO I SNIVEL! I jist set there with my fat big heinie planted contiguous against this old cold wall and blubber and whine and snivel! I got no ideal where my tears ends and PK's yellow horrid pee begins!

"You can jist tell your skinny old whoor that the next time she gives me any shit I'll jist wipe it all over you!" hollers PK. "And I mean real shit like what comes out of a asshole, you fat asshole! And I'll beat the shit outta you too and make you eat it!"

PK hollers on and on and on and as I am blubbering so hard I ain't able to ponder Fred's weenie nor Mr Jimmy's nor Burt's neither for my traditional Blessed Relief.

Then PK takes a old dirty brick out from a wall and I ponder he has became a Homocidal Maniac which is going to murder me but instead he bashes the front wheel on my Schwinn blue bicycle in horrid and gives me The Finger and exits out from said desserted Mayonnaise Warehouse with my poor 2 dollars.

I jist set here and blubber and blubber as I ain't able to impede it. I guess I blubber for one full duration.

"Danny?!"

I wipe my eyes on my shirt's sleeve and oscillate my head up and there in the doorway in his Dungarees with his conspicuous perky weenie tucked sideways and pointed Heavenwords loiters A NOBLE ANGEL!

"M-Mr J-Jimmy!"

"I was passin' by and I heard some awful cryin!"

Mr Jimmy comes over and squats down adjacent besides of me.

"What happened, Danny?"

"He p-peed on me plus b-busted m-my b-bike t-too."

"Who peed on you?"

"I b-better not s-say."

"OK, if you don't want to you don't have to. Nobody ain't gonna make you," says Mr Jimmy Infinitely genteel and soft.

He helps me up from these puddles of PK's pee in which I set in plus picks my busted bicycle up and slings it in to his auto's trunk which is parked jist around the corner and we get in to said which is a brand new metallic green 1947 Dodge 4 door sedan which is as convivial as Mr Jimmy hisself.

Mr Jimmy sticks his key in and his beauteous auto starts excessively fast. Not like our 1936 old Plymouth which takes one full duration to commence plus Mr Jimmy don't even care if I get PK's pee on his auto's brand new seat's covers as I am me myself more important to him then his auto's brand new seat's covers!

"Your a real big boy, Danny."

"Y-Yes, s-sir. I am inordinantly t-tall due to my H-Hormonal Uh-Unbalance."

"Was he bigger then you, this guy that peed on you?"

We drive away from the curb and start down the road towards our respectable homes.

"J-Jist a s-small bit l-littler then m-me."

OH MY GOSH! Is this Mortifying to Divulge!

"B-But he is one f-full y-year older," I add additionally. Maybe I should of lied and said PK is a whole alots bigger and older but I jist can not lie to Mr Jimmy even if I could of.

"You know," kindly says Mr Jimmy, "You didn't have to jist set there and let him pee on you."

"I w-was a-scared. He p-picks on m-me all the time p-plus s-slams his b-boot on my h-head."

"Don't your Dad help you none?" utters Mr Jimmy real soft and lowly. **OH MY GOSH!** I desire to jist fold up insides of Mr Jimmy's big 2 arms and go right to sleep all joyous plus safe in Full Bliss.

"Don't he help you none? He was almost a heavyweight champion boxer once, wasn't he? Why don't he teach you how to defend yourself?"

"H-He's a Inebriant. H-He c-can't."

Mr Jimmy pulls his beauteous auto over to the side of the road and stops and sticks his muscly warm arm on the top of my shoulders plus hugs me and utters:

"You pore boy. You pore, pore boy."

OH MY GOSH! IS THIS CONTENTING!

"You ever heard the story about the buffalo and the lion, Danny?"

"N-No," I say as I do not know a whole alots about buffalos nor lions but Mr Jimmy can jist Chat ceaselessly to me and I will listen untill the cows come home!

"Well," says Mr Jimmy, "Once there was this big old buffalo that was bein' chased all over the place by this lion that wanted to eat him."

I guess Mr Jimmy must mean a Mountain Lion as regular every day run of the mill average lions with big Mains do not reside in our country of the United States Of America excepting in Zoos where they are Fully Insulated.

"And this big old buffalo had to be on the run *all* the time just to get away from this lion that never give him no peace. Everywhere this big old buffalo would roam this lion would run right after him biting at his tail the whole darn time."

I guess said is like PK's boot on my head but I bet lions would never of peed on buffalos as their Standards is higher. And their The Kings Of The Jungles and Kings don't pee.

"But one day this old buffalo says to hisself: Why should I keep runnin' away all the time? I am a whole lot bigger than this here lion and weigh alot more too. And I got two real big buffalo horns which is alot more horns than I ever seen on any lion!"

Mr Jimmy kindly notes me for one full duration with his kind 2 eyes.

"'Maybe if I just poke my horns out at this lion, says the buffalo to hisself, and put all my weight behind 'em I could just chase him away from me for all time.' So the next time that lion chased him our buffalo friend ran for a while just to pick up some speed and then turned around all of a sudden and stuck out his big buffalo horns and put all the weight of his big heavy buffalo body behind 'em and knocked that lion clean in to the next county!"

Mr Jimmy smiles a Glimmering smile plus says:

"Well, Danny, what do you think of that?"

"C-Could that r-really occur in r-real actuality?"

"Buffalos have got the potential to knock the poop outta any lion in the world. A buffalo has just gotta make their mind up. Know what I mean? Then he's jist got to do it! It's all in a buffalo's head!"

"B-But I n-never heard of a b-buffalo b-beating up a lion. B-Buffalos would always g-get ate up. It's always th-the other w-way around."

"Yeah it is," utters Mr Jimmy which hugs me real tight, "And that's the whole point. But it don't have to be that way. Don't you see?"

Now ain't that kind? Firstly he tells me a private tale then he hugs me. But his surprise hug propels me to blubber again! Please do not ask me why. As I can not tell you. As I do not know. But sometimes I sporadically feel that if I had to take pills like The Lonely Gal I might not take them on purpose too and it would be Curtains for me!

Mr Jimmy jist hugs me in his big 2 arms and rocks me backwords and fourwords which impedes my blubbering. Then he starts his auto up again and I lean my head contiguous on to him and fasten my piglet 2 eyes on to his perky weenie in a exceptional State of Bliss and Mr Jimmy drives me home with his muscley arm on my shoulder and I instantaneously know that nobody on the whole Cosmos will be permitted to pee on me! At least not Daily.

29. MISS FISHLOCK AND HER SLOW BASTARD

I am exceptionally nerve racked today which is the 3rd week of Summer Vacation as it is exceedingly hot and Bull is extremely Inebriated and Jarleen is excessively mad at him plus has jist poured water on said's head as he called her Joe again. She is currantly commencing to go out bowling on her white big leg and crutches with Jack Shanks. (Ha. Ha.) (That old mattress is jist laying there awaiting for the 2 of them in the Rear of Jack Shanks' Pick-Up Deluxe with Baited Breath!)

I have jist Consummated ironing my Bright Blue Corduroys in which I am currantly garbed in along with my 100 Percent red nylon seersucker long-sleeved no-iron shirt. I washed said peedupon items last night which turned out exceptionally Exemplary plus free from fowl fragrance as I employed Duz Soap as Duz Does Everything. (Plus did!)

I am awaiting for dear Miranda Cosmonopolis and her singing teacher old Miss Fishlock plus am exceptionally nerve racked as Miranda asked me if could I sing a duet with her at The Old Timers Club and I wisht I had not of told her I can as I do not desire to stand up in front of no Bevy of Old Timers and sing even if said Bevy is all over seventy years of age due to my incessant obeseness.

However. I Acquiesced to Miranda's request With Alacrity as the broke down old Hotel LaVernia in which The Old Timers live in is jist one stone's throw from The Jolly Jug which I seen on my way to said Jug. So I will additionally strive to Drop In plus say hello to The Steamrollers. (ET. *AL!*)

I am currantly sweating like a stuck pig plus am on the Look

Out for PK which I seen prior this morning sneaking around contiguous and which might feasibly jump out and grab me as I waddle out through our front gate.

Anyhow. Miss Fishlock and dear Miranda and Miss Fishlock's handsome big 18 years of age Slow Son which is as old as I purport to appear to be plus possesses a Multi-protrusive weenie and is weak in the head all drive right up in Miss Fishlock's broke down old Studebaker auto which is as broke down almost as our 1936 old Plymouth which is Infinitely older due to it's Abizmol (Sp?!) State of Neglection.

Miss Fishlock's auto horn is Duly honked so I say goodbye to Jarleen which is piddling through our bathroom door plus waddle fast past Bull which is snoring on our Davenport currantly among Raisins and exit out and shut our front door closed real quiet.

I am exceedingly careful to note in all of the 4 Established directions in case PK is contiguous. He ain't. So I waddle fast to Miss Fishlock's auto as she has jist additionally honked. I jump in plus lock it's door jist as PK comes running down my street right at us!

Miss Fishlock tramps on her gas pedal as she knows that poor misguided PK is a Conventional Bully of mine and PK gives The Finger to all of us as we zoom away from him!

Miranda which oscillates her round little dear head on to me utters:

"What a thoroughly unpleasant boy!"

"I thoroughly agree!" says Miss Fishlock.

I thoroughly agree additionally but as it is hard to utter that sentence quick I remain Mutantly silent.

"What did you ever do to him, Danny, that he should be so vindictive towards you?" says Miss Fishlock.

"N-Nothing, Miss F-Fishlock. I g-guess he jist hates me as he d-don't like w-who I am."

Miss Fishlock looks over Miranda's round little head right at me as us 3 set in the front seat of her auto which is a real tight fit. Her handsome big Slow Son sets in the Rear segment of said broke down auto with a behemoth stack of Miss Fishlock's Music Volumes and it is hard to note his Multi-protrusive weenie with Impunity. (Unfortunately.)

Miss Fishlock says:

"Doesn't, Danny. Say he *doesn't* like who you are, not *don't* like who you are."

"I like who you are, Danny," says dear Miranda which ain't got no ideal about my Affiliations or she feasibly would not of said said but ain't that a kind thing which to say anyhow?

"And who are you, Danny?" utters Miss Fishlock which squinches her eyes at me in a Courteous although nosey Mode.

"He is Danny," says Miss Fishlock's 18 years of age Slow Son and it is real hard to yank my piglet 2 eyes off from his weenie but as he is setting in the Rear seat and I am setting in the front seat I ain't able to keep my head eternally oscillated around backwords like a darn corkscrew noting said.

"*Who* are you?" repeats Miss Fishlock repetitiously. This is exceedingly Puzzling as she knows darn well who I am.

"M-M-Me."

"Ummmn," she says plus smiles like she *knows* I would suck one weenie At The Drop Of One Hat! This is nerve racking and impels me to Prespire profusely but I like poor Miss Fishlock which would of been a whole alots happier if she didn't have no Slow Son Bastard born outsides of wedlock which ruined her reputation in The Opera World and propelled her to reside in Lemon Gulch and be Fully Unrecognized as dear Miranda Divulged at a Wednesday Club Dance prior. (To me alone.) (As said is a behemoth secret with Consequences!)

Said son is Slow due to falling out from Miss Fishlock's auto when In Motion on top of his head while Infantile. But dear Miranda says said Son was put on The Good Earth for some personalized reason by god almighty which is feasible.

Anyhow. Miranda requests to practice her solo song 'BECAUSE' so Miss Fishlock grabs a little Whistle which she wears on a string around her neck and blows on said as Miranda needs the correct music note with which to commence to sing with. So Miranda puffs up her little lips plus Opera Sings:

"Because God made thee mine
I'll cherish theeeeee..."

Dear Miranda is the kindest girl I ever met in my total life and possesses a exceedingly beauteous voice. When you listen to her sing it is excessively easy to forget all about her fatness and round little head. Dear Miranda now Opera Sings *real* loud:

"Through light and darkness

Through all time to beeeeee..."

"Thank you, Miranda," says Miss Fishlock.

"And pray His love may make
Our love divine!
BECAUSE GOD MADE THEE MINE!"
(Opera Sings Miranda *real, real* loud.)

"That will do just *fine*, Miranda!" hollers Miss Fishlock.

"Just fine!" says Miss Fishlock's Slow Son.

We arrive up to the broke down old Hotel LaVernia in Port City and all of us dismount. I am contented that Miss Fishlock's old auto ain't broke down on our journey as I am Fatigued of every Vehicle I ride in breaking down! Explicitly Major Ones inclusive of busses. (As said.)

Anyhow. I got to pee like a hound sucking eggs so I excuse myself Courteously.

"Five minutes, Danny," hollers Miss Fishlock as her and dear Miranda gether Miss Fishlock's music Volumes up from her auto's Rear seat where her Slow Son has recently prior set.

"Five minutes," says said Son which follows me as he additionally requires alleviation too.

"We will be in The LaVernia Entertainment Lounge on the third floor," hollers Miss Fishlock.

"Third floor," hollers said Son right on to my darn ear. (The sore one which Thwarted Bull whacked previous!)

Said Son and me find the Men's Room and go in but then he stops and jist loiters here right in front of the white Three Anchors Double Urinal plus utters:

"I got to pee. I got to pee. I got to pee!"

Now ain't that a dumb item which to utter?! Of course he has got to pee! That is why he has came here in the 1st place ain't it?! But he don't do nothing about it. He jist loiters here uttering said.

"I got to pee," he utters additionally plus continues not to do nothing about it.

"Y-You g-got to unbutton and t-take your weenie out or y-you'll jist p-pee on to yourself."

"I cain't. I cain't. My Mama always unbuttons me."

OH MY GOSH!! He is 18 years of age and he can not even unbutton hisself!

"Will you unbutton me, Danny?"

"M-Me?!"

He looks jist like he is about to blubber and I know jist how he feels so I commence to unbutton the 5 buttons on his fly. **HOWEVER!** I only unbutton 2 buttons when I note a Lump which is a whole alots bigger then the Lump I seen when I commenced to unbutton said. I unbutton the 3rd button and the Lump arises up abrupt like a chicken with their head chopped off! So I terminate unbuttoning instantaneously plus jist note said raising Lump and hold my breath plus feel my own dear weenie twitch in Awe And Fascination.

"You got to take my weenie out too," says Miss Fishlock's Slow Son, "My Mama always takes my weenie out for me."

OH MY GOSH! His Mama traditionally unbuttons him **PLUS** takes his weenie out and he is 18 years of age! I am real glad that I ain't slow among my brains as I would Loathe to get Jarleen's Carmen Red long fingernails on to my Private Segmants! **OH MY GOSH!**

Anyhow. I reach real helpful down insides of this Slow Son's Y-fronts and feel a behemoth Boner **WHICH IS BIGGER THEN ANY PENILE ITEM PRIOR FELT!** Plus is all squirmy and slippery underneath of it's Silken Fourskin which is a sure Premonition of Pre-Coital Slippage! I yank at it and said flops right out on to my hand like a fat tunafish plus it's Silken Fourskin zips right back with a behemoth snap which impels it's shiny pink weenie head to smile up at me like one true friend!

But that is not all which is preceding! This Slow Son has currently got his big hand way down insides of my Y-fronts and is squeezing my own dear Boner like a hog in slops! Then he squats right over and yanks my Bright Blue Corduroys right down without even unbuttoning said as I suppose he can't *never* unbutton *nothing* by hisself and my Boner pops up through my access slot and he slams his mouth on over it and slaps his tongue around it like a hound sucking eggs! **OH MY GOSH!!** I instantaneously squirt right on to his mouth and he squirts a sticky big handful on to my own hand in joyous Bliss!

"Danny! There you are! I said five minutes not ten! Are you ready for a sing-through before the Old Timers get here?" utters Miss Fishlock at me as I enter in to The Entertainment Lounge on the 3rd floor of The Hotel LaVernia.

"Sing-through," says Miss Fishlock's Slow Son which is setting

138

contiguous by Miranda in the 1st row of chairs with his 2 legs wide apart and his Multi-protrusive weenie Lump poking up underneath of his brown Corduroys like it was a Sacred Shrine! I ponder for one interval if he really knows how to button and unbutton his own pants plus take a lightning quick note at the crotch of my Bright Blue Corduroys. Fortunately no Osmosis occured due to my prior Fully Insulated Onanation in said Men's Room as I wiped my weenie up Scrupulous while listening to a sudden Enigmatic jangle of keys which come from one of the toilet Cubicles and sounded a whole alots like the keys which Fred Foster wears on a ring on his Dungarees belt loop! (But I Digress.)

I now strive to help dear Miranda mount up on to The LaVernia Lounge Entertainment Platform with one Mighty Effort as she ain't able to do said alone as she is impelled to bend over so far to take such a big step up that her fat big 2 titties yank her off balance although her fat big heinie does it's leveling best as Ballast.

Miss Fishlock sets down at the piano and stretches her skinny 10 fingers out which gets ready to play but her Slow Son whines:

"I want candy!"

"No," utters Miss Fishlock to her Bastard, "Absolutely not!"

"I want candy!" whines this Son repetitiously. Miss Fishlock pats her Prespiring brows with her hanky and notes her watch. Miranda is worried and Prespiring too plus her round little braided head looks littler even then as per as traditional which is Indubitably due to said merciless sun's heat which swells up the Remainder of her fat segmants a whole alots jist like it does mine.

"Oh, Danny," says Miss Fishlock, "would you be so kind and go downstairs to the Confectionary Counter in the lobby and purchase some soda pop and candy and perhaps some shelled peanuts? I believe we can all do with a lift. It is so infernally hot! Here is eighty-five cents, dear."

Miss Fishlock yanks 3 quarters and a dime out from her yellow small coin purse and pokes said Coinage at me. "Refreshed, Danny," she utters, "we can all give a superb performance. Thank you so much, dear."

Although I am still puffing from my recent Onanation I am always at the services of old kind ladies with funds.

I dismount off from said Entertainment Platform and grab Miss Fishlock's Coinage and commence to waddle throughout the hall to The Hotel LaVernia's elevater when I see this guy which comes running out from the Men's Room which turns and runs down the fire excape stairs which looks a whole alots like My Divine Fred Foster but ain't as why would Fred Foster be here in the Men's Room of The Hotel LaVernia in which he don't reside in?

Then **OH MY GOSH!!** Who is this skinny lady in the pink chenille bathrobe sashaying out from room 301?!

30. FLO PLUS THE LONELY GAL

"Miss F-Flo!" I holler!

"Why Danny!" says Flo, "It's *you*!"

Flo is real delightful to see me which is contenting in the extremes.

"Jist a sec, hon," says Flo, "I'll be back in 2 shakes of a lamb's tail. One's got to go relieve one's self."

Flo goes in to the Guest's Toilet's Room 2 doors down said hall as her own room feasibly ain't Equipped with no Overt toilet. I lean against The Hotel LaVernia's hall wall and loiter while I wait for Flo as she alleviates. Then suddenly:

"Floooooooo! Flooooooooo!" hollers this here goofy voice out from the room from which Flo has came out from. The door is currantly one small crack open so I peer in and here laying on the bed is The Lonely Gal! **OH MY GOSH AM I SURPRISED!**

"Floooooooo!" she hollers, "Floooooo! Where the fuck are you, you skinny sonofabitch?!"

"H-Hello, L-Lonely G-Gal," I utter as I push the door open wider so as she can note me.

"Who the fuck are you, fatty?!" hollers said Gal.

"D-Danny."

"Yeah?" she says, "Yeah? And who the fuck said you can come barging in like this disturbing my fucking privacy?!"

Dire tears squirts right out from my piglet darn 2 eyes. "D-Don't you r-reminisce m-me?"

"Reminisce?!" she hollers, "Remin-fucking-nisce?!"

She looks goofy for one interval.

"No I do not re-mi-nisce you!" hollers said Gal which throws a handful of Kleenexs from a Kleenex box at me. Said box sits on a table adjacent besides of her bed contiguous of a full almost bottle plus a fully empty bottle of Vat 69 which is the implicit beverage which Bull drinks relentless.

140

"Blow your fucking nose and stop bawling like a fucking child!" hollers The Gal.

"I *am* a ch-ch-child!"

I blow my nose plus wipe my piglet 2 eyes with the Kleenexs which she has threw at me.

"You're eighteen if you're a day!"

Her goofy 2 eyes cross and then uncross and I note that she is *exceptionally* Inebriated!

"I ain't n-neither 18," I utter real soft so as to Lull her down.

"Fucking *seventeen* then!"

"I am t-twelve y-years of age!"

My tears is squirting Direly out and I can not do nothing to impede them. "I am G-Grotesque d-due to my R-Relentless P-Pubescence!" I holler, "W-Which is impelled b-by A H-Hormonal Uh-Unbalance Of The H-Highest Order w-which has r-ran in our f-family for Eons!"

"What the *fuck*?!"

She flops backwords and whacks her head on the Iron bedstead.

"What is goin' *on* in here?!" hollers Flo which comes busting through this room's doorway.

"This fat Sissy bastard tried to fucking molest me!" hollers this Self-Same Lonely Gal which uttered she loved me on my battery radio every singular night at 10 PM excepting Mondays for *months* and which kissed me right on my upper lip **ONE WEEK PRIOR!** Plus told me right to my piglet pimply face that she **LOVED** me!

I sop up my old darn tears with The Gal's Kleenexs which was flang right through the air at me as she can't hardly hand *nothing* to one Courteous and genteel plus I strive to forget her bad manners and fowl language.

Said Gal arises up on to her 2 elbows and takes a big swig from the full almost bottle of Vat 69 plus flops back and whacks her head again and both of her 2 eyes closes shut and she commences to snore louder even then My Dad Bull on our Davenport!

"She has got herself a drinking problem," says Flo real serious, "and I am attempting to nurse her back to a full and happy life. I'm *real* good with alcoholics."

"Th-That's r-real kind of y-you, F-Flo."

Suddenly Miss Fishlock's Slow Son which is born outside of wedlock (As said.) pokes his handsome head through our door frame plus walks right in and whines loud:

"I want candy!"

"Who's *that* bastard?!" says Flo.

"M-Miss F-Fishlock's s-slow s-son."

"Oh," says Flo, "*Hung*, ain't he?"

"Y-Yes," I say as this is a Phrase with which I am framiliar with as it is habitually uttered by My Beauteous Mom in Collaboration with variegated indeterminant Genitalias.

"M-Miranda C-Cosmo-n-nopolis and me is s-singing a d-duet f-for The Old T-Timers C-Club in The L-LaVernia L-Lounge today." I utter Informatively plus blow my nose on said prior flang Kleenexs.

"I want candy!" whines Miss Fishlock's Slow Son additionally.

"I g-got to g-go," I say, "and p-procure c-candy and s-soda p-pop and sh-shelled peanuts for us b-before we p-practice our s-song numbers."

"I want candy!" hollers Miss Fishlock's Slow Son which grabs my hand plus yanks.

"What the *fuck*?!" hollers The Lonely Gal which don't even bother to open up her 2 eyes.

"W-Well, goodbye M-Miss F-Flo," I say, "P-Please take real good care of The L-Lonely G-Gal."

"Oh, I will," says Flo, "I'll take real good care of her. You bet I will! Count on it! Yessiree! So long, Danny."

Flo sways to the bed table and slurps a big swig from the Vat 69 plus thumps The Lonely Gal on her head with her knuckles.

"What the *fuck*?" says said Gal.

Flo hands her subsequential this full almost bottle from which The Gal takes a big swig from. I ain't too sure that more quantities of Vat 69 will nurse this Gal back to A Full And Happy Life as it ain't Aided nor Abetted Bull none at all.

I am about to ask Flo how her poetry writing is preceding but said Slow Son is literately yanking me right out from the door!

The Slow Bastard and me go down to the lobby and procure said candy and soda pop and shelled peanuts at the Confectionary Counter and return to The Entertainment Lounge and Vicariously consume said. Then we practice our song numbers. (Miranda and me *only* and not inclusive of said Son which ain't a accurate entertainer as he ain't even able to feasibly unbutton hisself!)

Multiple Old Timers is currantly setting on their chairs contiguous around the Entertainment Lounge's Platform plus doing Tasks as per old persons should ought to do such as knitting and reading and scratching at varigated segmants of their old selves which itch Insidious.

Miss Fishlock is jist terminating playing a Appropriate Modern Medley Of Songs including Don't Get Around Much Anymore and Old Rocking Chair's Got Me and As Time Goes By and Home Alone By The Telephone so as to warm up The Old Timers for I and Miranda's Duet.

Said Timers gets all riled up plus commences to clap for us like hogs in slops and if I was not so nerve racked I am sure my piglet 2 eyes would of squirted tears of gratuity as I ain't never been so appreciated by The Multitudes nor ain't never saw so many poor Down And Out beat up old persons in one room anywheres prior in A Often Uncaring World!

31. A TRAGEDY AT THE HOTEL LAVERNIA ENTERTAINMENT LOUNGE

It is now time for I and dear Miranda to sing our duet for which we worked out a Unique small dance for. Miss Fishlock currently plays our Introductory Music (Dance Ballerina Dance!) on The Entertainment Lounge's Piano as I and Miranda mounts up on to said Lounge's Entertainment Platform with me helping Miranda up on to said like previous as this procedure must be Adhered To every time due to dear Miranda's Overweaning 2 titties which disbalance her.

Suddenly Flo and The Lonely Gal comes right through the Lounge's swinging doors marching in behemoth Nazi Goose-steps plus sets down at the back giggling and scraping their chairs on to the floor a whole alots as their both Indisputably Inebriated in the extremes and suffering of exceptional Disarray!

As The Show Must Go On I and dear Miranda curtsies to The Old Timers and Miranda shakes her finger at me plus grins as it is one segmant of our Unique small dance. All of said Old Timers jist set there Glaring at me like they know all about my Affiliations due to my girlish waddle which impels me to sweat like a stuck pig. However. Miss Fishlock plays our Melody and Miranda instantaneously sings in her beauteous Opera voice:

"I wonder who came walking
In my dreams last night!"

I swing back and fourth to Miss Fishlock's piano playing even
although my yellow little teeth is chattering and my tummy jiggles
like a hog in slops! Plus I wink at Miranda as it is a traditional
segmant of our duet plus sing:

"It could of been me alright, alright!"

(I never stutter when singing songs.) (As said.) Miranda shakes
her finger at me again and grins plus I sing:

"I wonder who said 'sweetheart'
In the bright moonlight!"

I wink at Miranda again. (As per as Rehearsed.) Plus Miranda
Opera Sings:

"It could of been me alright, alright!"

Miranda slams her dainty 2 hands on to her waste plus sticks
her nose up like she is stuck-up although this is only to certify that
we was Strangers plus she Opera Sings:

"Seems impossible we were strangers
A couple of kisses ago!"

I wink at Miranda by mistake as I am still nerve racked and
forget that I should of tried to hold her hand instead of. (A assigned
segmant of this dance number also!) But I am Negligent. However
I sing:

"Gee, if this is a dream
I never dreamed..."

Dear Miranda grabs my hand as I didn't grab hers like I should
ought to of plus she Opera Sings:

"...That you and I would ever say hello!"

We nod a whole alots at each other then collectively sing in to each other's faces:

"Now we know who came walking
In our dreams last night!
It must have been us alright, alright!"

Plus Miranda Opera Sings real high:

"It must have been us alrighhhhhhhhht!"

I put my arms around Miranda's waste but not around the whole waste as the obese fat on our communal wastes continuously impedes this tender act. (Explicitly like at the Wednesday Club Dance.) (As said.) Then dear Miranda sticks her fat 2 arms around my waste. (Almost!) Plus we both sing collectively:

"It must have been us alrighhhhhhhhht!"

I and Miranda strive to do some more of our Unique small dance and we sort of tap-dance and jiggle a whole alots due to said Mutual obesities.

Then suddenly I hear from the back row of chairs a excessively loud: **"WHAT THE *FUCK*?!"**

It is The Lonely Gal which is standing up and waving her arms and wobbling back and fourth and pointing at I and Miranda! **AM I MORTIFIED!**

"JESUS H CHRIST!" hollers The Lonely Gal which points her finger right at I and Miranda, **"WHAT THE FUCK IS *THAT* SUPPOSED TO BE?!"**

Flo laughs too! Real loud plus squawky! And variegated Old Timers which thinks that our dance is supposed to be a Comedy Routine also laughs horridly loudly.

I got to admit that Miranda and me has got a whole alots of flopping up and down going on amid us as her big 2 titties plus my fat big tummy plus both of our behemoth heinies shakes like chickens with their heads chopped off!

Then all of The Old Timers commences to laugh and I suddenly note old big tears squirting out from dear Miranda's little dear eyes even although she keeps right on dancing as The Show Must Go On! And Miss Fishlock keeps right on playing as she don't note nothing Irreconcilable as she is Submerged in her Arts.

Then The Lonely Gal falls right off from her chair with a whack and Flo squats down to help her get up but falls also down and jist lays there. What a Dire mess! Then a Old Timer hollers at I and Miranda:

"Take it off! Take it all off! Take it *all* off, will ya?!"

It is like I and Miranda is supposed to be in a Burlesque Strip Tease show!

"I wanna see me some tittie!" hollers this indeterminant Old Timer additionally.

Poor Miranda's little mouth flops right open!

"**TITS! TITS! TITS!**" hollers said Timer plus another Old Timer in a tore hairnet looks right at me and hollers:

"Take it all off! Show us what you got, big boy!"

I can not hardly believe my own ears! Here is these poor down and out Old Timers hollering at I and dear poor Miranda like we was Strippers instead of children! Down and out exceptionally old persons is jist as unkind as any! **IRREGARDLESS OF!**

AM I MAD! I grab dear poor Miranda and drag her right off from that Entertainment Platform and set her down behind of it and she blubbers and blubbers.

Erstwhile The Lonely Gal lays on her back supinely on the floor contiguous by Flo which is additionally prone and snoring loud. However. Said Gal instantaneously commences to flop up and down plus froth!

Miss Fishlock calls The Hotel LaVernia Official Manageresse plus a Bell Boy with no protrusive weenie to speak of and said 2 loiters while The Lonely Gal terminates her Fit and immediately afterwords hollers Thrice:

"What the *fuck*?! What the *fuck*?! What the *fuck*?!"

Which is almost as Dire as The Old Timers hollering "Take it off!" and "Tits! Tits! Tits!" and "Take it all off! Show us what you got, big boy!" and "What The *Fuck*" is coming from a Established Acquaintance of mine!

The Manageresse and the Bell Boy grabs Flo and The Gal off from the floor which is real hard to Facilitate as said 2 Inebriants don't neither of them currantly wish to arise up from said floor. However. Both of said is carried back to their Cohabitated LaVernia hotel room In Due Course.

It takes me and Miss Fishlock implicitly 12 total minutes to impel dear poor Miranda to terminate blubbering as Miss Fishlock

146

utters real firm:

"Miranda, you have been crying for exactly twelve minutes!"

"My eyes hurt," whines poor Miranda. Miss Fishlock dabs at Miranda's red dear 2 eyes with a white nice hanky. "My throat hurts and I can't sing anymore," whines Miranda. Her pigtails has fell down too but said dangly pigtails at least makes her round little head look bigger and is A Marked Improvement over prior little-headishness.

"My hair hurts," whines Miranda as her hair is pulled real tight back by said braided duo In Perpetuity, "and I am humiliated!"

"You poor children," utters Miss Fishlock, "you were doing such a splendid job, too."

"Splendid," says Miss Fishlock's Slow Son.

By now all of the Old Timers has went fortunately away due to being impelled to by the Irate Manageresse which apologized to I and Miranda and Miss Fishlock. (So did the Bellboy which did have a weenie to speak of which protruded fine when he stuck his leg up on a chair during said apologizing.)

"M-Miss F-Fishlock, w-would you like to m-meet some g-good friends of m-mine?" I utter.

Miss Fishlock's eyes Transmogrifys theirselves in to 2 skinny slits instantaneously as she has jist prior met 2 of my friends plus says:

"Who *are* these friends?"

"Friends?" says Miss Fishlock's Slow Son, "Who *are* these friends?"

"The S-Steam r-rollers", I utter, "A l-lady's b-bowling team which is jist around the c-corner at The J-Jolly J-Jug.

"Oh, let's *do*!" utters Miranda although her eyes is still wet and reddish and one pigtail is still down plus flopping, "Let's *do* meet them!"

"Well," says Miss Fishlock, "as it's on our way. We can certainly all use a little cheering up."

We gether Miss Fishlock's Music Volumes up and exit out from The Hotel LaVernia then drive around the corner and here is The Jolly Jug at the end of the street. I am chock full of jolly ponderings on my dear friends The Steamrollers plus the concerned short lady.

Miss Fishlock stops her auto in front of said Jug and I jump out and waddle to the front door and stop Stock Still in Awe! Said door is locked with a behemoth pad lock plus here is a red big sign!

"CLOSED UNTIL FURTHER NOTICE BY ORDER OF THE VICE SQUAD OF THE PORT CITY POLICE DEPARTMENT"

Closed?! Am I disappointed! I waddle back on to the Rear seat of Miss Fishlock's auto and set by Miss Fishlock's Slow Son.

"Th-They're c-closed," I say, "Untill f-farther n-notice".

"C-Closed," says Miss Fishlock's Bastard from right adjacent, "until f-farther n-notice."

"How disappointing," says Miss Fishlock which don't seem disappointed at all.

OH MY GOSH!! I hope my personalized friends ain't became interred by The Port City Police Department but as The Keyhole (Which I read Voluminously.) ain't said nothing about knives and stripteases at The Jolly Jug yet I ponder they ain't. (Became interred.)

Miss Fishlock starts her auto up and we drive away plus Miranda Contemporaneously says:

"I have a wonderful idea!"

"And what is that, Miranda?" says Miss Fishlock which ain't contented at all due to our Hotel LaVernia Entertainment Lounge tragedy.

"Let's sing Are You Sleeping, Brother John," says Miranda.

"What a *good* idea!" says Miss Fishlock, "It will cheer us and help pass the time."

"The time," says Miss Fishlock's Slow Son which sits so contiguously adjacent besides of me that I can smell his weenie which Miss Fishlock must of forgot to wash sporadically today.

"You begin, Miss Fishlock!" says Miranda, "then I'll come in then Danny will come in."

"I want to sing," says the handsome Bastard contiguous, "too."

"No, dear," says Miss Fishlock. "You don't know the words."

"Or the *melody*," says Miranda real kind, "dear."

Miss Fishlock's Slow Son grins at Miranda as he likes her a whole alots and feasibly relishes to be called Dear. Which would *not*?! (Inclusive of me!)

"Shall I begin?" says Miss Fishlock.

"Yes," says Miranda so Miss Fishlock takes her whistle from around her neck and blows a Music Note Tone and commences to Opera Sing:

"Are you sleeping?
Are you sleeping?"

And Miranda Opera Sings:

"Brother John?
Brother John?"

plus points to me and I sing:

"Morning bells are ringing!
Morning bells are ringing!"

And Miranda points to I and Miss Fishlock and we all sing:

"Ding Dong Dong!
Ding Dong Dong!"

Miss Fishlock and Miranda laughs joyous and Miss Fishlock's Bastard laughs Ditto and sticks his hand right out and pats the round little top of Miranda's round little braided head. Plus utters:
"Please marry me, Miranda."
Plus he attains a Erection feasibly due to said patting of dear Miranda's round little braided head. (I guess.) (But I ain't certain. As I ain't no mind-reader!)
Miranda and Miss Fishlock laughs joyously additionally and do not note said Son's instantaneous behemoth Erection neither as their setting on the front seat and singing the next Verses from our song but I ain't as I forget all the Verses plus am Undergoing a additional Erection which I conceal Covertly underneath of a pile of Miss Fishlock's sheet music Volumes which hurts as I am impelled to compress said Vicariously down with the Toppermost Volume on to my protrusive Bright Blue Corduroys.
As Miss Fishlock's auto is so old we got to drive exceedingly slow back to Lemon Gulch which is OK by me as her Slow Son's convivial Boner is Acutely contiguous and A Joy Which To Behold.
I open said Toppermost Volume of Miss Fishlock's music up with which I currantly conceal my Erection with and appear to purport to Browse said Volume. However. While opening said up I poke one of my 2 elbows right on to the Slow Son's behemoth Boner real slow and sneaky and can feel said twitch although said

Son don't note nothing irreconcilable as he is Dozing plus feasibly dreaming of dear Miranda's round little braided head which he patted genteely prior.

Anyhow. Every time Miss Fishlock's auto jumps over a bump on our road I jab my elbow into the Son's behemoth Boner with Impunity. **BUT OH MY GOSH** after one interval I note that the Outtermost end of my elbow feels hot and damp as a hog in slops as said Son has squirted Spermatozoans all over the insides of his brown Corduroys which is seeping out on to his fly in a State of Full Osmosis. I myself squirt abruptly insides of my own Y-fronts which was in a State of Matriculation due to my moving hand which no person can observe accurate as said was gesticulating underneath of Miss Fishlock's music Volumes. **THANK GOSH!**

HOWEVER! The Slow Son's Boner don't un-Tumesce like a traditional Boner rendition should ought to of but jist remains behemoth. So I shove my fat big thigh right up contiguous on to this Son's damp leg and feast my piglet 2 eyes on his Boner all the way back home to Lemon Gulch Ecstatically in Bliss. I squirt one more additional time jist as we drive past The Big Lemon and it's Best Climate In The Cosmos sign.

All of this Covert ejecting is beneficial for one's Humane Condition in A Often Uncaring World.

32. PEELING BANANAS AT THE MAJOR MOTION PICTURE

A exceedingly handsome guy is setting jist 3 empty seats away from me at the Gulch Theater to which I have came to subsequential after being brung home by Miss Fishlock which has gave me 25 cents as I deeply require to get cheered up after our tragedy at The Hotel LaVernia Entertainment Lounge but the Major Motion Picture ain't commenced as of per yet.

This exceedingly handsome guy of which I am Chatting of is a Senior at Lemon Gulch Unified High School plus wears a silver cross around his neck and must be 17 years of age as all Seniors habitually is. I seen him Perusing The Holy Bible continually plus consuming a marshmallow Soda once (Which could of feasibly been vanilla as they are of the same colors and I was not close enough to smell said.) while garbed in his Senior's Special

Edition Lemon Gulch Unified High School's Sweater at The Saga Of The West Drugstore And Fountain Grill with his Dungarees exceptionally Tumesced Up. Plus he kindly smiled which satisfied me in the extremes as I myself consumed a Frosty-Cold Tom Crumpler Famous Extra-Thick Marshmallow Malt. (Paid for I might add with funds which I found in between of the Cushions on our Davenport which had fell out from Bull's pocket. Bull was not in occupation of said at that implicit minute.) (Obviously!) (Or I would of got whacked!) (Said funds should of however went on to the purchase of a new battery for my radio but I was Ravishing for a Tom Crumpler Famous Marshmallow Malt!) (But I Digress.)

I ponder I better not currently stare at this Senior which now sets in my Theater Vicinity as it might propel me to attain a Erection in Remembrance of his prior Tumescence. So I ponder dear poor Miranda and our LaVernia Lounge tragedy instead of so as to impede my weenie down. Them darn Old Timers missed out on hearing Miranda's main Opera song 'BECAUSE' which is sure to propel dear poor Miranda on in to the future! (So to speak.)

At The Hotel LaVernia Entertainment Lounge I learnt sadly that old persons ain't any different from young persons as every fool plus their brother is sporadically unkind irregardless of one's ages!

Anyhow. Here I set in The Gulch Theater and the Main Feature stars Gene Kelly and my all time favorite Dancer dear Vera Ellen which is eternally sweet and grinning. (Excepting while sporadically Distraught.) (I know jist how she feels!) (On Aces!)

However. A serial of Hopalong Cassidy has jist commenced which is exhibiting prior to the main feature which makes me excessively Vexed as today's serial should really of been Captain Marvel in his red tight costume with his protrusive weenie As Prior Announced. But it ain't as it is Cowboys instead of and ain't so heightening up although weenie Lumps is sporadically glimpsed underneath of variegated tight Cowboy pants on the serial's actors which is Gripping although guns plus their fights ain't. (I Abhor Violent Disarray.) (As said.)

However. At my piglet 2 eye's corners I keep noting this here Lemon Gulch Unified High Senior in his Silver Cross which has now moved one empty Theater's seat closer!

Then my black and white small dog Tinker sneaks down the aisle and Pinpoints my location by sniffling my sweaty fragrances and jumps right on to my lap as this is a Theatrical Tradition of hers. So here she is on my lap all cozy and Ameliorating as I note from said Corners that this Senior is now one additional empty Theater's seat *closer* up to me which leaves only *one* empty Theater's seat in between us! He is holding a banana on his lap from which he peels off from real often of.

Tinker snores on my lap as she possesses a sporadic breathing implication jist like Miss McCoy's although she herself don't wheeze none but jist breathes raspy like a black and white small dog with a breathing implication should ought to of.

The Main Feature commences and the Senior flops on to the seat *contiguous* plus I note that the banana he is peeling ain't. But is a Boner instead which he is yanking up and down Surreptitious like a hog in slops! This Intrigues me. Plus impels a State of Full Instantaneous Erection in my Bright Blue Corduroys!

There is sailors in the Main Feature which commences to sing as this Motion Picture is a Rousing Musical. I hope Fervantly that my fully Tumesced Boner don't jab and wake up my sleeping black and white small dog which lays Somnolent on my lap.

Said Picture continues With Alacrity and I note with exceptional satisfaction the jiggling weenie Lumps underneath of the white uniforms of the variegated convivial sailors which now tapdances.

As said Senior peels on said banana (Ha. Ha.) he eats popcorn from a striped red big box which he sticks out at me from which to help myself from which I do as I am excessively hungry as I ain't got no Coinage for Milky-Ways as almost most of my funds was stold by PK immediately prior to peeing on me.

As I am reaching in to the Senior's popcorn's box he hisself is grabbing for my Boner which lays smashed up against my excessively damp Y-fronts insides of my Semi-damp Bright Blue Corduroys (Due to multiple Onanations contiguous by The Slow Son.) which I ain't changed out from as of per yet as I desired to get straight out from our home and in to this Major Motion Picture as fast as humanely feasible due to severe sadness about The tragedy at The Hotel LaVernia Entertainment Lounge which compressed dear poor Miranda down even worst due to her Intense Femininity.

The Senior's hand now comes adjacent on to my garbed Boner but Tinker awakens up and growls at said and the Senior yanks it back. (His hand not my Boner!) I would of Relished a good Feel-Up too as I am Moderately blue and lowly and nobody never touches me down there excepting for myself. (And Little Norman on our

152

Mutual past.)

"Can you please move your little dog?" utters the Senior Courteously.

I nod yes plus push Tinker on to the contiguous Theater's seat and the Senior sticks out his hand but Tinker growls at said hand again and climbs back on to my lap and growls a whole alots more at the Senior which keeps yanking his hand back in exceptional Fear. This occurs a Multitude of times but I finally propel my black and white small dog on to the other Theater's seat again and the Senior and me watch said Picture for one full interval so as to let dear Tinker fall Somnolent. In Due Course when she commences to rasp plus snore the Senior covers both of our Boners up with his light summer jacket and finally gets his hand on to my Boner and gives said a strong big squeeze and **OH MY GOSH!** don't it jist feel Esoteric!

Then the Senior unbuttons my Bright Blue Corduroys and yanks my Boner fully out and feels it a whole alots more then takes my hand and shoves it down on to his Boner and don't his feel convivial and sticky right on the tip of it! (A added Plus.) Then he propels my hand up and down on his Silken Fourskin so as I can peel his banana too. (Ha. Ha.)

This is my 1st authentic Feel-Up in real actuality of a Marginal Adult Boner of which I have only saw once in a old beat up photo of a fucking man and lady although one ball only of said man's Genitalias was notable as his Boner segmant was sunk in a State of Full Insertion insides of the lady's Pewdendas which was a disappointment. (But I Digress.)

I note from the corner of my piglet 2 eyes that the Senior has got his eyes squinched shut as he is feeling exceptionally Compassionate. Then Tinker wakes up and jumps back on my lap and emits a fart plus growls and makes the Senior yank his hand off from my Boner With Alacrity.

Then a old lady comes and sets down contiguous and chews Carmels plus takes a Bevy of teeth out from her mouth and pulls a glob of gooey Carmels out from between them and notes me and the Senior.

Anyhow. I take my hand off from the Senior's Boner even although it is Obliterated underneath of the Senior's summer jacket as said old chewing lady might note something Irreconcilable and Divulge it to The Zealous Authorities which is what habitually occurs when Policemen traps Preverts in The Keyhole.

153

(That Periodical which additionally features horrid stories about Individuals which is Assaulted plus cut up in to little segments and left in variegated suitcases in Bus's Stations!)

So me and the Senior jist set there for the rest of said Picture and watch it. Although it is a real good Major Motion Picture I would of rather of had this Senior's hand on my Boner and my hand on his in Full Bliss. But instead here lays my black and white small dog on my lap snoring and emitting sporadic farts Intermittently.

The old chewing lady with the Bevy of gooey teeth gives me and the Senior a goofy look when we exit out after said Major Motion Picture although I am sure she ain't saw nothing Irreconcilable.

Jist before we get to the Lobby the Senior asks me if I desire to meet him out behind of the old Tangy Mayo desserted Warehouse plus utters:

"Please don't bring your little dog."

I answer yes that I will meet him and no that I ain't bringing my black and white small dog so he exits out from the Gulch Theater and I oscillate my head around to make sure that PK ain't contiguous nor even adjacent. He ain't neither. So I stick Tinker on to the basket of my bicycle and ride towards the old Tangy Mayo desserted Warehouse which is on my way home then stop and sit Tinker on the street and tell her to run on home as she knows the way which is only a few blocks which she Duly does.

When I get to said desserted Warehouse I shiver horrid due to Reprehensable Reminiscences from the PK Peeing Episode which occured on it's Vicinity. However. The Senior is setting on a wood old Lemon box and smoking a cigarette of which he asks if I wish a puff of.

"N-No, th-thank y-you, I ain't s-started to c-commence s-smoking as of y-yet."

It is Indisputable that he thinks I am purported to be at least 18 as I am jist as tall as he although fat as one hog.

"Felt good, didn't it? Felt good what we did at the movie," says the Senior real jovial.

"Y-Yes, r-real g-good."

I waddle on to a shadow Emanating from a behemoth stack of old wood big crates so as this Senior won't note how fat and reddish and pimply I am as he has only saw me up close in the dark prior. He takes one big suck on his cigarette plus kindly utters:

"Suit yourself," then unbuttons his Dungarees plus kindly

requests:

"Come over here please."

DO I COMPLY! Then he takes my hand and sticks it on to his Silken Fourskin which impels my yellow little teeth to chatter like traditional.

"What's your name?"

"D-Danny O'R-Rourke," I say real nerve racked, "B-But d-do not t-tell n-nobody or I'll get in t-trouble as M-My B-Beauteous M-Mom d-don't l-like me t-to do n-nothin' w-with m-my w-weenie but p-pee."

"We'd both of us get into trouble. My name's Shawn," he utters plus takes my piglet fat fingers and Entwines them around his Boner plus moves my hand up and down tender and soft. His dear Boner is exceedingly warm and excessively hard and I laugh joyous as it is like all of the admirable Boner renditions on which I ever Ruminated on. He unbuttons my Bright Blue Corduroys plus says:

"Why are you laughing?"

"I f-feel r-real g-good!"

"So do I."

He yanks my Boner out from it's access slot and squats right down in front of me and commences to suck on said like a hound sucking eggs!

Then he stands up and requests me to suck on his for one duration so I squat right down and comply. Said tastes excessively good and warm!

"Geeeee," hollers my dear Senior, "Geeeee! I'm coming!"

My mouth fills Spontaneously up as he squirts and Spermatozoans rolls down right off from my chin and I ponder I will blubber in joyous Bliss! Then he wipes hisself with his hanky plus wipes my mouth and squats down in front of me again and sucks on me like a piglet sucking at a sow tittie and I feel so...I can't think of *no* word to utter how I feel so I jist blubber and he utters:

"Gee, did I hurt you?"

Then I squirt promptly plus commence to blubber excessively hard as squirting ain't never felt like this prior. I feel so admirable that I blubber and blubber and The Senior looks real a-scared.

"Danny, how old are you?!"

"T-Twelve," I blubber.

"Oh God, Danny!" he says, "You look *eighteen!*"

OH MY GOSH! He uses my personalized name jist like I was a accurate human! I jist can't help myself so I holler:

"I L-LOVE Y-YOU! I L-L-LOVE Y-Y-YOU!"

Does he look a-scared *then*!

"I've got to go!" he says, "Pipe down, Danny, please! And don't tell anyone about this or we'll both of us be in real trouble jist like you said!"

"I L-L-LOVE Y-Y-YOU!" I holler. As he *cares* about me! He even asked if he *hurt* me! He said my own name and he don't even *know* me! **OH MY GOSH!** is he wondrous! But he currantly looks at me real nerve racked plus says:

"I've got to go! Promise you won't tell anyone about this!"

"I p-promise," I say, "C-Can I p-please meet up with y-you t-tomorrow f-for a R-Repeat P-Performance?"

But he is already running up the alley away from me jist as fast as he can run. "Hey!" I holler, **"I L-L-LOVVVVVE Y-Y-YOU!"**

As this is my 1st Fully Esoteric Venture in real actuality I am real heightened up! **"I L-L-LOVE Y-YOU!"** I holler, "Hey! C-Come b-back, **C-COME B-BAAAAACK! SHAWWWWWN! I L-L-LOVVVVVE YOU!"**

I got to admit that I over do it and it sounds like a Major Motion Picture but I do not care so I holler additionally:

"C-C-COME B-BACK, SHAWN! P-P-PLEEEEEASE! I L-LOVVVVVVVE Y-Y-YOU!"

But my dear Shawn the Senior with the little silver cross whipping around his neck like a Sacred Shrine runs away. So I jist loiter here blubbering with my weenie dingling out from my Bright Blue damp Corduroys.

I am blubbering real hard still as I button up and **THANK GOSH** it is dark and the only light is a street lamp which is almost a whole block away or else unspecified persons might note something Irreconcilable and Divulge me and I would end up in The Keyhole as Exhibit "A" which would print my name in their Weekly Preverts List and Jarleen and Bull would read it and I might even be impelled to Commit Suicide like multiple Preverts always does while interred!

I wipe my piglet 2 eyes and snotted nose plus terminate blubbering instantaneously as I note the Inexorable PK Benderson coming down the alley right at me! He must of jist missed grabbing me at the Motion Picture!

Even although it is dark he can still note me as I am so big and shiny all over with sweaty Prespiration. I jump on to my bicycle and pedal as fast as I can away. **OH MY GOSH!** I wisht my dear Senior was here as he is a whole alots older then poor misguided PK plus is a Highschool Senior.

As I pedal away I ponder if I will ever see my dear Senior again as he must of closed his eyes when he looked at me or he else wouldn't of touched me with a ten foot pole.

"Some little girl telephoned you," utters Jarleen as I enter in to our home. "She ain't no little bad girl, is she? You ain't had none of your fingers up insides of her panties?"

"N-No."

"You *sure*?" says Jarleen which looks surprised as I ain't. I wisht I could Divulge to her that I had jist had my fingers up insides of my dear Senior's Y-fronts and my piglet mouth smack on to his convivial weenie joyous but do not as she might feasibly whack me.

"It w-was M-Miranda C-Cosmopolis. The g-girl with wh-which I s-sing w-with. D-Did s-she l-leave a m-message for m-me?"

"She says to telephone her tomorrow as she has went to bed as she is plum wore out and don't feel good."

"Our s-singing d-didn't g-go r-real w-well. They w-wasn't k-kind to us."

"Oh," says Jarleen which picks at a Hangnail on her Carmen Red long fingernail, jist "Oh."

"M-Miranda b-blubbered w-when they all l-laughed at our d-dancing n-number."

"I am going bowling with Jack Shanks which will be here any minute," says Jarleen which snips off said Hangnail with a pair of Cutey-Cure scissors plus don't even note me as she is all heightened up by the Impending Arrival of the Ostensibly weeniless Jack Shanks.

Jarleen currantly loiters contiguous leaning on her 2 crutches and panting like Tinker almost and looking out from our window for Jack which drives right up and honks on his horn.

"Comin' Sugar!" hollers My Beauteous Mom loud.

She clumps out on her white big leg and crutches without even shutting our home's front door as she traditionally forgets to shut doors while heightened up and her and Jack Shanks drives right off. I shut said door and note that Bull ain't sleeping on the top of our Davenport so I waddle to Jarleen's bedroom to see if he has snuck in to said but he ain't. He don't even *try* to. Do not ask me why. As I can not tell you. As I do not know. I would of snuck sporadically in for Recuperation on a soft bed if I was he. But ain't. (Obviously!)

I waddle to our kitchen for food and here is Bull which is laying underneath of the kitchen table on his back with his 2 feet which is Encased in his Lurid socks poking out prone jist like The Lonely Gal's done sadly prior. Why do Inebriants continuously Seek Shelter underneath of tables?

I gobble up a whole Pint carton of cottage cheese which I find in our icebox plus lick out what butter is left on our butter dish as there ain't nothing on which to spread said butter on. Nor nothing clean with which to spread said with. Lucky for me I gobbled up a whole alots of my dear Senior's popcorn prior at the Gulch Theater or I would be Omnivorous!

I waddle to my bedroom with my flashlight and strike a match and light my kerosene lamp plus let my black and white small dog Tinker in through my bedroom window which jumps right on to my bed as she has came home on her own as demanded. She goes right to sleep adjacent on my 2 feet. She must of terminated her Oestrus as no variegated dogs followed her home from The Gulch Theater nor none jumps through my bedroom's window which strives to mount her like last Christmas.

I am laying in bed garbed in said orange horridly tight pajamas and it is time for The Lonely Gal's radio show so I turn off said kerosene lamp and switch on my battery radio even although it's battery is currently in A Dangerously Low State. A radio announcer says:

DUE TO TECHNICAL REASONS THE LONELY GAL WILL NOT BE HEARD TONIGHT. IN HER PLACE WE WILL HEAR A MEDLEY OF SEMI OPERATIC FAVORITES.

Said Favorites comes on and they ain't so bad and I do not even miss hearing The Lonely Gal neither. Please do not ask me why. As I can not tell you. As I do not know. (Mayhaps I have jist became Dangerously Cynical.) (Like the Handsome Coach would have became if he had not of adapted them 2 Orphans!) (But I am too young to adapt *anybody!*) (Alas!)

One explicit Semi Operatic on my radio sounds almost like Lottie Venable's Long Diseased Composer which is a comfort.

158

Suddenly a Dire ideal hits me on the head like one Ton Of Bricks and I am blue and lowly instantaneously as I ponder that I should not of told my dear Senior that I loved him! **AS I DON'T! AS TO TELL THE TRUTH THE WHOLE TRUTH AND NOTHING BUT THE TRUTH I LOVE MY DIVINE FRED FOSTER!**

33. BULL STIRS SHIT

I am currantly laying on my bed this morning pondering my dear Senior plus how I should not of Inferred to him I Love You as I love Fred Foster plus was jist hollering said at the Senior as I was heightened up like in a Major Motion Picture plus feasibly on a Acute State of Imfatuation. However. I desire to feel heightened up sporadically as it is good for my Humane Condition sometimes.

Jarleen opens my bedroom door up Spontaneously without knocking and tells me that Bull possesses a job which is a behemoth shock as Bull ain't never had no job in Living Remembrances as firstly he was in the Navy for a full duration plus shot straight on to said Missing Limbs benefits subsequential to that Japanese Locomotive which whacked off his authentic one. (As sadly said.) However. What Bull done prior when I was Infantile is a Enigma as nobody hardly never tells me nothing anyhow.

"It is a real easy job," utters Jarleen which polishes her fingernails Carmen Red (As per as always.) as she has got to look her best even while not working due to the white big cast on her leg which yanks the attentions of persons away from her glamorous teeth. (ET. AL!) Anyhow. I gobble my Oatmeal and ponder dear Fred's weenie Mute. (Like traditional.)

"It was Jack Shanks' idea," utters My Beauteous Mom, "He knows this guy at the Gulch Sewer Works and this sewer guy told him that they got to get somebody to set up insides of this red box over their big pond of sewerage to shift the gears on a giant mechanical arm which stirs everything so as to facilitate a cleansing process."

Jarleen blows at her red wet fingernails. "And Bull is jist the guy to stir the shit!"

Jarleen laughs real hard plus says:

"Ain't that right, Danny?"

"I g-guess s-so. B-But how c-can B-Bull d-drink his V-Vat

S-Sixty N-Nine if he is s-stuck up in s-some red little b-box over a b-bunch of s-sewerage?"

"Why he can jist take his big old whisky bottle with him! As Jack Shanks says that this guy at the sewer plant says that there is a itsy-bitsy alarm buzzer up there insides of this shitbox which will buzz and wake up Bull when he is required to reverse the gears on his giant shit stirrer."

This is exceptionally Intriguing as I ain't never seen a Giant Shit Stirring Accoutrements!

"A added plus is that although this sewerage shit stinks to high heaven Bull won't smell nothin' as he lost his sense o' smell as a small child. Which is a blessing in disguise. Did you know that your daddy was a boy Gasoline Sniffer, Danny? Like your poor cousin Gregory?"

"N-No. I d-didn't."

As nobody hardly never tells me nothing. (As said.)

"It has ran in our family for eons. And Boy Gasoline Sniffers indubitably lose their sense o' smell. Do you sniff gasoline, Danny?"

"N-No."

"Good. As it can make you lose your sense o' smell or make you stick your fingers up insides of some little bad girl's panties!"

Jarleen laughs like a crazy donkey and screws on the cap of her Carmen Red fingernail polish plus says:

"Why it's perfect, this here job for Bull! This sewer guy which is a member of The United Veterans of America knows that Bull drinks and can't smell nothing. As Jack Shanks told him so. And this sewer guy desires to give Bull a chance at a full and happy life. As Bull is a veteran hisself although he ain't a member of the UVA. Ain't that jist too sweet to be true?"

Jarleen blows on one Carmen Red wet finger nail and laughs additionally! I ain't noted her laugh so much for a excessively long interval and it makes me real contented as I love her as she is My Beauteous Mom. (Plus hope she loves me.) (Which ain't no Certainty.) (By no Matter of Means!) (Alas.) (And Alack.) (Unfortunately.) (For all implicated.)

Suddenly I note that clean pants and a shirt is all laid out for Bull on our dining room table which Jarleen must of ironed which is shocking as she only ever irons the puffy sleeves on her Tangy Mayo uniform.

Jarleen tells me that I got to help Bull garb hisself as he is Inebriated (Behemoth surprise!) and she has got said big cast on

160

her leg which is itchy plus her beauteous finger nails ain't fully dry as of per yet. So I commence to Do As Requested as it is Courteous plus Jarleen impels me to which says:

"Jack Shanks will be here any minute to pick Bull up and take him down to his new job so get to it, damn it!"

DO I COMPLY!

Firstly I wake Bull up which is Arduous in the extremes as he keeps falling back down on to his back severely prone. Secondly I strive to buckle his phony leg on to him but he keeps falling asleep and kicking it off while Somnolent. 3rdly I ain't even sure that Bull *knows* that he has got hisself a sewer job today neither. (This is Highly Problematical!)

However. I finally get Bull garbed in said ironed working garb even although he is snoring and swinging his arms and Stump all over the place which is unfortunate as he whacks me right on my mouth and breaks a segmant off from one front tooth which is all I need for total extreme Frontal ugliness on my piglet face!

I almost commence to blubber but do not as he only done said as he is Thwarted due to his one Legged State plus I am Fully Accustomized to Brutality. (PK Benderson **ET. AL!**) (Plus yellow horrid pee.) Then Jarleen comes in and laughs and Bull wakes up and says to her:

"Hello Joe!" plus takes a swing at her with his phony leg but she jumps back jist in time and he misses and she jist keeps laughing. Unfortunately as I am loitering contiguous he whacks me on the head but not on my bad ear **THANK GOSH**.

Poor Bull jist don't know what he is doing and Jarleen jist keeps on laughing but I have got myself Molested 2 times in 2 minutes! The Laws Of Average Indubitably ain't on my side. Anyhow I finally get his phony leg buckled on.

Then the muscular Jack Shanks drives up and enters in to our home and carries Bull out to his Chevy Pick-up Deluxe and crams him in to the Rear segmant of said on top of the mattress real easy as he possesses a whole alots of practice with said cramming in on said mattress. Ha. Ha. (Sex Joke.) (Pertaining explicitly to Jarleen's and Jack Shank's State of Fucking.)

Jarleen throws her crutches on to the Rear of said Deluxe which whacks Bull right on his head but he don't notice nothing as he is Somnolently snoring. Then Jarleen climbs on to the front seat then Jack Shanks gets in behind of the wheel and they drive right off.

Then **OH MY GOSH!** I suddenly note Bull's phony leg laying on the street in front of our home which he must of kicked off! So I grab it up so as a approaching auto will not Annihilate it. Setting in said auto is Mr Jimmy which kindly smiles the sweetest smile I have ever saw on a humane face plus stops and looks out from his auto's window and says:

"Hi, Danny! Howya keepin?"

"H-Hi, M-Mr J-Jimmy!" I utter in a State of Full Joy.

"Everything goin' all right?" says Mr Jimmy with his kind smile incessant.

"J-Jist f-fine, M-Mr J-Jimmy. H-How are y-y-you?"

"Jist fine. How's the old bicycle runnin'? Did I get your wheel straightened out Kopasetic?"

Mr Jimmy Utilizes this ancient Navel word for OK as he was in the Navy prior plus was A Born Leader Of Men plus a hero. (I have hearby quoted his son Little Norman which told me so.)

"My bike's j-jist f-fine, M-Mr J-Jimmy. Y-Your a life s-saver!"

Mr Jimmy laughs plus utters:

"You mean I got a big round hole in my little round head?" he says inferring to that little do-nut shaped mint candy.

"Oh n-no! I m-mean..."

I jiggle a whole alots plus am exceedingly Mortified as I do not desire for this wondrous kind man to think I would ever utter that he possesses a hole in his head!

Mr Jimmy laughs additionally and his white glamorous teeth glitter jist as glamorous as Jarleen's almost. Although you would have to go a real long way to find a tooth as glamorous as My Beauteous Mom's is.

"Jist kiddin', Danny. Whatcha got there under your arm?"

Suddenly I reminisce that I got Bull's phony leg plus utter:

"M-My Dad B-Bull's ph-phony l-leg."

"Don't he need it?"

"H-He l-lost it. He m-must of k-kicked it off. He h-has j-jist left for w-work."

I am real proud as Bull has got a accurate job for the 1st time in my life!

Mr Jimmy reaches out from his auto and pats me on my arm.

"Good for him! I bet your real happy."

"I s-sure am! B-But I c-can not t-talk c-currantly as I g-got to d-deliver this l-leg d-down to the Gulch S-Sewer W-Works w-where B-Bull is at as h-he m-might n-need it to p-procure his

162

P-Perfect B-Balance."

"I think he jist might! Hop in, Danny. I'll take you down there."

OH MY GOSH! Another ride in Mr Jimmy's new almost auto!

Mr Jimmy opens his auto's brand new door and I sit Bull's phony leg on the auto's floor plus get in and strive to set real close to Mr Jimmy so as to note his conspicuous perky weenie Lump jist below his steering wheel in Perpetuity.

"That is a real nice phony leg you got there, Danny. Yes, a real nice phony leg."

Mr Jimmy **SUDDENLY** lays his warm big hand right on the top of my garbed weenie! I attain a Erection instantaneously plus unbutton his Dungarees like Greased Lightning and one perky Boner pokes right up which glows Gorgeous and convivial! I peel back said's Silken Fourskin and ponder for one interval how plump and pink and pretty it is while Mr Jimmy Courteously Feels me Up Spontaneous but is Contemporaneously excessively careful to note in the direction in which he is driving his auto in **FOR SAFETY'S SAKE.**

Anyhow. I flop right over and shove my mouth on to Mr Jimmy's Boner and suck away in a State of Full Bliss then suddenly here is Bull's phony leg poking right in to my piglet face!

"Here you go, Danny, here's your dad's leg," says Mr Jimmy which stands outside his auto with said leg, "Tell him I said good luck on his new job."

I get out and grab Bull's phony leg and thank Mr Jimmy for the ride plus hold said leg over my crotch to impede his noting my traditional Boner which I can not never impede when he is on my Vicinity! Anyhow. I wave goodbye to Mr Jimmy which drives away as I Contemporaneously note Jack Shanks and Jarleen which is driving away additionally. As I ascertain they are going back to find Bull's leg I holler at them but they do not hear nothing plus drive away Heedless as heck.

So I waddle in to The Lemon Gulch Sewer Works to find my Thwarted one-legged Dad. **OH MY GOSH! DOES IT STINK!** It is lucky for Bull that he lost his State of Smelling due to Gasoline Sniffing in youthful times.

I stick his phony leg up in the air plus holler real loud as said stink fragrance is Dire:

"C-Can any p-person p-please tell m-me w-where my D-Dad is? As h-he n-needs his ph-phony l-leg!"

"I should think *so!*" says this lady which Sashays out from behind of a big sign on which is printed on:

"SEWAGE IS EVERYBODY'S BUSINESS."

There is black goggles over her eyes plus a skinny rubber clamp on her nose so as to impede said stinking fragrances.

"Follow me," says said lady which sounds goofy as her nose clamp impels her to.

"Th-Thank y-you," I say real Courteous. (As per as per usual.)

Said lady leads me to a big segmant of said sewer plant which stinks even worst!

"Up there, in The Shit Box. That there's your Dad. It was hell getting him up there on his one leg!"

The black goggles nose-clamped lady exits away and I climb a stepladder up a big cement wall and look up and note my Dad Bull insides of a red box high up over this behemoth whirly pond of stinking sewerage which is greyish brown of color with yellowish horrid Lumps which gurgles all over it like chickens with their heads chopped off. Said Lumps is getting stirred up by a behemoth iron mixer 7 trillion times bigger then Jarleen's electric food mixer which she don't use currantly as we ain't got no electricity but which she don't use anyhow even if we had of got it as she don't like to mix up variegated food. (As said.)

Anyhow. Bull is high up setting in his Shit Box as he is now Head Shit Stirrer at The Lemon Gulch Sewer Works. Am I proud!

As Bull is snoring up there in said red Box and no other Individual ain't nowheres in this behemoth stinking room I guess it don't make no difference that he is in a State of Full Somnolence as he ain't got nobody to Lord It Over him like Miss Snelgrove which is Jarleen's boss at Tangy Mayo does due to Jarleen being beauteous which Miss Snelgrove ain't plus she ain't never married and ain't likely to as Jarleen says due to her Unoperatable Wart which is as big as a snail's shell by her left nostril. So she Lords It Over Jarleen as per as Recompense. (So To Speak.) (Anyhow that's what Jarleen says.)

I ponder for one interval on how they got Bull way high up over said Shit Pond with his phony leg absent then I note a elevater behind of afourmentioned Shit Box which must of been how.

However. As Bull is hunched over and snoring he don't need to procure his Perfect Balance jist now plus I got to inquire how to use said elevater so I require a assistant and I seen this sewer man kindly smile at me as I was following said lady with the black goggles and nose-clamp on in. Said kind sewer man might inform me on how to Utilize this elevater plus might even possess a protrusive weenie on to the bargain!

So I lie Bull's phony leg contiguous on to the high cement side of this behemoth Shit Pond plus note a Surreal Number stamped on said Shit Pond's wall which says: **VAT 69! OH MY GOSH!** Jist like Bull's all-time favorite beverage which is comforting as he can now drink it and stir it additionally! (Ha. Ha.) (Sewerage Joke!)

I waddle off to look for this kind sewer man for assistance but he ain't where I seen him prior so I go through a door upon which is printed upon:

LOCKER ROOM

I note around for one full interval and there ain't nobody here neither and I am jist about to exit out from said room when I hear the trinkle of a Bevy of coins falling on to the cement floor. I Glare down a hall of garbing lockers and here is this kind sewer man which currantly smiles at me as he yanks down his overalls from which said Bevy of coins has recently prior fell from. I waddle over and squat down contiguous and pick up said coins which I hand back to him excessively Courteous.

"Thank you, son," he utters. I set down adjacent besides of him on the bench plus note that his dear weenie is poking out from it's Y-front's access slot in a friendly Mode as he feasibly has jist alleviated hisself prior to commencing to disgarb plus has neglected to re-install same insides of said Fronts. (Similar to the situation surrounding the Handsome Careless Bus's Driver's.) (Weenie.) This impels my own dear weenie to creep out Surreptitious.

"What brings you to our fair Sewer Works?" says this kind sewer man Courteously.

"M-My D-Dad n-needed his ph-phony l-leg."

"I can sure see how he would of, son," he says which Infers to Bull's ceaseless requirements on his phony leg as I note with joy said man's convivial Penile Ejection Slit.

"Hey what're y'all looking at?" utters said man which smiles additionally, "...my little friend?"

Now ain't that a kind thing which to say?! Explicitly In View Of my behemoth masses which is anything but little!

Said kind man instantaneously yanks his overalls off from his

165

2 legs which is covered all over with gold little hairs. (His legs not his overalls.) (Obviously!) Plus stands up and oscillates towards me and poking right out from his Y-fronts is a exceptionally convivial Boner which wobbles like a hound sucking eggs! Plus his Silken Fourskin is all stretched back as said Boner has attained it's maximum Magnitudes.

Suddenly he shoves said Boner square in to my piglet mouth and I squirt all over his shoeless bare foot!

"JESUS CHRIST!"
"OH MY GOD!"
"WHAT THE HELL HAPPENED?!"

I hear 3 hollers through the door of the Men's Toilet as I wipe my weenie and fat tummy dry with subsequential toilet tissues plus am a-scared that all of The Sewerage Personnel has heard me in a State of Full Onanation behind of said Toilet's door!

I yank my Dungarees as fast as I can up which is real slow due to their exceptional tightness on my sausage fat thighs plus waddle out from said toilet room!

Here is the lady with the black goggles and clamped nose and the kind sewer man which I had saw when I had came in. They are both on top of step ladders looking down on to the behemoth Shit Pond.

"JESUS H CHRIST!" hollers the kind sewer man with the kind smile which ain't currantly smiling.

"HOW'D IT HAPPEN?!" hollers the nose-clamped lady which takes off her black goggles so as to get a better look at something which I ain't able to note as I ain't got no step ladder from which to note it from.

"W-What oc-c-curred?!"

"Stay back, son!" utters the kind sewer man.

"Don't come up here, kid!" utters the black goggles nose-clamped lady with the goofy voice. (Due to said clamp.) (As said.)

"W-What oc-c-curred?!" I holler repetitious as I am exceptionally interested in that Shit Pond as my Dad Bull is it's Head Stirrer.

"Is that there your daddy's wooden leg?" says the kind sewer man which pokes one finger at Bull's phony leg.

"Y-Yes," I utter although said leg ain't wood but is Flesh-Colored BAKELITE. (Which is stamped on it's phony ankle.) I waddle over and pick up said leg from where it lays contiguous on this cement

166

wall adjacent besides of the VAT 69 Surreal Number.

The kind sewer man climbs down off from his step ladder and sticks his hand on to my shoulder. I note real quick that he possesses a protrusive weenie right down his left pants leg which means he ain't garbed in Y-fronts after all but Boxer Shorts. I am real contented as it is always refreshing to get a change of Shorts.

"What's your name, son?" says said kind sewer man.

"D-Danny O'Rourke."

The kind sewer man Genteely grabs Bull's phony leg away from me and utters soft and lowly:

"Your Dad won't be needin' this no more, Danny O'Rourke."

34. THE KIND SEWER MAN

I look up at the Shit Box and it's door which is open swings back and fourth. **THAT SHIT BOX IS EMPTY!**

"You pore boy," says the black goggles nose-clamped lady real high as her nose clamp continually impels this necessity, "You pore, pore boy."

"Your pore Dad is drownded, son," says the kind sewer man.

"Drownded in shit," says said Clamped lady highly, "Ain't it a shame?"

"He musta fell outta the Shit Box," says the kind sewer man.

"He musta," says the Clamped lady, "And drownded hisself."

"H-He ain't g-got h-his P-Perfect B-Balance w-without h-his ph-phony l-leg," I add additionally plus get woozy in the head from the Dire fragrances instantaneously.

"I better take you on home, son," says the kind sewer man jist as I commence to get woozier even.

"Yes," utters the nose-clamped lady which yanks off her black goggles and notes me sad plus whines:

"Get the pore boy outta here! I'll call in the po-leece."

In his auto I tell the kind sewer man the Vicinity on which my home is located on and we drive right off.

I am blue and lowly as I do not desire for no person to croak. None of them! Not even Bull. I did not desire for said Granddad to croak neither even although he was a unkind Liar which emitted farts. (Live And Let Live is my Motto!) (one of them.) (As said.)

The kind sewer man sticks his arm contiguous on my shoulder as we drive along. Bull never done that. Only dear Mr Jimmy ever done that. I flop my head down on to the kind sewer man's lap and as he is kind he permits said head to lay here adjacent besides of his weenie which is only one inch away from my piglet nose. I move my nose over a small bit and touch said weenie with said nose. As I am blubbering the kind sewer man don't notice nothing Irreconcilable plus jist says:

"You pore boy."

His garbed weenie twitches and protrudes a small bit more but as he is infinitely kind he don't know he is Tumescing so he jist utters:

"Pore boy. Pore boy."

I commence to blubber harder then I ever blubbered in my whole life and do I wobble! Do I jiggle!

The kind sewer man pats me on the head plus keeps right on uttering:

"Pore boy, pore boy."

His weenie which gets relentlessly poked by my wet nose is in a State of Full Tumescence when we finally drive up to my home's front gate in front of which is parked Jack Shank's Chevy Pick-up Deluxe in front of. But the kind sewer man still don't seem to note said Tumescence for which I take Full Responsibility for.

I hide my own Fully Erected Erection behind of Bull's phony leg plus hop out from the kind sewer man's auto and holler:

"J-Jarleen! J-Jarleen!"

After a interval My Beauteous Mom which is garbed in her Chartreuse Chenille house robe and white big leg wobbles out on to our front porch on her crutches. I stick Bull's phony leg out at her and she grabs it and the kind sewer man who's Genitalias has shrank fortunately down prior Chats to her about our communal tragedy.

Jarleen jist looks goofy at him as he Divulges what he has came to Divulge then she jist starts hollering:

"Jack! Jack, Sugar! Come quick!"

Jack Shanks runs out on to our front porch with a towel wrapped around his waste and sticks his arm contiguous on to Jarleen's shoulder which still looks goofy. My Unsolicited Arrival has impeded their Esoteric Ventures Indubitably.

"Goddamn it. Bull is drownded," says Jarleen which notes Jack Shanks then pats at her glittering beauteous Pompadour which is sheltered underneath of her hair net of Glorious sequins.

"Poor old Bull," utters Jack Shanks which scratches at his Ostensible weenie through his towel, "Bad luck."

"Yeah," says Jarleen, "But I git a Veteran's widow's pension."

Even although I am exceptionally woozy I ponder if PK Benderson is out there somewheres adjacent getting ready to slam his boot on to my head. What a Dementing item to ponder at a Tragic Time like this is!

35. AMONG SAID SAD CYPRESSES OF ELYSIUM LTD.

We are all of us setting here at Bull's funeral at Cypresses Of Elysium Ltd. Dear Miss Lela McCoy is our songstress which sweetly sings:

> "Oh Danny Boy
> the pipes, the pipes
> are calling
> from glen to glen
> and down the mountainside
> The summer's gone
> and all the rose is falling
> 'Tis you, 'tis you must go
> and I must bide."

I am named for this explicit song which kind dear Lottie Venables plays on the Pump Organ as it is Bull's favorite song which my Deeply Departed Grandma which was Bull's dear mother used to sing and propel I and Bull to blubber which I am doing currantly. Miss McCoy sings and Lottie Venables plays incessantly:

> "But come ye back
> when summer's in the meadow
> Or when the valley's hushed
> and white with snow."

Jarleen and me and Jack Shanks set in row one plus Jarleen has got a big pillow underneath of her knees so as to procure her Perfect Balance as her white big leg impels her to flop fourwords

Against Her Will.

> "'Tis I'll be there
> in sunshine or in shadow
> Oh Danny Boy, Oh Danny Boy,
> I love you so." (Sings kind dear Lela McCoy.) (Sweetly.) (As
per as per usual.)

Mr Jimmy sets jist behind of us in row 2 with his Spouse Miss Brenda. I oscillate my head around to Glare at Mr Jimmy's perky weenie which is always one sure contentment and he notes my old big tears and pats me on the head which impels my weenie to twitch which I ain't able to impede even at funerals. However. I got no desires to attain no Tumescences currantly as this is Bull's last funeral but I Tumesce anyhow as Mr Jimmy smiles with his glamorous teeth and procures his white nice hanky from a pocket contiguous on to his dear weenie and pats my 2 eyes with said sweet weenie-warmed item. Now ain't that a kind thing which to do?

> "And when ye come
> and all the flowers are dying
> If I am dead
> as dead I well may be..."

sings Miss Lela McCoy which clinches both of her fists right over her 2 titties and which don't wheeze none at all.

> "You'll come and find
> the place where I am lying
> and kneel and say
> an Ave there for me..."

My cousin Gregory sets in row 3. He don't like me but I do not care as he bores me Shitless plus is a Gasoline Sniffer without no future excepting Mayhaps as a Shit Stirrer which feasibly ain't too kind of a item to utter as my Deeply Departed Dad Bull was one immediately prior to Departure.

Right adjacent besides of said Sniffer sets his Mom Aunt Edna May which is Bull's sister plus which don't like me neither. But I am impelled to be kind to her as she is one of god's Creatures and kindness is my Motto. (One of them.) (As said.)

However. She is exceptionally boring. Explicitly like what she said to Jarleen when she visited us for 15 minutes after Jarleen had broke her leg in 3 places. Aunt Edna May said:

"Well, Jarleen. Let's face it. Now you got a broke leg."

"Yeah," says My Beauteous Mom, "you can say that again."

"A broke leg ain't the nicest thing in the world," says Aunt Edna May.

"You can say that again," says Jarleen.

"How's your *used* electrical appliances functioning, Jarleen?" says Aunt Edna May like it is a Sin to own Second-Hand Products as her and her Spouse Plumber always purchases Fully New items Whenever Applicable.

Before My Beauteous Mom can utter that *none* of our used electrical appliances is functioning as our electrical wires is Fully Absent Aunt Edna May says:

"Your used electric mixer, Jarleen, how's that *used* electric mixer of yours functioning?"

"OK," says My Beauteous Mom which don't care one way nor the other as she don't never use this mixer anyhow even when we got electrical wires which functions Kopasetic. (As said.)

"Your toaster," says Aunt Edna May, "How's that *used* toaster of yours a-doin'?"

"OK," says Jarleen which scratches on the insides of her white big cast with her straightened out wire coat hanger. (The one with which she prior whacked Flo with and propelled her to bleed.)

"Your *used* washer all right?" says Aunt Edna May after Jarleen don't utter nothing for one full duration as she is bored Shitless.

"Yeah," finally says Jarleen. It's OK too."

"Let's face it. You got lucky," says Aunt Edna May, "it could be a whole lot worse."

"Worse then *what*?" says My Beauteous Mom which pokes her coat hanger real far down insides of her white big leg cast and yawns.

Now ain't that as boring as all heck?

Aunt Edna May's Spouse Earl which is a Plumber ain't came to this funeral neither as he is out Plumbing elsewheres. But he don't like Bull nor me neither which is sad as he possesses a fat weenie which I noted once when he peed in our back yard followed by Barfing prior as he had drank too much. He ain't the smartest Individual here on God's Green Earth as my Deeply Departed

Grandma used to say.

Lottie Venables currently plays said Pump Organ and Miss Lela McCoy ain't hesitated to sing:

> "And I shall hear
> tho' soft you tread above me
> And all my grave
> will warmer, sweeter be..."

The rest of the rows at Cypresses Of Elysium Ltd is all empty excepting for the very last row in which sets Flo and The Lonely Gal in as My Beauteous Mom will not permit Flo to set in row 4 behind of Aunt Edna May and The Gasoline Sniffer as she desires to have a maximum of 3 empty rows between Flo and we. I note that poor Flo is blubbering like a hog in slops.

Jack Shanks is holding Jarleen's hand which ain't blubbering at all as she told me that tears impels her Mascara to run wild. Flo don't care if *hers* runs wild.

Lottie plays said organ and Miss McCoy sings sweet and relentless:

> "If you will bend
> and tell me that you love me
> Then I shall sleep in peace
> until you come to me."

Miss McCoy terminates her singing and blubbers and wheezes Tempestuously as her Implications has came back to Haunt her. Plus so is Lottie Venables which currantly still sets at said Pump Organ. (Blubbering not wheezing.) Lottie is playing the music-only end of said sad song.

Flo is still blubbering but The Lonely Gal ain't but is snoring Somnolently which is typical of one's Fatigued Inebriants.

Mr Jimmy's 2 eyes is red and so is the additional 2 of his Spouse's but they do not blubber. But set Sedate. Like a accurate family should ought to of.

I am really blubbering but more from this sad song then from the croaking. But I hope to blubber due to said croaking in Due Course although I blubbered prior in the kind sewer man's auto. Which could of been proficient. (Ain't sure.)

As the funeral is all over almost every fool plus their brother has got up and went although here in The Garden Of Contemplation Flo loiters besides of a Statuette of The Rod of Moses behind of which The Lonely Gal squats as she desires to pee not Contemplate.

Anyhow. Here I additionally loiter in said Garden Of holding Bull's Celebratory Funerary Urn in which Bull's ashes lays in. Said Urn was gave to *me* as Jarleen and Jack Shanks is long gone as they was impelled to leave early.

Bull was creamated instantaneously on a wood fire like a Hindu as the Deeply Departed's Refrigerator and oven at said Cypresses ain't functioning legitimately due to their electrical lines which was blew down jist like ours and it is real hot and Bull would of rotted Poste Haste.

Anyhow. Here I loiter with said Urn even although Mr Jimmy offered me a ride home in his new auto which I would of loved to have did but did not because as I am loitering in The Garden Of Contemplation I might as well Contemplate. As it was feasibly not the kindest thing in the world for me to be in a State of Full Onanation while my Deeply Departed Dad was drownding in shit.

But as I ain't able to swim I could not of rescued him anyhow. As the shit was way over my head.

36. MEAN AUNT EDNA MAY'S PRESENTIMINT

So here I loiter when up runs mean Aunt Edna May with the goofiest look on her mean face which I have ever saw suddenly!

"Let's face it! We are all of us real broke up about Bull!" hollers said Aunt right at me. **AM I SHOCKED!** As she *never* Chats to me if she can help it but as I am currantly standing right smack in the middle of the Archway Of Peace I guess she is impelled to as she could not jist shove me sideways and run right on by A Deeply Bereaved which Clutches a Celebratory Funerary Urn without uttering nothing!

The Gasoline Sniffer don't utter nothing however but jist ignores me and loiters against a Cypress Of Elysium and listens to his battery radio which should of been mine but *ain't*! (Due to said diseased Granddad's Treachery.)

"I had me a presentimint last week," utters mean Aunt Edna

May right on to my face, "Everything was foretold by The Forces That Be!"

What the heck is she Chatting on?!

"Come on Mom," whines her Gasoline Sniffer, "I got football practice."

"Shut up, Gregory!" hollers said Aunt, "I gotta tell your cousin about my presentimint!"

"Geeez, Mom," whines Gregory which is one year older then I, "Why do you got to talk to that fat sissy?! I wouldn't touch him with a ten foot pole!"

What a rude cousin I got!

"I got to tell him about my presentimint, that's why!" hollers said Aunt, "As it pertains to his poor dead Daddy who was my own dead brother! So *shut* up!"

"Geeez, Mom!"

"We all know jist how your Daddy died, don't we?" hollers Aunt Edna May.

"Y-Yes M-Ma'am."

"Let's face it! Drownding in poopoo ain't no picnic, is it?"

"N-No, M-Ma'am. It s-sure ain't."

"If your Daddy had of had two legs he could of swam, couldn't he of? And kept his head above the poopoo, couldn't he of?"

"Y-Yes, M-Ma'am. P-Plus if he h-hadn't of b-been Inebriated."

"Well, that's as may be! Only God Almighty knows that!"

"*I* kn-kn-kn-know th-that," I say but said Aunt ain't listening to me as per as usual.

"I had me a presentimint," says said Aunt.

I still ain't got no ideal what the heck A Presentimint is!

Aunt Edna May shoots her 2 eyes up like she is noting the big crack in the top of The Archway Of Peace and hollers:

"I dreamed I was a horse, I did! A big black *stallion* horse! And some mean sonofabitch tied me to a post and beat me!"

"Ah Mom!" hollers her Sniffer, "Let's go! I'm gonna be late for practice!"

"You jist shut up, Gregory, and listen to your battery radio that your poor dead Granddad give to *you*!"

What a unkind thing which to say right in front of *me*!

"Anyway," says said Aunt, "After I had got beat senseless by this horse-hating sonofabitch as I was a horse you see as I was dreamin', I jist neighed and whinnied and neighed! And I pawed the ground with my horse's hoofs and pawed and pawed and pawed!"

Her goofy 2 eyes go goofier even and she don't utter nothing for one full duration but jist keeps on looking up at that crack on the top of The Archway Of Peace like a Cock At Dawn. I Glare up there too but do not note nothing Irreconcilable. Then she pokes her mean dried up face real close plus hollers:

"Well! I pawed the ground two or three more times with my hoofs! And then...I shat! And SHAT and SHAT! And then I pawed and neighed and whinnied and SHAT some more! And pawed and SHAT and pawed and SHAT and pawed and SHAT!"

Aunt Edna May's eyes has became excessively big and goofy!

"Then this here mean sonofabitch beat me some more! And I pawed the ground some more and SHAT some more! As I was a horse, you see, still a poor defenceless horse as I was dreamin'. Well I pawed and SHAT and neighed and SHAT and pawed! Then I jist whinnied and SHAT and SHAT and SHAT and SHAT! And do you know what?" hollers said Aunt, "Do you know what?!"

Said Aunt jerks in exceptionally contiguous and screams right on to my piglet face:

"The next mornin' when I waked up I really *HAD* SHAT!"

"Oh, come on, Mom, goddamn it," whines said Sniffer.

"Shut up Greg you selfish little runt!" hollers Aunt Edna May, which sticks her thumb at her poor misguided son real mean and says to me:

"It's jist a phrase he's a-goin' through."

"Ah Mom," whines Gregory which turns the Volume dial up on our Lying Granddad's battery radio and I am *real real* contented to note that said radio's battery is getting *real real* low.

"So here I was the morning after my terrible dream. I had *pooped* everywhere!" hollers my Aunt which don't wish to be discommoded, "My and Earl's bed looked like a big ole bowl of chocolate pudding! Here I was drownding in poopoo! Jist like my poor dead brother! And this was two whole days before poor Bull drownded hisself! TWO WHOLE DAYS!"

Aunt Edna May notes me like I am supposed to say something about drownding in poopoo but if I had of shat on my bed the way she shat on her bed I would of kept this Shitting Information to myself! Anyhow. My Deeply Departed Grandma always said that we was swimming in shit from the day we was born. So it ain't any big deal. As hogs live their total lives among it and ain't None The Worse For Wear.

175

Aunt Edna May nods her head at me up and down and up and down real slow but don't say nothing and still looks goofy.

"Mom! Fer chrissakes! I'm late for my practice!"

But Aunt Edna May don't pay no attention to The Sniffer but jist grabs Bull's Celebratory Funerary Urn right away from me and yanks off it's lid and pokes her skinny finger in!

"Ashes to ashes!" she hollers, "Dust to Dust! You jist remember that, Danny."

She sniffs her skinny finger then wipes Bull's ashes off on to her puffy Calico sleeve and shoves his Celebratory Funerary Urn back at me.

"Re-m-member w-what?"

"My presentimint!" shrieks Aunt Edna May, "My goddamned presentiment!"

"I s-sure w-will, Aunt Edna M-M-May," I utter Alacrously.

Gregory gives me The Finger and pokes his battery radio up in to the air for every fool plus their brother to note and then her and him go off and get in to their auto and exit away and I say to myself: Presentimint. Presentimint. Plus make Mental Notations to look it up on my Severely Abridged Webster's. This takes my brains off from what mean Individuals them two is. (Plus her Spouse Earl even although he possesses a fat weenie and is presently absent.)

I note around to see if PK Benderson is anywheres contiguous and am jist commencing to exit out from The Garden Of Contemplation through The Archway Of Peace when Flo and The Lonely Gal comes up and Flo says Infinitely kind:

"I am real sorry about poor Bull."

"Me too," says The Lonely Gal which Glares at Flo, "though I've never had the pleasure of meeting him."

"Pleasure is correct!" says Flo which wipes at a black big tear as her Mascara has ran wild out from one eye, "He was a real pleasurable guy."

The Lonely Gal don't seem exceedingly contented with Flo's prior sentence as her face has went all reddish and her eyes squints plus she says:

"He was a *job*. A job is a job is a job, *Florence*."

"Flo," says Flo, "My name is Firenze and they call me *Flo*."

"I will call you whatever the fucking fuck I please to call you, *Florence*!"

I get a exceptionally Stalwart whiff of Alcoholic Whisky from The Gal's premises which reminds me of Bull and I hug his

Celebratory Funerary Urn tight adjacently contiguous up against of my fat big jiggly tummy. Please do not ask me why. As I can not tell you. As I do not know.

"Shut your mouth, honey," says Flo to The Gal, "or I will cut off your flapping tongue."

Flo opens her purse and takes out her horrid knife and snaps it open plus says:

"This is a *funeral* and don't you forget it! And we are speaking to *The Bereaved!*"

The Lonely Gal sways real far over and real far back and I wonder why I ever cared if she loved me or not as her Humane Condition ain't like mine at all. As she jist ain't kind! **PLUS ONLY SAYS I LOVE YOU WHEN SHE IS INEBRIATED! OR ON THE RADIO WHERE IT DON'T COUNT!** This is exceptionally Disillusioning.

"I wish to apologize, Danny, for The Lonely Gal today and for the both of us the other day at The Hotel LaVernia Entertainment Lounge. I am real ashamed of myself and I'm sorry that we made your little girlfriend cry and broke up your entertainment show."

"M-Miranda cries e-e-exceedingly e-easy," I say real Courteous as I do not desire for Flo to feel Reprehensable for her bad behavior prior as she is so currantly kind.

Then The Lonely Gal wobbles through The Archway Of Peace over to a explicit Cypress Of Elysium and I hope she ain't about to squat plus additionally pee nor Barf nor have one of her Frothing Fits. (Ladies is a Enigma.) (Explicitly inebriated Inebriants with fowl languages.)

"What the *fuck*?!" she hollers at this poor Cypress tree like she is talking to it, "What the fucking *fuck*?!"

She sticks her nose on to said tree plus sniffs real loud.

"Cypresses?! Cypresses of fucking Elysium?! You're a fucking *Eucalyptus!*"

I am laying on my bed Ruminating as it is night. I don't guess I am *real* sad like I should ought to purport to be but only Quasi-sad which I guess is OK although I feasibly should be a whole alots sadder. But ain't. (Sadly.)

Bull won't never hit me on my ear no more nor break my tooth by a accident nor compel my lip to bleed nor snore on the top of our Davenport neither nor never say Hello Joe. What do you know? What are a-cookin' in Tokio? Plus make his eyes on to 2 slits like a

Japanese Individual's.

I ponder that it is jist too bad that Bull got Thwarted as I know jist how bad he must of felt as I am Thwarted too and if I was Fully Thwarted In Perpetuity like Bull was due to his leg lack maybe I might be propelled to be a Inebriant too or even a Homocidal Sex Maniac and end up like Exhibit "A" on a slab in a courtroom. Who knows what a Fully Accurate Thwarting can lead to?

OH MY GOSH! I GOTTA BARF!

37. CONDOLATIONS

I Barfed my darn guts out last night! The 1st big Barf puddle squirted right on to the floor of my bedroom as I could not waddle to our bathroom in time plus Barfed variegated more times while In-Transit.

I got all variegated Barf wiped up *finally* plus was able to shoot subsequential Barf Squirts in to our toilet jist prior to when Jarleen and Jack Shanks had came back from their bowling to which they had went to when exiting out from Bull's funeral early as Jack Shanks preserved a bowling alley as Gulch Alleys possesses only 6 of which 3 of which is being sanded down as they was Out Of Kilter and the residents of Lemon Gulch adore the State of Bowling which is a Thriving Industry. (But I Digress.)

Lucky for me Jarleen could not smell none of my Barf due to her Evening in Paris which was squirted on Exuberant on account of old poor Thwarted Bull's funeral.

However. Jarleen did not permit Jack Shanks to enter in to our home neither as Jarleen says Bull's Corpse ain't even cold as of per yet. But as Bull is currantly sprinkled in to his Celebratory Funerary Urn I ain't sure what Jarleen means by Cold. Ladies is a Enigma. (As sporadically said.)

The telephone rings. As Jarleen is sleeping in her bedroom and not working at Tangy as of per yet due to her broke leg and as I always almost answer anyhow I pick up it's receiver and utter:

"H-Hello?"

"Danny?"

"Th-This is h-him."

"It's Miranda."

"H-Hello, M-Miranda."

"I'm awfully sorry about your father, Danny."

"Th-Thank y-you."

"I'm sorry I could not come to the funeral but I have influenza."

"I'm s-sorry th-that y-your s-sick, dear M-Miranda."

"Thank you. I'm in bed. I have a very high temperature too."

"Gee, th-that's too b-bad."

"I just wanted you to know that I would have come to the funeral if I hadn't have had influenza."

"Th-Thank you. Th-That's real n-nice of you to s-say so."

"I started to get it the other day when we sang at The Hotel LaVernia for The Old Timers which is possibly why I cried for twelve minutes."

"Y-Yeah. Th-That is r-real f-feasible."

"It took a very long time to come down with it because this particular influenza has a very long incubation period."

"I h-heard of th-those," I say although I ain't never but desire to be extra kind as Miranda suffered a whole alots from The Hotel LaVernia Entertainment Lounge tragedy due to her most tender Sensitivities plus is currently Severely Incapacitated.

"D-Did you v-v-v-v-v-b-barf?"

"Yes. A little. I vomited a little bit.

"I v-v-v-v-v-b-barfed all l-last n-night."

"You *did*?!"

"D-Do you th-think I g-got the in-fl-fluenza too?"

"Have you got a temperature?"

"I d-do not th-think so."

But I note that my brows feels a small bit hot simultaneously as I slap it with my hand. However. I do not utter nothing about it to Miranda as she might think I am a bigger baby then I am in real actuality!

"Then you probably don't. Not if you don't have a temperature. Why do you think you vomited?" says Miranda which Infers kindly to my Barfing.

"I d-do not kn-know."

"Do you think you vomited from...grief? Lots of people do. Do you think you vomited from...grief?"

"I d-do not th-think s-so," I say as I ain't positive I got said yet. (Accurate Grief.) (Although I did feel woozy at the Sewer Works but said wooziness could of been due to the stinking fragrances and not undeniable Grief.)

"Oh," utters Miranda.

Then there is a exceptionally long interval when nobody ain't saying nothing to nobody and I ascertain that dear Miranda is in a Full State of Fatigue and requires instantaneous Relaxation so I utter:

"W-Well. Th-Thank you for c-calling, dear M-Miranda. It is r-real k-kind of y-you."

"I had to call, Danny. Because you're a very sweet boy and you didn't deserve for your father to die."

Miranda ain't never even met my father personal **THANK GOSH!** But what a kind thing which to say anyhow.

Then Miranda coughs a whole alots which hurts my ear plus says:

"Goodbye, Danny."

"G-Goodbye, d-dear M-Miranda."

I hang up the receiver and my brows gets real hot but I reminisce suddenly that as it is Thursday I got to get my Ass In Gear and mow dear Lottie Venables' lawn!

So I squeeze my horridly tight Dungarees up on to my fat sausage 2 legs but said Dungarees is so horridly tight that I attain a instantaneous Erection as I ain't Onanated recently due to Bull's funeral and Barfing. So I ascertain to Onanate Fourthwith and I ponder My Divine Fred Foster which is 14 plus reach for my can of Peanut Oil.

When said Onanation is terminant I take a cup of coffee to Jarleen which is in bed as she is still Somnolent. I sit the coffee on her bedside's table and waddle back to the kitchen to boil my Oatmeal but as I feel Dire currantly I ascertain not to boil none plus ain't hungry and I got to go over right now and mow Lottie's lawn before I keel over as it is Thursday and the sun is merciless plus getting More-So.

As I waddle out from our home I note that My Divine Fred Foster is watering their lawn with a water hose with a Water-Saver Sprinkler head due to our Drought. Plus he is garbed in his cut-off Dungarees with his Bevy of keys hanging on to his key ring on his belt holder with no shirt on nor nothing and is oscillating way-over-backwords In Order To spray water on the top of a exceedingly wilty Jackaranda tree as although it is morning only it is boiling hot. (As said.) (Due to said.) (Sun.)

Fred's weenie Juts out real nice in it's currant posture and I Glare at it intensely for one full interval plus utter:

"H-Hi, F-Fred my old p-pal," and waddle closer for a better

peep at said dear weenie.

"Hi, Danny. How's it goin'?"

"OK, I g-guess, m-my old p-pal."

My tummy jiggles and my heinie wobbles due to Fred's Incongruity and my racked nerves plus other items such as funerals plus **I AM LITERATELY BURNING UP!** But I desire to kindly Chat with My Divine Fred so say:

"H-Hey, old p-pal. D-Didn't I s-see you the other d-day at The Hotel La V-Vernia? C-Coming out f-from the M-Men's Room?"

Fred gets red on his face for one interval but takes a deep big breath of Oxygen and smiles real kind plus utters:

"My Mom says she is awful sorry for what she hollered at you. *Awful* sorry. 'Cause she don't think you didn't mean to do what you done with them spiders."

"M-My D-Dad's d-dead," I utter plus am so Overwhelmed that I got to lean on our Mesh Wire fence to procure my Perfect Balance. Said prior sentence sounds goofy insides of my brains which is making Dire whistling noises insides of my ears.

"Yeah," says Fred which Infers to said croaking, "I know."

"H-He croaked th-three d-days ago. P-Plus w-was c-creamated instant-t-taneously as it w-was s-so h-hot he would of r-rotted if they h-hadn't of d-due to th-their D-Dearth of R-Refrigeration."

"Gee. That's too bad, Danny. We would of come to the funeral but was out of town as my Grandma was sick."

"Y-Yes," I say. I love Fred to look at me so kind and I currantly note his Alluring blue beauteous 2 eyes even more then his garbed dear Genitalias. Do not ask me why. As I can not tell you. As I do not know.

"I'm sure sorry."

"Th-thank you F-Fred," I utter with exceptional sincerity, "W-Well. I g-got to go m-mow L-Lottie V-Venable's l-lawn."

"Even though your Dad jist died?"

"As he is a c-corpse c-currantly and w-we k-keep h-him in h-his C-Celebratory F-Funerary Urn it d-don't m-make n-no d-difference to h-him."

My head is whirling all over the place like some indeterminant Individual has jist hit me on the top of it with a Blunt Instrument! (Like in The Keyhole.) Fred notes me real blue and lowly.

"Don't you miss your Dad?"

"N-Not y-yet. I g-guess he ain't b-been d-dead l-long enough."

"Yeah. I guess so."

"Anyhow. H-He n-never s-said n-nothing excepting H-Hello J-Joe. W-What d-do you kn-know? W-What are a-cookin' in T-Tokio."

"Tokyo?"

"Y-Yeah."

"Why Tokyo?"

"I d-do n-not kn-know. If I had of h-had any ideal about w-what he w-was t-talkin' about I w-would of kn-knew..."

I almost keel over plus grab our fence post in a Flurry, "I d-don't." I utter which completes my prior sentence.

Fred jist notes me peculiar for a interval then utters:

"Well, I got to go get dressed as I got to go shoppin' with Mom. Oh yeah, I want to thank you for keeping my secret. You know? What happened on the bus?"

"I w-won't n-never tell n-nobody, F-Fred my old p-pal."

"Your a good man, Danny. See ya later."

I got to hold on to our Wire Mesh Fence post jist so as to keep from keeling over as that was such a kind thing which to say but I feel like keeling over anyhow. But Fred don't note nothing Irreconcilable and turns off their water and puts down his Water-Saver hose sprinkler plus goes insides of his home.

I note his closed shut front door for a exceedingly long duration after he has went in. As I love him Dire.

38. POOR MISGUIDED PK BENDERSON

I waddle out from our front gate as I got to mow Lottie Venables's lawn Come Rain Or Come Shine but suddenly PK Benderson sneaks out from behind of our broke down 1936 old Plymouth behind of which he has hid behind of and grabs me!

"Where do you think your goin' you fat Sissy Prevert!"

"I g-got to mow M-Miss V-Venable's L-lawn," I utter Feverish.

My poor brows is hot as a Corn Fritter in July and I am sweating like a stuck pig plus wobbling like a hound sucking eggs!

"*That* old dike!" hollers PK.

"D-Dike? W-What's d-dike?"

"What do you c-c-c-c-care, you f-f-f-f-fat c-c-c-c-c-cocksucking s-s-sissy b-b-bastard!" hollers PK which Ridicules my horrid stutter!

182

I hope My Divine Fred Foster can not hear these Barbarious words which PK is hollering as I ain't no Bastard although he is correct about the Fat and the Sissy and the Cocksucker as my fondest wishes is to suck said in general and Fred Foster's implicitly. Please do not ask me why. As I can not tell you. As I do not know.

Then PK sticks out his leg and shoves me right over it! So here I am laying flat on my back prone on my own street supinely in front of my own front gate in front of my own home! What a Humane Condition!

My yellow little teeth is all chattering like they traditionally do Underneath Of Duress plus I ponder I will Barf and my head feels even hotter plus my black and white small dog Tinker which has jist ran up is barking at PK like a chicken with their head chopped off and I hope he don't Maim her!

PK now slams his big boot on to my jiggling tummy and shoves the air out from all my Oracles in one behemoth **WHOOSH!**

I strive to ponder some contenting nice item like the multiple weenies of Fred or Mr Jimmy or Burt or poor Wolfgang or Miss Fishlock's Slow Son or my dear Senior or the kind sewer man! Or even dear Miranda Cosmonopolis or Lottie Venables and Miss McCoy or The Steamrollers which is weeniless in the extremes! But as my head feels so hot and goofy I ain't able to ponder nothing excepting PK's big boot on my fat big tummy. I hope to gosh he ain't going to slam said boot on to my head! But *is*! Plus *does*! **OWWWWWWWW! DOES THIS HURT!**

"Fat Sissy cocksuckers jist adorrrrrrre eatin' shit!" hollers PK which shoves my head right at a dog turd on our road which probably belongs to my very own dear black and white small dog. Why is there so much shit in Lemon Gulch?! Even from *good* dogs?

"Hey! You fat Sissy bastard!" hollers PK which Glares down on to me, "Didn't your lazy asshole daddy jist kick the bucket?! Didn't that shitty old drunk jist croak in shit?!"

"M-My Dad ain't n-no d-drunk," I holler, "H-He was a C-Certified Inebriant!"

I am currently blubbering as per as usual and my head feels like some unspecified person has sat it on fire!

"He was a dumb old one-legged drunk!" hollers PK which punches me in my fat jiggly tummy with his big boot. "Everbody in Lemon Gulch knows it! It ain't no fuckin' secret!"

"Th-that ain't a-accurate!" I holler plus blubber relentlessly.

183

"It j-jist ain't a-accurate t-to t-talk th-that w-way t-to the D-Deeply Bereaved about his D-Deeply D-Departed!"

"Oh, *ain't* it? Well your Mom's a whore too!" he Insinuates, "She fucked ever man at Tangy who could git it up! Everbody knows it! I even fucked her with my little finger!"

"Y-Your a L-LIAR!"

"What did you say to me?! What did you say, you big fat prevert?!"

I have became Teaming with shivers plus am covered all over with more sweaty Prespiration then traditional but PK don't show me no Mercy and keeps on shoving his boot in to my tummy and impelling it to whoosh. I ponder I will Barf but don't but jist lay here in the dirt plus blubber Dire.

THEN SOMETHING OCCURS! It is like a whole alots of itsy-bitsy explosions insides of my head! Suddenly my fat 2 hands grab PK's boot! PK Glares down at me real surprized and falls backwords almost!

"Why you fat bastard!"

He pushes my piglet face right in to said dog's turd and kicks Tinker which is striving to bite his leg!

"G-Go away T-Tinker!" I holler and wipe the dog turd off from my cheek with my sleeve plus oscillate sideways so fast that PK flops on his back FLAT on to the ground with a behemoth whack which scares Tinker right back through our front gate!

"I'm gonna kill you! I'm gonna kill you!" hollers PK which don't have time to holler nothing else! As:

2 LEGS JUMPS ME UP AND STANDS ME RIGHT OVER PK AS HE LAYS FLAT ON HIS BACK ON OUR ROAD!

THESE 2 LEGS TAKES A BIG JUMP UP IN THE AIR AND DOWN COMES A FAT BIG HEINIE RIGHT ON TO PK'S TUMMY AND ALL HIS AIR WHOOSHES OUT FROM ALL HIS ORACLES JIST LIKE MINE DONE PRIOR!

WHAT IS OCCURRING?! HERE I AM SETTING RIGHT ON THE TOP OF PK BENDERSON AND I DO NOT KNOW HOW I COME HERE! AND WHO'S LEGS IS THESE?! AND WHO'S HEINIE IS THIS?!

PK LOOKS AT ME GOOFY AS HE IS EXCEPTIONALLY SHOCKED BY THIS UNSOLICITED ASSAULT!

THEN INSTANTANEOUSLY I SEE 2 HANDS TRANSMOGRIFY THEIRSELVES IN TO 2 FISTS AND DOWN DEEP INSIDES OF MY BRAINS I SEE FLO THROWING

HER SCARY KNIFE AT THAT POLICEMAN AND ALL THEM SMOKING LADIES IS WAVING BEER CANS AND HOLLERING FOWL LANGUAGE! AND THEM MEAN OLD TIMERS IS HOLLERING AT ME AND DEAR POOR MIRANDA! AND I SEE THE MEAN FACE OF THE FATTER EVEN THEN I BOY AND THE UNKIND RECEPTIONIST!

THEN WHIZZING THROUGH MY BRAINS WHIZZES A WHOLE ALOTS OF MEAN WORDS LIKE HURT AND MAIM AND GET EVEN AND MEAN ASSHOLE BASTARD AND VICTIMS LEFT IN LITTLE SEGMANTS IN SUITCASES IN BUS'S STATIONS PLUS UNKIND FEELINGS LIKE SMASHING AND PULVERIZING AND BASHING PERSON'S FACES IN AND MAKING PERSONS BLUBBER! AND MORE MUTILATIONS LIKE IN THE KEYHOLE THEN I FEEL TWO BEHEMOTH BUFFALO HORNS POKE OUT ON TO EACH SIDE OF MY HEAD!

"Let me up," says PK in a Itsy-Bitsy voice.

But a hollering horrid voice hollers:

"N-NO! N-NOOOOOOOOO!"

It seems like it is me which hollers but it ain't! As I don't never holler so mean nor so loud! It jist ain't me which is hollering:

"N-NOOOOOOOO! I WILL N-NOT L-LET YOU UP!"

Then these 2 fists which ain't mine commences to pound right down on to the middle of PK's face. SMACK! SMACK! SMACK!

PK tries real hard to arise hisself up but these goofy fat 2 legs which is attached to this fat big heinie clamps right down over his 2 sides and pins him flat and the 2 fists keeps on pounding! SMACK! SMACK! SMACK!

"Stop!" utters PK. But this horrid unkind hollering voice which sounds like me but ain't hollers:

"N-N-N-N-NOOOOOOOOOO! I W-W-WILL N-NOT S-S-STOP!"

I hear a big **WHACK** and PK's nose goes goofy and blood shoots out! I look down at his face and his 2 eyes jist look up at me like they ain't got no ideal what the heck is occurring! I do not know what is occurring neither as my head is hurting and I feel Barfy plus woozy in the extremes!

But these 2 fists keeps pounding away and pounding away! These fists which ain't mine as I can not do nothing to impede them!

Pretty soon PK's eyes gets exceptionally swelled up and

shut but these 2 fists keeps pounding away! **SMACK! SMACK! SMACK!** There is blood all over PK's shirt and a bloody big split on his lip!

SMACK! SMACK! SMACK! Here is a tooth which jist hangs sideways out from PK's bleedy lip!

"Please stop, Danny."

I note that this little voice comes from this bloody squinched up face which used to look a whole alots like PK. But why should said say my name Danny as *I* ain't doing nothing at all. I am jist setting on top of PK noting these whacking 2 fists whacking. **WHACKING! WHACKING! WHACKING!**

"Please stop, Danny O'Rourke," utters PK's itsy-bitsy voice which utters Danny O'Rourke not Queer nor Prevert nor Fat Ass Sissy Bastard! But *Danny O'Rourke*!

"Danny! Danny! Your killin' him!"

IT IS FRED FOSTER! His warm arms is right around my neck and his hot nice face is instantaneously contiguous on to my sweaty piglet cheek! **OH MY GOSH!** His sweet hot breath is wondrous!

But everything is fuzzy plus like in a slow-motion Major Motion Picture.

Fred has currantly got his 2 arms on to both sides of me and is striving to hold them 2 fists still!

THEN I NOTE INSTANTANEOUSLY THAT IT IS MY OWN 2 FISTS WHICH IS POUNDING AWAY AT THIS BLOODY POOR FACE!

"Danny! You got to stop! Your killin' him!"

Fred Foster hugs me *real* tight and my fists stops whacking and my piglet eyes clinch tight shut and my head feels hot and my weenie feels hot and I attain a behemoth Erection as Fred which is 14 hugs me *real* tight! Then every item goes jist as black as Flo's dyed black hair.

Then here I am laying on my fat tummy with my nose poking right in to the mattress in the Rear of Jack Shanks' Deluxe which is whizzing down The Port City Highway plus Evening In Paris perfume comes whooshing out from said mattress. Then everything goes black again. Exceedingly black. Excessively black. REAL REAL *REAL* **BLACK**.

39. THE HANDSOME 2 HOSPITAL SAILORS

I wake up plus am exceptionally groggy and so weak that Vicarious motion ain't perfectly feasible. I note that I am in a white nice bed in a white nice room which smells jist like clean nice soap. At the other side of said room is 2 additional beds which Comprise 2 handsome guys insides of them which is sailors as they got sailor's uniforms dingling on 2 hooks contiguous.

One handsome sailor says to the other handsome sailor:

"Hey, Bob, the kid's awake!"

"Hey nurse!" hollers Bob, "the kid's awake!"

"Of c-course I'm a-w-wake!" I utter, "I g-got to f-fix m-my Oatmeal and J-Jarleen's c-coffee!"

Then I Ruminate instantaneously that my own bed and own room ain't never been so white nor so clean nor so nice smelling and with never no handsome 2 sailors insides of it so I ascertain I am laying prone in a hospital. Or else dreaming.

Anyhow. I hope said handsome 2 hospital sailors will arise up out from their respectable beds and garb theirselves as I desire to note their weenies as all sailors possess excessively protrusive ones due to a wondrous flap-fly on their sailor's pants which buttons on each side and over the top and impels their weenies to lay fully down one leg or fully down the other. There jist ain't no go-between on a sailor's crotch. (But I Digress!)

Then a nurse comes in which says:

"Oh thank God!" plus yanks a plastic tube out from my arm and wheels a funny bottle hanging off from a hanger away and exits out so I ponder I *am* in a hospital plus ain't dreaming but ain't sure how I could of came here so sudden.

Then the nurse comes right back in plus is followed by Jarleen and Jack Shanks! **OH MY GOSH!**

"I see your better," utters Jarleen, "We was real worried."

Now ain't that a kind thing for My Beauteous Mom which to utter?!

"Jack brung me over when the hospital called this morning and said you was mumblin' in your sleep. We jist got here," says My Beauteous Mom.

"W-Where am I?"

"Your in Port City Navel Hospital," says Jarleen which takes a behemoth puff on her cigarette and blows said right on to my piglet face, "In which you got a perfect right to be in. As your dad Bull was a Navel veteran. You been here a month. Don't you remember *nothing*?"

"N-Nothin'," I utter plus ponder that somebody is making a behemoth mistake as how could I of been here for one total month?!

"You got brain fever," says Jarleen. It's a-goin' around."

"Yeah," says Jack Shanks which hardly never ever says nothing, "Sure is."

"You was dee-lerious," says Jarleen, "We could of lost you. Firstly Bull and now you."

I suddenly reminisce that Bull was drownded plus feel blue and lowly for one full interval plus hope that Jarleen feasibly might commence to blubber due to these here sad Circumstances but don't but jist notes in to her little Pancake Make-Up Compact Mirror and yanks a hunk of Raging Ruby Lipstick out from besides of a glamorous tooth plus snaps said Compact shut and says:

"You realize where that would of left *me*, Danny? All alone in this mean old world? You got the time, Jack?"

"Yeah." says Jack Shanks.

"Well what time *is* it?!" hollers My Beauteous Mom which snaps open her Compact again and pokes her glamorous teeth in to it's mirror plus yanks a hunk of cigarette's tobacco off from one additional tooth.

"Ten-forty-five," says Jack Shanks which Infers to Jarleen's time Query.

Jarleen notes me for one interval then squinches up her brows and drops her cigarette on the floor and smashes it out with one of her clear plastic nice high heeled shoes with the Polka Dot roses on their opened toes. (My all time favorites.) (As said.)

"We got to go, Danny, ain't we Jack?" says Jarleen which intensely notes the handsome 2 hospital sailors like they was the last 2 Compatriots on God's Green Earth.

"Yeah. We got a alley preserved at Gulch Alleys," says Jack Shanks which scratches at something indeterminant among the 33 Billion pleats on his Zoot-Suit pants.

Then Jarleen gives me jist about the contentest smile I ever seen and I feel wondrous as she don't do this real Repetitiously. I ponder she is going to squat right down and kiss me so I pucker up my lip real content and shut my eyes and await said kind Act. However. She don't kiss me but jist kicks her leg way up in the air and hollers:

"See?!"

Her white big leg cast has went!

"Weeeeeh!" she hollers, "They took it off last week, didn't they, Jack?"

"Yeah. Last week."

Jarleen winks at Jack plus says:

"Now we can *really* bowl can't we, sugar?"

Jack Shanks don't utter nothing but jist nods his head up and down and I note real hard at his crotch but still ain't able to note no weenie Lump amidst all of them pleats. I guess that lump I seen when he was wrapped in a towel on our front porch jist after Bull was drownded in shit was a Rarified Episode.

Jarleen comes real close to me again and then looks excessively serious.

"There is something I forgot to tell you, Danny. Something I should of oughta of told you when I and Jack first come in."

My heart commences to thump like a chicken with their head chopped off as I ascertain My Beauteous Mom is about to Divulge that she loves me as I been so sick and all.

Well. She squats down real adjacent plus puts her mouth contiguous. Will I now receive my Peck on the cheek for which I traditionally awaited by our front door every morning when Jarleen exited out for work for?! I jist shut my piglet 2 eyes and await joyous for said Peck and/or variegated kind words which is sure to compel me into a State of Full Bliss.

But My Beauteous Mom jist hollers:

"Our regular electrical wires has been set up! I can currently operate my electrical leg razor! Ain't that jist wonnnnnnnderful?!"

She shoves one of her shaved legs in my face and yanks my hand out so as I can feel how smooth and beauteous it is.

"Y-Yes," I say plus jerk my hand back and poke my fingers in to my ears as they hurt something awful from her hollering!

Then Jack Shanks notes me for one interval plus squinches up his brows and says:

"Your skinny," which impels Jarleen to yank her eyes off from the handsome 2 hospital sailors at which she has been Glaring at plus utter:

"Why your skinny! Your not fat no more!"

I note my abdomenal segmants. Where is my fat tummy? I *am* dreaming! But it is a exceptionally Adequate dream!

Jarleen says she will come and see me the day after tomorrow plus is contented I did not croak and her and Jack Shanks exits out from my hospital's room.

Am I *really* skinny? I ponder that my fat heinie is jist sagging deep down in to my hospital's bed's soft springs and dragging my fat tummy right on down with it. But I ascertain anyhow to jump right out from my bed so as to note one's total Torso In Perpetuity. So I jump right out! But keel right on over instantaneously!

Before I can ponder what is occurring them handsome 2 hospital sailors jumps up from their respectable beds and runs over to me and commences to lift me up off from this Navel hospital's room's floor.

As said kind 2 lifts me my head oscillates back and fourth and I Glare right up their 2 hospital's shirts in Unison and note a convivial Boner underneath of each which impels me to attain a additional one of my own plus grab theirs Capricious!

"Hey pal!" hollers one handsome hospital sailor, "Jist what the heck do you think *your* doin'?!"

"Hey pal!" hollers this other handsome hospital sailor, "My sailor pal is right! What the heck do you think *your* doin'?!"

But both of said sailors lift up their 2 hospital's shirts convenient so as I got Infinitive Access to both of them 2 convivial Penile items!

Anyhow. Here I am Supinely squishing up and down 2 Silken Fourskins as both of said loiter on each side of my hospital's bed with their white nice lifted up hospital's shirts! Instantaneously we are a squirting trio! But this joyous event occurs among my brains only as only me is squirting due to one silently Mute Onanation underneath of my blanket in a State of Full Insulation as I ain't never got out from my bed in the 1st place as I feel so darn weak I couldn't of.

I grab 6 Kleenexs from a Kleenex box which lays contiguous plus wipe up my wet weenie and tummy.

Then one handsome sailor looks up from the funnybook he is Perusing and notes me plus utters:

"Your a real good looking kid, Danny."

What?! **ME** goodlooking?! Is said sailor crazy?!

Then am I surprised! Dear Miranda Cosmonopolis Spontaneously waddles right in!

"Hello, Danny," she says and sets down on a chair which squeaks like a chicken with their head chopped off.

"H-Hello, dear M-Miranda. R-Real k-kind of y-you to c-come."

"Miss Fishlock brought me. She is buying sheet music at

Thearle's Music. It's open on Saturdays, you know, all day. We ran in to your mother on the street and she said you were awake. Danny! I am *so* happy as we were worried sick!"

Now ain't that a kind thing which to say?!

"Th-Thank you, M-Miranda."

"H-How is M-Miss F-Fishlock and her S-Slow S-Son?"

I ponder the handsome Bastard's Loquacious weenie which I had the Delectation of Feeling Up for one full duration with my elbow. And said delighted pondering impels my own weenie to Snap To Attention so I lift up my knees so as so dear Miranda can not note nothing Irreconcilable poking out from underneath of my hospital's bed's blanket. (Like one behemoth BONER for a example!)

"Fine," says Miranda which don't note my arising up Boner but answers my Inquisition about the respectable conditions of Miss Fishlock and her Slow Son.

"H-How is y-your influenza g-going, M-Miranda?"

"How kind of you to ask. I have been really well for two weeks."

Dear Miranda wipes a old big tear out from her eye plus utters:

"I have been so worried about you Danny that I almost died."

"S-So d-did I," I utter Jovial so as dear Miranda will see it is a joke and will laugh too and not be so blue and lowly. As it might Debilitate her Sensitivities. But Miranda which looks real serious for one full interval jist utters:

"Did you know that Paul K Benderson is in this hospital?"

OH MY GOSH! PK has came to slam his boot on my head and/or tummy!

"I g-guess he has c-came t-to t-torment me," I utter With Alacrity.

"Has *come* to torment you, Danny. Not has *came*. But he isn't strong enough to torment anybody. Not now."

"W-Where is h-he?" I utter real soft so as if PK is hiding adjacent he won't hear nothing.

"He is just down the hall. The doctors are going to make him a new nose. His was badly broken. It has not healed properly. They will have to break it again and start all over from scratch. He also has multiple fractures of an arm and leg which have had to be re-broken and set again too. And he needs two new front teeth. His were..."

"D-Did h-he have a accident?"

Miranda don't utter nothing at all for one interval. Then hollers almost:

"Don't you remember what happened, Danny?!"

"I'm sorry, dear," says the Navel hospital's nurse which has jist came in, "Danny needs to rest now."

Now ain't that a kind thing which to say? As no Individual *never* notes my sporadic Lassitudes!

Miranda gets up off from her chair plus says:

"Well goodbye, Danny. I'll try and come and see you tomorrow if Miss Fishlock is driving to Port City. She sometimes leads choir practice at the First Prebyterian church. Otherwise, I'll try and get a bus by myself."

Now ain't that a kind thing for her which to do?!

"G-Goodbye, dear M-Miranda. Th-thank you f-for c-coming."

"You're a very nice boy, Danny. Please...please..."

Dear Miranda notes me for one full duration and looks blue and lowly and purports to note my tummy which ain't there no more as it has sank way down. (As said.) (Among bed Springs and/or Mattress **ET. AL!**)

"Please don't ever change, Danny."

Miranda blows me a kiss from her hand plus commences to blubber hard and exits instantaneous simultaneous out.

Now why did dear Miranda blubber?! I am better for gosh's sake. Plus why did she note so hard and get so blue and lowly when noting my tummy? **OH MY GOSH!** She feasibly noted my Slow Son impelled Boner!

Said nurse shoves a paper Dixie cup at me in which a blue big pill resides in.

"Take this, honey, it will help you to rest. You have been awful, awful sick."

I put said blue big pill in to my mouth and the kind nurse hands me a glass of water with which to swallow said with then exits out.

I commence to get woozy plus wonder what Miranda means by: Don't I Remember What Happened? Then jist like some indeterminant person has hit me over the head with a ax and throwed me in a ditch **WHACK!** I get Spontaneously Somnolent! Plus sleep.

40. MURDER IN THE NAVEL HOSPITAL !

It is excessively dark when I awake up. The handsome 2 hospital sailors is each sleeping on their respectable hospital's beds and I got to alleviate one's self like a chicken with their head chopped off and ain't got no hospital's bedpan. So due to said alleviation Implication I arise up real quiet so as not to Raffle the handsome 2 hospital sailors up plus waddle towards my hospital's room's door.

But jist as I get contiguous by said sailors I note that what I thought was one sailor on his bed is jist 3 pillows piled up underneath of a blanket and said 2 hospital sailors is both in the very Self-Same bed flopping up and down on top of each other like chickens with their heads chopped off!

Plus I hear Chatting:

"Golly, Bob, this is real neat! Don't y'all think so?"

"I sure do, Jim, my old pal! You got a ship-shape heinie!"

"Your Boner ain't nothing to be sneezed at neither, Bob!" utters Jim kindly.

"Why thank you, buddy!" says Bob, "It surely does feel commendable Corn-Holing you! This is my all time favorite task!"

Prior said is my 1st contenting confrontation with Corn-Holing. (About which I heard about from Little Norman as although little he is Erudite in multiple Esoteric items.)

I am real content for my handsome 2 hospital sailors as they got each other to Corn-Hole in Full Bliss and be true friends of.

I ponder in joy for one full interval on getting Fred Foster's or Mr Jimmy's or Burt's or even Miss Fishlock's Slow Bastard's Boner stuck right up my fat big heinie plus commence to attain a Erection. But as I got to pee real bad I waddle soft past the Corn-Holing handsome 2 hospital sailors so as not to impede their pleasures plus open our room's door and exit out Mutantly silent.

I note up and down said hospital's hallway so as to be positive that PK ain't hiding hisself adjacent behind of no water cooler as he is Inexorable even with a broke arm and leg plus is so unkind that nothing can Prohibit him. However. I wonder how he got all of them broke body segments?

I note a TOILETS sign towards which I waddle towards subsequential as my alleviation can not no longer be impeded farther. I relieve one's self and exit out to the hall again plus hear 2 moans moaning:

"Ohhhhhh!......Ohhhhhh!" which Emanates out from behind of one closed hospital's room's door. I smash my piglet ear up contiguous against this here door and listen plus open said up real quiet and note in.

Here in a bed is a indeterminant Individual which is laying supinely on one's back prone with a whole alots of bandages stuck all over the place plus a goofy Utensil strapped right over their nose and mouth with a long tube coming out from it which whooshes in and out jist like when PK traditionally slams his big boot in to my tummy. Said whooshing tube is stuck on to a big tank with a sign on it which says: OXYGEN.

This moaning laying down indeterminant prone Individual possesses one white big leg jist like Jarleen's was which hangs up in to the air on a skinny chain. Plus has got 2 white big casts on it's 2 arms.

Suddenly I note a sign on the end of said Individual's hospital's bed:

"Paul K Benderson. One Bully.
In Execrable condition!"

Do I concur! Attached to said sign with a behemoth paper clip is a additional sign which says:

"Plus not a real kind boy neither!
In other words: one Inexorable Bully. As sadly said."

I go right on over to this laying down moaning Individual which is PK! plus squat down and note that he has terminated from his moaning and went right to sleep with said whooshing Oxygen Utinsel strapped over his nose plus mouth. (As said.)

I grab the behemoth paper clip off from the Additional Sign and clip it on to the whooshing Oxygen Tube which stops whooshing instantaneously. This paper clip terminates PK's Oxygen and he commences to wheeze Tempestuously like Miss McCoy when she squats up subsequential to squatting down.

So here I set in joy noting PK which flops up and down multiple times like The Lonely Gal done in her Fit! Then he don't move at all but jist lays there jist like Flo done when Jarleen whacked her. Like he has croaked!

194

41. EXPLICIT FRIENDS

"Danny. Wake up. You got visitors."

I open my piglet Somnolent eyes and note the kind nurse which is poking her face so close adjacent that I can smell her nice Dentyne Chewing Gum breath plus am real content I ain't no Homocidal Maniac but was jist dreaming A Murderous dream only. (Like in The Keyhole.) (Which has got a Murderous Dreams Department.) (Including the one about Individuals which is cut up In A Frenzy in to little segmants and stuck in to variegated suitcases and Abandoned in Bus's Stations.) (As said?)

Then said nurse takes her face out from in front of me and I note Lottie Venables and her dear friend of her heart Miss Lela McCoy kindly loitering there!

"Oh, Danny! *Dear* Danny," says kind Lottie with glittering eyes, "We were *so* worried about you! We've been here time and again but you were always..."

Lottie hides her face and snivels.

"Sleeping," utters Miss McCoy which wipes a tear which has flopped down on to her cheek away.

"You *must* get well soon," says Lela McCoy, "I have various new electric products to display and you're *just* the boy to do it!"

Lottie and Lela set here for one full interval and utter variegated kind items at me one after the other! Lottie says that I am thin but I say I ain't as I only look thin as I am laying supinely and my fat tummy is in a State of being drug down into my soft hospital's mattress by my relentless fat heinie. (As said.) Lottie and Lela nod their multiple heads kindly in Acclimation plus give me 5 Milky-Ways and Raisins but I ain't currently hungry like I used to be. (Alas.)

After said kind 2 has exited out one of the handsome 2 hospital sailors utters:

"Your sure a popular guy, Danny!"

"You sure got a whole lot of friends," utters the additional handsome hospital sailor. Now ain't them 2 kind things which to utter? And one right after the other!

3 specified persons has visited me anyhow not counting Jarleen and Jack Shanks which ain't explicitly accurate persons as she is My Beauteous Mom and he is *her* Paramount (As said.) and

not my own personalized friend but is OK by me as he impels Jarleen to smile and exhibit her glamorous teeth which contents me and indeterminant others in the extremes.

However. The only visiting person which is on my own age Bracket is dear Miranda Cosmonopolis which I cherish Irregardless from her Gender as a girl as she is the only person which likes me on my own true Bracket. Plus I would cherish her anyhow due to her most tender Sensitivities. (As said.) (Plus I am one Devotee of hers!) (As said!)

However. I desire friends of one's similar Gender with nice weenies in my Bracket. Please do not ask me why. As I can not tell you. As I do not know.

The handsome 2 hospital sailors depart out to attend their Physical Therapies. Therefour I am Fully Insulated plus as I been so sick for so long I commence to ponder my Humane Condition. This is a excessively Depressive Pursuit and as I am additionally compressed down due to Fatigue and Lassitudes I strive to make a Cursory List of all persons with which I am on acquaintance with which was kind to me Irregardless of their Brackets.

1. My Divine Fred. (Foster.) (Convivial weenie.) (Wondrous Dream secret.) (Handsome in the extremes.) (Am in love with.) (Don't love me in no weenie way.) (As it ain't his Humane Condition.) (Unfortunately.) (Alas.) (What was he doing insides of the Men's Room of The Hotel LaVernia?) (As he don't reside there.) (Visiting a kind friend?) (But was it really *he*?)

2. Dear Miranda Cosmonopolis. (Kind.) (Variegated Tender Sensitivities.) (A month older then I but Fully in my Bracket.) (Cherished.) (Why did she exit out from my hospital's room blubbering?) (Have I did something bad?) (Opera Sings good.) (Am one Devotee of.) (Visits me in the hospital.) (No weenie.)

3. Mr Jimmy. (Exceedingly kind.) (Exceedingly handsome.) (one conspicuous weenie!) (Condolated me after my PK Benderson Pee Tragedy.) (Tells Zoological Stories.) (Fixed my Schwinn blue bicycle!)

4. Lottie Venables. (Old.) (Exceedingly kind.) (Plays good music.) (Nice bathroom!) (Likes Long Diseased Composers.) (Says my hair is like flames!) (Visits me in the hospital.) (Brings Milky-Ways.) (No

weenie.)

5. Miss Lela McCoy. (Old.) (Exceedingly kind.) (Apt at Friendship.) (Sings good.) (Implicitly at funerals.) (My employer.) (Wheezes.) (After squatting up.) (Due to Implications.) (Visits me in the hospital.) (Brings Raisins.) (No weenie.)

6. Miss Fishlock. (Old.) (Kind although A Enigma.) (Musical Experience.) (Tragic life due to her Bastard.) (Unbuttons Slow Son's Corduroys prior to alleviation?!) (No weenie.)

7. Miss Fishlock's Slow Son. (6 years older then I myself.) (Slow.) (Very handsome.) (Protrusive weenie.) (Desirable to Feel-Up with elbows on variegated broke down auto journeys of long duration.)

8. Burt. (Exceedingly friendly.) (Gap in Levi's fly.) (Gap in between of front 2 teeth.) (Convivial weenie. One segmant of which which was saw in real actuality in his weenie creepers.) (Silken Fourskin!) (He is Other Directed.) (*Which* direction?!) (!)

9. The Kind Sewer Man. (Kind.) (Possesses the convivial weenie in to which I poked my nose contiguous in to.) (Kept saying Pore Boy Pore Boy multiple times.) (Contenting.) (Divulges Drowndings efficiently.) (Bull's.) (To Jarleen and Jack Shanks.) (Jack Shanks is OK too.) (Explicitly wrapped in towels.)

10. My dear Senior. (Possesses the only Marginally Mature Boner I ever sucked in real actuality.) (But run away when I hollered I loved him.) (Although I really love Fred.) (Was jist being Dramatic.) (Me.) (Like in a Major Motion Picture.) (I was only Imfatuated.) (Almost forgot! He sucked me additionally!) (My black and white small dog Abhors him Obstensible.)

11. Little Norman. (Possesses the weenie on which I Debuted on.) (One suck only.) (No Spermatozoans Whatsoever.) (As Little Norman could not as of per yet eject.) (Almost one year ago.) (We was both jist kids.) (He sucked mine too plus got a mouthful of Spermatozoans.) (As I got Relentless Pubescence.) (As said.) (He is Sired by a conspicuous perky weenied kind father.) (Mr Jimmy Tomlin!) (Ex Hero!) (A Fully Kopasetic Adult Individual!)

12. Flo. (Washed dog shit off from my 100 Percent red nylon seer-sucker long-sleeved no-iron shirt.) (Saved me from PK.) (Endorses my behemoth vocabulary.) (Carries a knife.) (Sporadically gives me The Willies but has variegated qualities.) (Learns Epic Pomes by heart by The Memorization Method.) (Strives to impel The Lonely Gal away from her Inebriations.) (Is Reviled by Jarleen.) (Fucked my Dad.) (No weenie.)

13. The Lonely Gal. (A Inebriant.) (Employs fowl language like a chicken with their head chopped off!) (Kind to me on radio only.) (Multiple variegated occurences however which must be Taken Into Account.) (So should be included on this list In All Fairness due to Multiplicity.) (Hollered she loved me in the back room.) (But was Inebriated during said Confession.) (Is one big let down due to generalized insincerity.) (She lies.) (Has Fits plus froths on suitable occasions.) (Plus Barfs.) (On pool table.) (Small puddles only.) (Writes own songs which she subsequential sings.) (No weenie!)

14. The Steamrollers. (Some exceedingly kind ladies.) (2 of prior said drove me home in a beauteous auto plus sung beauteous.) (Purchased 2 previous Dr Peppers for me.) (Contenting.) (One of said whacked me on the top of my head with Pool balls.) (By accident.) (But bought me one subsequential Milky-Way.) (All of said seen me keel over plus pee my pants!) (Was still kind irregardless!) (Including the concerned short lady.) (Not one weenie in the Bevy.)

Said list impels me to note that A Often Uncaring World maybe ain't as bad as pondered prior as a specified number of variegated persons is kind irregardless of My Humane Condition although said persons ain't got my secret weenie Affiliations information on their fingertips nor ain't all of them in my Bracket. However. The Lonely Gal Inferred that I was a Cocksucker which was comforting.

PK Benderson ain't on said list as he ain't never been kind to me but is Diagonally Opposed. (Although I should visit him in his hospital's room as he is wounded.) (But not jist yet!)

Anyhow. As I am laying here on my hospital's bed I commence to Ruminate about a real bad dream in which I was setting on PK's tummy in and in which I noted 2 fists which kept pounding away on PK's face in. Then dear Miranda's voice flops right in to my brains plus hollers:

"Don't you remember what happened, Danny?!"

THEN IN FLOPS ALL THIS DIRE INFORMATION! OH MY GOSH! It was me which beat Paul K Benderson up! It was me which slammed him to the Earth and set on his tummy and broke up his nose and whacked his 2 eyes untill they was swelled shut plus knocked his front 2 teeth out and broke his arms and leg! Is this why Miranda blubbered jist prior to exiting out from my hospital's room?! Because I myself am a bigger Bully then poor misguided Paul K Benderson?! (Plus even more Inexorable even?!)

I commence to blubber as my Dire recent History Repugs me! How *could* I Thrash another person when I myself desire to be kind?! I am a horrid Hippocrates!

Even although Paul K Molested me relentlessly I shouldn't of hadda oughta never of Thrashed him mercilessly as 2 Wrongs Ain't Never Made one Right as my Deeply Departed Grandma traditionally uttered.

Pondering my dear Grandma's Deeply Departed Words impels me to blubber harder even so I jist lay here and blubber and blubber and blubber as us fat big Sissies is Veteran blubbers. (And don't ever let no Individual tell you that we ain't!)

The handsome 2 hospital sailors come back from their Physical Therapies and as I ain't able to impede my blubbering they come over to me and loiter contiguous and I note the contenting Lumps underneath of their hospital's shirts joyous but blubber anyhow.

"What's the matter, Danny?" says one handsome hospital sailor.

"I b-beat a g-guy up!" I say, "P-Plus Th-Thrashed him m-mercilessly."

"Yeah," says said handsome sailor, "We heard about that, didn't we, Jim?"

"Sure did," says Jim, "But he got what was comin' to him from what we heard about it."

Jim moves in contiguous and pats me right on my head. I Glare joyously at his weenie Lump underneath of his hospital's shirt plus hope said 2 sailors do not note my Acute interest on their respectable Lower Pelvic Torsal regions among my tears.

"That damned bully beat up on you all the time," says Bob.

"He got what was comin' to him," says Jim.

"W-Who told y-you th-that?"

"A kid named Fred," says Jim.

"F-F-FRED?!"

"Fred Foster," says Bob.

"He has came to see you ever darn day since we been here," says Jim.

"FRED FOSTER HAS CAME TO SEE ME EVERY DAY?!" I holler Rapaciously!

"Ever darn day," says Jim.

"And we been here four weeks." says Bob.

SOMETHING FEELS EXCESSIVELY GOOFY INSIDES OF MY BRAINS!

WAY DOWN DEEP SOMETHING IS CRACKLING AWAY AND SPARKING LIKE A 4TH OF JULY SPARKLER!

"Yeah," says Jim, "Affirmative. Fred come to visit you ever darn day for four weeks."

"Affirmative," says Bob, "Ever darn day since we been here."

"We been recuperatin' from Brain Fever too," says Jim.

"It is goin' around," says Bob.

"And this Fred kid has came to see you every day and talked a whole lot about you to us," says Jim.

"A real good looking kid too," says Bob, "Ain't he, Jim?"

"Sure is," says Jim.

"That's for *dang* sure," says Bob.

Am I joyous! My Divine Fred Foster has came to see me every day while Somnolent!

"He sure has gotta be a good friend of yours to visit you all of them times. That's fer sure!" says Jim.

"That's fer dang sure!" says Bob. "ain't it, Jim?"

"You can say that agin!" says Jim.

42. A ANGEL'S FACE

The handsome 2 hospital sailors go back to their respectable beds and I commence to ponder My Divine Fred which has came to see me every darn day for 4 weeks!

I attain a Erection due to the Fourgoing Ruminations explicitly when I ponder Fred's blue beauteous 2 eyes and Lump plus am impelled to Onanate additionally covertly underneath of my Hospital's bed's blanket but as the handsome 2 hospital sailors is currantly Somnolent due to prior Zealous Therapies they don't hear nothing Irreconcilable from this explicit Onanation In Progress.

Said terminates successful and after wiping myself up with subsequentual Kleenexs I lay back sort of goofy and grunting on my hospital's bed.

"Danny," says the kind hospital's nurse which enters in, "Here is a mirror so as you can fix yourself up as it is visiting hour. There is a comb on your bed table."

Said nurse exits out.

As Fred Foster might arrive any minute on his traditional Pilgimage I grab said mirror and stick it in front of my piglet face.

OH MY GOSH! IT AIN'T ME MYSELF WHICH IS GLARING BACK FROM SAID MIRROR!

The face at which I look at ain't a piglet face with slitty little piglet eyes and pimples but is all smooth and pink and pretty and ain't reddish but jist a delighted pink! **IT IS A ANGEL'S FACE!** plus almost as beauteous as my Angel Mr Jimmy! Or My Divine Fred Foster which is 14. And my hair ain't greasy but is shiny red and wavy and Fully Flame-like as if some indeterminant Individual must of sneaked in and washed it during Somnolence.

I yank the blankets off from my bed so as to note my variegated body segmants plus set up on the edge of said bed and await for my floppy fat big tummy to swing back out on to it's fat traditional posture but it don't! There ain't no tummy here at all! I yank up my hospital's shirt! **OH MY GOSH! AM I SKINNY!** I jump up!

Where is my fat 2 thighs? I take one step! **NO WADDLE!** I take a additional step. **WHERE IS MY WADDLE?!** I ain't propelled to stick my arms out like a girl to procure my Perfect Balance neither as there ain't no fat 2 thighs which to rub Chafeingly together contiguous nor disbalance me! I take another additional step! Still no waddle! Where is my horrid sweaty Prespiration?! *Am* I dreaming?! **OH MY GOSH!**

I wobble back to my hospital's bed and flop back down on to said as although I do not waddle no more I do *wobble* a whole alots as my skinny new 2 legs ain't excessively Robust as per as yet due to my Recuperation which is In Full Progress.

I can not await untill Fred notes me awakened up and Fully Conscientous!

I squinch my beauteous new 2 eyes tight shut plus ponder for a full duration. Nothing makes no sense! How could My Humane Condition change so much?!

And this here goofy 4th of July sparkler insides of my brains! What on God's Green Earth was that?! **OH MY GOSH!**

"Danny?"

I open my new beauteous 2 eyes which was squinched shut up. It is My Old Pal Fred Foster!

"Danny!" says Fred, "Your awake! Hello, old pal!"

"Hello, Fred old pal," I utter in a State of Full Bliss.

But something is different so I utter said again:

"Hello, Fred old pal."

Something feels wondrous deep among my brains! What the heck is it?!

"Your real skinny, Danny. I thought it jist looked like you was thin as you was laying down and was all flattened out when I seen you before when you was sleepin'. But now that your sittin' up your real skinny!"

Fred sets down on a chair which squashes up his Suppliant Genitalias real nice.

"Yeah," I say, "I sure have gone and lost a whole alots of weight Interred in this here hospital."

I feel excessively heightened up and joyous and everything seems so wondrous plus so easy! Is it jist because My Divine Fred has came to visit me every darn day for 4 weeks?!

"You can surely say that again," says My Old Pal Fred which Infers to my being skinny currantly plus then Digresses:

"I come to visit you lots of times, Danny."

"Yeah. The 2 sailors told me."

My words! **MY WORDS!** It's jist like singing!

"You don't stutter no more, Danny!" says Fred.

That is it! **I DO NOT STUTTER NO MORE!** That is why it is jist like singing as I do not stutter when I sing!

Fred notes me for one interval.

"You didn't do no talkin' in your sleep, did you, Danny? While you was conked out, I mean."

Dear Fred is worried.

"I jist mumbled as I was dee-lirious," I utter and the words jist flop right out from my mouth! My tongue knows jist what it wishes to utter plus goes right on ahead and utters it!

"'Cause I was real worried that you would dream and talk in your sleep and tell everbody about my wet dream." says Fred in a exceptionally hushed-up Tone and then *real* soft: "Or that you seen me at the Hotel Lavernia."

He squats over and pulls one of his socks up and squinches his convivial weenie up again off from which I ain't able to yank my 2 eyes from off.

"I ain't had no dreams about you, Fred old pal, while Somnolent.
"Danny..."

Fred stops as he ain't able to utter no more of this explicit sentence.

"Yes, Fred my old pal?"

"You didn't have not even one dream about me? You was sleeping a whole month. You must of dreamed of something."

"Jist one dream Fred. But it was not about you."

"I dreamed about *you*, Danny."

Fred sort of squirms around on his chair and gets red on his neck and I note that his weenie is protruding more then it protruded at our conversation's Outset.

"You did?" I say real easy due to my Dearth of stuttering.
"Yeah."

Fred pushes his Tumescing weenie down by crossing over one of his legs, "And they was...good dreams."

OH MY GOSH! I am commencing to attain a Erection too! I poke my new skinny 2 legs up underneath of my hospital's bed's blankets so as to Enshroud said from Prying Eyes. (Possible Navel Hospital's nurse's if she enters unsuspected.)

"I am real proud of you, Danny," says Fred, "Your sure a brave guy! It was real good that you didn't let PK get away with sayin' what he said about your Mom and your poor old dead Dad!"

I do not remember nothing about what PK said but am joyous that at least one Individual is contented that I done what I done as *I* ain't! As said Beating Up on Paul K Benderson was not kind plus impels me to feel blue and lowly.

"I thought, Danny, I thought that maybe when you get outta the hospital you and me can kinda pal around together? Huh? Be buddies? I mean as we already live right next door to each other and all."

"That would be real good, Fred old Pal."

OH MY GOSH! WHEN YOUR KIND NOBODY CARES

ABOUT YOU BUT WHEN YOUR NOT THEY SURE DO! JIST BEAT ONE PERSON UP AND THE MULTITUDES LOVES YOU! WHAT A WORLD! WHAT A WORLD!

"And you can come over to my place at night when Mom and Dad is off at their PTA meetings," says Fred, "and we can kinda... goof off together. You know. Jist us two buddies?" utters Fred which is 14. (As said!)

Fred is currantly Tumesced right up to his Hilt and there ain't nothing he can do about it! The kind nurse comes in to take the temperatures of the handsome 2 hospital sailors but don't fortunately note us even although I myself am in a State of Full Erection underneath of my blanket which can be saw! (By Hostile Eyes Whenever Applicable!)

Anyhow. Fred and me jist keep noting each other's Boners plus smiling Munificent smiles as the nurse takes the temperatures from the respectable 2 Ass Holes of the handsome 2 hospital sailors.

43. SUCH PEOPLE !

"Well, Danny," says Fred after the handsome 2 hospital sailor's temperatures has been took and the kind nurse has went, "I guess I better oughta go now. As your likely to get more visitors and I don't want to tire you out none."

"I guess your right, Fred my old pal," I utter even although I do not desire for My Dear Old Pal Fred to exit out but as I feel excessively weak plus have Onanated twice immediately prior I Acquiesce for Fred's departure plus utter:

"Okay, old pal, whatever you say."

Fred shakes my hand which impels my Boner to arise up additional plus twitch Interminably!

"Goodbye for now, buddy," says Fred which kindly notes my Boner.

BUDDY! Fred calls me his **BUDDY!**

"You ain't gonna forget what I said about us bein' good buddies? Are you buddy?"

"**OH MY GOSH** no, Fred my dear old pal. I mean buddy!"

Fred stands up exceptionally contiguous to my hand which is laying on the edge of my hospital's bed and pokes his garbed

Boner on to it!

I Feel-Up said real genteel and joyous as it wiggles and suddenly Fred squats down by my bed and sticks his mouth adjacent on my ear plus whispers:

"I lied to you, Danny."

"Huh?"

"All that stuff about how I wouldn't tell nobody how you looked at my peter in the mensroom at the Port City Bus Station. I wasn't in Port City to see my girlfriend, Danny."

"You wasn't?"

"No. I come to Port City sometimes...to look for... friends."

"I'm your friend, Fred, I *always* been."

Fred oscillates his head down and shuts his eyes closed and don't utter nothing for one full interval plus then notes me and says real soft and lowly:

"I ain't got no girlfriends."

"You ain't?"

"No."

"I ain't neither."

"What about Miranda Cosmonopolis? Your always hangin' around with her."

"I cherish her. But I ain't in love."

"You ain't?" Not even a little bit?"

"No. I'm jist her Devotee."

"I'm real glad."

"You won't have to go to Port City no more for friends, will you, old pal?"

"No. No more. Well. I guess I better leave now."

Fred stands up and pats me right on my Shapely shoulders.

"Your a real brave guy beating up that Bully PK Benderson."

Hi Brave Guy I reminisce which is what The Lonely Gal said on the radio when I was jist a fat big Sissy nearly almost 2 months ago. (Fred has called me brave twice!)

"A real brave guy," says Fred additionally. (**THRICE!**)

"I jist turned around. Plus used my horns. We all got 'em, Fred."

My Dear Old Pal And Buddy Fred looks around to see if any person is watching which they ain't so he squats down again and sticks his hand underneath of my blanket and grabs my Boner and Feels it Up.

"Well. Goodbye for now, buddy," utters Fred which stands up

205

plus covers his own Boner with a magazine.

"Goodbye, My Buddy!" I utter joyous in the extremes.

Fred holds said magazine over his Boner and exits out plus dear Miranda Cosmonopolis waddles in Spontaneously bearing a behemoth Volume!

"Hello, Danny," says Miranda which looks excessively blue and lowly.

"Hello, Miranda, how nice of you to come," I gladly utter Fully Devoted.

"Who was that good looking boy who just came out of your room?"

"Fred Foster. My best buddy and pal."

"Oh," says Miranda, "he is *beautiful*."

As boys is supposed to be handsome and not beautiful I utter "I guess so," as it ain't a good ideal to Divulge one's Affiliations by adding nothing additional.

"Miss Fishlock is buying a used Baldwin piano at Borgen's Pianos and brought me over. She is coming to see you later. Everyone knows you're awake now."

Poor Miranda which looks even bluer and lower set down in a chair with a big grunt plus chair-creaking and says:

"You don't stutter anymore. Why?"

"I guess my Fever took it away," I say but I know insides of my brains that it was Fred's 31 visits which did it **AS LOVE CONQUERS ALL!**

"Oh," says Miranda which looks like she will commence to blubber any minute, "You're so...handsome now."

I reminisce my Angel's new face in the mirror.

"Where are your pimples?"

"They have jist went, I guess."

Then am I surprised! Miranda which should of been joyous for me commences to blubber plus throws the behemoth Volume she is bearing right at me jist like The Lonely Gal traditionally throwed Kleenexs and hankies!

"Oh, Danny!" hollers Miranda, "Now that you're thin and handsome and don't stutter you'll never dance with me again at The Wednesday Club!"

OH MY GOSH!

"Or sing with me at The Hotel LaVernia Entertainment Lounge! You probably won't even like me any more as I am so fat! **AND I KNOW I HAVE A VERY SMALL HEAD!** But my head is in *perfect* proportion to my body! It only *looks* small! Because... because... because I am so... **FAAAAAAAT!**"

"But dear Miranda..."

"You probably wish I would just go away right now! This very minute! You probably wish I would just disappear! So you won't have to be embarrassed to be seen with big fat me!"

"But dear Miranda..."

"And you beat up poor PK! It was *awful!* That poor boy is just down the hall! He is miserable! And scheduled for extremely serious nose surgery tomorrow! He can't breathe properly! He can't walk! He can't even feed himself because his arms had to be re-broken and set *again!* And he is forced to use a bed pan because he can not leave his bed! I didn't know you were so mean and cruel, Danny!"

"But dear Miranda..."

"We should turn the other cheek, Danny! When we suffer under tribulation we should just turn the other cheek!" hollers Miranda which squirts a Admixture of spray-snot and tears all over my hospital's blanket!

OH MY GOSH is she blubbering and she can hardly get her breath she is so blue and lowly!

"But dear Miranda, I did not mean to beat PK up! Honest! I was jist a water buffalo which turned around and defended hisself!

"A *what*?!" hollers Miranda.

"A water buffalo, Miranda, which defended hisself from a lion!"

"Water buffalos should turn the other cheek, Danny!" hollers Miranda louder even among her squirting tears plus spray-snot!

"They always do and they get bit right on the rump and eat up subsequential!"

"*Eaten* up," hollers Miranda, "**EATEN up SUBSEQUENTIALLY!** Oh what's the use?! You'll never speak to me again now that you're so good looking! You'll probably be the most popular boy in school now!"

"But dear Miranda, I promise I will converse to you again! I cherish you! You are my *only almost friend!* Jist because I ain't fat ain't no reason not to like you! I am explicitly the same insides of my brains plus jist as soon as I am disinterred from this hospital I will strive to dance with you at The Wednesday Club every darn Wednesday!"

(I hope that my handsome 2 hospital sailors ain't impeded by all of this hollering so I oscillate my head to note. They ain't as they are Somnolent.)

Dear poor Miranda jist loiters here and notes me for a full duration and I can see all of her white little teeth as her mouth is open through which she is impelled to breathe through as she has got big snot-clogs in her poor nose's little nostrils.

She wipes her eyes up with a Kleenex which she procures from a Kleenex box contiguous plus says:

"Do you mean that? Do you really mean that? About dancing with me? Scout's honor?"

"I ain't no Boy Scout, Miranda. They would not let me be one as they said I was too big and too Sissified plus might Molest my Compatriots."

Miranda looks surprised for a interval then wipes up her tears then utters:

"I am sorry I shouted at you. I know you're a nice, kind boy and you didn't mean to hurt PK."

Miranda takes said behemoth Volume off from the floor to which it had fell to when prior flang. She opens said Volume up to a big bookmark in it plus says:

"Here is something you should read, Danny. I marked it for you. I thought of it when I saw you yesterday and you were so handsome. And so very, very changed."

Miranda breathes real hard and fastly and holds this big Volume jist underneath of her Rollicking 2 titties for a interval as she reads it to herself then she sits it on the table by my hospital's bed plus utters:

"I have to do some shopping for my mother."

Miranda gets up with a additional big grunt and traditional chair-creaking and utters from insides the doorframe jist before she exits out:

"You were a very sweet boy, Danny. And I sincerely hope you always will be."

As Miranda has went and the handsome 2 hospital sailors is sleeping I walk (Not waddle!) over and look on to my hospital's room's wall's mirror to see if I really *am* dreaming.

But my pimples is still gone. My heinie is still tiny. My slitty piglet 2 eyes ain't. Plus is still big and blue and looks like they have grew new gold eyelashes. Even my yellow little teeth is white (As the kind nurse impelled me to brush said thoroughly.) although one front tooth still possesses a broke little corner due to Deeply

Departed Bull's prior Thwarted whack. Plus I am still inordinantly tall and skinny but not too skinny as I am **FULLY SWANIFIED!** I wisht My Deeply Departed Grandma could see me now!

Suddenly the mirror commences to get all fuzzy and my Gorgeous new self disappears and my fat big Sissy face Glares back at me all sweaty and pimply! And my fat big tummy pokes traditionally out and my fat big heinie jiggles! **OH MY GOSH!** Everything good which happened to me is jist a darned dream! **OH MY GOSH!** I feel like keeling over! Then my old fat as one hog face utters:

"NO MATTER HOW HANDSOME YOU ARE, DANNY, THE ONLY THING WHICH COUNTS IS WHAT LAYS DEEP INSIDES OF YOU BECAUSE WHAT LAYS DEEP INSIDES STAYS THERE INCESSANTLY. YOU WILL ALWAYS BE A FAT BIG SISSY DEEP INSIDES! REMEMBER THAT!"

"Oh I will! Oh I will!"

"AND ALWAYS BE KIND TO ALL PERSONS!"

"Yes I will!" I holler additionally.

Said mirror gets all fuzzy again and my new Angel Face comes back and smiles right at me.

But this gets me all nerve racked up! So I walk Sedately back to my bed and set there graciously and commence to ponder items which will impel me on to a State of Domestic Tranquility.

I ponder dear Miranda Cosmonopolis which I will perpetually cherish devotedly.

And Mr Jimmy which smiled kindly and rescued me from pee and hugged me and told me a Zoo Story.

And Lottie Venables and her true friend of her heart Miss Lela McCoy which give me Tea For 3 and one Long Diseased Composer's Music and 6 multiple colored cupcakes plus 2 jobs. (Skinny Lawn's Mowing and Display Window's Decor.)

And Miss Fishlock which Promulgates my Culture and her Bastard which permitted me to touch his weenie with my elbow all the way from Port City to Lemon Gulch in a State of Full Bliss.

And the handsome 2 hospital sailors which possess convivial protrusive weenies and told me that My Dear Old Buddy Fred had came to see me every day for one total month which terminated my stuttering Prompt.

And Poor Wolfgang which stuttered jist like me and which hugged me even although he did not Chat the English language.

And the kind sewer man which drove me home as I stuck my piglet nose contiguous on to his weenie with Impunity.

And My Beauteous Mom which is beauteous and I guess that is enough.

And Jack Shanks which is not such a bad guy and which got my Dad a job even although said was Short-Lived.

And Flo which rescued me once from PK Benderson plus give me funds and a Marshmallow Soda. (And washed Dog Shit off from my 100 Percent red seersucker nylon no-iron long-sleeved shirt.)

And The Lonely Gal which ain't so bad as all that and which said she loved me a whole alots of times on the radio and once in person. Even although she is a Inebriant plus says Fuck she is only Humane.

And The Steamrollers which is Babe and Lorraine and Reggie and Marie plus the concerned short lady which all kindly smiled and treated me jist like a accurate humane being as they seen what lays deep insides of me even although I keeled over and peed my pants. (A Unfortunate Detail.)

And the kind elevater lady which give me Detailed Directions to The Jolly Jug where I met them exceedingly kind ladies.

Oh yes! And My Deeply Departed Grandma which I cherished as much as any person on this Cosmos.

And last but not least My Divine Fred Foster which wishes to Goof-Off with me jist like a accurate Pal while his parents attend their Parent Teachers Association Meetings! (As said.) Plus which this morning Felt-Up my Genitalias in real actuality plus uttered that he dreamed about me while his weenie Tumesced up right before my very eyes! My Beauteous Fred which thinks I'm brave for Beating Up the Inexorable PK Benderson! My wondrous blue-eyed Fred which wants to be *my* Buddy!

I terminate said pondering finally which has lasted one full duration and which has Rendered me on to a State of Full Domestic Tranquility and I walk *Sedately* (No waddling for me!) over to the Hospital's mirror and note my Wondrous new self again jist to make sure it ain't desserted me! It ain't! **AM I BEAUTEOUS! BUT STILL INFINITELY KIND UNDERNEATH OF IT ALL!**

So I go back to my bed and set my gracious Slim Bottom down and pick up this here Volume which dear Miranda has gave me which I ain't never Perused before even although I heard of it's Author which has wrote said while co-habiting our school library.

I open said Volume up at this here book-marked page in it which Miranda has marked and right acrosst from where she has drew little red arrows on the book mark I read:

"How beauteous mankind is!
O brave new world
That hath such people in it!"

Now ain't that a kind thing which to say?!

44. AFTERWORDS

Lottie Venables and her friend of the heart, Miss Lela McCoy, now live together. Miss McCoy was eventually forced to sell LG Radios for health reasons and an inability to squat up after squatting down. She is faring better under the tender loving care of Lottie.

These two kind ladies are perfectly content and often have Musical Evenings to which Danny, when he is in Lemon Gulch on a visit, and Miranda Cosmonopolis, when she is not on a world tour, are always cordially invited.

Burt, with his business partner, an older man, Mr Albee, who has kept his good looks and physique, were the lucky buyers of LG Radios which flourished as Television came in and everybody in Lemon Gulch bought a television set just as soon as humanly possible.

Poor Wolfgang learned English at breakneck speed and got an excellent job as an apprentice for a noted but lonely inventor.

Wolfgang, ever practical, always stays at the YMCA whenever he is out of town on business. He still stutters.

Danny's teacher, the bitter Mrs Vealfoy, divorced her Marine husband, was immediately married again but soon after was widowed when her new husband was struck down by a huge box of feather-boas flung at him from a great height.

Miss Fishlock's slow son fell on an icy road, struck his head, lay there till morning, as dead. But wasn't, and now became exceedingly clever, had a vision, developed a Wonder Diet and tried it on Miranda Cosmonopolis who became extremely thin *without* losing her meltingly lovely operatic voice. Her little round head was now perfectly in scale with her svelte new appearance and she and Miss Fishlock's no longer slow son were married. He is Miranda's exceptionally astute manager and Miranda is an up and coming opera singer to whom Danny is still devoted though necessarily at a distance as Miranda and company are seldom in one place for very long.

Miss Fishlock lives with this successful, much travelled couple but of course is no longer impelled to unbutton her son's trousers when he alleviates (if indeed she ever was!).

The Steamrollers started their own mesh wire fence company. The concerned short lady who is still concerned, though somewhat taller on her new platform heels, is their accountant. They are so successful that Babe and Lorraine reopened The Jolly Jug a few years later as The New Maiden's Head and it became a leading meeting place for Women's Liberation, later to be known as Feminism.

Jarleen and Jack Shanks got married and soon after stopped bowling. Jarleen, at forty-four, is still the most beautiful woman at Tangy Mayo, if not in Lemon Gulch. However, she now walks with a slight limp due to her accident with the Convenient Picnic Size Tangy Mayonnaise display.

Incidentally, Danny finally got a big juicy kiss from his beautiful Mom when, handsome, assured and unstuttering (some years ago), he returned home from The Port City Naval Hospital. It contented him (and her!).

Ignoring his mother Edna May's vehement warnings, Gregory the Gasoline Sniffer continued to sniff gasoline until one day he accidentally set himself on fire in their garage -- at the same time dropping his battery radio which shattered into 666 pieces on the concrete floor. He was not seriously injured but he never again sniffed gasoline and never again simultaneously stuck his fingers up the panties of that particular bad little girl who, fortunately unhurt, fled the fire but thereafter would not touch Gregory with a ten foot pole.

Aunt Edna May had several additional bowel-related presentiments which occurred sporadically until, desperate, she sought medical assistance and was provided with a heavy-duty colostomy bag which must be, in the interests of good hygiene, emptied several times each day. Unfortunately.

Fifi and Collette still teach French but not at a Junior College. They are now fully tenured language professors at one of California's leading universities where Fifi is head and Collette is deputy head of the French department. They are exceptionally active in Women's causes. Neither woman feels nearly so *de trop* these days.

Mr Jimmy Tomlin, as a reward for his hard, honest work, his intimate knowledge of machines, his deep and abiding understanding of people, his ability to lead men, and his all-around common decency, was made Personnel Manager in an ICBM factory in Texas. He and his wife, Brenda, who continues to make the best Pecan Panochy fudge in the world, and their children, Little Norman and Bunny Lois and their dog Rags, moved away from Lemon Gulch to live in a sumptuous house with swimming pool on a glossy edge of Dallas where Little Norman and Bunny Lois began, with Mr Jimmy's kind encouragement, to study ballet. Little Norman is no longer little but very well endowed. Particularly when noted in his leotards. He is soon to marry Natasha, an equally talented fellow dance student.

Everything is Kopasetic for the happy Tomlins who, incidentally, were in Texas for a month during Danny's Brain Fever hospitalization but showered him with get-well cards and Pecan Panochy fudge upon their return.

The kind elevator lady lost her position when an automatic elevator was installed in her building but was offered the job of the unkind Receptionist who had continued to make an extremely bad impression on people, particularly children. In the interests of solidarity the kind elevator lady refused to take the job of her co-worker but soon won an astounding amount of money in the Irish Sweepstakes and retired in luxury.

The unkind Receptionist, however, fell off her receptionist's high stool one day, shattered her horn-rimmed glasses and fractured her hip. The hip did not heal well. Although she still works as a Receptionist she has not known two days together without moderate hip pain.

The kind sewer man, profoundly altered by Bull's tragic drowning in the Lemon Gulch Sewer Works' primary sewage cleansing Vat 69, quit his job, acquired ten acres of exceedingly barren Lemon Gulch land dirt-cheap, fertilized it by means of his special contacts at the sewer plant and is today the chief supplier of lemons which ensure the tang in Tangy Mayonnaise. He married the woman with the black goggles and nose-clamp who was delighted.

Michelangelo Da vinci Martinez, who daily swept the Bus Terminal section of The Saga of the West Drugstore and Fountain Grill/Bus Terminal, bought-out The Saga of the West's proprietors, Sebastien and Violet Melmoth when they retired. The exceedingly thrifty Martinez maintains an excellent selection of Physical Culture periodicals on the magazine and newspapers shelves but adamantly (and admirably) refuses to sell The Keyhole.

The two handsome hospital sailors, already great buddies, became ever closer and after their respective Honorable Discharges from the U.S. Navy moved in together. They have been together ever since.
    What Danny assumed to be a dream that night in the Port City Naval Hospital, wasn't. At least the part pertaining to Bob and Jim's nocturnal corn-holing activities.

The Senior became a priest and gave up smoking. But, a deeply frustrated man, he soon started again.

The advance of laser surgery finally enabled Miss Snelgrove, Jarleen's supervisor at Tangy Mayo, to have her disfiguring wart safely removed. She smiles often now -- even at Jarleen -- and is exceedingly solicitous of Jarleen's slight limp which she, Miss Snelgrove, seems in some small, odd way even to enjoy.

Lightning vaporized Danny's Granddad's tombstone, at the same time bringing down the main Lemon Gulch electrical line yet again. Jarleen, lacking power for her electric razor, was forced, for five more grueling days, to shave her legs with Jack Shank's straight-razor and highly perfumed shaving cream.

The fatter-even-than-Danny-boy became even fatter. Then even fatter. Then even fatter. He frowns alot. And deserves *everything* he gets.

The Lonely Gal, with the healthy encouragement of Flo, joined Alcoholics Anonymous and made a complete recovery. She sings for a Port City dance band and occasionally at The New Maiden's Head and tapes her radio broadcasts for midnight listeners as, decidedly middleaged, she now requires a good night's sleep.

She and Flo lived together for a few months but it didn't work so they split up. They got back together for a few months but again it didn't work as, sober, The Lonely Gal was a *completely* different person. So they split up permanently.

The Lonely Gal lives alone but always remembers to take her medication. She occasionally sees the concerned short lady with whom she has for several years carried on a low-key affair and rarely says "What the *fuck*?!" and then, only when exceptionally perturbed.

Flo is a full-time manicurist for a beauty salon chain with shops in Lemon Gulch, Port City and Fresno. Her long black hair is now its natural silver-grey and she wears it severely pulled back in a chignon. She is convinced she will one day be apprehended for the slaughter-murder of the bossy older guy she lived with so long ago, the guy who wrote her Epic Poem and whom she deposited in *very* small pieces in three cheap cardboard suitcases at the Port City Bus Terminal.

The devious policeman who raided The Jolly Jug and attempted unsuccessfully to arrest Flo was promoted to The Port City Vice Squad and gleefully harassed homosexual men and women for several years. Until, it is rumoured, he was accidentally neutered climbing an 8ft mesh wire fence while attempting to elude an irate Drag Queen he had attempted to molest.

The Hotel LaVernia, which was being completely renovated, burned to the ground one night taking the Entertainment Lounge with it. Fortunately, the hotel's only remaining occupants, The Old Timers, and the entire LaVernia management were on a bus tour playing the slot machines of Las Vegas (courtesy of The Port City Community Fund). No one was injured in the fire. The Old Timers now live in The St James Home for the Recalcitrant Elderly, formerly The Tales Of Hoffman Memorial Hospital, in conditions not so genial as those of the ill-fated Hotel LaVernia.

Miranda Cosmonopolis, in spite of her hectic concert schedule and certain bitter memories of The Hotel LaVernia Entertainment Lounge debacle, always manages to give at least one recital a year for The Old Timers (when traveling in this hemisphere -- For old time's sake).

Paul K Benderson's broken nose, arms and leg were successfully repaired, though he unfortunately sextupled in weight while recuperating.

PK became a highschool drop-out one year later due to the incessant "Fatty, Fatty/two-by-four" taunts of his highschool colleagues and now spends his days -- *though he has an extremely acute sense of smell* -- in that Sewer Works Shitbox so long ago abruptly vacated by Bull, and his nights in the bushes contiguous to The Big Lemon, where, to supplement his meagre income, he services older other-directed gentlemen for an *exceptionally* reasonable fee. He is also a cheap spy for The Keyhole which, unfortunately but not surprisingly, continues to thrive. PK is known these days in the Homosexual Underground as "Fatty St Paul".

Danny, while in hospital, never got around to visiting the new PK who was exceedingly grateful for this omission as he was ever after terrified of Danny.

Danny made a complete recovery and became, as said, clear-skinned, handsome, slim, a non-stutterer and no longer reddish (except for his flamelike curls). He seldom if ever blubbers anymore and everybody seems to care *fervantly* about "what lays deep insides of him". But Danny cares for only one person, his divine Fred Foster. The feeling is mutual.

Danny and Fred attended highschool then college, where they both graduated with much better than average grades and remained, and are currently still the best possible of buddies (In a manner of speaking).

"The best possible!" says Danny, sipping his ice cold Dr Pepper under a merciless sun.

"That's for darn sure," says Fred who takes Danny's hand and squeezes it hard after making exceedingly sure no one in the restaurant's patio is watching. After all, it is only 1957!

Oh yes! Tinker: Danny's loyal black and white small dog, after producing innumerable puppies, passed gracefully away of old age and is buried, courtesy of kind Lottie Venables and kind Lela McCoy, in the Pet Paradise section of Cypresses of Elysium Ltd.

When Danny is in Lemon Gulch visiting his beautiful Mom and Jack Shanks and Lottie and Lela he always says a prayer by Tinker's grave which lies not a stone's throw from Bull's tiny memorial marker over which Danny once kneeled and whispered:

"Hello Joe. What do you know? What are a-cookin' in Tokio?"

Please do not ask Danny O'Rourke why he said that. As he can not tell you. As he does not know.

Lightning Source UK Ltd.
Milton Keynes UK
UKOW04f0627110915

258435UK00001B/12/P